*Three*
*passionate*

MISTRE

*Blackmail*

Exciting new books from reader
favourites Kim Lawrence,
Melanie Milburne & Day Leclaire

# MISTRESSES BY

# *Blackmail*

### KIM LAWRENCE
### MELANIE MILBURNE
### DAY LECLAIRE

*M&B™ and M&B™ with the Rose Device
are trademarks of the publisher.
Harlequin Mills & Boon Limited, Eton House,
18-24 Paradise Road, Richmond, Surrey TW9 1SR*

MISTRESSES BY BLACKMAIL
© by Harlequin Enterprises II B.V./S.à.r.l. 2009

*Desert Prince, Blackmailed Bride* © Kim Lawrence 2009
*The Marcolini Blackmail Marriage* © Melanie Milburne 2009
*Dante's Blackmailed Bride* © Day Totten Smith 2008

ISBN: 978 0 263 87526 3

009-0509

*Printed and bound in Spain
by Litografia Rosés S.A., Barcelona*

# Desert Prince, Blackmailed Bride

## KIM LAWRENCE

**Kim Lawrence** lives on a farm in rural Anglesey. She runs two miles daily and finds this an excellent opportunity to unwind and seek inspiration for her writing! It also helps her keep up with her husband, two active sons, and the various stray animals which have adopted them. Always a fanatical consumer of fiction, she is now equally enthusiastic about writing. She loves a happy ending!

I'd like to dedicate this book to the memory of my mum, Ann Shirley - lovely lady, best friend, kindest critic and the real-life feisty heroine.

# CHAPTER ONE

RAFIQ slid his arms into his linen shirt and sat straddling the chair. The pale fabric gaped to reveal the perfectly delineated muscles of his deep gold upper torso—a lot more delineated since he'd dropped almost fifteen pounds.

None of the turbulent seething in his chest was reflected in his expression as, his hands clenched into fists, he fought to control his totally irrational compulsion to drag the grey-haired Frenchman from his seat and throttle a retraction from him.

He was lying—he *had* to be lying!

He didn't, and not just because the doctor was a good twenty years his senior, but because he recognised denial even when he was the one doing the denying. Rafiq knew the man wasn't lying. It was the truth. Not a truth anyone wanted to hear, but the truth.

He wasn't going to see his fiftieth birthday—or, for that matter, his thirty-third!

Once the drumming in his ears had softened to a dull roar a phrase separated itself from the disconnected jumble of thoughts swirling in his head: *roll with the punches.*

It sounded so easy.

Years of practice at rigidly disciplining himself helped, and slowly an icy calm settled over him.

'How long?'

Pierre Henri adjusted his suit jacket—no white coat; he was far too celebrated to need a uniform to establish his authority—and got up slowly. He walked across the room and pulled the X-rays down from the screen, sliding them back into their envelope while he struggled to select his words carefully.

Breaking bad news was a part of the job that he did not enjoy, but it was an integral part of that job and he was considered good at it. He did not normally struggle for words in these circumstances.

He knew the importance of positive body language—it wasn't just what you said but the way you said it—and he knew how emphasising the positive even when there was precious little to be positive about could make a world of difference to the way the person listening felt.

Everyone was different, but years of experience had given him an insight that enabled him to tailor his response to what an individual patient needed from him.

Of course there were exceptions. And this man, he thought, retaking a seat opposite his patient, was one of them!

As his patient's dark eyes locked on to his Pierre felt sweat break out along his upper lip. Insecurity was not something that troubled the eminent physician, yet as he met the pewter-flecked inscrutable gaze of the Crown Prince of Zantara he felt the roles of patient and doctor were oddly reversed.

This man—despite the fact he had just dropped the worst news possible on him—was the one in control.

It was pointless, he knew, to try and understand Rafiq Al Kamil. He was a one-off, a maverick, and neither quality was a feature of his wealth and status—although even for someone like Pierre, who was accustomed to being consulted by the rich and powerful, the sheer scale of the Zantaran royal family's assets was almost surreal.

Pierre was out of his professional comfort zone. Shock, denial, anger—there were as many reactions as there were people. But never in his professional life had he encountered anyone who showed such a total lack of response, and he was thrown.

It was desperately hard to be supportive to someone who appeared not to require any support.

A nicely timed warm handclasp to the shoulder often did wonders, but in this instance he felt any such attempt would be treated as a sign of disrespect—it might even be treasonable!

'I will have to push you, Doctor.'

Pierre started, and coloured at the younger man's prompt.

For the first time the Prince was showing some emotion—and it was impatience. Such control was daunting. This wasn't a display of dispassion, it was… Pierre shook his head slightly as his professional vocabulary failed him. It was *spooky*, he concluded!

*He* was conscious of feeling more anger and bitterness than this young man was displaying. He had never been able to deliver this sort of news and not feel failure, and this went doubly so when the person concerned should have had his whole life ahead of him, when he was full of life and vigour. It seemed such a tragic waste.

It suddenly occurred to the doctor that the Prince's attitude could stem from the fact that he did not fully comprehend the gravity of his situation. Pierre pushed his glasses further up his nose and angled a kindly look at the tall heir to the throne of Zantara.

'Perhaps I did not explain myself fully, Prince Rafiq?'

'I admit some of the technical language passed over my head.'

I doubt that, thought the Frenchman, not fooled by the self-deprecating response. The intelligence shining in the younger man's eyes was one of the first things he had noticed. And even if he hadn't noticed, it had become clear from the battery of searching questions he had asked that this man had mind like a steel trap.

'Correct me if I am wrong,' Rafiq invited, thinking, *Please correct me. Let this all be a massive misunderstanding.* 'I have a rare blood disorder, and it has reached an advanced stage where there is no hope of cure?' His dark brows lifted towards his hairline. 'There is something else I need to know?' His gesture invited the older man to expand.

Pierre Henri cleared his throat. 'You are probably thinking *Why me?*'

Rafiq's broad shoulders lifted as he stood to tuck the hem of his shirt into the waistband of his trousers. He paused to consider the question before replying. At six-five he towered over the seated man. Broad of shoulder and long of leg, Rafiq's streamlined, muscle-packed frame was athletically formed, and it would have made him stand out even had he *not* possessed a face of star-tling, symmetrical male beauty, of the type normally seen on classical statues.

'Why not me?' Why should he be exempt from the capricious cruelty of fate? Innocents were given far worse to bear, and he was no innocent—but he *was* a man with a job to do.

He supposed that everyone in his position felt they needed longer—but he really *did* need longer.

'Just so. A very…erm…*healthy* attitude—marvel-lous philosophy.'

'So, how long do I have?'

Information was power—so they said. Even informa-tion you'd have been happier to remain in ignorance of. In Rafiq's mind he equated power with control, and that was a commodity in short supply. He could feel it slipping through his fingers like grains of sand. He could definitely use a little top-up.

The older man's eyes fell. 'Well…erm…these things are very hard to gauge with any precision.'

In other words the news was not good. Rafiq mentally squared his shoulders. 'Make an educated guess.'

'You can, if you wish, have a second opinion.'

Many patients confronted by a diagnosis they did not wish to believe did so—especially those who had the finances to fly doctors from Paris by private jet for a consultation.

'Are you not the best in your field?'

Rafiq was conscious that he ought to be feeling… feeling *what*? More, he supposed. But after the initial kick in the gut moment when he had realised the truth, he had felt very little except a sense of urgency.

'How long do I have?'

'It is hard to be definitive, but I'd say six…'

Rafiq recognised the man's discomfort but felt little sympathy for it. Instead he was conscious of a growing sense of impatience. 'Days? Weeks…? Months…?' None would be long enough to prepare his little brother to step into his shoes.

'Months.'

Nothing in the younger man's demeanour suggested that he had just been given a death sentence.

'Of course the progression of the disease can vary, and if you accepted the palliative treatment we spoke of…'

'This treatment could affect my faculties, my memory?'

The doctor conceded the possibility with a nod. 'It could extend six months to possibly a year, though.'

Rafiq dismissed the suggestion with a wave of his hand. 'Out of the question.'

'I can review your case weekly.'

'As you wish, Doctor.'

'I am so very sorry, Your Highness.'

The offer of sympathy drew a look of cold disdain from the younger man, who sketched a smile and murmured 'You're kind' before excusing himself.

Out in the corridor Rafiq Al Kamil allowed his mask to slip, and his emotions bubbled to the surface in one vicious, corrosive explosion. With a curse he slammed his clenched fist into an innocent wall.

Through his closed eyelids he could still see the pity

in the Frenchman's face. Pity. It was one thing that he could not, *would* not endure. He recoiled from the idea of seeing that same expression on the faces of people when they met him.

His jaw hardened and a look of steely determination and pride settled on his patrician features. That wasn't going to happen. Eyes closed, Rafiq expelled the pent-up emotion in one long, sibilant breath. He refused to give way to terror or pity. He would die as he would live—on his own terms. But first there was much to do.

His face set in lines of ruthless resolve, he made his way out into the sunlight. Half an hour later he found himself in the stables, with no recollection of how he came to be there.

Hassan, the groom who had put him on his first horse as a boy, approached.

'Prince Rafiq.' The older man's manner was deferential but not obsequious as he bowed his head.

'Hassan.' Rafiq's smile left his dark eyes bleak.

'You wish me to saddle a horse?'

Rafiq reached out and touched the flank of the mare in the nearest stall. He nodded and said carelessly, 'Why not?'

Riding in the desert was to him the most life-affirming experience possible—and for the moment at least he was still alive. The desert was where he always found himself at times of stress. The sight and sounds of the ageless landscape always cleared his head and restored his focus.

'He is not in the best of moods,' Hassan warned. 'Restless and in need of exercise.' He was looking at the Prince as he said this.

The information was unnecessary as the black stallion being led towards him rolled his eyes, reared up on his hind legs and pawed the air.

'I think perhaps you both are...?' The older man's eyes held a concern he knew better than to express as they scanned the Prince's face.

He had watched the Prince grow from a lively, animated child into the man he was today—strong, resolute, decisive and strong-minded. Yet he was capable of compassion—for all but himself. A man, in short, who embodied all the qualities people expected of a leader, though occasionally in an unguarded moment Hassan fancied he glimpsed briefly the mischievous little boy who had once haunted the stables. The little boy whose passing he regretted.

A man, Hassan reflected, should have a place he could let down his guard, and it saddened him that for his Prince the stables were the closest thing he had to such a sanctuary.

Rafiq stepped forward with a grin. 'I think you are right.' He flashed the groom a warm smile. 'Thank you, Hassan. I will go and change.'

'It is always a pleasure to be of service, Prince Rafiq.'

Gabby identified herself politely. Little option, really, when her path was blocked by two big, bearded men wearing black flowing robes. It had always been her policy to be polite to very large men dressed in black—especially when they were both gripping the jewelled handles of scimitars. Common sense told her the barbaric-looking weapons were purely ornamental—*she hoped*.

Actually, this entire venture was a lesson in hope, but she always had been a 'glass half full' sort of person—though the last two days had cut deeply into her natural optimism.

It was impossible to tell from the larger of the two men's stony expression if he understood a word she was saying, so Gabby repeated herself—this time speaking more slowly and waving her hands descriptively.

'I have an appointment,' she lied. 'I got lost. The King is expecting me.'

The man looked at her in silence, his glance sliding briefly over her dishevelled figure. Gabby was sure guilt and desperation must be written all over her face—she had never really mastered the art of hiding her feelings.

It occurred to her that she should have dressed for the occasion, then her story might not have been met with such obvious scepticism. It was likely people did not take tea with the King of Zantara wearing grubby jeans and a torn shirt.

'I had a slight accident on the way here,' she told the silent man as she lifted a hand to smooth hair that at the best of times refused to be tamed, but just now probably gave her the appearance of an extra in a film that involved mad women and lunatic asylums.

When the man did break his silence it was not to speak to Gabby, whom he regarded with deep suspicion, but to the similarly clad man with him. They conversed briefly in Arabic, then the second man, after sliding a stern look in Gabby's direction, gave a deferential nod of his head to the first and vanished through a door she had not noticed to the left.

Gabby smiled. It was rare that Gabby's smile did not evoke a response from its recipient, but the man in the black robe seemed unfortunately immune to the infectious warmth and her dimple.

'Children and animals like me.'

The limp quip did not draw any response.

He had, she decided, very poor people skills. Maybe being miserable came with the job of protecting the Zantaran royal family from contact with ordinary people? Did they ever step down from their ivory towers?

On the other hand, she conceded, it was possible he knew who she was, and this was the way he treated relatives of almost convicted felons—not that the *almost*, according to the man at the embassy, was anything more than a formality.

As far as he was concerned Paul was as guilty as hell—and this was the man who was meant to be on her brother's side!

'Your brother was caught carrying the drugs, Miss Barton,' he had reminded Gabby, in response to her angry diatribe on the justice system in this dustbowl of a country. 'And Zantara is *not* actually a dustbowl. There are desert areas, obviously, but due to the mountain range to the east and—' He had caught Gabby's eye and cut short the geography lesson, concluding apologetically, 'And in fairness the zero tolerance attitude to drugs here is well known to visitors. Our own government guidelines to travellers actually—'

Gabby, who was not interested in fairness, had cut in, explaining she was not there to read government guidelines but to get her brother out of jail and back home, where she had every intention of throttling him personally.

'My brother is not a drug runner. Stupid, yes,' she conceded. '*Very* stupid,' she added grimly. Only a total imbecile would carry a stuffed toy through Customs for a girl just because she'd smiled at him and looked helpless.

Gabby could see how people found his defence story lame, but they didn't *know* Paul. He had spent his entire adult life being made a fool of by pretty girls, and still he retained his child-like faith in the basic goodness of human nature—especially the human nature of pretty girls. It was left to his sister to be cynical for him.

Predictably, the pretty girl in question this time had vanished without trace, and now her brother was incarcerated behind prison walls, where he was likely to stay for a very long time unless Gabby pulled off some sort of miracle. And that was looking about as likely as this guard smiling back at her.

She felt the stirrings of despair, and took a deep and sustaining breath before adding another hundred volts to her smile. Stay positive, Gabby, she chided herself. She had to, for Paul's sake, and so far being positive had got her further than any of the embassy man's depressing predictions.

When she had explained her embryonic plan the man at the embassy had laughed. He'd actually given her a patronising pat on the head while explaining that she had to be realistic. It was totally impossible, he'd explained patiently, for her to gain access to the royal palace. As for an audience with the King—well, he had been here twelve months, and that honour had not as yet been granted *him*.

Gabby had asked him if he had any better ideas.

Once he'd starting talking about tact and diplomacy she had tuned him out, deciding there and then she would get into the royal palace if it killed her.

It hadn't—though she did have a few bruises to show for her efforts. She was inside—just—and the place looked as though it was straight from the pages of a fairy tale, complete with minarets that glistened with gold and lapis lazuli in the relentlessly fierce sun that shone down from the dizzyingly blue sky. Another time Gabby might have been enchanted by her surroundings, but she had no time for enchantment. She was on a mission.

First impossible step achieved. The next was to see the man himself—because, as her dad always said, if you wanted something you didn't mess around with the little people, you went right to the top.

And the King seemed about as top as you could get in this oil-rich desert state, and Gabby had every intention of pleading her brother's case to the man himself.

It had been simply bad luck, walking straight into two guards, but hopefully it was only a minor setback.

In deference to her aching face muscles she stopped smiling. She was wondering if it might actually be more useful to play dumb—though it went against the grain—when another granite-faced black-clad figure appeared—thankfully minus a scimitar.

The man with the face like granite looked Gabby up and down. You could almost hear him mentally filing her as harmless before he announced in perfect English that he was going to escort her from the premises.

'I have an appointment with the King.' The more

often she said it, Gabby reflected, the less convincing and more crazy it sounded.

'So I have been told. But there appears to have been a blunder, which I will look into immediately. The King does not have an appointment scheduled today. I am sorry for the inconvenience, Miss…?'

'Barton.'

'Miss Barton. I will have to ask you to leave and reschedule.'

He was scrupulously polite, but clearly—despite the lovely manners—not a man to be messed with. A winning smile was not going to work here.

'Good idea. I'll do that.'

'A wise decision.'

Gabby, who was not renowned for her ability to take no for an answer went meekly, keeping up a steady stream of inanity which after the first few minutes he did not bother responding to, and waited for her chance. Hoping she'd know what to do with it if and when it arrived.

She did.

They had entered a square mosaic-floored hallway—one of several they had passed through—when her escort stopped in response to a call from a short man who was one of the few Gabby had seen not armed to the teeth. As he left her side to speak to the man framed in the arched doorway, it clearly did not cross his mind that his instruction to Gabby to 'Wait there, please' would be ignored.

Gabby flashed her best meek, dumb smile, and waited until he'd reached the other man—then she hit the ground running, and carried on doing just that, ignoring the cries and sounds that followed her as she took the first turning off the wide corridor. Within seconds she was in a maze of narrow corridors, the echo of her heels loud in the silent hallways.

She ran along corridors and up stairs until her knees were jelly, then flopped forward, her long honey-blonde hair brushing the floor as, hands clasped to her thighs, she struggled to drag oxygen into her lungs.

Trying very hard not to think about the abundance of armed men she had seen, she slipped off her shoes, shoving them in the back pocket of her jeans, and continued more cautiously. The corridors were a regular maze, and there were miles of them. Only twice in half an hour did she hear the sound of raised voices and footsteps—presumably a search party after her blood, thought Gabby, though she sincerely hoped not literally.

The third time she heard voices and footsteps they were much closer. Heart pounding, she flattened herself against the wall—as though that was going to make her invisible, she thought, as the pause gave her time to consider her actions.

Her father, who always gave her the benefit of the doubt, would have said she was impetuous. More like reckless and irresponsible, her mother would have retorted, and on this occasion Gabby could see she might have had a point.

What had she achieved?

Beyond the very real possibility there would be two Bartons behind bars by this evening?

Gabby was mad with herself. She knew she ought to have done more research, but when opportunity in the shape of a distracted driver and an open delivery van had presented itself she had reacted without thinking. If she had had more time to plan she might now have an idea of the palace layout.

The sound of a footfall close by interrupted her gloomy analysis of the situation and sent her instinctively for the worn flight of spiral stone steps to her right. She flew up them in breathless haste.

At the top Gabby found herself in a small foyer, with a large metal-studded, ancient-looking door in front of her. At the sound of steps behind her Gabby took a deep breath and pushed it. Relieved when it swung inwards, she stepped inside and, hastily closing it behind her, turned the big key in the lock, shooting home a couple of heavy-duty bolts before leaning back against the solid wood, her chest heaving.

For the first time she looked around the room she stood in. It was curiously shaped—octagonal—but, more importantly from her point of view, it was empty.

As her racing heart slowed Gabby's eyes adjusted to the gloom and she surveyed her sanctuary. Unlike the other rooms she had glimpsed inside the palace it was informally furnished, with an eclectic mix of antique and modern items. One wall appeared to be lined with books, several of which lay open on a large inlaid table, and another wall had heavy curtains pulled across. The light that filtered though the gaps suggested there was a window behind it.

The adrenaline rush that had got her this far abruptly receded, and her knees folded. Spine pressed to the door, she slid down to the floor until she sat, her knees drawn up to her chin, shaking.

# CHAPTER TWO

STANDING on the balcony, Rafiq gazed out over the palace's luminous gilded towers and beyond to the city, with its graceful avenues lined by waving palms, its white geometric buildings spreading out into the neatly cultivated fields that had once been desert, and further on again to the purple haze that was the mountain range that ran across the eastern border of Zantara.

It was a view he had looked at countless times, but never before had his appreciation of the beauty held this bitter poignancy.

Zantara had grown beyond recognition in the last few years, but there was still so much to be done—and he had assumed he would be there to do it, to guide his country into the twenty-first century, treading the delicate path between tradition and progress... Frustration and a sense of loss so profound he had no words to describe it clenched around his heart like an iron fist. He closed his eyes, his strong-boned features reflecting the emotions he had fought to subdue since receiving the prognosis earlier.

He jaw hardened, and he dragged a hand through his

dark hair while squaring his broad shoulders. He could not afford to indulge in emotional reaction. He needed to stay focused. There was much to do and very little time to do it in.

His task and his title would fall on the shoulders of his younger brother, and his affection for his likeable sibling did not blind him to the fact that Hakim was utterly unsuited to the task.

Zantara was a land richly endowed with natural resources. As well as oil, there were vast mineral deposits as yet untouched. Properly managed, they guaranteed the long-term prosperity of Zantara and its people—but there were many in high places who only paid lip service to the long-term aims that he and his father had always worked towards.

They smiled and applauded reform, but given the chance they would not let morality or ideals get in the way of exploiting the country for their personal gain.

As the heir, over the years Rafiq had been the target of influential families on the make, who would have liked nothing better than to see him marry one of their own, thus automatically gaining—or so they imagined—unprecedented access to the throne.

Zantara had a political stability that was the envy of surrounding countries, but Rafiq was only too aware of how easily things could change—how little it would take to unbalance that delicate harmony. Introducing a perceived advantage to one of the country's powerful families might be all it took.

Rafiq, who had no intention of allowing that situation to occur, was amused rather than threatened by political manoeuvring. But Hakim was so eager to please, so malleable—in fact all the things that made his brother so much more likeable a person than he was—and he would be putty in the hands of those circling sharks. When Hakim became heir he would become their new target… It was a disaster waiting to happen.

What Hakim needed, he mused, was someone to guide him—someone with backbone, someone behind the throne giving his brother the strength to make tough decisions and see through the sycophants and con-men.

It came to Rafiq in a blinding flash. It was simple, but obvious. His brother needed a wife—the right sort of wife, obviously—who could be groomed for the role of power behind the throne.

Rafiq straightened up as he mentally skimmed the list of possible candidates…

A frown of dissatisfaction furrowed his brow as he methodically discarded them all. It would take a very special woman.

He rubbed a hand over the brown skin of his neck, feeling the grit that remained after his solitary ride through the desert earlier.

It had required all his considerable skill to stay in the saddle as his Arab stallion, the pride of the stables, possibly picking up on the mood of his master, had spent all the time he wasn't thundering across the desert as though pursued by devils trying to unseat his rider.

The only possible candidate who even began to fill his requirements was—

Rafiq did not complete the thought, because at that

moment he heard a voice—a very distinct and very feminine voice.

*'So what happens next, Gabby?'*

Rafiq knew what was going to happen next, but he could identify with the desperation in that voice.

Either auditory hallucinations were a symptom of the disease the doctor had forgotten to mention, or someone had had the audacity to invade what was his private sanctum. The tower room was the place he retreated to when the weight of the formality involved in fulfilling his duties became too stifling and oppressive—it was his retreat, tucked away in this remote corner of the palace, simply furnished and totally out of bounds.

Utterly astounded that anyone would have such impudence, and curious to see the owner of the very English voice, Rafiq pulled aside the heavy curtain that screened the small balcony from the room beyond.

Chin resting on her knees, Gabby's eyes lifted as the big heavy curtain was swept back, flooding the room with golden light and revealing a balcony surrounded by an elaborately carved railing.

Gabby's eyes carried on up. The golden-skinned man who stood framed in the light-filled arch was seriously tall.

He was also quite spectacularly good to look at.

He wore a knee-length robe in a thin white fabric— thin enough, as a gust of wind plastered it close to his lean torso, for her to make out the shadow of a dark drift of body hair across his broad chest. The riding breeches he wore beneath the robe were tucked into dusty boots. His head was bare and the dusky gloss of his hair outlined by a nimbus of sunlight—which seemed appropriate, as there was something of the fallen angel about his achingly perfect features. Gabby was disastrously sidetracked from her personal dilemma by the combined impact of chiselled cheekbones, a clean-shaven square jaw, a broad, intelligent forehead, aquiline nose, a wide and disturbingly sensual mouth, and incredible wide-spaced black eyes shot with flecks of platinum and framed by long curling sooty lashes.

*Wow!*

No man had a right to be *that* good-looking.

He arched a dark brow and drawled. 'Gabby…?'

His voice was deep, and the velvet tones only slightly accented, but for some reason it made the hairs on the nape of Gabby's neck stand on end. Probably the male arrogance he was oozing had got under her skin. Something had. She rubbed her hands along her forearms, troubled by the prickling sensation under her skin.

'No… Yes…' Aware that she was blushing like a schoolgirl, she closed her mouth. Unable to break the mesmeric hold of his bold pewter-flecked stare, she gave up trying to sound like someone with an IQ in single figures.

'You are perhaps bad with names?'

It was not unusual to see a woman in Zantara wearing Western clothes, even though less commonly they wore jeans. But it was very unusual to find one who was blue-eyed or blonde. The young woman sitting on the floor was both.

The startled azure eyes fixed on his face suggested

their owner was just as surprised to see him as he was to see her—so this *wasn't* an engineered meeting…

That had been his initial assumption, and Rafiq still reserved judgement. He had been frequently pursued over the years, and the women who set their sights on him constantly managed to surprise him with their ingenuity—not to mention their acting ability.

His vanity, or lack of it, was such that he didn't imagine for one second that it was his personal magnetism that made these women humiliate themselves by going to such embarrassingly elaborate lengths to gain his attention. It was his title, his position that attracted them. The old adage that power was a strong aphrodisiac was not far from the mark.

He had occasionally wondered in the past if he would ever find a woman who wanted him and not what he represented, or even wanted him *despite* what he represented.

Those thoughts had never gone beyond casual speculation, because he had always known that in reality his choice of bride would be a political decision, not a romantic one. His own parents' marriage had been such a one, and despite a considerable age-gap the marriage had been a success. They both respected one another, and neither had entered into the arrangement with any false expectations.

The union had produced two sons, and had done much to negate the political fallout from his father's first marriage. That marriage *had* been a love-match—not in itself a problem, but King Zafir's first wife's inability to supply him with an heir had been. When the King had steadfastly refused to put aside the love of his life, the monarchy that had lasted so many generations had been in real danger. Then, against all the odds, the Queen had conceived, but the country's and the King's delight had been short-lived. Queen Sadira had gone into premature labour and died of complications. The baby—a boy— had died a week later.

By all accounts his father had been almost mad with grief, and without his powerful hand at the reins the country had divided into warring factions. It had been a time of deep political unrest.

Rafiq had never been able to imagine the man he knew today being so blindly besotted that he'd put romantic love ahead of duty. Even less could he imagine himself repeating that mistake.

Now, of course, the subject was irrelevant. For him there would be no marriage, no wife and no future.

Cutting short this line of thought before he became lost in a morass of despondency, Rafiq dragged a hand though his hair, smoothing the dark strands into the nape of his neck. A frown of distaste drew his brows into a straight line. He despised self-pity in himself even more than in others.

Besides being a pointless emotion, it smacked of self-indulgence—more productive by far to focus on things he could control. Like the blonde...

The blonde whose astonishing neon blue eyes had not yet left his face.

She really was not the sort of woman you would miss in a crowd—not with those eyes and that head of decadent blonde curls that spilled down her back, framing a vivid little face that reminded him of a Titian portrait. But below the neck, he decided, staying with the art analogy, she was pure Degas. Her slim, supple and gently rounded body might have belonged to one of that artist's ethereal ballet dancers.

She looked like a wilted rose, with her grubby face and the purple smudge of exhaustion beneath her eyes. She was the delicate, petite type of female that aroused the protective instinct in a lot of men.

Rafiq's assessing glance drifted from her stubborn chin and defiant, wary eyes to the pouting lower lip, and he thought they would be the same men who failed to notice that she had *stroppy* written all over her.

She began to struggle to her feet. Rafiq noted the tremor in the hand that reached to clutch for support and extended his own. She looked at it for a moment with the sort of enthusiasm that most people reserved for a striking snake, then deliberately ignored it, carrying on struggling.

Rafiq withdrew his hand and with a derisive shrug made no further attempt to help her, even though she looked about as weak and shaky as a newborn kitten.

He liked independent women—but not when they felt the need to make pointless displays of self-sufficiency.

Gretchen, his lover for twelve months previous to their non-acrimonious split in May, was a highly independent-minded woman, who made no apologies for being ambitious, but she took the little courtesies offered by a man as her due.

Gretchen was a divorce lawyer based in Paris; before her there had been Cynthia, a fashion designer in Milan—long-distance relationships, with women who'd wanted what he did: sex. Not casual, anonymous sex, but sex that came with no emotional strings attached.

Rafiq had never understood why people felt long-distance love affairs put a strain on relationships. For him, the arrangement was perfect. It made it easier to compartmentalise his personal and public life. He never had unrealistic calls on his time when he had duties to perform, there were no draining emotional melodramas, and there were no outside distractions—just mutually satisfying sex.

He was not even sure why he and Gretchen had split up. She was everything he wanted in a woman—totally self-absorbed, of course, but that had its advantages, and she didn't make small talk.

Gretchen hadn't changed, so why had boredom and dissatisfaction set in?

There was never more than one woman in his life at a time, but there generally was one. Sex was important—or it had been! He had put this barren period in his love life down to a jaded appetite. Had his life acquired a certain cyclical predictability? Was the effort worth the reward? But now, for the first time, he was confronted by the possibility that his recent loss of libido might be another insidious symptom of the disease that was robbing him of his future, of the opportunity to decide that he *wanted* the emotionally draining drama he had been actively avoiding.

He looked at the blonde's mouth and felt his body stir lustfully—and thought maybe not...

He had never been attracted to women who treated their femininity like an affliction, and he got the distinct

impression this woman would take it as an insult if a
man opened a door for her. She looked all prickles, aggression, and pink sulky lips, he decided, his critical
gaze lingering longer than was polite on those lips.

In short, not his type—physically or otherwise. But
by anyone's standards she'd definitely fulfil the role of
distraction.

It would be a simple matter to have her removed, and
that was clearly the logical course of action, but curiosity won out over practicality. How did a blue-eyed
blonde come to be in here?

He recognised it was a very poor piece of prioritis-
ing, but at that moment this was the mystery that had
captured his total attention—maybe he was attracted by
its light relief value?

He searched his brain for a plausible explanation for
her presence and came up empty. There simply wasn't
one. True, tourism was a developing industry in Zantara,
but to his knowledge they had not begun offering
escorted tours of the palace.

His father was in many ways a moderniser, but the
mental image of curious camera-clicking crowds being
shown around the King of Zantara's private apartments
caused the corner of Rafiq's stern mouth to twitch.

Gabby was conscious of his intense scrutiny—she now
understood why people spoke of *feeling* someone's eyes.

Reluctant to reveal her weakened condition to this
stranger, she surreptitiously leaned her elbow against an
armoire set against the wall. Being a fugitive was certainly exhausting!

It wasn't just her reluctance to show vulnerability

that had made her reject his offer of assistance. She couldn't explain it, but the idea of those long brown fingers touching her... She frowned and shook her head, confused by the violence of her gut rejection.

The sound of his bitter-chocolate voice made her jump. 'You are well?'

She tilted her head. He didn't look as if he'd lose much sleep if she said *No, I'm damned well not*. This was not a man who oozed empathy. Under the cool exterior she sensed an explosive, combustible quality that was reflected in his dark stare.

Some women might find that quality attractive, but she had never felt drawn to dangerous or brooding moody men. He probably practised that expression in front of the mirror, she decided uncharitably.

Gabby dragged a tangled skein of blonde hair back from her face and threw it over her shoulder, pushing back stray tendrils of hair from her sweat-dampened face.

'I'm fine,' she lied, trying to straighten her creased and torn shirt as she continued to regard him warily.

It was a struggle not to show that she was slightly intimidated—all right, a lot more than slightly—by his raw physical presence. Of their own volition her eyes travelled to his toes and made the journey up to his face. A little shudder traced a shivery path up her spine— God, the man had an aura that was almost electric. She had never encountered anything like it—or like him!

'You startled me. I didn't know anyone was in here.'

Not that he was *anyone*. This man was definitely *someone*. She breathed in the outdoorsy scent that drifted from his direction and felt her stomach flip.

His arrogant self-assurance was that of a man who had never heard the word *no* from a woman in his life. This was an alpha male, with raw sex appeal oozing from every pore. He was a man women were programmed to want to say yes to—a man they'd want to father their children. And my goodness, she thought with an inner sigh, as her eyes travelled back to his face, with his gene pool they would be extremely beautiful children.

And so far the utterly gorgeous creature had not opened the door and invited her to leave.

Maybe he wasn't meant to be there either…? she speculated hopefully.

This was an idea she could warm to—and after the last forty-eight hours she needed a break.

She let her fertile imagination go into overdrive. Could this be an upstairs-downstairs situation? Maybe he didn't want to be found out any more than she did? His were definitely the first dusty boots gracing the marble floors she had seen, so it was a real possibility. Had she intruded on a secret assignation?

Admittedly he didn't look like star-crossed lover material—it was sensuality and not sentiment that you saw when you looked at his mouth. Its wide, firm contours sent out a conflicting message of control and passion.

Before Gabby could drag her distracted gaze from his lips and summon up an inventive explanation for her own presence there was a loud bang on the door behind her. Gabby turned and, staring fearfully at the door, began to back away.

'Miss Barton, if you don't open this door immediately I will be forced to break it down.'

No need for that explanation, then.

She wondered uneasily how the tall stranger would react now her fugitive status had been established. She turned her head and was none the wiser. He had a great poker face—actually, he had a great face… Her eyes dropped… A great body…

A great everything!

Despite the uncustomary harassed note, Rafiq immediately identified the voice as belonging to Rashid, a senior member of his father's personal bodyguard—not an easy man to rattle.

He turned his head in time to see a flash of despair and fear in the blonde's wide blue eyes. It only lasted seconds, before she literally and mentally squared her slender shoulders, stuck out her softly rounded chin and adopted an air of studied defiance.

Gabby muttered, 'You and whose army?'

The door looked pretty solid to her. Solid enough to withstand an earthquake. She was trapped, but for the moment safe—if you discounted her companion. Not an easy thing to do. The man was a distraction she could do without.

'Who *are* you?'

A frown of concentration on her face, Gabby glared at the door. She did not turn her head, and therefore missed the look of stark incredulity that chased across Rafiq's lean dark features when she waved a hand in impatient dismissal.

'Not now, *please*—I'm trying to think,' she snapped. Trying, but not really getting far. And she blamed this partly on her rotten luck.

There might be times when being trapped in an enclosed space with a man who appeared to have been gifted with a dangerously generous share of phero-mones was not a hardship, but this wasn't one of those times. Actually, that wasn't true. She had never been at-tracted to overtly macho men. She went more for the in-tellectual type, a man who wasn't afraid to show his emotions and his vulnerability, but such men were thin on the ground. Actually, she was unsure whether they existed outside literature and her imagination—it could be she was doomed to settle or remain single.

Rafiq was accustomed to being treated with a level of deference by virtually everybody he met. He had not been so casually dismissed since he was a boy—and then the only woman in a position to do so had been his mother. It was an irrational response to rudeness, but he found himself even more curious about the blonde.

*Why not invite her for a dinner date as you have so much time to waste?*

He frowned in unappreciative response to the ironic voice in his head, and allowed his glance to wander to the neatly trimmed pearly fingertips she was rubbing along the slightly tip-tilted end of her small nose. This woman was like none he had encountered in his thirty-two years. And he wasn't talking about her dress code—though it was nothing short of a miracle that she still managed to look feminine dressed like *that*!

He watched as she lifted her hand and dashed it across her face. Her hair was honey-gold, with paler shades woven in with the silky mesh that fell to her shoulders.

As his eyes slid down her body it became obvious

that his curiosity was not the only thing this woman had
awoken. The ache in his groin was increasingly hard to
ignore. He might be dying, but nobody had told his
libido, it seemed!

Gabby turned her head at the sound of his laugh, her
darting blue gaze moving indignantly across his lean
features. 'You think this is *funny*?'

'I think it is extraordinary that I am laughing.' Not to
mention lusting.

Gabby glared, bemused by the cryptic response.

'Who are you, Gabby Barton?'

Feathery brows several shades darker than her hair
twitched into a straight line above her neat nose. The intensity of his narrowed stare made her uneasy. 'Not a
thief, if that's what you're thinking. I didn't come to
steal the family silver.'

'I believe you,' he soothed. 'But you have a purpose...what have you come here for?'

Gabby was gripped by a sudden irrational compulsion to pour out her troubles to this total stranger. Tell
him the whole tangled tale... Appalled that she was
about to go all weak—little woman crying on the
shoulder of a big strong man—she closed her mouth
with an audible snap and shook her head.

Of course if her problem could be solved by brute
force it might well be worth getting him on her side. But
she wasn't the type of person who off-loaded her problems
onto anyone—least of all someone she had just met!

## CHAPTER THREE

RAFIQ watched as she lowered her eyes, causing the tips of her lashes to brush against her slightly grubby cheek. She remained silent.

'A woman of mystery...'

'No mystery,' she denied, shaking her head.

'How did you get into the palace?'

'How do you know I wasn't invited?'

One black brow slanted satirically as he glanced towards the door.

Gabby's slender shoulders lifted. 'All right,' she conceded. 'I wasn't. I sort of *slipped* in.'

His brows hit his hairline. '*Slipped in?*' He shook his head in a firm negative motion. 'That isn't possible.' Incredulity deepened his voice a husky octave, and it feathered across Gabby's nerve-endings as he repeated, 'You *slipped in* past Security?'

'In the back of a delivery van.' It had been one of those moments when you acted on instinct and didn't have time to think about the consequences. That came later, she thought bitterly, when you were trapped in a room with armed men outside the door. Not that she regretted it for a second. If she hadn't at least tried she would never have forgiven herself.

Rafiq thought about the substantial budget earmarked each year for palace security, and a muscle clenched in his lean cheek once more as he fought the unexpected desire to laugh. The girl was more than unusual, she was unique—though he had not dismissed the possibility she was mentally unbalanced just yet.

'And when it slowed down I...I got out...'

This casual confidence sent Rafiq's eyebrows in the direction of his dark hairline. 'It was moving?' He tried to imagine any of the women he knew leaping out of a moving vehicle and failed.

He felt reluctant admiration stir once more. Whoever this woman was, she did not lack courage—or for that matter recklessness. And today had taught Rafiq that when all other alternatives were exhausted *reckless* was sometimes the only thing left.

'Not very fast...' She lifted a hand to the shoulder seam of her shirt. The skin beneath was grazed and starting to bruise.

His brow furrowed in concern as he saw the specks of bright blood on the cotton. 'You are injured?'

He didn't wait for her denial. Gabby watched with horror as he strode with purpose towards the door, his white robe billowing around his tall frame.

He was going to let them in!

She acted without thinking and threw herself between him and the door. Shrill panic threaded her voice as she caught his arm.

Their eyes met, and there was a long, still, nerve-shredding silence, Gabby's world narrowed until the only things she was conscious of were his mesmerising sloe-dark eyes and the thunderous beat of her heart as it pounded in her ears.

It was Rafiq who broke the tableau, the breath expelled from his lungs in one slow, audible hiss as his dark glance moved from her wide, beseeching eyes to the small pale hand on his arm.

Gabby saw the direction of his gaze, saw the inexplicable astonishment in his expression, but she didn't let go. If anything she clung harder, her fingers tightening into the taut, rock-hard muscle of his arm.

Her breath came in panicky gasps as she appealed with husky urgency, 'Please—don't let them in.'

Rafiq's glance flickered across the soft contours of her face. Her full lips trembled, and under the smudges of dirt the freckles across the bridge of her nose stood out against the dramatic pallor of her skin. Her electric blue eyes held the zealot-like glow of sheer desperation.

He shook his head. 'I must. You need a doctor.'

Gabby unpeeled her fingers from his arm, finding her digits strangely reluctant to respond to her commands. Mission accomplished, she absently rubbed her palm across her thigh. The impression of sinewy strength in his forearm seemed to have imprinted itself on her hand.

'It's nothing,' she promised, ripping the fabric of her shirt a little more than it already was to prove her point, revealing the smooth curve of her shoulder and the beginning of a large area of bruising in the process.

'I can't feel it,' she said, between clenched teeth.

But she could feel the brown fingertip he slid down

the exposed curve. And her nervous system's reaction to a touch that was so light it barely stirred the soft invisible down on her pale skin was totally disproportionate. Every nerve-ending in her body came alive, and a heavy, creeping warm lethargy invaded her suddenly uncooperative limbs.

There was not a breath of air in the room. She doubted this sort of stillness existed outside the eye of a hurricane, where the fragile illusion of security was coloured with the anticipation of the storm that was just waiting to break.

She could feel the pressure in her eardrums as her heart-rate began to race. The air thrummed with tension—unacknowledged and almost tangible.

Gabby struggled to maintain her indifferent pose, and to control her shallow, uneven breathing as his fingertip moved upwards, tracing the angle of her collarbone in a light, feathery motion. Unable to bear the prickling heat under her skin and the dragging sensation low in her belly another second, she pulled away.

'I told you—I'm fine.' Gabby glared at him, resentment shining in her eyes as they connected with his and stayed connected. She was utterly mesmerised by the febrile glow smouldering deep in his dark eyes.

Rafiq did not speak until the heat in his blood had cooled—which meant he was silent for some time.

What he had felt when he touched her skin had been raw and primitive. It didn't take enormous powers of analytical deduction to conclude it was some form of delayed reaction, because he was not a man who allowed his passions to rule him, but it was easy to understand why some men finding themselves in his position might chose to blot out the bleak reality of their situation. They might turn to alcohol, jump in the driver's seat of a fast car or sit astride a horse and try and outrun the devils within.

And then others might bury themselves physically and mentally in the soft body of a desirable woman…

His eyes brushed the slender white column of her neck before reaching the full curve of her wide mouth. His chest lifted as he dragged in a fractured breath. *A woman like this one.*

'Do you imagine that the men outside are going to go away? Why can't you admit defeat gracefully?'

'There's nothing graceful about defeat,' she retorted scornfully.

Her apparent inability to see that she had lost irritated him. But the irritation melted into antagonism as the memory of the raw desire, the tidal swell of devouring hunger that had washed over him moments earlier surfaced.

'Not admitting you have lost does not make it any less a reality.'

*Nice sermon*, admitted the ironic voice in his head. *Is it intended for her or you, Rafiq?*

Gabby compressed her lips, regarding him with seething resentment. Did he think she didn't *know* that her situation was impossible? Did he think she didn't *know* she only had herself to blame?

Her lips curled into a derisive smile. '*Lost…?* I'm not playing a game.'

'You are delaying the inevitable.'

'Thank you for that pearl of wisdom,' she snapped sarcastically. 'If you want to be helpful you could go out there and tell them I'm not here…'

'Why would I lie for you?'

Gabby scowled at him. 'Maybe they don't know you're here either?'

'I imagine they will be shocked to find me present.'

The admission drew a *hah* from Gabby. 'I thought as much! You're not meant to be here either, are you?'

His lashes, jet and lustrously curled, swept downwards, concealing the satirical gleam in his dark eyes from Gabby as they brushed the slashing angle of his cheekbones.

'This room is off-limits to everyone but the Crown Prince.'

The information made her examine her surroundings with fresh interest. 'Really?' Her voice echoed her surprise. 'A sort of bolthole?' she mused.

Compared with the parts of the palace she'd seen, this was as plain as a monk's cell—a well-read monk who liked comfy chairs.

'Maybe he gets bored with the glitter? He likes books,' she added, running her finger along the spine of a thick leather-bound volume open on the table. She read the title and her eyebrows shot up. 'Not what I'd call light reading, so he's not just a pretty face.'

'You are familiar with the Prince?'

Gabby laughed and folded her arms across her chest. 'What do you think?' She rolled her eyes. 'If you must know, I read an article.'

'Was it a critical article?'

The suggestion drew a laugh from Gabby.

'Hardly! Either your Prince Rafiq has just stepped directly off Mount Olympus, or someone paid the journalist to write nice things, or she had a massive crush on him—because *nobody* is that marvellous. Personally it made me queasy to read all that gushy stuff.'

The odd look on his face made her recall the embassy man's warning.

*'The people here are very protective of their royal family, so avoid saying anything that could offend.'*

'*Gushy*...? I must have missed that one.'

The admission was delivered in a flat tone, but she had the impression that far from being offended he was amused. It just showed that the embassy man had been wrong—people here did have a sense of humour.

His dark eyes scanned her face. 'I am going to open the door you know. Sooner or later.'

Gabby gave a resigned sigh, compressed her lips and nodded. Short of sprouting wings, there was no other way out, and he was right: she was delaying the inevitable. It had also crossed her mind that the longer she kept the men outside waiting the less likely they were to be sympathetic.

Sympathetic? Ever the optimist, Gabby. They'll probably fling you into a cell next to Paul.

'I suggest you stay there, be quiet, and restrain any impulses you have to do something dramatic or foolish.'

'I suppose you're going to be in trouble too...?' She struggled to feel some genuine sympathy, but it was hard when he didn't look perturbed by his predicament, and she couldn't rid herself of the suspicion that he was the type of man who liked to break the odd rule once in a while just for the hell of it.

Under a tightly controlled surface, she decided, studying the lean hard lines of his face, he had a combustible quality. But then he was a man of contradictions. Like his mouth, she thought, her eyes straying in that direction. The stern upper lip and the full sexy lower lip, sending two opposing messages…

'I am already in trouble.'

The cryptic response made her frown. 'I'll make it clear you didn't help me or anything.'

He inclined his dark head, and something she could not interpret flickered at the back of his eyes. 'Thank you.'

'Why are you here?'

'Why are *you* here?' he shot back seamlessly.

'I was looking for someone.'

'The Crown Prince?'

'At a pinch he'd do, I suppose, but, no—not really. I need someone with more clout.' A choking sound made her tilt her head to look at him.

'I think you'll find that the Crown Prince has a little…*clout*.'

'Maybe,' she conceded, dismissing the absent royal with a shrug, and a worried glance towards the door that was the only thing between her and total failure— maybe even imprisonment. 'But he isn't here, is he? There's just you and me.' Which sounded a lot cosier than it was. 'No insult intended, but I need someone important to hear what I have to say. Don't panic—I won't bore you with the details.'

Without the belligerence she seemed much smaller,

more delicate, and the bleak note of resignation in her flat voice stirred something he refused to recognise as concern.

'I will tell you if I'm bored,' he promised.

'Nice offer.' If he meant it—which she doubted. 'I came here to see the King.'

It sounded so absurd, even to her, that Gabby wouldn't have been surprised if he had laughed. He didn't, though she was willing to bet he would look pretty incredible if he *did* laugh, or even smile, she thought, trying to imagine the lines bracketing his stern, incredibly sexy mouth relaxing. Actually, now she thought about it, it might be easier to concentrate if he didn't laugh.

'There are official channels to receive an audience with the King, if that is your plan.' He did not add that there was also a long list for those waiting to be granted an audience with his father.

'I've no time for official channels and plans,' she admitted. 'I'm kind of winging it.'

The desperation in her manner was tinged with obstinacy as she looked around the room. There *had* to be another way out. She refused to believe that her attempt to save her brother could end in such ignominious failure.

'Are you sure there isn't any other way out of here? What about the balcony?' Without waiting for a response, her urgency fuelled by another bang on the door, followed by a second volley of threats, Gabby, her eyes sparkling, rushed headlong past him and out of the open double doors.

The balcony was not large—little more than six feet in width—and the impetus of her dash sent Gabby right up to the scrolled wrought-iron railing that came up to waist-height.

As she found herself staring down at a dizzying drop, her vision blurred and the world far below spun. A mewling sound locked in her throat as she closed her eyes.

# CHAPTER FOUR

RAFIQ emerged on the balcony just as Gabby loosened her grip on the rail and her body swayed forward. A violent curse was drawn from his lips as he surged forward, his fingers closing like steel bands around her upper arms as he jerked her back to safety.

Gabby's knees had gone. Head spinning, she was only vaguely conscious of her heels dragging across the floor in the moment before she found herself hauled upwards. With a sigh she leaned back into him, her heart pounding after her near escape. His arms came up around her waist, anchoring her there, drawing her closer.

'Don't worry—I'm not going to jump.' Now that the moment of sheer terror was over she was becoming a lot more conscious of other details—disturbing details, like the hot, hard imprint of his body where her spine curved into his lean length. She was tempted to stay where she was and prolong the moment. 'Thank you,' she said huskily. 'I'm not good with heights.'

'I'm disappointed. I thought nothing frightened this jumping-from-moving-vehicles action woman.'

One arm still wrapped in a supportive band across her

midriff, Rafiq felt her ribcage rise as she sought to suck in a deep breath before responding huskily, but with a lot less attitude than she had shown so far.

'So sorry to be a disappointment, but we all have our weaknesses.' It seemed a good time for her to remember that her weaknesses did not usually include being attracted by obvious beefcake—even the exotic variety.

*Very* exotic, she thought as the clean, musky and very male scent of his body teased her quivering nostrils. Her eyelashes brushed her cheeks as her gaze fastened onto his fingers, long and tapering where they lay on her arm. A large red stone set in a thick gold band decorated one finger. If the stone had been real it would have been worth a small fortune.

Was he married?

Did he have a brood of children and an adoring doe-eyed wife who worshipped him? The images of domestic harmony that passed before her eyes made Gabby feel vaguely dissatisfied.

Was it envy? Obviously not of the woman who was married to this total stranger, but Gabby was twenty-four, and she had never even met anyone she cared enough about to have a serious relationship with—this was one area of her life where she was risk-averse.

As recently as the previous weekend Gabby had produced a jokey response when her friend Rachel had made an exasperated suggestion that she should lower the bar and maybe have a little fun.

Gabby was no prude, but she wasn't sure she wanted the 'fun' her friend was talking about—and she wasn't about to admit that she was a closet romantic. And anyway, everyone would treat her confession as a joke. She was simply not the type of girl anyone expected to admit she believed there was someone special for everyone—someone worth waiting for.

But she couldn't help but occasionally wistfully wonder if there actually *was* anyone out there for her, and she found it increasingly difficult to even imagine meeting someone she wanted to share her life with. Maybe Rachel was right? she mused. Maybe she was just making life difficult for herself…?

It could be she was doomed to stay single. Oh, well—there were worse things—things like being married to a man every woman under a hundred lusted after, she thought.

As she sucked in another tremulous breath Rafiq could feel the tremors running through her body. She felt soft, warm, scarily delicate. The man in him recognised that he was strongly attracted to her; the Prince in him knew that even had circumstances been different, even if he hadn't just been given a death sentence, a woman like this would not be for him.

There had never been any room for distraction in his life, and that went double now. His glance flickered across the top of the blonde's tousled head. There was no doubt this woman had distraction written all over her.

Her colour heightened, Gabby pulled away and walked back in to the octagonal room. She couldn't decide if her legs felt as shaky as those of a newborn colt due to her fear of heights and the accumulated stress of the last two days, or to this badly timed *visceral* reaction to a stranger.

Now, that was weird—because she had never been attracted to men like him, who projected animal magnetism. As she tilted her chin to meet his level dark gaze she was forced to acknowledge she had never actually *met* men like him before.

Her lips twisted into a wry smile. She was guessing there *were* no other men like him…

'Why do you want to speak to the King?'

Self-recrimination tautened her soft face as his question made her realise she was in danger of losing focus here.

'I really don't see why that would be any of your business.'

There was another bang on the door—loud enough to make Gabby flinch.

Without taking his eyes from Gabby's face, he nodded towards the door. 'It is possibly *his* business.'

Gabby glared at him. 'Well, if you must know I want the King to intercede. It's my brother—he's under arrest, awaiting trial.'

Gabby watched comprehension and distaste spread across his lean face. Her chin lifted. She had seen this response before, but most people attempted to conceal it. He did not.

'Your brother is the English drug-smuggler?'

Indignation sparkled in her eyes as she retorted, 'My brother is *not* a smuggler.' She saw the look of cynical contempt in the tall Arab's face and struggled to stop her eyes falling guiltily from his. 'What's the point?' she said, throwing up her hands in disgust. 'You've already made up your mind,' she accused angrily. '*Everyone* in this stupid place has already made up their minds,' she added, with an emotional quiver in her voice as she realised Paul didn't stand a chance.

The embassy man had been right—his fate was sealed.

The idea hit him like the classic bolt from the blue. He had been searching for an answer to his problems and the answer had come looking for him—or as good as.

He smiled, and his answer glared back at him with loathing.

Had he gone mad?

Admittedly on the surface it seemed a crazy, desperate idea, but sometimes you had to think outside the box—something he was famed for, though admittedly he had never ventured this far outside on previous occasions.

He'd never had to.

His thoughts raced. This girl possessed the qualities his brother was lacking: toughness, resourcefulness and a healthy lack of respect for people in authority. And loyalty was a quality you could not buy. How many people would have gone to the lengths she had for a brother? And even now, when she knew deep down it was hopeless, she refused to give up.

And he had something she needed.

Looking at the defeated slump of her slender shoulders, and at the tears sparkling on her cheeks, Rafiq felt a moment's doubt about his intentions. He quickly pushed aside the disquiet and walked towards the door. This was about the future of his country. He could not afford sentiment.

Gabby lifted her head at the sound of the lock being clicked.

With the door half open he turned back to look at her, and Gabby lifted her chin. She had not realised until this moment that she had hoped, quite irrationally, that this stranger might be on her side. Which probably made her certifiably stupid.

Gabby waited, sickly anticipating armed men appearing. When they didn't she moved towards the door, but any tentative hope she had that the coast might miraculously be clear for her to make her escape vanished when she heard the sound of deep male voices outside.

One belonged to the man who had just walked out, the other possibly to the man who had been escorting her from the premises—though it was hard to tell, because he wasn't sounding cold or dismissive now.

If anything he was sounding…well, deferential.

Gabby was still trying to make sense of this conundrum when the tall Arab reappeared. He closed the door.

Gabby noticed immediately that the air of hauteur she had noticed in his manner was now more pronounced. She folded her arms protectively across her chest as she regarded him with deep suspicion. She was missing something.

He waved a hand towards a low divan covered in tumbled silk cushions. 'Have a seat, Miss Barton.'

Gabby didn't miss the significant fact that this was not a suggestion. 'What's going on? The guard—where is—?'

'I have convinced Rashid that you offer no immediate threat to security.'

She gave a dubious shake of her head. 'And your word was enough to make him go away?'

'Perhaps I should introduce myself?' Without breaking eye contact with Gabby, he bowed fractionally at the waist and said, 'I am Prince Rafiq Al Kamil.'

The hot colour flew once again to Gabby's cheeks.

If the introduction had come from anyone else she would have thought them delusional and politely asked if they had taken their medication, but as her gaze travelled up the length of the tall figure, from his dusty feet to his gleaming dark head, she had to bite back a groan at her own stupidity.

She might have been looking for royalty, but in her own defence she hadn't been expecting to find it so literally. If she had been thinking straight she might have worked it out herself—his whole manner proclaimed that he was speaking the truth.

So this was what the end result of centuries of breeding looked like... She had to admit that even to someone who felt a natural repugnance for arranged marriages he was a pretty good advert.

A mortified flush climbed to her cheeks. '*You're* the Crown Prince?' she said, feeling stupid.

He inclined his head in regal acknowledgement and drawled sardonically, 'A poor second, I realise, to the King, but my father is at present out of the country. You don't look very pleased,' he mused, studying her flushed face and sparkling eyes. 'Is this not what you wanted? A chance to plead your brother's case at the highest level?'

Despite the fact she had what she wanted, instead of taking this heaven-sent opportunity to ingratiate herself and plead Paul's case, she remained on her feet and shouted angrily, 'Why didn't you tell me who you were?' Adding, 'And how do I know you even *are* who you say you are? You could be anyone.'

A look of astonishment chased across his lean features. 'You wish me to *prove* who I am?'

Their eyes connected, and Gabby's short burst of irrational anger subsided. She shook her head, retracting the challenge before taking the seat he had previously proffered. She would have infinitely preferred the dark wood chair beside it to this low divan that would not have looked out of place in a harem.

How did harems work?

Did *he* have one?

The questions popped unbidden into her head, and it was hard to mentally drop the theme as she watched him lower his long, lean length into the slatted designer chair she would have preferred herself. It was not exactly difficult to see him in the role of desert predator.

'Would you like some refreshment?'

She shook her head, and took a deep breath before launching into her practised impassioned plea. He didn't interrupt, even when—despite her intention to make her argument with dispassionate cool and not come across as a hysterical female—her voice became suspended by tears and she had to wipe her wet face on the hem of her shirt.

'And so,' she finished, having presented what she hoped was a compelling argument, 'my brother was foolish—really stupid,' she conceded. 'But he didn't do anything criminal. You could say he's the victim here.'

'You could. But I would not.' If the man she spoke of had been a youth, a teenager, he might have felt more sympathy, but it was incomprehensible to Rafiq that a man of thirty could be as naive as the man she described.

Gabby bit her lip. 'He made a mistake. But he doesn't deserve to go to jail for twenty-five years. If it helps, I can promise to make his life a living hell if you let him come home.'

Gabby could see no softening in his attitude as he wondered aloud, 'Does your brother appreciate what a powerful advocate he has in you, I wonder?'

Frustration robbed her retort of diplomacy. 'I'm not here to ask for favours. I'm here to demand justice. And if that doesn't work—'

He raised a brow. *'Demand?'*

'All right,' she conceded, back-pedalling. 'I'll grovel and tell you you're marvelous—even though you don't seem to have heard a word I've said.' Had anything she'd said made *any* impact on him? 'Oh, and I have these,' she added, lifting her bottom from the divan and extracting the papers she had stuffed in her back pocket. 'Character references. I'm not saying that Paul is a saint, because he isn't, and quite honestly he doesn't have the sense he was born with. But there isn't an ounce of vice or malice in him,' she promised sincerely. She smoothed the papers before extending her hand.

There was a pause before Prince Rafiq took them from her, but he made no attempt to look at them. His eyes remained directed with an intensity she found unnerving on her face.

'Aren't you going to look at them?'

'I'm sure they show your brother in a favourable light. You would hardly bring me anything that did not do so.'

Frustration bubbled up in Gabby. 'If you weren't going to take me seriously why did you let me waste my time talking?'

'Because I wanted to see how much your brother's freedom means to you.'

'Like a lab rat, you mean?' she suggested, her tone of polite enquiry at stark variance with the militant sparkle in her eyes. 'You were dangling candy?'

His eyes slid over her body and he gave a shrug. 'I can think of more flattering analogies,' he observed drily.

'Don't tell me—dog? Donkey…?' He, she thought, her eyes sweeping his face from under the protective sweep of her eyelashes, would be something lean, sleek and unpredictable… A panther, perhaps—although there was something wolfish about him now, as he bared his teeth in a smile that left his remarkable eyes cold.

Ignoring her cranky interjection, he conceded, 'I wanted to gauge what you might do to gain him a pardon.' His dark eyes narrowed as he scanned her face. His voice was soft as he asked, 'What *would* you do, Miss Barton?'

Gabby shook her head in bewilderment. 'What do you mean, *do*?'

'I mean what price do you put on your brother's freedom?'

She felt the first flicker of real hope, but remained cautious as she asked, 'Are you saying you could get Paul released?'

'I could.'

'But will you?'

The pause stretched, and Gabby held her breath.

'That is…negotiable.'

Shaking with relief, she surged to her feet. If he had been anyone else she would have kissed him. Her eyes brushed his mouth, and the image that flashed in her head sent her stomach into a rollercoaster dip.

She tried to pretend the heat rush was an air-conditioning fault rather than hormones, and trained her gaze on a relatively non-fantasy-provoking area of his anatomy. Although there was nothing aesthetically unpleasing about middle of his chest.

'I'll do anything!' she pronounced.

# CHAPTER FIVE

HER unquestioning response caused Rafiq to experience an inconvenient spasm of guilt.

'This is something you should think about,' he cautioned.

He could not be fairer—there was no question of deception or taking advantage of her obvious fatigue. She could choose to walk away. He would not stop her.

Gabby frowned as he rose to his feet and stood there, towering over her. She hastily followed his example—but with a lot less towering and none of the co-ordinated animal grace that epitomised all his movements.

'I don't have to think about it. I would do anyth—' Her confident assurance was cut short by the single finger pressed to her lips. Gabby's blue eyes flew wide. The contact didn't just silence her tongue, it shut down every link between her brain and her limbs. She was literally paralysed...*with lust?*

Gabby immediately dismissed this laughable theory. She was clearly suffering the physical symptoms of stress and exhaustion—he wasn't even her type.

*Why exactly,* asked the voice in her head, *do you feel*

*the need to tell yourself that again? It's not as if you're fooling anyone,* it pointed out, *least of all him.*

Gabby's wide blue gaze lifted to the Prince's lean face. Previously she had been so mesmerised by him that she had failed to notice how deep the lines bracketing his mouth were, how tightly the smooth golden flesh was drawn across the sharp planes and angles of his face, how there was a grey tinge to his complexion.

She felt a flash of concern that vanished the moment their glances connected. This man was the very last person in the universe who needed her sympathy.

'Do not commit yourself until you know what the price is…' His finger left the cushiony softness of her pink lips and trailed lightly across her cheek before falling away.

The menace in his cryptic advice sent a shiver of fear trickling down Gabby's sweat-dampened back. She asked apprehensively, 'What do you mean, *price*?'

'Miss Barton, there is no such thing as a free lunch. Speaking of which—I will arrange refreshments.'

'No!' Gabby grabbed his arm and Rafiq turned his head.

Aware of the rapid progress of the deep flush that was working its way up her neck, Gabby dropped her hand. She resented the way that with the quirk of one flyaway black brow he could make an innocent tactile gesture seem something a lot more complicated.

'I don't want food, I want…' *I want my legs to start working, so that I can run somewhere I don't have to deal with someone with weird pewter-shot eyes making it hard to concentrate.*

Gabby was instantly ashamed of her selfish reaction. This was about Paul. This man could save him—and what was she doing? Turning accepting his hospitality into a battle of wills. It wasn't going to kill her to be civil to the man, was it?

'Nevertheless you will have lunch.'

She bit her lip. Civil was fine in theory, but did he have to present everything as a damned ultimatum?

'The decision I will ask you to make should not be made when you are suffering from exhaustion.'

'I am not exhausted.' Even as she spoke Gabby was conscious of the uncontrollable tremor in her limbs and the cotton wool sensation in her head.

'No?' He raised a brow and studied her face objectively. 'When did you last sleep? Eat?'

It wasn't until he introduced the subject that Gabby realised that it was a long time since she had done either. Once her adrenaline levels dropped she recognised she was not going to be able to negotiate her way out of a paper bag! Food was probably a good idea—and caffeine was an even better one.

'Or, for that matter, bathe?'

Gabby sucked in an offended breath. 'Are you saying I smell?'

The memory of the floral-scented female smell that had teased his nostrils when she had been in his arms came back to Rafiq, and without warning desire slammed through his body. An image formed in his mind of her, soft and warm, lying beneath him, her arms wrapped around him and her long blonde hair spread out on a pillow…

The image was so strong that he was sucked into a wild sensual vortex as the room and reality receded.

Gabby knew she was not drop-dead gorgeous, but she was vain enough to resent his pointed reminder that she looked like a wreck—especially when the comment had been made by the most spectacularly gorgeous man on the planet.

'And you're one to talk,' she snapped, studying the drawn lines of his patrician face with a speculative frown. 'When did *you* last have a decent night's sleep?' And how unfair, she reflected, her gaze lingering on the sensual upper curve of his mouth, that being sleep-deprived didn't stop him looking incredible.

Her challenging expression morphed into one of be-musement as he continued to stare at her. There was a sheen of moisture on his broad brow, and the expression in his dilated eyes was oddly blank.

'Are you all right…?'

Rafiq blinked, the effort causing beads of moisture to break out along his upper lip as he dragged himself clear of the sensual scene playing out in his head. A man who normally prided himself on his control, he was shocked to be caught displaying the restraint of a teenage schoolboy with raging hormones.

A muscle in his lean cheek clenched. 'I'm fine.'

'If you say so.' Gabby did not bother to hide her scepticism. 'But if you ask me, if anyone looks like they need a good feed it's you.'

It was not the observation that startled Rafiq but the person it came from. His weight loss had gone totally unnoticed by those close to him.

It seemed ironic that a total stranger had noticed what they had missed and he—he had ignored. If he hadn't...

He shook his head fractionally. There was no point going there. Such perception, however, would be useful for the role he had in mind for Gabby Barton.

'It doesn't matter who you are, you can only get away with burning the candle at both ends for so long,' she pointed out, oblivious to the fact that people did *not* rebuke the Crown Prince of Zantara.

'My life is one long party,' Rafiq drawled sardonically.

A party that probably involved a lot of women— the sleek, sexy sort. Well, they weren't going to be ugly, were they?

Gabby's lips formed a moue of distaste. 'You can swing from the chandeliers for all I care,' she said, with a shrug that was intended to establish her total uninterest in his social life. 'What do I know? All that inbreeding has probably bred out your need for sleep.'

That would have been convenient, Rafiq reflected, giving a hard laugh. The night sweats and insomnia and his resulting constant fatigue had been some of the collection of insidious symptoms that had made him eventually seek medical advice.

Having never suffered a day's illness in his entire life, it had not crossed his mind that the doctors would discover any sinister cause.

'Have I said something funny?'

He shook his head. 'Not funny, just insightful.'

'You mean you *don't* need sleep?'

Only too aware of how badly he needed to sleep, Rafiq ignored the question. 'Our gene pool is really not so stagnant as you appear to think. Over the years there have been many infusions of fresh blood.'

And had those infusions been willing additions to the gene pool? Gabby speculated. Or had his relations—the ones he had inherited that mouth and eyes from—ridden around the desert abducting nubile maidens who caught their fancy?

It was not exactly a big stretch to see Rafiq Al Kamil in the role of desert Sheikh, astride some high-bred stallion, his flowing desert robes flying as he scooped up another victim before riding off into the sunset with his prize and installing her in some silken tent.

Gabby had only the faintest mental image of the tent, but a very vivid representation in her head of the sleek-bodied, bold-eyed seducer of innocents as he tore off his robes.

Her waking fantasy was interrupted by his bored drawl. 'I am merely offering you hospitality. I would like you to be rested and lucid when we discuss this matter further. Do not be rash, Miss Barton, because I will hold you to any promises you make.'

Gabby didn't know if the sinister note in his warning was a creation of her fertile imagination, but after he had swept away to God knew where, without offering her even a crumb of explanation, she sat reflecting on his departing comment.

For the first time she asked herself what the price he put on her brother's freedom was. What did she have that a prince who had everything wanted?

She was sitting pondering this when her lolling head hit her chest, and she jerked upright with a cry. The last thing she wanted to do was fall asleep. She needed to keep her wits about her. Shaking her head to clear her muzzy thoughts, she got up and scrubbed her eyes with her fists. She began to pace the room.

Of all the places she could have ended up when she ran she had found herself here—was it fate?

What *could* she have that the Prince wanted?

Catching sight of her reflection as she passed a full-length mirror in a heavily carved ornate frame, she let out a groan of startled dismay.

Her hair that had started the day—or was it yester-day? She had lost track—secured at the nape of her neck in a ponytail now streamed down her back and curled in wild disarray around her face. Any trace of make-up was gone, and her face and wrecked clothes were liberally smeared with dirt from where she had landed face down in the dust when she had rolled from the delivery truck.

'Oh, Lord!' Easy to see now why the man had suggested she needed a wash!

One hand lifted to her head, she approached the mirror. Well, one thing she could rule out was him asking for sexual favours in return for Paul's freedom—not that she had ever ruled it *in*.

Remembering the paralysing stab of lust that had immobilised her when he had touched her, she just prayed he had no inkling of her mortifying reaction. God, to think she had actually imagined for a split second that it had been mutual...

Gabby grimaced at her reflection. Talk about deluded! Unless possibly the Prince had a thing for bag ladies...?

Licking her finger, she tried to rub a smear of dirt off her cheek. Besides, even if he had been smitten with terminal lust at the sight of her—a low chuckle of self-deprecation escaped her throat at the thought—he didn't strike her as the sort of man who traded for sexual favours.

Why would he, when he had probably been fighting off women with a stick all his adult life? Or maybe *not* fighting? This possibility made her frown severely at her reflection.

Running her fingers through her hair in an attempt to tame the wild waves, she did not at first see the young woman who had appeared quietly in the room, and when she did she jumped.

'Oh—I didn't see you there.'

'Sorry, miss.' The girl bowed her veiled head. She was young and very pretty, and regarded Gabby with ill-concealed curiosity. 'The Prince has asked me to show you to your rooms.'

*I have rooms?* Gabby decided not to question it, though the alteration in her status from unwanted intruder to honoured guest was hard to get her head around. In a lot of ways she had felt more comfortable when they were trying to throw her out. That at least had had the feel of normality, whereas what was happening now was deeply surreal.

'Lead the way,' Gabby said, wondering what she'd let herself in for.

Gabby tried, but all her attempts at making conversation with her guide drew only a nervous laugh or a startled look from the big fawn eyes, so eventually she lapsed into awed silence.

It was hard *not* to be awed by the sheer scale and splendour of the palace—a splendour that Gabby had not had the time to appreciate during her earlier flight.

The young girl led Gabby through a maze of wide corridors and splendid ornate courtyards to an area of the palace her earlier wanderings had not led her near. Here, the splendour went up to a new level.

They turned a corner, and Gabby drew a startled breath. The wall to her left was fitted with a vast floor-to-ceiling stained glass window. Light streamed through, casting a vibrant shadow that danced on the ceiling and trickled down like liquid gold fingers onto the floor.

The girl looked around in enquiry when Gabby stopped, apparently oblivious to the breathtaking magnificence.

'It's beautiful,' Gabby said, gesturing to the glass panel.

The girl looked puzzled, but flashed Gabby a sweet smile. She gestured to a wide sweeping staircase that led to the floor above, the dozens of thin gold bangles on her wrist jangling musically.

She walked along the corridor so quickly that Gabby, whose legs felt like lead, lagged behind. At the far end she opened a door and gestured for Gabby to enter.

'Your rooms, miss.'

The sitting room alone had about three times the floor space of the entire tiny flat her parents had converted for her on the top storey of the Edwardian house where she and Paul had grown up.

Their homing pigeon, her parents called her. Gabby had never felt any impulse to travel to far exotic places. Straight out of college a job in the local primary school had come up, and she had been delighted to get it. Some people were adventurous, but she just wasn't one of them. She didn't dream about faraway places. Ironic, really, because here she was, in a place more exotic than she'd imagined existed...

She did a full three-hundred-and-sixty twirl and let out a silent whistle. 'This is incredible.'

Her guide smiled with pleasure and gestured towards the doors that were flung open onto a wide balcony.

'You would like to see the view? Many admire it. When your Prime Minister stayed his wife took many photographs.'

Gabby smiled at the girl, impressed. *Prime Minister!* 'No, thank you,' she said. She had had enough of views—and this time there would be no strong male arms to pull her back from danger.

It was a classic case of out of the frying pan into the fire, because Rafiq Al Kamil did not represent safety except for Paul, she thought, squeezing her eyes shut and crossing her fingers as she murmured fiercely under her breath, *'Please* free Paul.'

A smile tugged the corner of her mouth as an image of her brother popped into her head. He was smiling, and then he wasn't, and then he wasn't blond and he wasn't Paul.

Gabby opened her eyes with a snap, and rubbed her upper arms vigorously to dispel the rash of goosebumps that had broken out over her skin. The cold that had made her shiver had turned her thoughts in the dangerous direction of the heat that had burned through the layers of clothing when Rafiq had hauled her back from the brink.

It seemed to Gabby that she was still on the brink—
the brink of going quietly crazy. She extended her hand
to push back her hair and saw she was shaking again.
She felt a surge of relief. She wasn't going mad—she
was just experiencing a severe blood sugar dip. She had
felt like this before, when she had skipped a meal or two
because she was busy.

Well, that accounted for some of it. But she had to
admit missing a meal had never caused her to look at a man
and feel the shameful slow burn of desire low in her belly.

She turned with an over-bright smile to the girl. 'Do
you think I could have a cup of tea?'

'Your meal will be here presently. I will make sure
that there is tea, miss. You will have time to bathe, if you
wish, and there are fresh clothes in the bedroom.'

Gabby smiled in acknowledgement of the offer, even
as she thought *no thanks*.

Once alone, she explored. She bounced on the
enormous bed and pulled back the counterpane to
admire the finest Egyptian cotton linen, then pressed a
selection of buttons on a panel she discovered. One of
them caused curtains to silently swish across the
windows, and another filled the room with the sound of
a blues tune that had always been one of her favourites.

She didn't have a clue how to switch it off, so she let it
play. The background sound was soothing, and it actually
made her feel a bit less lost. She turned up the volume,
thinking she needed all the help she could get. She was so
totally out of her depth. The question was, how long could
she carry on treading water before she sank like a stone?

The entire suite of rooms was sumptuously furnished, but it was the bathroom that really made her eyes pop. The sight of an utterly decadent sunken bath that could have fitted an entire soccer team brought a wistful gleam to her eyes…

The girl had said there was time. What could be the harm?

She turned on the taps and struggled to recall the title of the song now playing as she began to strip off her soiled clothes.

She took a little while to select a bath oil she liked from the vast selection on offer, before tipping in the contents of a blue crystal flagon. The room was immediately filled with the aroma of roses as the water foamed.

Gabby inhaled and smiled in anticipation as she walked down the flight of shallow steps that led into the foaming water. In the middle of all this craziness, taking a bath seemed so marvellously normal.

She actually giggled as the water begin to lap around her ankles, then waded deeper, dropping to her knees and scooping the water in both hands. She threw it over her back and shoulders, wincing a little as it touched her bruises and grazed skin.

Then with a sigh she switched off the gushing water and stretched out, resting her head on a conveniently situated padded headrest. The effect on her body was almost instant. She could actually feel the tension begin to ease from her body as if by magic. Smiling, she ducked her head under, and emerged moments later, with water streaming down her wet face. Pushing her saturated hair from her face, Gabby lay back again.

As she floated in the warm scented water a self-protective instinct kicked in, and her overtaxed brain went numb. Staring up at the elaborate gold-embellished carvings on the ceiling, Gabby didn't feel concerned when they began slipping in and out of focus. Her eyelids felt as though they had lead weights attached—so heavy that finally she had to close them.

Just for a minute…

The combination of warm water and music had the obvious effect. Her mind emptied and she slept.

Rafiq consulted his watch as he knocked on the door of the guest suite to announce his presence. It had been an hour since he'd left Gabriella Barton, and he had not wasted that time.

Considering the time factor, the file that now lay on his desk was actually quite comprehensive. What he had read about her brother suggested, rather to his surprise, that the young man might actually *be* innocent. Skimming the pages, he had seen that Paul Barton was a perfect example of arrested development.

Innocent, perhaps, but Rafiq had little sympathy. He saw nothing to admire in the hedonistic existence of those who drifted aimlessly through life, avoiding responsibility and leaving chaos in their wake, expecting other people to pick up the pieces.

He knew all the essential facts about Paul Barton. But the information on his sister—the information that actually interested him—was less complete. It was frustrating, but he could fill in the gaps later. As nothing he had read negated his plan or made it unworkable, he was pushing on regardless.

When there was no reply to his knock he stepped inside. The music system was playing some moody jazz piece he was vaguely familiar with, but the salon was empty. The food attractively laid out on a low table was untouched and cold.

'Miss Barton! Gabby!' He flicked the 'off' switch on the music system and repeated his call. When this elicited no response either, he moved to the bedroom door and knocked loudly.

When this too yielded no result, he went inside. The canopied bed was not disturbed. The only sign that the room had been entered was the neat pile of fresh clothes he had left instructions for the maid to provide, which still lay folded on a chair.

He called out again. She had to have heard him. The novelty of being ignored did not amuse him—rudeness never amused him—and her not responding was irritatingly childish.

He laid his hand palm flat on the bathroom door, and it swung inwards.

There was no indignant screech when, after the slightest of hesitations, he stepped inside. The room was filled with steam that misted the reflective surfaces, and it took Rafiq's eyes a few moments to adjust and see the woman in the bath.

He turned his head abruptly—though perhaps not as quickly as he might have. The heightened colour along the crests of his cheekbones was hidden by the fog of steam.

He stared fixedly at the wall, still seeing the image of pale limbs and a slim body that had imprinted itself on his retina. He reaction had been that of a green schoolboy catching his first sight of the naked female form. She had made no attempt to cover herself.

'Sorry, but I did call out. When you are ready I will be in the salon.'

He was approaching the door when a soft gurgling sigh from the direction of the bath made him frown. 'Miss Barton?' He turned his head, and in a flash realised that the reason she had not replied was because she was either sound asleep or unconscious.

With a curse he crossed the room and strode straight into the water. She was lying so still that for a split second he thought she wasn't breathing. When he saw the lift of her ribcage and small breasts he felt a rush of relief that was quickly replaced by anger—furious, molten anger.

Even as he called out her name he saw the ripple of water wash over her face. Sucking in a breath through clenched teeth, he bent and placed his hand under her head, lifting her face clear of the water. She stirred sleepily and muttered something unintelligible as he picked her up. It took two attempts. She weighed nothing, but even nothing, when it was wet and slippery and uncooperative, was hard to get a grip on.

As he heaved her bodily into his arms she opened her eyes and looked at him, her gaze big and blue as a summer sky. If he hadn't come in when he had those eyes might have been permanently closed—sheer carelessness could have resulted in tragedy.

It was incandescent fury that Gabby saw on his face when she opened her eyes. She instinctively recoiled from the blaze of rage, but for several seconds there was no recognition in her eyes. Her sleep-fuddled mind was a total blank. Then events of the past two days came rushing back, and all the condensed misery and emotional turmoil hit her with the force of a brick wall.

She blinked up at the dark, lean features of Rafiq Al Kamil... He was going to help Paul, but she still didn't know whether to put him in her friend or foe file... He was actually a bit big to fit in *any* file.

He was carrying her as though she weighed nothing, and there was no element of softness about him. Physically he felt all hard bone and muscle, and mentally his gaze was as unforgiving as tungsten steel.

Hold on! She blinked, frustrated at the time it was taking her brain to assimilate the most basic information. Then abruptly the time-lag between her seeing something and interpreting it narrowed, and her eyes widened to their fullest extent. He was *carrying* her!

'What are you doing?' She looked down and saw her naked body. She froze. 'And why—' her voice quivered '—am I naked?'

Gabby's eyes slowly lifted. Wild panic was triggered as they connected with his, and she was swallowed up by a tide of mind-numbing horror. She began to struggle wildly, hitting out and screaming at the top of her lungs. She landed several blows before he responded to her shrill commands to put her down!

'Be still!'

Panting from her exertion, Gabby looked at the towel held out to her with deep suspicion, before grabbing it and wrapping it around herself. Swathed from head to toe, she felt slightly more secure, but she was still shaking as she angled him a look of withering contempt, struggling to stop her teeth chattering.

She directed a narrow stare at his dark face. 'T…take another step closer…touch me and I'll…' *What?* Gabby asked herself. *Scream? Because that's done so much good so far, hasn't it?*

# CHAPTER SIX

'LET me ease your mind. There is no incentive you could offer that would make me come within five feet of you.'

He had always been drawn to cool goddesses, so in theory Rafiq knew that holding a wet, screaming, squirming, volatile virago should not have aroused him.

He dug his hands deep in his pockets in a vain attempt to disguise the fact that he was in fact deeply aroused. It was a case of theory losing out yet again when it collided with reality—especially wet, slippery reality.

Her smooth brow pleated in a deep frown as she tried to follow the sequence of events that had landed her naked in his arms. 'How did I...?'

The last thing she remembered was soaking in the tub.

'I was taking a bath...' She shook her head and threw him an accusing glare. 'Do you make a habit of sneaking up on women when they're taking a bath?'

His nostrils flared. 'I did not *sneak*.'

'Well, you sure as hell didn't knock!'

'I did.'

This was getting childish—though there was nothing adolescent about his body in that suit, or presumably out of it—not that it was a subject that interested Gabby. She rolled her eyes, radiating a scorn she was far from feeling. She had lost time…how long?

Her thoughts were in a spiralling loop of bemusement. Had someone drugged her tea…? No, she hadn't had any tea. Her dry throat reminded her of that. Or was it the result of the terror she had experienced when she'd found herself naked in a desert sheikh's arms?

So he was now wearing a very western suit, and the tailor who had cut it to fit his frame must have been kissing the ground he walked on—but the desert sheikh thing still applied. It didn't matter about the wrappings or the sophisticated, urbane demeanor. Deep down this man was a total barbarian—she had every right to feel terror.

Just terror…?

Gabby evaded his dark eyes and closed down that line of thought before it got going.

'You were asleep.'

Gabby's eyes lifted. She opened her mouth to refute the crazy claim, then closed it again. A few hazy memories came slipping back, but she ignored them and produced a disdainful sniff.

*Asleep!* Couldn't the lecherous rat come up with a better story? Or was it possible that in some moment of insanity brought on by stress and emotion she *had* been responsible for ending up naked in his arms?

It seemed about as likely as him being overcome by lust and going Neanderthal. This man had control—iron control that it would take a lot to snap.

'I might have dozed off for a moment,' she conceded reluctantly. 'But that doesn't give you the right to—'

'Save your life?'

This drew a laugh from Gabby. 'My hero! Save my life? Pooh!' she muttered, even as the realisation that he had seen her naked hit her again. The thought kept going around in her head, and every time it did she had to fight the urge to curl up into a mortified foetal ball and pretend this was all a dream—correction, *nightmare!*

'You could have drowned.' As he thought of how close she had been, he felt anger crowding in on him again.

About to pour scorn on this, Gabby closed her mouth with an audible click. She swallowed. 'I only closed my eyes for a minute.'

Rafiq could hear the uncertainty in her voice.

His nasty smile was to Gabby's mind unnecessarily smug.

'When I got in the tub the water was stone-cold.' His sweeping gesture drew her gaze downwards, and Gabby saw the bottoms of his beautifully tailored trousers were wet to above the knee. There were dark water stains on his shirt and jacket from where he had held her.

He had held her naked in his arms. She shook her head to dispel the image that was a distraction she did not need just now—though she knew she was going to be thinking about it later.

The colour flooded her face. 'I fell asleep...? That was... I was...'

'Stupid,' he supplied helpfully.

She bit her lip, totally mortified. 'I didn't do it on purpose.' She covered her face with her hands and groaned. 'God, this is so embarrassing.'

He looked confused by her choice of words. 'Why?'

She looked at him through her fingers. Was he dense, or what? 'Because I was…'

'Naked?' he suggested, looking amused. 'Better to be embarrassed, Gabby,' he declared, 'than dead. If it helps, I *have* seen naked women before.' None of them were imprinted on his retina, though.

'It doesn't,' she hissed, thinking of women with Hollywood gloss and perfect bodies he no doubt normally swept into his arms. She wanted badly for the floor to open up and swallow her. 'Now, if you don't mind, I'd like to get dressed.' He didn't move, so she added pointedly, 'Without an audience.'

'Of course.' He inclined his head and turned to leave her.

'And…thank you' she called, as he stood with his hand extended towards the door.

He swung back. 'It was my pleasure.'

'That's what bothers me,' she muttered as the door closed. He must have heard her because she heard him laugh, which just about made her humiliation complete.

Gabby was tempted to put her own clothes back on, but her shirt had just about disintegrated.

'Damn,' she muttered, shaking out the dress that had been left for her. The floor-length gown unfolded with a soft swish. Her eyes widened. 'Wow!'

A dreamy expression drifted across Gabby's face as she gazed at it. Layers of the finest silk in varying shades of blue, it was just about the loveliest thing she had ever seen. She had never in her life imagined wearing anything like it.

It probably wouldn't fit.

It did.

It fitted perfectly. Gabby found herself smiling stupidly as she looked at her reflection in the full-length mirror. She swung her hips and the dress belled out from her knees, the silk swishing seductively against her skin.

'My God, I almost have a cleavage!'

Not that the illusion was going to fool the man waiting for her in the next room. He already *knew* that she wasn't exactly lushly endowed. Although she had read somewhere that when it came to the naked female form men did not demand the perfection that women imagined...

Her expression sobered abruptly and she took a step back. Paul was rotting in a prison cell and she was wondering what the Crown Prince of Zantara had thought about her naked—wondering what he would say when he saw she scrubbed up quite well. How shallow and selfish did that make her?

Not to mention delusional. An infant-school teacher from Cheshire would not even register on his radar.

She shook her head and refused to think about the heat she had seen in his eyes.

Taking a deep breath, she walked into the salon. The first thing that hit her was the smell of food—she was ravenous—and then she turned, and the second thing hit her.

Rafiq Al Kamil was sitting on one of the sofas. He rose politely to his feet when he saw her. Ineffably elegant, he radiated a confidence that was totally unaffected—an integral part of him, as was the raw sexuality that hit an unprepared Gabby with the impact of a physical blow.

What a time to discover a weakness for tall, dark and brooding, Gabby thought as she struggled to mentally shift gear. She was ashamed that she had to struggle. Her brother's dilemma should be the first thing on her mind—not some stranger who had made the whole brooding hero thing his own.

He didn't speak, just stared at Gabby—who stared back. She felt his eyes as they slid down her body, and she lifted a self-conscious hand to the silk bodice of the dress.

'My clothes were a write-off. This isn't really my style, but thanks.' She lowered her eyes. What was she doing thanking the man? It wasn't as if he'd picked it out personally.

'It is an improvement.'

The iridescent shades of blue in the gown she wore reflected but did not outshine the brilliance of her blue gaze. Her skin, scrubbed clean of make-up and dirt, was revealed as flawless and porcelain-pale, and her hair, freshly washed and still damp, fell down her back in soft rippling waves

'Anything would be.' She shrugged.

'That is not what I meant,' Rafiq said, as he struggled to erase the image in his head of her in the bathtub, her pale skin gleaming and wet. It wasn't just his body that was weakened, it seemed, but also his brain.

Was he going to *say* what he meant?

She noticed that his glance had dropped to the creamy vee that hinted at her cleavage, and to hide the fact her heart had started hammering she let her hair fall forward to hide the flush on her cheeks.

'It is true that what you are wearing is not suitable

for travelling in the backs of delivery trucks. You appear uncomfortable…are you still embarrassed?' He sounded mildly amused by the possibility. 'Shall we agree to forget the…*incident* ever happened?'

'It was a total non-incident as far as I'm concerned,' she grunted. 'So, tell me what this is about. What do you want?' *Not your body, Gabby, so stop fantasising.*

Rafiq shook his head. 'First you must eat something.' He gestured towards the table. While she had been dressing the cold food had been removed, and fresh hot dishes were set in their place.

'I'm not hungry.' Her stomach chose that moment to growl loudly.

He looked smug and walked across and lifted the lid on one of the dishes. An aromatic spicy smell drifted across to Gabby, whose mouth immediately began to water.

'Sit.'

Gabby thought about ignoring him, but decided the rebellion was pretty pointless. The sooner she humoured him the sooner she would find out what she had to do to secure Paul's release.

'And what are *you* going to do? Watch me eat?' she asked as she sat down. If so, indigestion was assured.

'I think I will join you,' he said, gracefully lowering himself with the ease of long practice onto one of the very low divan seats around the circular table.

'How cosy—a date, almost.' She piled some food onto a plate and forked some into her mouth—it was delicious.

She swallowed and felt a large pang of guilt. She was living in the lap of luxury, albeit temporarily, and Paul was probably on a diet of bread and water.

'I don't know about you, but I can eat and talk.'

But not look at him and think straight. So she didn't. She kept her eyes trained on her plate as she adopted a brisk, business-like tone.

'They're talking about putting my brother behind bars for twenty-five years, so as far as I'm concerned no price is too steep. Stop being so damned mysterious and tell me what you want. My soul?' She laughed at the suggestion, but he didn't join in—which did not seem like a good sign to Gabby.

'What do you think of my country?'

Gabby's impatience showed as she snapped back, 'I've not actually had a lot of time for sightseeing.'

'I will call you Gabriella.'

'And what will I call *you*?' She could think of several things, but most of them would probably get her arrested for treason.

'My name,' he said, laying a hand lightly on his chest, 'is Rafiq.'

'I can't call you that!'

He looked mildly surprised by her appalled denial. 'Why not?'

Gabby, who couldn't think of a single reason beyond the uncomfortable implied intimacy of using his name, ignored the question.

'Look, why have you brought me here? What is this about? The food, the dress, the…' She stopped, suddenly realising that there wasn't a soul in the world who knew where she was. The fork stopped halfway to her mouth. She had lost her appetite. She'd practically been kidnapped and she hadn't even noticed.

'I told the man at the embassy...' She scoured her memory and triumphantly produced his name. 'I told Mr Park I would telephone him at six. If I don't he will come and collect me.'

'Really? He did not mention it when I spoke to him.'

Her eyes widened. 'You spoke to the man at the embassy? You told him I'm here?' Gabby grimaced. When she had left the bespectacled diplomat she had promised she wouldn't do anything rash. Her eyes suddenly widened 'Did you make a complaint about me?'

'I spoke to Mr *Parker*,' Rafiq confirmed. 'And I made no complaint.'

Gabby expelled a relieved sigh. She didn't want to alienate one of the few people who might be on Paul's side, even if he was hopeless.

'When I told him you were here it was news that caused him some alarm,' he informed her. 'He was under the impression that you were happy to let him act on your behalf.'

Gabby wrinkled her nose. 'Well, the man was about as much use as a wet lettuce leaf. All he could talk about were diplomatic channels and how these things take time. I couldn't wait.'

Something flickered in the back of his deepset eyes. Gabby was struggling to interpret it when he said, surprisingly, 'It so happens that I share your sense of urgency.'

She regarded him with a wary frown. 'You do?'

'I do, and for the record I am not trying to kidnap you, Gabriella.'

Mortified colour flew to her cheeks. 'I didn't say that.'

'But you thought it. The door is open.' He gestured

towards the double doors. 'Or at least it will be if you decide to leave. You are quite at liberty to do so whenever you wish. There are no locks, no guards... But I feel I should remind you that it was you who sought me out—or at least my father. Which was a prime example of optimism winning out over common sense.'

Gabby gritted her teeth in frustration and didn't move. 'Are you just playing with me? Is this some sort of game for you or are you actually going to help my brother?'

'That is up to you.'

'Rafiq, what do you want?'

'You are a kindergarten teacher.'

Her feathery brows shot up. 'How on earth did you know that?' she gasped.

Ignoring the indignant question, he continued. 'And you are not emotionally entangled at present. In fact you have never been seriously involved. I find this hard to believe,' he admitted. However, if his information was accurate, it did remove one impediment that might have been an obstacle to his plan.

Of course the perfect bride for a future king would be a virgin, but even his father, who attached a great deal of importance to such things, recognised that modern morality made this desirable rather than essential.

The colour climbed to Gabby's cheeks. 'Look, where are you getting this information? How—?'

'Do not be naive, Gabby. I have used the time while you were resting to make myself familiar with your brother's case.'

She gave a sigh of relief. 'So you know he's innocent?'

'I do not know this.'

She laid down her fork and fixed him with a narrow-eyed glare. 'Well, I *do* know it.'

'Shall we leave the matter of your brother's innocence out of this discussion?'

She regarded him in disgust. 'You're not the least bit interested in justice, are you?'

'I do not make a habit of interfering with the judicial system of my country. However, in this instance I am willing to make an exception.'

Gabby's lip curled. 'Yes, you're an opportunist—I get that,' she inserted impatiently. 'But what do you *want*?'

She saw the jolt of shock that stiffened his body at her less than deferential attitude. Sticking out her chin, she folded her arms across her chest and met his dark implacable gaze. She wasn't going to pretend a respect she didn't feel.

'You want your brother released from prison, his name cleared and the slate wiped clean. I want *my* brother married.'

Gabby struggled and failed to make the connection between the two. She shook her head and pushed away a silky skein of fair hair that had drifted across her face.

'What does that have to do with me?'

'I will help you achieve your objective if you help me achieve mine, Miss Barton.'

'But how can I help? Do you want me to talk to your brother's girlfriend?'

'My brother does not have a girlfriend. Well, actually he has several, but none would make a suitable consort for the future King of Zantara.'

Gabby was struggling to follow, but immediately identified a discrepancy. 'But aren't *you* the future King?'

He appeared to tense, but ignored the question and successfully diverted her attention by declaring, 'I have decided that *you* would be a suitable bride for my brother.'

Gabby blinked. 'Is that meant to be some sort of twisted joke? My God, you never had any intention of helping Paul, did you?' Throwing him a look of disgust, she folded her napkin with slow deliberation and got to her feet. 'What do you and your friends do for after-dinner entertainment? Watch traffic accidents?'

Rafiq rose to his feet and stood there towering over her. 'You asked me about the succession. You are correct. I am next in line, but I will not be King, Miss Barton.'

An expression of overt suspicion in her narrowed eyes, she folded her arms across her chest. What was this? she wondered. Another example of his warped sense of humour?

'Why not?'

A man born to be King, he looked the part—which was pretty rare in royal circles. He was regal down to his fingertips, and on the evidence so far he'd have no major problem with the ordering-people-around element of the job.

Before she had finished reflecting on his princely attributes, he had covered the space between them in two easy strides. Planting a hand on the wall behind her head, he leaned over her.

His sheer physical presence was incredibly intimidating, but Gabby was determined not to give him the

KIM LAWRENCE 89

satisfaction of showing him how painfully aware of
him she was.

'I need your word that what I am about to tell you
will not leave this room.'

The intensity of his manner unnerved Gabby even
more.

'Or what?' she squeaked.

He arched a brow and gave her a look of mock
surprise. 'You are in a position to threaten me?'

Gabby, who was in a position to fall in a shaking heap
at his feet, shook her head and gulped. Barely audibly,
she forced her response past her frozen vocal cords.

'No.'

'I *am* next in line of succession. My father was not
young when I was born, and five years ago he had two
heart attacks. The second was fairly major and he had
surgery. He could live for a long time or he might not.'

Gabby was unsure how to respond to this information. She ducked under his arm and put some distance
between them. 'The same could be said of everyone.'

'Not of me.'

'Why? Are you going to live for ever?' She gave a
scornful laugh and began to turn.

'I am dying, Gabby.'

# CHAPTER SEVEN

His words made her swing back. 'You're sick, all right—sick in the sense of humour department.' She pointed at her face. 'Does it look like I'm laughing?' She stopped.

He wasn't laughing either. Conscious of a knot of something close to panic building in her chest, she scanned his face, her unease growing.

'My God!' The colour drained from her face and her hand came up to cover her trembling lips. 'You're telling the truth!'

'I have perhaps six months to live. I have that time to prepare my brother for the role which will be his.'

Gabby shook her head in a negative motion and staggered backwards, until the back of her knees hit a chair. She slid into it. 'But there must be something?'

'No.' His closed expression made it clear that he found the subject uncomfortable.

'But you're young and fit...' she protested, her eyes travelling the long, lean length of him. She had never actually seen anyone who looked more alive.

'This is not something we need to discuss. The facts are clear—not to accept them would lack...dignity.'

She was utterly bemused by his attitude. *'Dignity?'*

'There is nothing that can be done.'

She felt something snap inside her. Suddenly Gabby was so angry that for several heartbeats she couldn't speak. 'How can you be so calm about it?'

Rafiq shrugged in response and looked visibly taken aback by her reaction. 'Why should it matter to you? We are strangers.'

The question and the shrug fanned the flames of the anger that held her in its grip. Hands on the arms of the chair, Gabby pulled herself to her feet.

She tilted her head back to look into his dark, impassive face, and as she studied the strong, cleanly sculpted lines and planes of his symmetrical features she thought, He *can't* be dying! It simply wasn't possible. It had to be a mistake. She had never seen anyone look *less* weak or *more* invulnerable.

Vitality seeped from every gorgeous pore—or was that nervous energy? she wondered, the indentation between her bows deepening as her glance lingered on the dark smudges beneath his spectacular eyes.

'There *must* be something—'

He cut her off with a flat, 'There is not.' Looking irritated by her insistence, he added with horrid finality, 'I *am* dying.'

Their eyes met, and her hand went to her mouth as a tiny cry was wrenched from her throat. 'But you *can't* be ill. You don't *look* ill,' Even as she spoke she was seeing the shadows under his eyes, the lines of strain bracketing his mouth.

'I do not at present feel ill.' The doctor had explained

that this was the reason why so many people who presented with this disease were already beyond treatment. The onset was insidious, and the symptoms were often limited to general fatigue, night sweats, and weight loss—not specific.

'But that's a good sign, isn't it? They are making advances in medical science every day of the week. Things that once seemed impossible—'

A muscle clenched in his jaw. 'There is nothing that can be done beyond the occasional blood transfusion as a short-term fix later on, when my energy levels drop.'

'How can you accept it this way?' she reproached him incredulously. She looked at him—tall, vital-looking, the embodiment of masculine vigour—and shook her head in utter rejection.

Rafiq's lashes dipped to hide the emotion that flared hotly in his hooded eyes. A nerve clenched in his jaw. *Accept?* Did she imagine he had any choice? Did she imagine he would not have preferred to yell and bellow?

He could not allow himself the indulgence. He needed to focus and do what had to be done for his country. His chest lifted as he expelled a deep breath and subdued the sudden irrational impulse he had to shake her or kiss her or both.

'It is a path we are all on, Gabriella.'

'Spare me the homespun philosophy, please,' she begged, rolling her eyes. In the grip of emotions she didn't even recognise, she was barely conscious that she had laid her hands flat against his chest. 'I don't call it brave—I call it defeatist and pathetic. Aren't you angry? God, if it was me I'd be *furious*!'

Rafiq lifted his eyes from the small hands that lay against his chest. 'You *appear* to be furious.'

His impassive manner further ignited her passion. 'I am,' she gritted.

'There is little point railing against fate.'

'I'm not mad at fate, I'm mad with you!' she exploded. 'You're just so, so...*passive*. It's feeble! You should be fighting! You're acting like you're dead already! But you're not.' Flexing the fingers pressed against his chest, she fixed him with a fierce sapphire stare. 'I can feel your heart beating...' She began to beat out the tattoo of the steady thud in his chest.

There was no conscious thought behind her action as she reached up impulsively, grabbing his head in her hands and dragging it down to her. Her eyes squeezed tight shut as she pressed her trembling lips to his warm firm mouth and kissed him hard. She felt a shudder pass through him, but he made no attempt to return the pressure.

She pulled clear after a moment. This wasn't about kissing him, or even wanting him to kiss her back, she told herself. It was about proving a point. The method was crude, and heavy on the drama, but she had done it.

She fixed him with a shimmering blue stare and shook her head, pressing a hand to her heaving bosom.

'*Now* do you believe you're alive?'

'You make an argument forcibly, Gabriella,' he observed thickly.

There was nothing forcible about the pressure of his mouth as it covered hers. Soft and seductive, his lips moved sensuously over hers. As his tongue traced the soft trembling outline they parted. He accepted the mute invitation and his tongue slid deep into her mouth. She felt the groan in his chest as his big hands moved to her waist and dragged her up hard against him.

The erotic pressure of his erection as it pressed into her soft belly made Gabby weak with wild desire. Her hips moved against him instinctively as she met the deep, stabbing incursions of his tongue with her own, hesitantly at first, and then with more confidence and urgency.

Then it stopped.

He put her away from him so abruptly that Gabby almost fell over. Her head spinning, she blinked up at him, waiting for the world to slide back into focus. You couldn't kiss a person that way and then act as though nothing had happened!

But he was. Could a man really turn it off that quickly? Other than the dark colour scoring his cheekbones there was nothing in his manner to suggest that moments earlier he had been fully aroused.

Maybe he still was? It was only by exerting every ounce of the will-power at her disposal that Gabby stopped her glance dropping. Unfortunately the blush she had no control over.

'A man has the right to face his death however he wishes, Gabriella.'

'Your rights! What about my rights?' Gabby, still shaking after the sensual invasion, shook her spinning head. 'It's not my *wish* to marry your brother. Or to be kissed by you,' she lied.

'That will not happen again,' he said with a formal inclination of his head. 'As delightful as the diversion was.'

In order to make true his promise Rafiq knew he

would have to take care to keep her literally at arm's length in future. For some reason his brain ceased to function around her.

He was still shocked to the core that for the first time in his life he had permitted carnal need to overrule common sense and logic.

'I think we should focus on the matter in hand. It *is* your wish to save your brother from a life behind bars?'

She gave an incredulous snort. 'You were serious? You're saying that if I agree to marry your brother the charges against Paul will go away?'

'In essence, yes.'

'You want me to marry your brother. So what was that?' Her hand went to her lips. They still felt swollen and over-sensitive. 'A test run?' she suggested bitterly. 'The royal bedroom test? Did I pass?'

Gabby took an involuntary step back as fury flashed in his eyes, the pewter flecks disappearing as they darkened.

'That was a mistake,' he gritted through clenched teeth.

*Mistake!* This man was a master of understatement. 'On that at least we are in total agreement.'

'We will discuss it no more.'

Gabby, who hadn't planned to discuss it all, stuck out her chin and tried to match his nonchalant uninterest in the subject. 'Fine by me.'

'I appreciate this is not a decision you can take lightly, and I would like to be able to give you more time, but the fact is time is the one luxury I do not have.'

Her anger fell away, to be replaced by the cold chill of dread. 'Don't say that,' she begged in a stricken whisper.

This was the point where Rafiq could no longer

pretend he was not playing dirty, so he stifled his natural sense of fair play and said, 'When you are making your decision remember that although obviously I cannot anticipate the judicial process…'

The blatant hypocrisy made her smile ironically. If he wasn't the law then he was definitely above it. 'Of course not,' she drawled.

'It seems likely, given the zero tolerance stance we take on drugs, that your brother will spend the next twenty to twenty-five years behind bars.'

Gabby's air of moral superiority evaporated. Her stomach churned sickly as an image of her sibling spending all those years incarcerated for a crime he didn't commit rose up before her.

'You're actually asking me to…?' She stopped and angled a bewildered look at his face. 'But why me?' She shook her head. 'I'm not exactly queen material. I'm sure you have a little black book filled with high-born virgins who would stab each other in the back to wear a crown.'

'Things have moved on since the little black book.'

'You're computerised? How progressive,' she drawled sarcastically. 'Then go open a file and look for another sacrificial lamb.'

'If *you* decide to make the *sacrifice* you would be spending the next twenty-five years living in some luxury. You would be respected, and you would have a position of power and influence that most people can only dream of.'

'I have never dreamt of power and influence.'

His perfect mouth twisted into an ironic smile. 'Think about it now,' he suggested.

'What about your brother? Doesn't he have a say?'

His nonplussed expression drew a frustrated groan of impatience from Gabby.

'What,' she asked, spelling it out slowly, 'if he doesn't want to marry me? He might hate me on sight. You cannot make him marry me,' she added, when there was no corresponding glimmer of recognition in his un-blinking regard. 'Unless you plan to blackmail him too?'

'My brother has lived the lifestyle of a playboy but he is aware of his responsibilities.'

'So you *do* plan to blackmail him?'

His bared his teeth in a white wolfish grin that to Gabby seemed utterly ruthless.

'I am hoping it will not be necessary.'

'Because he'll take one look at me and fall passion-ately in love?'

Instead of laughing, he swept his eyes from her feet to the top of her silky head.

'It is a possibility.' One that ought to fill him if not with joy then certainly satisfaction. But instead Rafiq was conscious of a vague sense of discontent.

Her lips twisted into a grimace. 'Right!' Now she *knew* he was being sarcastic, and his fixed, unblinking regard began to make her feel uncomfortable.

'You should not bite your nails.'

'I do not—' She stopped and realised that her finger was in her mouth. 'See—I'm a social liability.'

'I'm sure you can be very charming when you want to be.' The idea of her being charming to his brother caused Rafiq's vague discontent to escalate into strong displeasure.

'My brother, Gabriella, is not only a much nicer person than me—'

'Not exactly a big ask.'

'—he is quite…malleable.'

'You mean if you tell him to marry me he will?'

'I would not be that unsubtle. And I think you underestimate yourself…' he chided.

'You do know you have the moral scruples of a snake, don't you?'

His taunting smile died, and the expression that replaced it was implacable. 'I have no time for scruples, Gabriella. You and I, we both understand what few do in this world.'

'What is that?'

'Duty. How many sisters would have done what you have to save their brother from the consequences of his own foolish actions? You are a woman of resources, resolve and inner strength. You could never marry a man who is strong.'

'You mean a man like you?'

He looked startled by the suggestion. 'You and I?' he echoed, his eyes slowly tracing the wilful curve of her full upper lip. He released a scornful laugh and shook his head. 'It would be a total disaster.'

While his incredulous response irritated her, Gabby could not disagree with his scathing analysis. 'It would be a head-on collision,' she said, thinking of that kiss. That had been quite a collision.

'The modern way is to speak of marriage as a partnerships of equals.'

'And it isn't?' Gabby prompted, thinking that everything he was saying showed that at heart the 'modernising' Prince was nothing but a barbarian.

'One partner needs to take the lead.'

'You mean a leader and a follower?' No prizes for guessing which one he would be, but she wasn't exactly flattered that he tarred her with the same brush.

'I mean someone who is capable of making decisions and living with the consequences—someone who is capable of putting duty ahead of their personal desires and needs.'

Despite herself Gabby was fascinated by this insight into his belief system. 'Is that what you've done?' What, she wondered, were the desires this man had denied for the sake of duty? A woman?

She shook her head and gave a hard laugh. 'Sorry— stupid question. It's what you're still doing. You don't have a clue what I'm talking about, do you?' she added studying his face. 'Most people who knew they only had weeks to live would want to cram all the things they wanted to do but never had an opportunity to into that space of time.'

'I have led a privileged life and enjoyed opportunities beyond those that most people can dream of.'

She knew her heart ought to be aching for herself, for the choice he was forcing her to make, but instead she felt that irrational organ ache for him.

'The sort of life that you want me to embrace?' she suggested, tears thickening her voice to a husky whisper as helplessness swelled like a lump of lead in her chest.

Rafiq refused to acknowledge the misery in her voice, and reminded himself he was offering her a life that many would envy. His first duty was to secure the future and security of his country.

'It is your choice.'

Anger like blue flame flared in her eyes as she shook her head emphatically from side to side, fixing him with a sparkling sapphire stare.

'You know I don't have any choice.'

Rafiq refused to acknowledge the surge of guilt he felt as their eyes connected. 'There is always a choice, Gabriella. I am not forcing you to do anything.' It might be wise if he kept not just a physical distance between them but an emotional one too. Empathy could cause problems.

'Amazing, isn't it? But I'm not mad about this entire sacrificial lamb thing. I'm not thanking my lucky stars I met you either. But why are you even wasting your time with this obsession?'

'You call it obsession and I call it duty, Gabriella.'

She threw up her hands and covered her ears. 'Will you stop calling me that?' she yelled.

'Is it not your name?'

'Not the way you say it! *Gabriella!*' she spat in disgust, trying and failing to imitate his rich, resonant tone. 'I'm Gabby—plain Gabby. Not Queen of the May or Queen of anywhere else. When I marry I don't want to be some man's keeper.'

He quirked a dark brow. 'You have some fantasy of being dominated?'

The suggestion caused angry colour to rush to her face—or was that anger more closely connected with the graphic erotic mental image she blinked so hard to clear?

'No, I have some *fantasy* of being loved and cherished!' she yelled back, her voice shaking with the strength of her feelings. Despite that brief mental lapse, she had never had fantasies about lying naked beneath a man with a body that gleamed like oiled silk.

If she hadn't known he was totally incapable of it, she might have called the flicker of emotion that crossed his face guilt.

'My brother is a basically good man.'

'If he's nothing like you that's a head start,' she agreed, keeping her emotions and her imagination in check as she regarded him with cold disdain. 'So what's the plan? Are you going to use blackmail with him too?' she wondered, pretending great interest as she watched his lean face darken with annoyance. 'Are you going to play the "dying wish" card?'

The moment the words left her lips she wished them unsaid, and when she saw him flinch she felt even worse.

As she struggled to cling to her antagonism her stomach took a sickly lurching dive in utter rejection of the thought of this vital man being prematurely robbed of his life. Gabby had never met anyone who embodied life and vitality more. It was impossible for her to look at him and believe that he was dying.

Tears welled in Gabby's eyes and began to roll down her cheeks as she bit her lip.

Misinterpreting her silent misery, his undertaking to keep his distance forgotten, Rafiq started forward, his hand extended.

Gabby blew her nose and backed away, fending him off with one hand.

'I really don't want a shoulder to cry on—least of all

yours,' she spat. 'Let's face it—you're not sorry. If any of your remorse or sympathy was genuine—if you gave a damn for anything but your duty and your country—you wouldn't be doing this... Oh, and have a I mentioned it is a totally crazy idea?'

'We are both in a position we don't want to be, Gabriella. I ask this: meet my brother. He is at present out of the country, but I expect him back in two days' time.'

She regarded him warily. 'Just meet?'

'Think of it as a first date.'

'But you expect there to be a second?'

'It is no secret, Gabriella. I have made it clear what my wishes are. My brother needs support; you are a strong, resourceful woman.'

If she really was as resourceful as he imagined she would be able to think of another way to gain Paul's freedom. 'And you'll let Paul go home?'

He nodded. 'There are formalities to be—'

'How long?' she cut in.

'Thirty-six, forty-eight hours...and then he will be on a plane back to England.'

Gabby released a shuddering breath. The sooner the better, as far as she was concerned—before Rafiq woke up to the insanity of his scheme. And she had no doubt he would. This was just his way of trying to cope with what was happening to him. Playing along and humouring him felt almost like cheating.

'I'll meet your brother.'

She could tell from his satisfied smile that he had never doubted her agreement.

'Fine. Until then I suggest we put the time at our

disposal to good use.' His dark gaze drifted down her body, and he felt the lustful kick of his libido. Had the circumstances been different, that 'good use' would have involved a bed.

He inhaled and reminded himself that circumstances were *not* different, and it was *not* a good idea for a man to undress—even mentally—the woman destined to be his brother's bride.

'What sort of good use?'

Her frown, he reflected, would have been even more suspicious had she known of the carnal mental images he struggled to banish from his head.

'There are things about my country—the formalities that a princess must—'

Her jaw dropped. 'You want me to learn which fork to use?'

Her interruption brought an impatient frown to his face. 'There are customs, ceremonies…'

She rolled her eyes. 'I suddenly feel like Eliza Doolittle.'

His heavy-lidded eyes narrowed at her flippant insertion. 'One of the first things you might like to learn is that it is not generally considered good manners to interrupt a member of the royal family. I will see you tomorrow.'

'I can hardly wait.'

The worrying part was that her sarcastic parting shot as he left the room had an element of truth to it.

She had clearly lost her mind.

# CHAPTER EIGHT

GABBY did not actually see Rafiq until almost the following afternoon.

Her morning had been spent with someone called Sayed. She had no idea what his specific role was in the royal household—he had introduced himself simply as a member of the Prince's personal staff—but it was clear from the level of respect given him by others that he was a man of some influence.

Sayed had given her a tour of the palace—or at least as much as could be covered in a morning. It was impossible to tell from the man's manner towards her what he had been told about her, if anything. He was obviously too polite to express anything as vulgar as curiosity.

They had now reached the library—a room of such dazzling magnificence that even after all the splendour she had been exposed to that morning Gabby was stunned into awed silence. Then Rafiq finally appeared, and Gabby was struck dumb with awe for the second time.

She watched as he walked up the wooden steps that led to the upper mezzanine level of the room. Her breath snagged in her throat.

The man really was magnificent!

Her gaze swept in an arc from his toes to his dark bare head. He was wearing what seemed to be the norm for him—riding breeches, boots, and a white flowing desert robe, above which his burnished skin glowed golden. She gave her head a tiny shake of denial, still unable to reconcile his vitality with what she knew of his illness.

He nodded quite curtly to her, and then turned to Sayed.

The two men spoke in their own tongue for several minutes, and Gabby was left to twiddle her thumbs before the older man bowed low to her and excused himself.

Gabby turned to the tall Prince. 'So what's next?' she asked arching a brow. 'Cutlery lessons?'

'I will assess the need for those at lunch.'

Gabby's wrathful glare met his steady, sardonic gaze, and her expression melted into a reluctant grin. 'If you're serious,' she warned, 'I will slurp my soup.'

His dry response disconcerted her. 'I sense you will be a charming dinner companion.'

The humour in his eyes disconcerted her some more—and she struggled not to respond to his dry humour. 'Dinner and lunch?' she said, trying not to analyse her quickened heart-rate too closely. 'I do feel honoured.'

'I would have been here earlier, but a problem required by attention. I hope Sayed was an adequate deputy.'

'He was a preferable deputy.' He hadn't shaken loose odd, uncomfortable feelings inside her. 'Infinitely preferable,' she added, dragging her eyes from his mouth. 'How did you explain to him…?'

He shook his head and looked baffled. 'Explain?'

Gabby laid a hand flat on her chest. 'Me! How did you explain me being here?'

There was no answering flicker of comprehension in his face as he placed his hand on the back of a leather chair. Gabby's eyes were drawn to the dark red ring on his finger. He had lovely hands…strong and sensitive…and…

'Why would I explain anything?'

Gabby's eyes lifted to his face. Her distracted study of his hands had brought a flush to her cheeks. It remained there as she studied his lean, patrician features.

After a few seconds she laughed. 'Sorry—silly question.'

'Sayed tells me that you have asked a good many intelligent questions.'

'He does?' Gabby doused her smile and frowned, because she didn't want to make it seem as if she was eager to please. 'It was the novelty of receiving straight answers,' she observed crankily.

'I will try to be direct.' He extended his arm in invitation. 'Would you like to have lunch?'

Gabby gave a take-it-or-leave-it shrug and turned in the direction he indicated. As she did so she came face to face with a portrait that had caught her attention when she had first walked into the library. This close, the subject's beauty was even more startling.

'Her eyes really do follow you,' she murmured, studying the dark-haired beauty. Her skin seemed to glow and her eyes were as blue as the string of sapphires that hung around her slender throat. 'Who is she—or *was* she?'

'Was. Queen Sadira.'

Gabby's eyes left the painting as she tilted her head up to Rafiq. She found he was looking at her and not the portrait. 'Your mother?'

'No, she was my father's first wife. She was the love of his life.'

Gabby, who wasn't sure she would have enjoyed having the love of her husband's life looking down at her from such a prominent position, turned back to the portrait.

'But he loved your mother too?'

'No. I think he was fond of her, and he respected her, but a man only experiences that sort of…insanity once in his life.'

Gabby turned her head and found Rafiq was standing closer. She tilted her head further back and felt her stomach dip in reaction to the masculine aura he generated.

'He didn't love her?' His pragmatic observation shocked her.

'You sound scandalised,' he observed. 'You do not need to be. Not on my mother's behalf. She did not love my father—not in the romantic sense—but she respected him, and they shared a vision of what this country should be, and a strong sense of commitment and duty.'

Things, Gabby thought, studying his dark face, they had passed on to one of their sons at least. A son who even when he was dying did not think about it in personal terms but in terms of how it would affect the future of his damned country… She was conscious of anger building inside her. No one had ever given him the choice!

Why should Rafiq be expected to make such a sac-rifice?

'My parents' marriage was a successful union.' Annoyance flickered across Rafiq's face as he heard the defensive note in his own voice. 'When they married the country was in turmoil. My mother was instrumental in supporting my father when he undid the years of neglect following Sadira's death.'

'You think love is a form of insanity?' She studied his profile, her glance lingering on the passionate curve of his mouth, and wondered if Rafiq had ever known that insanity.

His eyes slid to the portrait. 'When Sadira could not bear children my father was expected to put her aside. He refused, even though the lack of a clear heir to the throne was creating major divisions.'

Gabby's tender heart bled for the tragic Queen. 'You think he should have put her aside?'

He shrugged. 'My father put his personal happiness ahead of his duty.'

'Is that a yes or a no?' It was a silly question. It was clear from his actions that Rafiq put his individual desires and needs below his duty and his country—duty had been bred into him, and he had never been allowed to be a carefree little boy or a reckless young man. He had always been the future King.

'The job of King comes with responsibilities.'

'The poor woman. She was so beautiful...' Even though her glance had drifted back to the portrait Gabby remained painfully conscious of the man beside her, and her empathy went bone-deep. 'And her eyes are incredible...so blue.'

'Not as blue as yours.'

The husky retort brought her swinging back to face him. As their eyes connected the air around them seemed to shimmer with the intensity of unspoken desires and emotions.

The only sounds in the massive room came from the mingled tick of a selection of antique time pieces and their breathing—hard to distinguish each from the other.

Gabby's stomach quivered, and her heart thundered as she struggled to breathe. Her feet seemed glued to the floor with lustful longing. She struggled to break free of the bonds of the sexual thrall that held her tight in its grip… Rafiq's eyes were so…*hot*… Oh, help!

'I… I… I'm hungry. For food,' she added, her face crimson with embarrassment.

Rafiq inhaled, his flared nostrils quivering as he scented her perfume. 'I too am *hungry*…' Ravenous described better the desire pounding through his veins.

He moved abruptly, and broke the tableau a split second before Sayed announced his return with a tentative knock.

'What is it, Sayed?' He assumed a neutral expression. She was a sensual banquet, but not his.

Standing in the vault of the room, Sayed raised his voice to reach the mezzanine level. 'I am afraid that there has been a landslip in Bahu.'

Gabby saw Rafiq stiffen as the two men continued their interchange in rapid Arabic. It didn't take an ability to understand the language to see that the situation they were discussing was serious.

Halfway to convincing herself that the entire sizzling moment had only existed in her head, Gabby was sure of it when Rafiq turned back to her, with no residual trace of warmth in his sombre manner.

'I am needed. I must leave you.'

'Take me with you,' she heard herself say. 'That is…'

'All right,' he said, telling himself that it was a good thing if she saw some of his country and fell under its spell.

It was not a good moment to think of spells.

Conversation was not possible due to the noise during the helicopter flight. It took them three quarters of an hour, but for Gabby, staring down at the fascinating and constantly changing scenery of this geographically diverse country, the time went quickly.

Gabby wrapped the silk scarf she had been given around her head as she stepped out into the sun. She shaded her eyes and stared.

A group of black tents were scattered around a green oasis, but what dominated the site was the towering ancient stone wall rising up behind them.

Rafiq watched her jaw drop.

'It is the remains of a Crusader castle. Like the Bedouin, the Crusaders were attracted by the water, and due to the height nobody—enemy or friend—can arrive unseen.'

It was clear from the small group who came to greet them that Rafiq fell into the latter category.

'There are no men.' Gabby voiced her observation out loud.

'The men are all helping in the rescue. My father gave permission for an archaeological dig to go ahead down in the valley.'

'That's where the landslip is?'

Rafiq nodded, his expression sombre. 'Yes, several young men from here were working on the site.'

'There are injuries?'

'It appears so. The rescue is being made more difficult by sheer inaccessibility. The overhanging cliffs make helicopter access impossible, and the track is too rough for four-wheel drives. That just leaves...' He nodded towards a distant dust cloud that as Gabby watched became a group of horsemen, approaching at great speed.

She felt her stomach lurch as she saw the spare horse they were leading.

'You're going in?'

He nodded, and looked surprised by the question. 'Of course.'

'Can I come with you?'

He shook his head, something close to tenderness flickering across his face as he looked at her. Gabby's stomach flipped.

'Not this time,' he said. His expression grew troubled as he focused on her face. Then, as he hooked a thumb under her chin and tilted her face up to his, it hardened into one of self-recrimination. 'I should not have brought you.'

'What if when you go with them—?' She nodded towards the men who had reined in their mounts close by. 'What if—' she repeated, unable to keep the anxiety from her voice. 'What if you get ill?'

'I won't.'

Not a very practical response, but one that seemed

to Gabby very typical of this man—this very hands-on
Prince, who took responsibility a lot more literally than
most.

'The women will look after you.' Rafiq had turned
away to speak to the group from the tents, varied in
age and all looking visibly comforted by what Rafiq
said to them.

He only looked back once as he strode out to the
waiting men and vaulted with lithe ease into the saddle
of the spare horse. Gabby watched until the riders
were nothing more than specks in the shimmering
desert landscape.

The women did look after Gabby, but as they spoke no
English and she spoke no Arabic, communication was
limited. Her anxiety levels were rising, and she had
almost chewed her nails off. When the braziers were lit,
sending clouds of smoke into the darkening sky, still
there was no sign of Rafiq.

She had tried several ways to ask the women when
they thought Rafiq might be back, but the mention of
his name had produced many giggles and smiles that
were pretty much the same in any language.

Dawn was breaking when Gabby curled up on a rug
beside one of the open camp fires, finally succumbing
to exhaustion. But that exhaustion paled into insignificance beside the pallor of fatigue in the grime-streaked
face of the man she saw when she awoke a couple of
hours later.

'Rafiq!'

He stretched his long legs in front of him and hooked

one ankle over the other, looking at her over the rim of his coffee cup.

'Good morning. I am sorry you were left for so long.'

Dismissing the apology with a wave of her hand, Gabby pushed aside the blanket someone had placed over her while she slept and shot into a sitting position, wincing as her cramped limbs complained.

'You should have woken me. How long have you been sitting there? You're hurt?' she asked, as her horrified gaze fastened on the blood seeping from a gash on his wide forehead.

'I am fine.'

From the way he said it Gabby knew the same could not be said of everyone. 'Were many hurt?' she asked quietly.

'One fatality,' he said, placing his cup down on a level stone with an exaggerated care that did not quite hide the tremor in his hand. He thought of the boy who had died in his arms. Later he must speak to the mother who had lost her son. 'Twenty injuries. Five of those are critical; one man lost an arm.'

She watched as he passed a hand across his eyes. The need to wrap her arms around him and offer the comfort that would obviously be rejected was so intense that it took every ounce of her self-control to stay put. She could feel his pain in her bones.

'I'm sorry.' This was a prince, she realised, who took duty to a very personal level. He really *cared*.

He flicked her a half-smile that was very white in his grime-streaked face. 'They have been airlifted out now. A helicopter will be back for you presently.'

'You're not coming?'

He shook his head. 'I must stay.'

She didn't even try and persuade him otherwise. It was obvious that he wasn't going to change his mind.

'What about my princess lessons?'

Rafiq felt something move and twist inside his chest as he looked at her, her hair a wild halo, the dark smudges under her eyes making them seem huge. Swallowing, he shook his head. 'I think you have had a baptism of fire into our culture, so we will skip the cutlery lesson.'

'Did I pass?'

He looked at her in silence for a moment, then rose to his feet. 'Yes, you passed.'

# CHAPTER NINE

PAUL'S good-looking face lit up when he saw her. He rushed forward and enfolded Gabby in a bear-like hug, before sweeping her off her feet and twirling her around in a circle.

'Put me down, you idiot,' she begged, laughing. 'Thank you,' she said, smoothing down her hair which, thanks to the ministrations of a hairdresser who must be famous because he only had one name, hung like a smooth silky curtain down to her waist.

'Thank me?' Paul shook his head. 'I don't think so. Thank *you*.' He shook his head in admiration. 'I don't know how you did it, sis—but, thanks.'

Her eyes slid from his. 'I didn't do anything,' she protested. She had wondered whether to tell Paul the truth, but had decided on balance not to. It would be pointless. Why make him feel guilty? Always supposing he actually took her seriously.

'That's not what the Parker guy said. He said you were Wonder Woman.'

'No, he didn't.'

'No,' Paul agreed, checking out his reflection in the

mirror. 'I might keep the beard,' he mused, rubbing his hand against the sparse, patchy growth on his lower face. He appealed to Gabby. 'What do you think?'

'I think no.'

Paul sighed. 'You're probably right. The chicks don't dig facial hair,' he added with a mock leer.

'Must you use that word?' she asked with distaste.

'While it annoys you—yes.'

Gabby rolled her eyes. 'So, what *did* Mr Parker say about me?'

'It's always about you, isn't it…?' Paul teased. 'Actually, the guy had an idea that you must have friends in high places. I put him straight. Mind you, I did start to wonder when they sent that car to pick me up. You should have seen it—about twenty feet long, and inside…' He let out a long whistle and shook his head. 'Then I realised.'

'You did?'

He nodded. 'They're buttering me up.'

'They are?'

'Obviously.'

Gabby shook her head and looked bemused.

'God, Gabby, you are so slow sometimes. They're afraid of bad publicity. And— Is that chocolate?' Distracted, he picked up a bar of chocolate that was amongst the contents that had spilled out of Gabby's bag onto the table.

He mimed a roll of drums and said dramatically, 'My first food as a free and exonerated man.' He shoved a large chunk into his mouth, rolled his eyes and groaned. 'Heaven,' he said, before adding, 'The thing is, they don't want me suing them for false imprisonment or something.'

Gabby's eyes widened in alarm. 'You're not thinking of doing anything like that, are you, Paul?' she asked uneasily.

'All I want to do is go home.'

Gabby's shoulders sagged in relief. 'You're booked on the six-thirty flight this evening.'

'Six-thirty? That barely gives me time to use room service.' Paul flung himself down on the nearest sofa and threw a grateful look at Gabby. 'You're a miracle-worker, sis.' His expression sobered as he asked, 'How are Mum and Dad?'

'You can ask them yourself later today.'

'It's been tough on them.'

She nodded. 'They've coped well enough.'

'Is there cable? Do you think I could get the match?' Paul wondered.

Gabby, thinking of the anxiety she'd suffered, imagining him in some cell with no window, regarded Paul with amused exasperation. He had just been through an experience that would have traumatised most and permanently scarred some for life, and all he could think of was a soccer match. And it wasn't an act either.

It must be nice, she reflected wistfully, to go through life with such a laid-back attitude.

'Was it terrible? Prison?' Gabby asked, feeling as usual like the responsible adult present, even though Paul was six years older than her.

Paul began to scroll through the channels, stopping when he found a cartoon he proclaimed to be his favourite.

'If you don't want to talk about it, I understand.'

'Turn down the empathy, Gabby, it's not good for your blood pressure. I've not got post-traumatic stress or anything. What is there to say? It's not meant to be nice, is it? It's prison. But it wasn't as bad as it might have been, and I knew I'd get out. I hadn't done anything, and anyhow I had the A team on the job.' He shot her an affectionate grin.

Gabby responded, marvelling at the way he had shrugged off his imprisonment the same way he shrugged off anything unpleasant that ever happened to him. Paul was, she reflected, nothing if not resilient.

'You look different.'

Gabby was amazed that he had noticed. 'You think so?'

'New dress?'

'Yes,' she agreed, thinking, New dress, new hair, new make-up… In fact when she had looked in the mirror before she had driven—or rather *been* driven—out of the palace earlier, she had hardly recognised the person who had looked back at her. If Paul, not the most observant of people, had noticed, the transformation must be even greater than she had thought.

'It's a different look,' Paul observed, fingering the blue filmy fabric of the skirt that fell in soft folds to her knees.

'But you don't like it?'

'Sure. I'm just used to seeing you in jeans. This makes you look a bit…um…untouchable,' he decided, studying her new look.

'Untouchable?'

Gabby was startled by the suggestion, but when she thought about it was not exactly displeased. The chances of Prince Hakim wanting to touch her were in her opinion fairly remote, and if she was cold and distant enough it would hopefully put him off her totally. Throwing many obstacles in the way of Rafiq's plan could only be a good thing. And if, as she suspected, Rafiq was overestimating his brother's sense of duty, it would not be long before Rafiq had to accept that people were not puppets.

But it was not her ability to be cold and distant to his brother that was troubling Gabby. Every time she thought of the way she had grabbed Rafiq and kissed him she wanted to curl up and die—and when she thought of him kissing her back the recognition that she hadn't wanted him to stop was more than humiliating, it was beyond belief!

How was it possible? The feelings he had aroused in her were terrifying, the hunger and excitement totally alien to her nature. Why, of all the men she had ever met, was this angry, tragic, *infuriating* man the one who had awoken the dormant sensual side to her nature?

Of course he had a good side. She kept seeing his tired, beautiful face as Sayed had arrived at the Bahu encampment to escort her back to the palace yesterday. He cared so passionately about his people and his country that she couldn't help but admire him and worry about him.

She clenched her teeth. No, she *wouldn't* worry! The wretched man hadn't even had the courtesy to let her know when or if he had returned to the palace. All she'd had was that stupid damned note this morning!

What was wrong with her? Was she one of those women who were attracted to what they couldn't have?

No. For that theory to work she would have to *want* Prince Rafiq, and obviously she didn't. Heat ignited low in her belly just thinking of him, but that was only a chemical reaction to a man who was the quintessence of everything male. Small wonder, really, that her hormones had been jolted out of their dormant state.

But she had them firmly under control now, so it was end of story, turn the darned page, Gabby, and get on with sorting out the next problem—namely, showing she was not queen material.

'Well, maybe not untouchable, but...' Paul replied.

'Regal?' Gabby suggested. Gabby, appalled by her thought, struggled with the urge to mess her hair and wipe off the beautifully applied make-up. All day she'd had the feeling of being trapped inside the body of someone else. Or maybe just trapped—which she was. *Temporarily* trapped.

Paul threw back his head and laughed. 'You? Regal? Now, that *is* a good one.' He chuckled at the joke, then asked, 'What time did you say the flight was?'

Gabby told him and he consulted his watch. 'So, no time for a nap?'

She shook her head. 'I don't suppose it was easy to sleep in prison?'

'Actually, there wasn't a lot else to do—and you know me. I can sleep anywhere, any time. The King of the Catnap!' he said, stretching out on the sofa and yawning. 'Haven't you got some packing to do or something? Shall I order a taxi?'

Gabby took a deep breath. 'Actually, Paul, I thought I might stay on for a while.'

'You're not coming home?'

*Home.* The emotional lump of loss in Gabby's throat swelled, and she blinked as she felt the prickle of tears behind her eyelids.

She could get on that plane with Paul.

She had given her word, but that had been under duress so it didn't count. There was nothing barring the integrity Rafiq seemed so convinced she possessed stopping her. She could sleep in her own bed tonight.

The idea held a lot of appeal.

What was to stop her? *Who* was to stop her?

Rafiq? Even Rafiq would stop short of boarding an international flight and hauling her off—wouldn't he? An image of Rafiq's face—the carved cheekbones, the sensually sculpted mouth and the implacable dark eyes—flashed into her mind.

It was the face of a man who would stop short of nothing to achieve the goal he had set himself. The man was so fixated and stubborn that she was wasting her time telling him his plan was crazy, but she was sure that the passage of time would prove what he didn't want to hear.

'I thought I'd take an extended holiday,' she said.

Just the odd twenty years or so, if things went according to Rafiq's plan. But it wouldn't—it *couldn't*. Gabby clung to her conviction. The alternative was something she couldn't bring herself to contemplate.

'But you don't *go* on holiday.'

'I don't go on holiday as often as you—but then who does?'

Paul worked only to pay for his trips, while their

parents lived in hope that he would outgrow his wanderlust, but so far it showed no signs of happening.

'I went to the Lake District last summer,' she reminded him.

Paul dismissed the Lake District with a grimace. 'You took a group of kids and you camped in the rain. I don't call that a holiday.'

'The Lake District is beautiful.'

Paul shook his head. 'You know, Gabby, sometimes I worry about you. Maybe I'll stay on with you.'

The word exploded from Gabby. *'No!'*

She felt Paul's astonished stare, and added in a more moderate tone, 'What I mean is, you have to go home. This has been traumatic for Mum and Dad, and they're not going to believe you're safe until they see you and hug you.'

Paul grimaced and looked contrite. 'Point taken. Poor Mum and Dad—I've given them a tough time over the years, haven't I? I never mean for these thing to happen, you know.'

Gabby's expression softened with affection. 'I know you don't.'

'Well, at least they have one kid who doesn't give them nightmares.'

Gabby dodged his gaze. She was still working on the assumption that Rafiq's plan would never actually come to fruition, but if it did it would not be just her own life that was affected.

She tuned back in from her worried analysis just in time to hear Paul say, 'Shame, though. I'd have liked to show you the sights... Not jail, obviously. Are you staying on at this hotel? How much are they asking a night? Let me speak to the management—I'll see if they'll do you a deal.'

'Thanks, Paul, but actually I've had an invite to stay with…a family.'

'Cool—the best way to see a country is to stay with locals. Or are they ex-pats?'

'No, they're local, actually. I've been invited to stay at the palace.'

Paul stared at her. After a long, startled silence he clapped his hands and gave a smug smile. 'See—I was right!'

'You were?' she said warily.

'Yeah. They're scared stiff I'll stir up trouble and they're pulling a charm offensive on you. I say go for it, sis. You might even get to see the Royals.'

'I can hardly wait.'

'I was just joking. That place is vast—and you're not likely to get invited to dinner with the King.'

Gabby, her mind very much on the ordeal awaiting her that evening, joined in weakly as Paul laughed heartily at his own joke.

'Come on,' she said, playfully knocking his foot down from the sofa. 'Shake a leg. You don't want to miss your flight.'

'What did I tell you?' Paul said as she climbed into the limo beside him. 'VIP treatment. I'm tempted to stay and milk it a bit.'

'They might be tempted to change their mind and throw you back into jail.'

Paul laughed and patted her hand. 'You're such a worrier, Gabby.'

At the airport the VIP treatment continued. They were even shown through to a private lounge and offered refreshments. Gabby had a few moments' panic when the flight was called and Paul was nowhere to be found, but he returned before she had gone into meltdown, looking pleased with himself.

'Where were you? The flight has been called.'

'First class,' he announced as she hustled him out of the lounge. 'Now do you believe me?'

She smiled and shook her head. 'You're incorrigible. But promise me one thing—don't talk to any strange women.'

'I've sworn off women.'

'I've heard that before,' Gabby muttered as she watched him go through security.

The relief she felt as she watched Paul's flight lift off was intense.

He was safe. She had achieved what she came out here to do. But at a price.

The heat outside the air-conditioned terminal building hit Gabby like a solid shimmering wall as she stepped onto the wide pavement in front.

There was no sign of the car that had deposited them, and Gabby was wondering what to do next when a long black limo with tinted windows pulled up.

The rear door opened.

'Get in,' a disembodied voice snapped.

It was the verbal equivalent of a click of the fingers. Gabby's lips thinned in displeasure. She would have given a lot not to jump in in response, but she had very little option.

'Is that an invitation or an order?'

'It's whichever works.'

With a snort, Gabby slid into the back seat. She arranged her skirts neatly around her knees and crossed her ankles, but she was only delaying the inevitable. She had to look at him some time.

'How did you find your brother? He is well?'

As if he actually cared. With anger in her eyes, Gabby turned her head and promptly forgot what she had been about to say.

Today, along with a traditional flowing white robe, his head was covered by a white *keffiyah*, held in place by a woven gold band. The only blemish on his face was the healing wound on his forehead. The traditional headgear emphasised the remarkable bones, the sybaritic purity and the strongly sensual quality of his face. Especially, she thought, the sensual quality of his mouth. Her eyes were irresistibly drawn to the blatantly sexual curve of his lips. It was obvious that a man with a mouth like that had to be a good kisser—and he was.

It was some time later that her drifting, dreamy gaze finally connected with his. He arched a questioning brow. Embarrassed colour flew to her pale cheeks.

She compressed her lips and tossed him a cold response. 'Considering what he's been through, he's remarkably well.' She sniffed and thought, *No thanks to you!*

'You have explained the situation?'

'You mean did I tell him I bought his freedom by relinquishing mine? Strangely enough, no, I didn't. This

may seem like some sort of business deal to you, but
to most people it would look like blackmail—and,
actually, that's how it feels.'

*And you're telling him this why? Rafiq is not inter-
ested in how you feel.*

Instead of answering her outburst with some cutting
riposte or sinister warning he didn't say anything at all.
But she could feel his eyes, even though she had
turned her head and was staring blindly out of the
window. Finally she could bear it no longer. She
turned her head.

Rafiq was scowling at her.

She lifted her hands like someone protesting their innocence. 'What? It's the truth. Can you say you *haven't*
blackmailed me?'

'What have you done to yourself?'

The seemingly unconnected criticism made her
blink. 'Done to myself? I haven't done anything.'

He lifted a hand and inscribed a motion above his
own head. 'Your hair…your face.'

'That wasn't me—that was your hit squad. You don't
like it?' She just managed to stop herself touching her hair.

'I do not like it.'

'How very rude of you to mention it.' And how totally
ridiculous that I actually care.

'Why did you let them do this to you?'

The utter unfairness took her breath away. 'Like me,
they were following orders—*yours*!'

Her orders had been delivered on a silver tray. Along
with details of her brother's flight and where she could
meet him, the handwritten note had also informed her

that she would be dining that evening with the two
Princes. The postscript had explained that a selection of
suitable outfits would be delivered to her room later.

They had been—along with a hairdresser, a stylist
and a make-up artist. They had admired her skin until
Gabby had let slip that her skincare regime was a bit hit
and miss, and depended greatly on what skincare
products were on special offer. The women had then discovered a lot more room for improvement.

Rafiq looked outraged. 'I did not tell them to do *this!*'

'*This?*' This time she couldn't stop herself touching
her hair. 'What's wrong with it? I've been styled,
made over...' And apparently I still don't make the
grade—great!

'You could be any woman in the street.'

Only the ones who could afford couture, she thought.
'No—any woman in the street could catch a plane and
go back home.'

'Your style is individual.' His frowning scrutiny
returned to her hair, which shone like glass and fell
river-straight down her back.

'That's what I thought you wanted to get rid of.'

Rafiq did not respond. His expression, as he continued to stare at her hair, was distracted. Then without
warning he reached out and swept a strand of shiny hair
from her cheek.

'That's what I thought too.' But he had changed his
mind.

Gabby stared at the blood-red stone on his finger
and shivered as his fingertips brushed her cheek.

'Yesterday your hair looked as if you hadn't combed

it. When you were sleeping, you…' He speared his fingers deeper into it, and remembered doing the same when he had kissed her. The memory made it hard to retain his detachment. It made him hard, full-stop.

Gabby hardly recognised the hoarse, husky voice as her own as she retorted, 'I don't always look that bad. Yesterday I had been sleeping in the desert.'

'And worrying about me.' His hand dropped and his hooded stare darkened as his long fingers curled around her throat.

Gabby felt the light touch like a burning brand on her skin. 'I was worried about everyone. How are…?'

The relief she felt when his hand fell away was so intense she had to bite back a bubble of hysterical laughter.

'Two are still on the critical list.'

'I'm sorry.' She was utterly bewildered, and had no way of articulating her helpless physical response to this man. She had never experienced anything like the sensations that were thrumming through her body. So much for taking control of her hormones!

She ran her tongue along her upper lip to blot the beads of moisture that had broken out there, fighting the desire to crawl out of her skin.

'Well, I suppose it's too late to do anything about your hair now.'

'You really know how to make a girl feel good about herself. You could always chuck me out of the car to try and get the look you apparently liked so much,' she said, reaching for the door handle.

With a curse he leaned across her and clamped his hand over hers.

Gabby shrank back in her seat, her senses spinning and her pulses leaping as his arm pressed her into the seat.

'I was joking,' she said. But not now. Now jumping seemed a pretty safe alternative to having him this close. She was overwhelmingly conscious at a cellular level of his hard male body, the heat, the scent, the raw, powerful masculinity of him.

His hand still covering hers, he turned his head. His face was so close she could feel his breath on her cheek and see the network of fine lines around his eyes. His dark hooded eyes were fierce and hypnotic.

And then it came. The forbidden thought she had walled away—*he's dying.*

A keening cry ached for escape from her tight throat. She shouldn't feel this terrible sense of loss—for God's sake, she didn't even like him, he was her enemy—but the empathic connection she felt with him was so strong she could feel the weight of his emotional isolation, and her foolish heart ached for him.

*How do I feel so close to this man?*

Their eyes connected and clung, and for a moment time seemed to slow, then freeze. It was Rafiq who leaned back in his seat, and the spell broke.

Gabby expelled a shaky sigh and sat on her hands, to hide the fact they were shaking. 'Talk about overreaction. You have no sense of humour.' She gave a light laugh and turned her head to look out of the window. Please let this journey be over!

The highway from the airport was wide, long and straight, cutting directly through miles of flat ochre-coloured desert, dotted with strange and weirdly shaped rock formations that rose up into the sky, casting even weirder shadows against the desert floor. There was a lot of traffic. She commented on the fact, because it seemed like a fairly safe and impersonal subject.

'It is a holiday here and it is tradition for people—families—to go to the sea. They are now returning to the city.'

'I know someone who took a diving holiday here a few a years ago.'

'Yes, there is good diving. The coast is littered with wrecks that are rich in sea life. I learnt to dive there myself.'

'And those green patches I keep seeing in the desert? What are they?' she asked, looking at his cut glass profile and not at the scenery rushing by.

'They are areas of irrigation, and most productive. We actually have a strong agricultural economy, and even without the hand of man the desert is not as arid and lifeless as it appears. Many species have adapted to the conditions and temperature fluctuations—I have even seen fig trees growing miles from water.'

Gabby listened, fascinated as much by the passion, enthusiasm and pride for his country she could hear in his voice as the information.

'In the south, where there is no shortage of rainfall, we have—' He stopped abruptly and turned his head. 'Are you actually interested?'

Gabby said the first thing that came into her head. Unfortunately it was the truth.

'No, I just like the sound of your voice.' Actually, *like* was far too tepid a term. 'And of course,' she continued, adopting a flippant attitude, 'I'm going to be Queen of all I survey…' *Quick recovery, Gabby.* Her mocking smile faded. 'You do know it's not going to happen, don't you, Rafiq?' she said quietly. 'Have you even told your family that you're ill?'

'I will tell them at the appropriate time,' he replied with deceptive calm. The problem was one that he knew he would have to face. But not yet.

His father was not young, and though he was not a physically demonstrative man Rafiq knew that his sons were his life. Once people knew he would be treated differently, and this was something he wanted to postpone for as long as possible.

'They have a right to know,' Gabby began earnestly. 'And you shouldn't be alone. You should have—'

Rafiq listened until he could bear no more. 'Enough!' He cut her dead with a jerky motion of his hand. 'I hardly need a support network when I have you, do I?'

His sarcasm made her flush and look away—but not before Rafiq had seen the glitter of tears in her eyes.

He studied her delicate profile and felt glad there was no woman in his life who would weep tears for him and mourn. What man could contemplate the prospect of the woman he had held in his arms and made love to watching him fade away by slow degrees without horror?

'Let me make it plain that I do not need your pity, your understanding, or your compassion. Is that clear?'

She swallowed and compressed her lips. 'As crystal.'

His voice soft with menace, he leaned in towards her, his dark eyes burning into hers. 'And if you have any ideas about telling anyone…'

'I won't blab.'

'Good,' he said, settling back in his seat as the car glided through the open palace gates.

# CHAPTER TEN

'WE ARE dining in the small family dining room.'

'Cosy. *Very* cosy,' she commented as he stood aside to let her precede him into the room. The 'small family dining room' was the size of a football pitch. The table set at one end, with gold candlesticks, heavy crystal and antique silver, was about thirty feet long, and they were walking on a mosaic floor that had to be centuries old.

Rafiq, upon whom her irony was wasted, saw her staring at the glowing mosaic and said casually, 'Byzantine,' before approaching the man sitting at the table with a newspaper propped in front of him.

Gabby looked curiously at the man she was meant to marry. *It just so was not going to happen.* He was around six feet tall and slim, and he wore his dark hair cropped short and spiky at the front. A black tee shirt under a silver-grey suit and scuffed trainers completed his ensemble.

The same individuality and lack of formality was evident in his greeting, as he clapped his elder brother on the back and regarded Gabby with open curiosity.

'Hello, I'm Hakim. You must be Gabriella. I've heard a lot about you.'

Gabby's eyes widened. 'You have?' She threw Rafiq a questioning glare before accepting the hand extended to her. Her fixed smile broadened when the young Prince held her eyes and raised it to his lips.

Gabby laughed, and realised that staying distant and cold was not going to be easy. 'Sorry—you just remind me of someone I know.'

His smile flashed white in his handsome face. 'Someone pretty marvelous—am I right?'

Gabby laughed again. 'My brother—and he would be the first to agree with you.' Her glance flickered between the two Princes. Rafiq scowled and Hakim winked. 'Gosh, you're not even a little bit alike, are you?' she gasped, thinking that the younger brother might be all style over substance, but he was charming and refreshingly uncomplicated to someone struggling to cope with the exhausting complexity, contradictions and convolutions of Rafiq's personality.

'You see, Rafiq, some people appreciate me.'

The duration of the meal followed the same pattern of light-hearted banter—though there was a slight hiccough when, in the middle of dessert, Hakim asked her how the research for her thesis was going.

Gabby played for time. *'Thesis?'*

'Gabriella has not yet had an opportunity to see first-hand the new initiative for the Bedouin children,' Rafiq inserted, in response to her raised eyebrow glare.

'Well, you're in safe hands with Rafiq, Gabriella.'

*Safe* was not exactly the word that sprang to mind when she thought of Rafiq's hands. She swallowed, thinking of them framing her face while he kissed her.

Her eyes were drawn unwisely to the sensuous, sexy curve of his lips. Rafiq saw her looking and his eyes went hot when he felt her gaze. Her stomach went into a dipping dive.

'Gabby,' she said at last, her voice a little too breathy and her smile several thousand volts too bright. To her relief Hakim seemed oblivious to the charged undercurrents that she could feel like a crackle under her skin.

'Gabby—I like that. Well, Gabby, the entire idea was Rafiq's brainchild. As you can imagine, there was a lot of local opposition to combat—especially when he insisted that females have full access to the scheme. So, you're in education, Gabby?'

'I'm an infant school teacher.'

'Really? You look nothing like any teacher I had. Does she, Rashid?'

His appeal to his brother was met with a blank stare. Just when the silence was getting awkward, Rafiq responded, 'Gabriella is very well qualified.'

'I'm sure she is. What I'm wondering is how you two met.'

'By accident.'

'A mutual friend.'

The two versions emerged simultaneously.

Gabby glared at Rafiq, who carried on eating—or actually not. She had already noted with some concern that all he did was push his food around the plate—a fact which seemed to have escaped the notice of his brother.

Hakim looked amused as he glanced from one to the other. 'Obviously it was a fate thing.'

Gabby's embarrassment increased when several more comments Hakim made through the meal revealed—to her at least—that he was obviously under the impression that she and Rafiq were an item.

Rafiq, whose contribution to social intercourse had shrunk to monosyllabic grunts by the end of the meal, seemed oblivious. And the gaps in conversation were ably filled by Hakim, who was happy to talk—especially about himself.

Having toyed with her dessert, and getting increasingly angry because she was concerned about Rafiq, Gabby excused herself and retired to her room. The man might be in terrible agony, and he was too stupid or stubborn to say a word. He'd just sat there looking noble and dignified because he didn't know how to act any other way.

After pacing the room making unflattering observations about the Crown Prince of Zantara, while fractured images and snatches of conversation played in her head, it hit her like the proverbial bolt from the blue.

She—the woman with the armour-plated heart—had fallen in love. With the wrong brother! How funny was that?

She didn't feel much like laughing as, hand pressed to her forehead, she fell full-length backwards onto the bed and lay there, staring blankly up at the ceiling.

She had fallen in love with a man who, even if he'd had a future, would have had no place for her in it. Did irony get any darker? Did life get any more darned unfair? Tears began to seep from beneath her eyelids, streaming unchecked down her face.

* * *

Rafiq nodded to the maid who had brought coffee and turned to his brother. 'You appeared to get on well with Miss Barton, Hakim? What did you think of her?'

He had to work hard to keep the note of accusation from his voice, and he was not entirely successful. It seemed an appropriate moment to remind himself that this was what he wanted, what he had actively engineered—more than he had in all honesty expected.

He had expected Gabriella to make herself as obnoxious as she knew how—and he knew from personal experience that was *very*. Instead she had laughed at his brother's jokes—even when they weren't funny. That damned dimple of hers had not taken a rest.

There had been an instant rapport between the two. His thoughts slipped back to a moment midway through the meal when he had seen their heads close together, fair and dark almost touching. Hakim had placed his hand on her shoulder and Rafiq had felt a savage compulsion to drag his brother from his seat.

Rafiq inhaled and closed his eyes, his nostrils flaring, the muscles along his angular jaw flexing and tensing, causing the sinews in his neck to stand out like steel cords.

He had been acting like an old wolf—the pack leader about to be replaced by young blood.

It was pathetic.

Why should he be jealous of his brother?

The answer was shocking in its simplicity: because Hakim would have Gabriella. She was everything that didn't attract Rafiq in a woman, and yet he wanted her more than any woman he had ever met. He could not look at her without thinking about touching her skin, inhaling her scent...

'Think of her?' Hakim looked startled by the question. 'It's not like you to ask my opinion.'

'Well, I'm asking now.'

'I haven't really thought...' Rafiq's dark accusing frown made Hakim backtrack. 'She's nice, very pretty—a bit *serious*...'

Rafiq's face went blank with utter astonishment. Were they talking about the same woman? 'Serious...? You mean *not* shallow? And this is a bad thing?'

'I didn't mean it that way. I meant...studious-serious,' Hakim corrected, thinking his brother must *really* like this English teacher to spring to her defence that way.

Not really news. A man would have had to be blind and deaf not to have noticed the obvious charge crackling between them. And in his experience only people who were *very* aware of one another ignored one another quite so determinedly.

It was not amazing that Rafiq was attracted to Gabby—she was pretty gorgeous—but it was amazing...actually, more than amazing...that Rafiq was discussing her with him. He had always kept his personal life strictly private, and there had been no male bonding sessions when they were younger, where they exchanged stories about the women who had broken their hearts.

Hakim's heart had frequently been broken, but if Rafiq had ever lost a night's sleep over a woman it was news to him.

'*Studious?*' Rafiq echoed, thinking of her soft, naked and pliant in his arms...while she was asleep at least. Awake, she had turned into a spitting little wild cat.

'All right, then, smart, clever. I find that a bit…intimidating.' He shrugged and grinned. 'Because, unlike you, brother, I'm not what you'd call intellectual, I generally go for girls who are more—'

Rafiq, looking pained, cut across his brother. 'Details are unnecessary. I have seen the sort of girls you *like*.'

Hakim grinned broadly. 'I'm what you'd could call a work in progress. But one of these days, brother, I might just surprise you.' *And sooner than you think*, he added silently. 'And I do like Gabby. What is not to like…? I presume that you're about to tell me?'

Rafiq lifted a brow. 'Is that what you think?'

'You usually warn me off unsuitable women. I'm amazed you introduced her to me—went out of your way to introduce her to me if she's got a skeleton in the closet. And since when were you interested in what *I* think?'

A spasm of regret crossed Rafiq's dark features. 'I am sorry if I have excluded you, Hakim,' he said abruptly.

Hakim stared. 'Well, if that sorrow is worth a new Porsche—great. I'm really not all that scarred because I haven't sat in on endless meetings on agricultural policy.' His eyes narrowed, and despite the levity of his manner there was some concern in his face as he asked, 'What is all this hair-shirt stuff, Rafiq?'

His eyes widened again as a fairly revolutionary possibility hit him. Was it possible Rafiq was asking his *advice*? Or at least asking for him to tell him to go for it, even if she didn't tick all the boxes?

He must *really* like her!

'What do you need my opinion for anyway? Are you trying to tell me that you haven't already got a file an inch thick on Gabby?' Hakim knew that his brother entered into relationships the same way he would a financial negotiation. He did his research and was not flexible. He did not make concessions.

But this time it looked as if whatever dirt he had on the girl in question had not put him off. But perhaps he thought it should? Who knew? Hakim thought. They were in new territory.

The file Hakim had spoken of had indeed arrived in its more complete form, on his desk that morning. Rafiq had put it straight in a locked drawer, telling himself that he would study it later.

But no matter what was in that file, no matter what or who lay in Gabriella's past, it would not alter the fact that she'd make a better wife than his brother deserved, and would be a queen that any country would be proud to boast of.

'What a woman did before she met you is hardly important.'

Hakim, in the act of stirring more sugar into his coffee, stopped and turned to stare at his brother in utter amazement. Rafiq was serious… How serious…? *Wife* serious?

'So if you decided to get married tomorrow you wouldn't want to know ahead of time if your prospective bride had any scandals that might be embarrassing?'

'The same premise applies.'

Hakim's jaw dropped. 'Is this the same man speaking who once told me that a royal bride needs to be squeaky clean, no unsavoury secrets, no skeletons in the closet. The next thing you'll be telling me is she doesn't have to be a virgin.'

Rafiq did not join in his brother's amused laughter. 'It is better to be the last man in a woman's life than the first.' Better, of course, to be both. But Rafiq appreciated that in the modern world that limited a man's choices. *His* choices were non-existent, but Hakim had a life of choices ahead of him. Of course he didn't know how lucky he was, because it was the human way not to appreciate what you had until it was being taken from you.

Hakim stopped laughing and stared. 'Will whatever alien that has taken over your body let me speak to my brother, Rafiq?'

'Do not be foolish,' Rafiq snapped, his brows knitting into an irritated frown.

'You know what you're talking like?' Hakim fixed his brother with a narrowed, speculative stare. 'You're talking like a man who's fallen in love. Have you ever been in love, Rafiq?'

'Not as often as you, little brother.'

'Clever,' Hakim admired. 'But you didn't answer the question.'

'And I am not going to.'

## CHAPTER ELEVEN

'GABBY—Gabby wherefore art thou...?'

Gabby, who had been sitting in a chair staring out over the palace illuminated against a deep velvet starry sky, got to her feet and, standing well back from the edge, looked down cautiously. Prince Hakim was standing beneath the balcony, his hand pressed to his heart and a grin on his handsome face.

'At school,' he called up, 'I always wanted to be Romeo, but being the prettiest boy in school, and until I was seventeen one of the shortest, I was always Juliet.'

'From what I hear you've had a lot of practice playing Romeo since.'

He grimaced. 'Ouch! Someone has been telling tales. If you leaned down I could climb up your hair.'

Gabby lifted a hand to her hair. After a shower it had reverted to type and gone its own sweet way. 'Make up your mind. Am I Juliet or Rapunzel?' she said, throwing a rope of silky blonde threads over her shoulder.

'I wish I could stay around and discover, but alas I'm flying back to Paris tonight.'

'Isn't that a bit unexpected?'

'As a matter of fact, yes. But something my brother said has made my mind up about something…'

'Something Rafiq said…?' Gabby's face fell. 'So he's told you…' She felt relief, and then almost immediately alarm and indignation. 'But you must realise that you can't go!'

'Why can't I go?'

Her words were jumbled in her anxiety to convince him that his dying brother needed him here. 'Oh, I know the stuff about me is a bit crazy, but don't worry—that will blow over. I think it's his way of coping, staying in control. He needs you here. I know he pushes people away, and acts as though he's invincible, but—'

Hakim's voice minus the mockery and laughter sounded much more like his brother's as he cut across her. 'Why does Rafiq need me here?'

'Why?' She closed her eyes and pressed her hand to her mouth—*a bit late now, Barton*. She groaned. 'You don't know, do you?' Oh, God, what had she done?

'Don't know what?'

'I can't tell you. I gave my word.'

Hakim swore at length and then, after first testing the strength of the wrought-iron support of the balcony, began to climb up it.

From above Gabby watched, her heart in her mouth.

Across the courtyard Rafiq, standing next to an ornate fountain, watched with very different feelings. He had arrived in time to watch the entire scene. Thanks to the noise from the fountain he hadn't been able to hear what was being said, but he had a pretty good idea. He couldn't see them now that Hakim had grabbed her and pushed into the bedroom, but he had a pretty good idea what was happening.

It wasn't going to happen. He wouldn't allow it!

The primal rage that surfaced in him lasted the time it took him to charge across the courtyard and reach the balcony. He stood in the exact spot his brother had. He could see the imprint of his footprints in the freshly watered grass. The rage turned to cold stone inside him.

What was he going to do? Climb up and claim her? Well, that made sense—he had so much more to offer a woman than Hakim. *Take me, because I'm a dying man.*

Half an hour later, when the sprinkler system switched on again, Rafiq was still standing in the same spot. The jets of water roused him from the dark place he had gone to. He let his head fall back and lifted his eyes to the sky as water streamed down his face, and he felt the pain of the primal scream locked in his throat.

He ached for a woman he had pushed into the arms of his brother. He couldn't even summon a smile to recognise the dark irony.


'I'm so, *so* sorry,' Gabby said, falling to her knees beside Prince Hakim, who sat hunched in a chair his face hidden in his hands. 'I thought he had told you.'

Hakim lifted his head. His face was chalk-white and his dark eyes stricken. 'I don't believe it. Rafiq is…he's never been ill a day in his life. Why the hell didn't he tell me?' He turned a resentful glare on Gabby. 'He told *you.*'

'That's because I'm a stranger.'

'I'm his brother.'

'That's the point,' Gabby cried, her tender heart

aching. She wasn't hurt by Hakim's hostility, she was just grateful that he hadn't got as far as wondering why she had agreed to Rafiq's scheme.

She laid her hand flat on her chest and said in as neutral a voice as possible, '*I* don't matter to him.' *Why should you, you idiot woman?* 'He wants to protect you for as long as he can,' she explained.

Hakim dragged a hand across his face, blotting the moisture from his red-rimmed eyes. 'He's been protecting me for twenty-four years,' he choked.

'I know,' Gabby said patting his hand. 'The thing is, now we—' She stopped and closed her eyes. There is no *we*, Gabby. There's *them*. Rafiq and his family. 'You, his family and his friends need to be there for him,' she finished quietly.

'You know, I thought all that stuff at dinner…you and him…I thought *he* wanted to marry you. When all along he thinks I'm so pathetic I can't do the job of king without someone to back me up.' Again his expression was tinged with resentment as he looked at Gabby. 'He must have a very high opinion of you.'

She shook her head. 'No, he thinks I'm a total pain.' She gave a shaky laugh. 'But he loves you,' she told Hakim earnestly. 'And he knows what a desperately hard job you'll have. He's had his whole life to prepare for it, but it's just being dropped on you. He wants to help and he's a control freak.'

Hakim sniffed and smiled. 'He is that. And I'm not offended he thinks I can't cut the mustard. He's right. I can't do it.'

'Do what?'

'Be King.' Hakim got to his feet and dragged a hand through his hair. He walked towards the door, leaving a dismayed Gabby sitting on the floor. 'He's right, Gabby. I can't do it alone. I know I can't.'

It had been almost six a.m. before Gabby had fallen asleep, and it was late when she emerged the next morning. She wasn't surprised to find herself alone eating breakfast.

Or actually not eating. Her stomach rebelled at the thought of food. She wished she knew what was going on. What had Hakim done? Had he gone straight to Rafiq and confronted him? Had he run away? No, she couldn't think that of him—she didn't want to.

Only a week ago she had been reading about this family in an article, a bit of hurried research, and now she had become so deeply embroiled in their lives her own would never be the same.

Damn, if only she'd thought to tell Hakim to wait until Rafiq was ready to tell him the truth. If only she'd kept her mouth shut to begin with and not jumped in with both big feet. She looked down at her size fours, shod in a pair of soft leather sandals, and asked herself, *Why am I blaming myself? I didn't ask to be in the middle of this. I didn't ask to be blackmailed. I didn't ask to fall in love! Damn, damn, damn! What am I going to do?*

Forehead creased against the pounding in her temples, Gabby clapped a hand to her aching head. She felt like a hamster in a wheel, going nowhere fast, her thoughts revolving around in ceaseless unproductive circles.

Bottom line: her life was chaos. She was standing in the middle of an emotional minefield and it didn't make any difference what choice she made, which direction she went—she was going to be hurt.

She didn't want to be a queen. She wanted to be with one man—a brave, stupid man, who was trying to push her into bed with his brother!

Expression stormy, she took a sip from her coffee cup and yelped as the liquid scalded her mouth. She slammed the cup down, splashing coffee all over the snowy table linen, and poured iced water from the pitcher into her glass.

She was greedily gulping it when she saw Sayed in the doorway.

'Miss Barton…? I am sorry to disturb you.'

Gabby's expression of polite enquiry morphed into one of apprehension when the normally imperturbable Sayed spoke again.

'I am very worried about the Crown Prince, miss.'

She dropped the glass, spilling water over the already ruined table linen.

Her manner was at stark variance to the icy dread that was creeping over her as she smiled politely and asked, 'Has something happened?'

If anything *had* happened she would be the only one, barring Hakim, who realised the ominous implications. Her jaw firmed and her hands balled into tight fists at her sides as she struggled to control her panic. Damn the man for a stubborn idiot.

'I think something must have, miss… He…the Crown Prince…is…angry.'

Gabby expelled a relieved sigh. At least he wasn't ill. 'Is that all? He's always angry.'

Even as she spoke Gabby realised he wasn't—at least not with everyone else. By comparison with his cranky, critical attitude to her, he was capable of displaying an almost supernatural degree of tolerance with other people. Not that he suffered fools gladly, but on the other hand he gave praise where it was due, and people went the extra mile just to receive one of his rare smiles.

Gabby pushed away the image of Rafiq smiling and concentrated on Sayed, who was shaking his head in an emphatic negative motion.

'No, this is serious. I have known the Crown Prince since he was a child, and I have never seen him like this. I am worried,' he confessed.

So was Gabby, though she struggled to hide it. 'Why are you telling me this, Sayed?'

'I thought you might—' He stopped, looking awkward, and began wringing his gnarled hands together.

Gabby took pity on him and suggested, 'You thought I might be stupid enough to risk getting my head chewed off?' Despite her joking tone the genuine anxiety in the older man's eyes filled her with increasing disquiet.

Sayed looked relieved. 'Exactly so, miss. He might listen to you.'

Gabby stared at the man, wondering if he had been out too long in the midday sun. Listen to her? Rafiq did not listen to anyone. But her... She was the very *last* person he would listen to. Somehow the staff here had got the wrong message from her presence.

'So he didn't seem ill at all?'

'Ill, miss?' He shook his head, looking puzzled,

adding with a touch of pride, 'No, the Crown Prince enjoys excellent health. He always has, even as a boy.'

Gabby's eyes fell. Even asking if he was ill went against the denial screaming inside her as she refused point-blank to contemplate a world that did not contain Rafiq.

It was bizarre. Not long ago she had not known he even existed, except as a name in the official guide-book. Now the idea of him not being here made bony, skeletal fingers of dread in her chest tighten until she couldn't breathe.

'I'll see what I can do.' She doubted it would be anything of substance, but Sayed obviously thought oth-erwise: his relief was obvious. The man clearly imagined she possessed supernatural powers. 'Where is he?'

'He is in his private room in the tower, miss. I think you know where it is.'

Gabby saw the man's secret little smile. Clearly the grapevine was alive and well in the Palace. And she for one didn't want to know what garbled version of the truth had been passed around.

Gabby had lifted her hand to tap on the door when she heard the sound of a loud, angry voice inside. She stopped and waited. There was a short silence after the rant ended, and then the even more alarming sound of crashing and smashing began.

Gabby gave up on the idea of announcing herself. Instead she pushed the door open cautiously. It gave. Wondering what on earth she was going to find, she squared her shoulders and stepped inside.

There was evidence of the destruction she had heard,

but there was nothing systematic about it as far as she could see. Rafiq, who was pacing the floor like a sleek, feral caged animal, wasn't simply walking around objects, but through them.

Rafiq turned, a snarl on his face. 'What are *you* doing here?'

Their glances connected, worried blue on wrathful and smouldering black, and her breath snagged painfully in her throat. In his primitive anger all pretence of civilisation was washed away and Rafiq was quite simply magnificent. Of course she had always known he was a man of strong passions, and she had even seen him strain at the emotional leash at times, but now it had snapped!

As their glances connected his eyes, blacker than the darkest starless night sky, lit from within by twin flames, drilled into her. Every individual fibre and muscle in his body was bunched and taut. He was an explosion about to happen.

She didn't want to supply the final trigger. Gabby ran her tongue lightly across her dry lips as something that was part trepidation and part excitement slid through her. Now that really *did* make her weird…

'What has happened, Rafiq? Are you ill? Is—?'

'Not ill—just dying.' He saw her flinch, but pushed away the shaft of inconvenient guilt that slipped like a dull blade between his ribs.

Gabby, her face pale, bit down on her quivering lip and tucked her hair behind her ears. It immediately sprang free. 'Well, something must have happened to put you in this mood.'

His upper lip curled into a sneer. 'Something? Oh,

yes, *something* has happened,' he agreed darkly as he swung away from her.

Gabby watched, her frustration growing as he recommenced his restless panther-like pacing of the room. She chased after him, catching him as he reached the doors that lay open to the balcony where she had lost her balance the first time they had met.

Without thinking she caught hold of his arm and tugged him to a stop.

He stood breathing hard, staring with a look she couldn't put a name on at her hand on his arm.

'Sorry—I'm a tactile person.' She sincerely hoped he didn't correctly translate this as *I can't keep my hands off you.* 'I keep forgetting people don't lay hands on the royal person without an invitation.'

She turned her head to one side and regarded him with a calm she was not feeling.

'Will you stop being so damned enigmatic and stay still for ten seconds? You can be snide and superior just as well when you're sitting down. I know this,' she said, placing her hands flat on her chest, 'because I've seen you do it.'

The fury still pounded inside his skull like a hammer, but Rafiq managed a flicker of a smile as he lowered himself into a chair.

'Thank you,' she said, dropping to her knees beside it. 'Now, you can tell me that it's none of my business,' she began, thinking he most probably would, 'but—'

'It *is* your business.'

That threw Gabby off balance. 'It is?'

'I received a note form Hakim this morning. He has flown back to Paris.'

Rafiq watched as the colour drained from her face. If his brother had been on the same continent at that moment he would not have been responsible for his actions.

'How could he? How could he leave now? After…?' Gabby, her face as pale as paper apart from two bright spots of angry colour on the apples of her cheeks, stopped and pressed a hand to her lips. How could he do this to Rafiq?

The pain in her horrified whisper penetrated a part of Rafiq's heart that had never previously been exposed.

She lifted swimming blue eyes to Rafiq. 'I really thought he had more—' Her voice broke as she considered Hakim's departure.

'My brother is a fool, and I am sorry for what he has done to you. His actions are those of a—' He used a word in his native tongue that she didn't understand, but his expression was translation enough.

'Done to *me*?' she echoed, confused.

Rafiq swallowed, the muscles in his throat visibly rippling under his brown skin and his eyes glowing as he contemplated the pleasure of throttling his own brother.

'You have suffered at the hands of the Al Kamil family.' He gave a grimace of self-recrimination. 'I have used you,' he admitted stiffly, his rage visibly growing as he spoke, 'but at least I haven't slept with you, knowing all along I had no intention—' He closed his eyes and cursed slowly and fluently in several languages.

Gabby, her eyes widening suddenly in angry comprehension, exclaimed, 'Slept with me! You think I slept with a man I'd only known five seconds?'

Why not just call me a slut and have done with it?

she thought, ignoring the sly voice in her head which suggested that *two* seconds would have done it if the man in question had been Rafiq.

A muscle clenched in his lean cheek as he shook his head in a stiff negative motion. 'You will not speak of it.'

He could not allow himself to think of it, to torture himself with images and allow the jealousy to bite like acid into him.

'But I—'

He cut off her protest with a look. 'I saw him climb into your room.'

Her jaw dropped. 'You saw...?' Her eyes narrowed. 'You were watching?'

'I had something I wished to discuss with you.'

Rafiq had been struggling throughout the day to keep his feelings of guilt at bay, but following their dinner he had come to a decision. He would release her from their bargain. The irony was that, having studied her brother's case in further detail, he doubted that the case against Paul Barton would have ever made it to court after the scheduled review.

Of course this irony had paled into insignificance beside his finding his own brother scaling her balcony— minus the rose between his teeth, but in all other ways the perfect romantic lover.

'I had planned to use the door.'

Gabby bit her lip. 'What did you want to discuss with me?'

'It is no longer relevant.' She was puzzling over his sharp retort when he added, 'To think that I pushed you into his arms!'

His snarled recrimination made Gabby flinch. 'I'm not some puppet. You've never made me do anything I didn't want to, Rafiq.'

Her clumsy attempt to soothe him had the opposite effect.

'So you have fallen in love with him?' he said heavily. It was nothing he had not already suspected. He had seen women fall for his brother's brand of charm before.

The absurd assumption made Gabby stare at this normally smart man. 'Of course not. It was just—'

'Sex?' he finished for her heavily, before closing his eyes and slipping seamlessly into a flood of Arabic she could not follow apart from some spectacular epithets. She watched him slam his fist into the carved arm of his chair.

A cry of alarm was wrenched from the watching Gabby's throat as she witnessed this loss of control.

'For goodness' sake, Rafiq,' she cried, tugging at his arm.

She saw with horror blood well along the line of his knuckles as he ground his flesh into the hard surface. It had to be hurting, but he didn't appear to notice—not the pain, nor her breathless panting efforts to pull his arm down. She could barely get a purchase. The muscles under her fingers were tense and bulging and they had about as much give as a steel bar. Her efforts were futile. He appeared not to even notice her.

He relaxed his arm suddenly, and, breathing a sigh of relief, Gabby knelt there, panting, her fingers still curled around his forearm.

'Your poor hand.' She winced, raising his hand to

examine the broken skin across his knuckles. 'You need—'

Rafiq sucked in a deep, shuddering breath and fixed her with a blazing stare so intense it stripped bare her defences, leaving her feeling emotionally exposed and trembling. *'Need...?'* he echoed, giving a laugh that made her heart twist in her chest in empathy.

Anger rose inside her as she lifted his hand to her chest and nursed it there. Tears filled her eyes. He needed life, and it was being denied him. Misery lodged in her chest like a lump of lead—there was simply nothing she could say that wasn't utterly clichéd.

'Sorry.'

Her whispered comment brought his eyes to her face. He felt tenderness twist his heart. No woman had ever touched him this deeply.

'I am sorry too. Sorry that I did not imagine for a heartbeat...not for a heartbeat—' He broke off, lifting the hand that she held to his own chest and pressing it against the area where his heart rested.

Gabby, her hand trapped beneath his, could feel the heat of his body and the steady thud of his heart.

*Oh, God, but I love him!* The anguished admission was drawn from her very soul.

'I did not imagine that a brother of mine could be so totally without honour. He actually left me a note,' he raged, lifting his other hand to frame her face with long brown fingers.

It struck Gabby that to the casual observer they would look like lovers. A shiver slid down her spine.

'What did Hakim say in the letter?' she asked, wondering if she ought to tell Rafiq *why* his brother had gone. It weighed heavily on her conscience that she had inadvertently broken her promise.

But, while unburdening herself might ease her guilt, it was not going to make Rafiq feel any better to know why his brother had run away.

Gabby felt livid every time she thought about the young Prince and his feeble behaviour. She was definitely not inclined to make excuses for him, especially as it seemed to her people had been making excuses for Hakim for too long.

She believed that everyone faced tests in their lives. This was the most important test Hakim had ever faced and he had flunked it! If she had Hakim here now she'd tell him exactly what she thought of him. Of course it hurt like hell to know someone you loved was in pain and that there wasn't a damn thing you could do to help, but you had to put your own feelings to one side.

That was simply what you did when you loved someone. Time enough later to indulge your own pain— too much time, she thought bleakly.

In that moment she was conscious of nothing but Rafiq. Every other thought was obliterated from her head as she soaked in sensations: the warmth radiating from his lean, hard body, his masculine strength, the fresh male scent of his skin.

'People use love as an excuse—as if that justifies everything.'

Gabby felt a moment of guilty panic—*had he guessed?*

Then he added with a sardonic sneer, 'My brother is apparently in love.' Rafiq's fingers fell away from her face, and his upper lip curled with contempt as he contended, 'He doesn't know the meaning of the word.'

Rafiq's eyes swept her face before he turned his head away from her, expelling a hissing breath through flared nostrils. 'He writes to say he is getting married to some woman—a divorcee. Apparently I have said something which has made him realise he has to do this. He never has been able to take responsibility for his own actions.' He flung up his hands in a gesture of disgust before giving a shrug and pronouncing, 'Their children will be idiots.'

'He's getting married?' Gabby cried, sinking back onto her heels. 'I didn't see that one coming,' she admitted, wondering if there really was a woman, or if Hakim had invented her to explain his absence.

Rafiq looked at her downbent head and felt a rush of emotion he avoided analysing. 'My brother is an idiot…' he said. He could have had Gabby, he thought. He is an imbecile!

'You're angry because all your careful plans have gone up in smoke,' she said.

'You think this is about my plans?' It seemed to Gabby that he looked inexplicably startled by her comment.

'But you have to look on the bright side.'

Rafiq followed her advice and realised he would not have to endure the agony of being forced to see her exchange vows with his brother.

'There *is* a bright side?' He was willing to play along. She was clearly putting a brave face on it, but her pride had to be in tatters.

She frowned at the sardonic interruption. 'He will

have a wife, and that's what you wanted. She might be good for him.'

'I no longer care.'

Gabby, who didn't for a second believe him, patted his hand—an action that made him stiffen. She would have pulled her hand away, had he not covered it with his own and kept it there.

'Hakim is never going to be you, Rafiq, no matter who his wife is.' She paused to let this sink in. 'You have to trust him.'

His fingers tightened over hers. 'You of all people can speak my brother's name and say the word trust in the same breath?'

'This isn't about me. I'm just saying you have to let him make his own mistakes, be his own man. This woman might be exactly the sort of wife he needs.'

Rafiq gave her of a look of utter disdain. 'She is—'

'I know—an idiot.'

Her bored drawl pulled him up short. He frowned. 'That is irrelevant.'

This change of tack made Gabby blink. 'Who runs your country is *irrelevant*? I wish you'd decided that before I handed in my notice and gave away my cat.'

He flushed under her sardonic glare. 'My brother's actions to you have been—'

Suddenly Gabby was furious—her temper going from stationary to sixty in the blink of an eye. Shaking with the force of her emotions, she stabbed a finger in the direction of his broad chest. 'Don't you *dare* suggest you're this angry because your brother used me. You're such a hypocrite, Rafiq! This sudden concern for my welfare is totally phoney. This is about the fact that for once you can't control everything!'

'Control?' The irony struck him forcibly. He had never felt as out of control in his life!

'You're a control freak. And you know something? *You're* the idiot!' She stopped and laughed at his stunned expression, barely conscious of the tears running down her cheeks. 'You're so busy preparing for after you're dead—'

She stopped, her voice cracking emotionally as she pulled her hand from his and angrily brushed the moisture from her cheek with the back of her hand.

'You're so busy preparing that you're not bothering to live the rest of your life. It's an utter waste!' she finished on a resentful quiver. 'You should be extracting every last ounce from—' Shaking her head, she turned away, her teeth drawing blood from her quivering lower lip.

There was silence as Rafiq looked at her slender shoulders shaking.

She started as he laid a hand on her shoulder. 'I'm fine,' she sniffed defensively, before he could say anything. 'I'm not the one dying,' she added thickly.

Oh, God, why had she said that?

# CHAPTER TWELVE

RAFIQ, his stern features set like stone, allowed his hand to fall from her shoulder.

'I suppose I'll be going home now?' Gabby said in a small voice.

'Home?'

Gabby turned, tilting her head and looking him directly in the face. She took a deep breath. Had she imagined it? The sizzle of electricity when their hands brushed? The gleam of hunger she had glimpsed in his face when she had felt his eyes on her? Was the entire sexual tension thing a figment of her imagination?

Was it all one-sided?

*You'll never know if you don't ask, Gabby. So ask, girl.*

'Well, there's no reason for me to stay around here any more—*is* there?'

He met her steady regard with a look that held about as much promise as a wet Monday morning. Gabby felt the metallic taste of humiliation and utter loss in her mouth as she pinned on a smile and gave a jaunty shrug.

'I'll just chalk this up to experience. I got what I came

here for—Paul is free—and I've had a nice little holiday thrown in.'

'You are going home?' he said, in the oddest voice.

'Yes, I'm going home!' she yelled in exasperation. 'Haven't I just been saying that for the past—?' She sniffed and blinked back the warm tears welling in her eyes.

The evidence of tears shimmering in her blue eyes drew a curse from his lips. 'You *want* to go home?'

His throaty drawl rasped across her nerve-endings like sandpaper. 'Never mind about what *I* want. For goodness' sake, Rafiq, what about what *you* want?' Her mouth twisted into a bitter smile when he looked at her blankly. 'You act as though I'm talking a foreign language... Well, I suppose I am in a way—not that your English isn't actually better than mine, and—'

His voice cut across her rambling dialogue. 'A man cannot always have what he wants,' he said heavily.

'Just for one minute pretend you can,' she suggested. 'Forget you're a prince, forget duty and family.' She looked at his face, stopped and shook her head. 'There's no point, is there? You can't. You'll always be a prince first and a man second.'

He swallowed. 'Do you think I do not wish it otherwise at times?' he asked harshly.

Her eyes, blue as cornflowers, flew to his face and clung. 'Then wish now,' she begged huskily. 'Forget your brother. You're the one,' she reminded him, 'who always says you don't waste time and effort over things outside your control.'

'I had no idea you had listened to what I say.'

'I hang on your every word,' she drawled sarcastically.

'Your logic is questionable.'

'So is my sanity, when I've been talking to *you* for more than thirty seconds. You know I'm right,' she claimed shakily. 'You just can't admit it. So try to stop being a control freak for two seconds. Forget about your family. I do know this is sacrilege I'm talking…'

'Since when has that stopped you?'

It wasn't the dry insert but the flash of amused warmth that for a brief moment lightened the tension in his features, making Gabby stumble over her words as she continued. 'Forget—f…forget about Zantara,' she recommended. 'Zantara will be here long after we are *all* gone. Think for once in your life about you.'

'Me?'

'Yes, think about Rafiq,' she said, her blue eyes earnestly scanning his face. 'What do you want? And I don't mean duty. I mean what do you *want*? If you could have whatever you want at this minute what would it be? I bet you haven't even thought about it.'

In a world where nothing was the way it should have been this was one thing she was determined to achieve. Rafiq was for once in his life going to do something selfish.

A nerve in his lean cheek jumped as his restless dark glance touched the soft curve of her full mouth. He had gone to sleep seeing her mouth, imagining tasting the sweetness within. He had woken up and the mental torture had continued.

The words were dragged from his throat against his will. 'Oh, I have thought about it.'

'You have? Great!' she enthused, offering him a smile of gentle encouragement. 'So what is it?'

There was a long, dragging silence as his heavy lids came down. Through the mesh of his lashes as they lay against his slashing cheekbones it was impossible for Gabby to read his expression, and he evinced a great interest in his hand-tooled leather riding boots before rising to his feet.

Gabby's soft features hardened into a mask of determination as she followed his example, and stood toe to toe with him. She planted her hands on her softly curved hips and angled her face up to his.

'I'm not moving until you tell me.'

Rafiq's heavy lids lifted. The intensity of his stare burned into Gabby as their eyes met. She was suddenly overwhelmingly conscious of his sheer physical presence as he towered over her. She had no control over the shiver of illicit excitement that trickled down her spine.

'This.'

Gabby's eyes flew wide in startled shock as he bent his dark head towards her. *He's going to kiss me.* The shocking realisation sent a wild rush of heat through her body.

Without thinking—why think about something she had been genetically programmed from birth to do?—she turned her mouth into his, shivering with anticipation at the first firm touch of his lips. A deep sigh shuddered through her body as her lips parted of their own volition under the firm pressure. Her lashes fluttered like trapped butterflies against her flushed cheeks as the kiss deepened and grew more intense, and a fractured lost moan was dragged from somewhere deep inside her.

The heat inside Gabby built as Rafiq continued to

kiss her, deepening the intimacy by slow, sensual incre-
ments as he explored the soft, sweet moistness of her
mouth like a starving man who had found sustenance.

She was burning up from the inside out, and the
flames of desire were searing away the last threads of
common sense from her brain. She knew it was only sex
for him, and he thought it was just as casual for her—
he believed she had slept with his brother the previous
night—but that didn't matter. None of it mattered.

If this was his way of blanking out the cruel cards
fate had dealt him, his way of forgetting what must
haunt his every waking moment, she didn't care. Gabby
wanted to give what comfort she could and take
whatever came her way.

Finally Rafiq's head lifted, but he stayed close—
close enough for her to be able to feel his warm breath
on her face, to see the network of lines radiating from
around his eyes.

Gabby looked up at him through half-closed eyes, the
hot summer blue almost swallowed up by her dilated
pupils. She was trembling, and she could feel the febrile
shudders that ran at irregular intervals through his grey-
hound-lean frame.

She felt a hot, heavy lethargy as he tangled his
fingers deep in her hair and ran a finger softly along
the curve of her cheek, lingering over the indentation
of her dimple.

'I have thought about it a *lot*,' he slurred thickly.

Gabby was intoxicated by the startling admission.
'Then why on earth didn't you do something sooner?' she
wailed, standing on her tiptoes to plant a kiss at the corner

of his fascinating mouth. He responded with a growl, and kissed her with a ferocity that sent her senses spinning.

'You were marrying my brother,' he reminded her, when he had kissed her into a state of blissful, aching submission.

Gabby looked up at him. Who would have guessed that surrender to her own needs and those of someone else could feel so perfect?

'And now I'm surplus to requirements?' Bless Hakim, she thought, smiling.

'Not *my* requirements.'

Rafiq turned a deaf ear to the voice in his head that told him he ought not to be doing this. Every fibre in his body told him he *had* to do this—he could no more *not* do this than he could stop his body dragging in its next breath. His brain supplied a plausible cover story that allowed him to go on. This was just sex.

The expression in his eyes made the heat in her blood pool low between her legs. 'Those requirements,' she admitted, with an uncharacteristic boldness she was actually getting the hang of quite quickly, 'are the only ones I'm actually concerned with right now.'

A sudden frown tautened his strong-boned features. 'You are offering yourself up as a sop to a dying man…?'

She reached up and took his face between her hands. Tears stood out in her eyes as she fixed him with a fierce glare. 'I don't want to talk about that!' she breathed. 'I've never seen anyone as alive as you are—and, for the record, there is nothing at all selfless about what I'm doing.'

Rafiq searched her face, and from the expression of predatory satisfaction that slowly spread across his bronzed features she could only assume he was satisfied with what he saw reflected there.

By some miracle he managed to keep his passion on its leash, though the immense effort made him shake like a highly strung racehorse in the slips.

'You know that I can offer you no future?' He refused to allow himself to think of what might have been. 'This is…'

'Sex,' Gabby inserted, stealing his earlier line. It was easier to say it herself than hear him do so.

Even so, the surgically stark pronouncement had instantly brought an emotional lump the size of a boulder to Gabby's throat. She struggled to speak past the aching occlusion.

'You think a woman cannot want uncomplicated sex?' she asked, thinking *Not this woman*. But there was no need to tell him that.

Her response should have eased his mind, but he looked less than pleased. Maybe he saw through her lie?

'All my relationships have been with women who wanted uncomplicated sex.' And that was the way he had wanted it. But now he wanted more, and he had no right to ask for it. He had no future. If she wanted the here and now he would give it to her—he didn't have the strength not to!

His admission had sent a jealous jab through Gabby.

'Then I'm no different.' Except for the style, elegance, sexual experience… The list of the things she didn't possess which they no doubt had was depressingly long.

Rafiq found himself responding without even thinking. 'You *are* different.' And so was he—very different from the man who had once wanted low-maintenance mistresses.

'I knew you'd realise eventually that I'm not royal material.'

He blinked, astonished at her interpretation of his words.

'But does that matter when there are just the two of us?'

He made no response, and she thought, *Hell, do I have to beg?* The knowledge that she would if need be was deeply shocking.

'You don't wear a crown in bed, do you?'

'I wear nothing in bed.'

The colour flew to her cheeks.

'And as for the future—nobody can predict what the future holds, Rafiq.'

'I have a better idea than most.' His mobile lips curled upwards in a smile that as far as she could see held no trace of self-pity. But while Gabby could admire his ability to find humour in this the blackest of situations she could not smile with him.

'I'm not interested in the future,' she claimed, trying not to think about life without Rafiq stretching dismally into the distance. 'I'm thinking about the present. You can give me the present, Rafiq.'

His eyes appeared illuminated from within as he began to speak in his own tongue. Gabby didn't have the faintest clue what he was saying, but the husky erotic flow and the glow in his eyes mesmerised her into a state of breathless compliance.

When he kissed her, bending her body back in an arc with the force of his onslaught, she melted. And when he lifted her into his arms she moulded herself fluidly to him, revelling in the strength of his muscular, masculine hardness, crooning things that under normal circumstances she would have blushed even to think in his ear.

Rafiq was breathing hard as he laid her on the low divan. His rapid, laboured inhalations registered at some level in her hormone-mushed brain. She struggled to raise herself on her elbow to ask anxiously, 'Are you all right? Should you be doing this?' The total selfishness of her actions suddenly struck her like an unwelcome splash of ice water. 'Your doctors—will they allow—?'

'I do not seek anyone's permission for my actions,' he declared, with the hauteur that she had come to associate so closely with him. His manner softened as he conceded with a negligent shrug, 'I might die...' His eyes slid over her slim body before returning to her lips, still wet and cherry-red from his kisses. 'But what a way to go!'

He responded to her gasp of horrified outrage with a white grin that was unapologetically devilish.

'How can you joke—?'

He slid his hand under the hem of her shirt and skimmed his fingertips along the soft curve of her stomach and her protest terminated in a husky moan.

It felt like a long time since he had been this close to a woman. 'Your skin is like silk,' he said thickly. 'You're so soft and warm and...' *I'm as selfish as hell.* He started to shake his head as a wave of self-disgust washed over him. He was worse than Hakim. 'I can't do this.'

Every muscle in Gabby body's clenched in silent agony at the suggestion of rejection. 'Why not? What's wrong with me?'

His eyes snapped open. 'Nothing,' he declared, his fierce eyes sliding greedily over her supine form. 'You're perfect.'

'So,' she retorted thickly, 'are you. Rafiq, I don't know if this is a good idea or not, and I don't care, but I'm perfectly willing to argue about it later. Not now— please, not now…'

The room was blotted out as he bent his head.

'Thank God,' Gabby breathed, as she lay shaking with feverish anticipation. Through the mesh of her lashes she saw a golden corona of sunlight around his dark head, and then he kissed her, and it wasn't just the room that was blotted out but everything that wasn't Rafiq.

Her entire world was filled with the sight, sound and smell of him, and desire, a deep primal need, roared in her veins like all-consuming fire.

Gabby, drowning in heavy, hot sensual languor, was not even conscious that he had unfastened her shirt until she felt the stir of air on her scalding hot skin as he peeled it aside.

One knee on the low divan and one foot braced on the floor, he arched over her, while his hands moved over the curves of her hips, drawing her up, moulding her body to his, letting her feel how much he wanted her as he kissed her as if he would drain the life from her.

She shivered as his lips slid wetly down her throat, his tongue tracing the line between her quivering breasts. He flicked the front fastening clasp of her bra and the fabric parted.

To cover the fact she was suddenly desperately self-conscious, scared stiff he'd find her wanting, she adopted a painfully awkward joky manner and laughed.

'You seem to know your way around women's underwear.' And around women too, she thought struggling against the compulsion to cover herself.

Rafiq seemed to see through her bravado—possibly because her jaw was clamped so tight it felt in danger of fracturing and her eyes were squeezed shut.

He curved his long fingers around her jaw and tilted her face up to him. 'Open your eyes.'

She did, and he smiled down at her, the tenderness in his dark face tinged by a fierce predatory hunger that made the liquid fire pooling low in her belly concentrate in a throbbing ache between her legs.

She wanted him so much that nothing in the world mattered.

She shifted restlessly, and caught her breath when, still holding her eyes, he cupped one small high breast in his hand, his thumb following the firm, gentle outer curve towards the rosily engorged nipple.

A cry was drawn from her throat as he ran his thumb back and forth across the ruched peak.

'You should be proud of your body. It is beautiful— all of it,' he growled thickly, and he lowered his head and took first one trembling nipple and then the other into his mouth. His tongue lashed the sensitised peaks, drawing a series of hoarse gasps from Gabby.

When he lifted his head there were dark lines of colour scoring the slashing angles of his high cheekbones.

'You should take pleasure in your body and from it— I do. See how much pleasure…'

Before Gabby realised his intention he took her hand in his and fed it onto his body, then curved his hand across hers, holding it there.

Her mouth opened in a startled O as she felt the hard, pulsing swell of his confined arousal through his clothes.

He laughed at her expression and released her hand, bending his head to kiss her. 'Do you believe now that I like what I see?'

Gabby, her heart hammering, nodded mutely, the memory of the surge of his body against her hand still making her weak with lust and sheer longing.

Rafiq carried on kissing her while unfastening her skirt and sliding it down her hips. Her pants followed. He disentangled her fingers from his hair and raised himself up on one hand to look down at her.

'You are so beautiful, Gabriella…' He pressed a hand hard to his chest and swallowed. 'So beautiful that it *hurts*.' He looked as astonished to hear himself make the confession as Gabby was.

'You are very good at multi-tasking,' she breathed against his lips.

He lifted his head, breathing hard, and flashed a white grin. 'I am good at many things.' Her blush drew a delighted throaty laugh from him. 'But sadly very out of practice.'

Because of his illness? She pushed aside the thought, and wondered what constituted 'out of practice' to Rafiq. A week? A month?

'Don't worry,' she said, literally shaking with need. 'I'm not a tough audience.'

Rafiq's eyes darkened as he read the glow of need in

her cerulean eyes. He stood up, drawing a protest from Gabby, who drew herself up on her knees to cling to his leg. She let go and settled back with a sigh as he began tearing off his clothes with flattering urgency.

After fighting his way out of his shirt he flung it over his shoulder, minus any buttons. His body had the sort of perfection that she had always imagined did not exist outside the creative powers of an artist. But he was no cold statue. And no artist, no matter how skilful, could have reproduced the earthy sexuality he projected.

His skin was an even gold, and as he stood in a pool of warm light it gleamed like oiled silk. The muscles in his upper body were impressively developed, and there was no surplus fat to mar the perfect muscular definition of his washboard-flat belly.

Holding her eyes, he unbuckled the belt of his trousers and let them fall. A moment later he kicked aside his shorts and sat on the side of the bed.

The breath snagged in her aching throat as her eyes slid down his body. She swallowed and looked away quickly when she reached his pulsating manhood.

He laughed and said, 'You are allowed to look and touch.' The smile died from his lips and he added in a hard, driven tone, 'Touch me, Gabriella. I need to feel your hands on me. I have been needing it from the moment I laid eyes on you.'

The raw need in his voice sent a fierce thrill through Gabby. She reached out and laid her hand on the hair-roughened skin of his chest. Then, leaning up, she kissed him on the mouth—a deep kiss with all of her heart in it. A soft fractured moan drifted from deep within her as they touched for the first time skin to skin, her breasts crushed against his chest. She ran her hands over his muscled thigh, then softly her fingers curled over his engorged shaft. The breath left her lungs in a shaky gasp of wonder.

The thought of all of him inside her burnt away the last threads of Gabby's control. She felt liberated. She felt alive.

His mouth was against hers. He was speaking— they were both speaking, but not necessarily in the same language. Their jerky, disconnected words were interspersed with frantic touching, hungry kisses and hoarse moans.

Gabby clung tight when Rafiq wrapped his arms around her and fell backwards, pulling her down on top of him as the silk cushions fell on the floor.

The tortured need throbbing inside him threatened his control as she pressed her lovely firm breasts against his chest and whispered, 'Please make it stop hurting, Rafiq.'

He held her hips and flipped her over, pulling her underneath him, and then he raised himself on one elbow and looked down into her face. Her pink lips were swollen, and in her big eyes the blue was only a thin band around her dilated pupils.

Gabby's heart was pounding so hard she wouldn't have heard if Rafiq had chosen that moment to speak. But he didn't. Without saying a word, his eyes burning into her, he took her wrists and pinioned them either side of her head.

He released one hand to stroke her, his fingers sliding over the damp skin of her hip and thigh while his knee nudged her legs apart. His fingers moved to her inner thighs, gradually moving with torturous slowness until he touched the moist heat between her legs.

Rafiq's body shuddered with the effort of not plunging straight into her sweet, wet heat. He watched her pale body writhe as he touched her, heard the fractured little sobs in her throat as she cried his name over and over, and it raised the heat roaring in his blood to fever pitch.

No woman had ever been so sensitive to his touch. He had never wanted to please a woman more. He had never wanted to possess a woman more. He shook quite literally with raw need. His nostrils flared as he bent his head and ran his tongue down the soft curve of her belly, smelling the scent of her arousal, breathing it in deeply.

Gabby's teeth sank deep into her lower lip. She could taste blood in her mouth but barely registered it as his fingers stroked her, flicking across her tight nub, driving her to the brink before sliding into her smooth slickness.

Her cheeks flushed bright, she was delirious with pleasure.

'You're so tight,' he murmured, biting softly into the curve of her neck, kissing the corner of her mouth, and her eyelids as he finally settled between her legs, the silky hard tip of his erection nudging her.

Then he was inside her. One long, deep thrust buried him deep in her very core. Gabby's untutored body convulsed with shock at this new and most shocking of all sensations, and above her Rafiq stilled.

Gabby, her senses glutted with new sensations, barely registered the cry that was torn from his throat.

Rafiq was filling her, stretching her, and when he moved, sinking in and withdrawing over and over, pushing deeper, touching the core of her, she lost all sense of self. All that was left was primal driving need and Rafiq.

When the climax hit her she called his name and clung to him. She felt close to losing consciousness as every pleasure-soaked cell of her body exploded. She heard him cry her name and felt the hot rush of his own release. They lay there, their sweat-slick bodies entwined, gasping for air.

Slowly reality seeped back, and Rafiq began to pull away.

'No!' she cried, throwing her arms across his broad back.

Rafiq turned his head to angle a questioning look into her flushed face. She looked like a wanton angel, her lips red and wet, her smooth cheeks flushed, her eyes bright and her wild blonde hair spread out on the bright silk pillows.

'Can we just stay like this for a little while?' she coaxed. 'You don't have to do anything, just…' She lowered her eyes and stroked his back. His skin felt like satin. 'You feel so good… Just a little while…please?'

Her wide eyes flew to his face as she felt him pulse inside her. 'Well, we *could* do something—if you like?'

He fixed her with a smouldering stare. 'Yes, you little witch—I like,' he growled. 'I have never felt this alive in my life.'

The second time was slower, their passion tinged with a sweet, aching tenderness that brought tears to her eyes—tears that overflowed when her climax claimed her. Rafiq accepted the tears and held her, rocking her back and forth slowly until they abated.

# CHAPTER THIRTEEN

THEIR lovemaking had been meant as a brief escape, a mechanical exercise—not something that was life-affirming, a confirmation that he was alive.

Rafiq had never wanted to live so much in his life!

As their sweat-slick bodies cooled his brain started functioning again, and he was furious with himself for allowing his emotions to become involved. Once he had called himself every word for a total bastard in his multilingual vocabulary his anger shifted to Gabriella—Gabriella, who had deceived him. Even now he could not believe that it was possible. There was a dream-like quality to the entire experience—he was living a forbidden fantasy.

Looking down at her tousled blonde head, he felt his anger slide away. Something twisted in his chest: a pain he avoided analysing. He smoothed down her hair, soft like silk. He breathed in the scent of her skin. It smelt of roses and of her and of him.

His arms tightened around her warm, pliant body, and she made a little noise in her throat like a contented kitten.

'Sorry about the crying, Rafiq.' Gabby was grateful

that he hadn't asked her to explain the overflow of emotions. 'Thank you,' she whispered, kissing his hand.

His racing mind slowed as he let her softness seep into him. He didn't want to move and he didn't want to think—because this was one conversation he didn't want to have. Not yet.

He ought to feel ashamed—well, he did. But the emotion was submerged beneath layer on layer of gloating male satisfaction. She was *his*.

In his arms she stirred again, running a hand down his hair-roughened chest and then circling his pebble-hard flat male nipple with her fingertip. The lustful surge of his body made it clear that if he put off the conversation much longer it wasn't going to happen for some time.

'How is this possible, Gabriella?'

With lazy, cat-like grace Gabby, who had been lying with her back curved into his chest, rolled over onto her stomach, sending a shower of silk cushions cascading onto the floor.

She propped herself up on one elbow, and with one hand under her chin looked enquiringly into his face.

'I was just asking myself the same thing,' she admitted. She knew he wanted this to be straightforward sex, but unable to stop herself, and frankly not caring if she came across as besotted and hero worshipping, she added huskily. 'That was—you are—utterly and totally incredible.'

'And you were a virgin,' he charged grimly.

While his shock and horror at the moment of discovery had been almost instantly swamped by an elemen-

tal surge of primal gratification that he was her first
lover it was now back in spades.

Gabby blinked as she registered the simmering
outrage in his voice and manner. His reaction struck her
as extremely unreasonable. What was she meant to do?
Deny it? Or produce some sort of defence?

'That bothers you?'

'Bothers me?' he echoed incredulously. 'What do
you think? A woman of your age would normally have
had many lovers.'

'You're the one with the file on me. You knew I didn't
have a boyfriend. You said—'

'No man in your life at present,' he cut in. 'I knew
you had not had a long-term relationship or a live-in
lover, not never had sex! It genuinely never even crossed
my mind that a woman who looks like you, who is so
obviously passionate...' He rolled onto his back and
propped a hand under his head. 'And last night I saw my
brother climb into your bed.'

'Bedroom—not bed. Big difference. It's not my fault
if you have a smutty imagination.' *He thinks I'm beautiful!* Gabby struggled to get her head around this
amazing fact.

'This is not something you were complaining
about earlier.'

Gabby turned a reproachful look on him.

'What is this? An interrogation? Hakim and I just
chatted.'

'Chatted?' Rafiq echoed. 'You *chatted*?' It was inexplicable to him that any man could be in her bedroom
and just chat.

'I didn't say we had sex. You just assumed...'

'You wanted me to assume.'

The accusation struck Gabby as deeply unfair. 'I hardly think you are in any position to criticise me. It's not my fault you were spying on me.'

'Do not be ridiculous!'

It was the first time she could recall Rafiq dodging her gaze. A sure sign of guilt.

'I did try to tell you nothing happened. You refused to listen.' Gabby glared at him. He had spoilt everything and her mellow glow of contentment had vanished.

And sex didn't seem to have made him very happy either, she thought, studying his face and noticing for the first time the greyish tinge beneath the surface of his usually vibrant skin.

Fear rushed through her. During the time when she had been in his arms, when they had been one, she had forgotten. Now the fear came rushing back.

'Oh, my God—this is all my fault.' She scrabbled into a kneeling position and began to pull the silken throw that had slipped to the floor over him.

Rafiq caught her hand and trapped it under his as he pressed it flat on his belly.

Her fingers spread and flexed as contact with his hair-roughened skin made things stir and shift lustfully deep inside her. What sort of woman did that make her? He was ill, and all she could think about was sex.

'What are you doing?'

Gabby shook her head. 'I don't know. I make a pretty clueless nurse,' she admitted ruefully. 'Can I get you something? Water and an aspirin...?' She lifted a hand to her head and groaned remorsefully. 'I'm so selfish. You should be conserving your strength, not…'

His smile was tinged with tenderness as he watched the blush spread across her face. His teasing expression abruptly faded. 'Not stealing your virginity?'

She squeezed her eyes tight shut and groaned. 'I don't know why you're acting like this is such a big deal. It was hardly stealing—I virtually begged you.'

'I'm not ill, Gabriella. I just didn't get much sleep last night.' Not much as in practically none. Rafiq had spent the night torturing himself, thinking of her in his brother's arms.

'Are you sure?'

He nodded.

'And do you expect to get much sleep tonight?'

Encouraged by his audible sharp intake of breath, she threw him a look of provocative challenge and, holding his eyes, ran a finger down the hard plane of his chest, before spreading her fingers across the hair-roughened skin of his washboard-hard belly, then lower.

'Stop that!' he growled, and Gabby stopped smiling.

The indentation between her brows deepened as her blue gaze fluttered questioningly to his face. 'What's wrong?'

'You can ask me that?' He sounded amazed and in-explicably angry as he lifted a hand and tucked it under his head. Refusing to acknowledge the hurt bewilderment in her eyes, his own eyes slipped downwards to the gentle sway of her coral-tipped breasts. He swore, and snapped, 'For pity's sake put some clothes on.'

Gabby flinched as though he had struck her. His

words had made her feel painfully self-conscious of her nakedness—a nakedness that moments earlier had felt empowering and natural.

'Why? Don't I come up to your high standards?' she asked, grabbing the cover she had draped over him and wrapping it around her own shoulders.

He looked at her as though she was insane. 'Because I can't think with your breasts in my face.' He couldn't think anyway. His brain was still refusing to move beyond the shock that she'd been a virgin.

Gabby blinked, and blushed again as her eyes slid to the tell-tale imprint of his arousal stirring beneath the fine silk covering.

'Oh!' she said, feeling slightly mollified. She was no expert, but for a man who was not in the most robust of health he appeared to have remarkable stamina. 'Is that a problem? You could think later.'

'You appear not to appreciate the seriousness of this situation.'

'*What* situation?'

'You were an innocent.'

'I realise that in your world not being a virgin lowers my market value, but in my world... Dear God, the way you're talking anyone would think I was pregnant.'

Rafiq froze. 'You could be.' He struck the heel of his hand to his head and groaned.

Watching him, Gabby was distracted by the rippling contraction of his stomach muscles as he sat upright in one fluid flowing motion. She watched covetously as he swung his legs over the side of the divan and continued to display a total lack of self-consciousness over his naked state.

'Could be?' she echoed vaguely.

'Of course you could be. You're not taking contraception.' Virgins did not need to. His voice was heavy with self-recrimination as he added, 'And I didn't take precautions.'

That this was the first time in his life he had been so criminally careless would not by his reckoning be a comfort to her, and it was certainly no excuse. There *was* no excuse!

Gabby opened her mouth to tell him he could relax, that there was no chance she was pregnant. Not that she had shown any more care of the consequences than he had. It was by pure chance not cautious foresight that she happened to be protected. She had started taking the contraceptive pill the previous month, when her doctor had prescribed it in the hope of regulating her irregular and painful periods.

Instead she heard herself say, 'Look, even if I was it wouldn't be the end of the world.'

He looked at her as though she had lost her mind. 'A life, a child, can never be dismissed so carelessly.'

She flushed at the reprimand. 'There is no child.'

'I don't think you have thought about the implications. If you are pregnant, the child would be heir to the throne.'

'Great—let's get married on the off-chance!'

He responded to her sarcasm with a nod of agreement. 'Obviously the child would only be heir if he was legitimate.'

Gabby couldn't believe what she was hearing. 'It might be a girl.'

He dismissed the possibility with a regal wave of his hand. The response drew a choked laugh from Gabby.

'Do you realise how crazy this is? We're discussing a child that doesn't even exist.'

'Maybe not now,' he continued, speaking his thoughts aloud, 'but it could. I have months to live yet.'

His unemotional observation sent a chill down Gabby's spine.

'I don't know why I haven't thought of this before,' he said.

Gabby couldn't believe he was suggesting what it sounded like. 'Possibly because you were still in touch with reality then?'

'It would secure the future of the throne. My father would guide you when the time comes—you would be regent for our son.'

She could almost see the scheme forming in his head. 'You have it all planned out, then?'

Her tone brought his attention to her face. 'Have I said something wrong?'

She arched a brow and hugged the throw tighter around her body. 'What could be wrong? I'm delighted if this little oversight might result in a solution to your heir problem. A sort of two birds with one stone scenario?' She swung her legs off the opposite side of the divan and sat with her back to him. 'My God, you're discussing a child that doesn't even exist—and thank God it doesn't. I've always thought that people who have a baby to paper over the cracks in a marriage are selfish and misguided, but this isn't just misguided—it's terribly wrong. Babies should be born out of *love*!'

'You're being emotional.'

The cold accusation drew a laugh from Gabby, who stood up still draped in the brightly coloured throw. 'Is that a crime?'

'Statistically, the majority of babies in your country are conceived by accident—does that mean they are any less loved by their parents?'

She gave a growl of utter frustration. 'I don't even know why we're discussing this.'

'You can't ignore the possibility you could be pregnant.'

'I'm not,' she said flatly. 'If you plan to go out and impregnate some willing incubator, fine! But personally I'd like the man I'm in bed with to be thinking of me, not of securing political stability for his country. Call me an old romantic, but there it is.'

As she spoke, Rafiq's face darkened. 'Have you quite finished?'

Gabby shrugged and began to walk away, but Rafiq bounded to his feet and spun her back to him.

'You have so much experience with being in bed with men?'

'I've had a shaky start,' she admitted. 'But I live in hope.' Actually, hope was in pretty short supply.

'You provoke me, Gabriella.' His hands slid down her shoulders, effectively clamping her arms to her sides as he yanked her towards him. It was defiance alone that enabled Gabby to hold his gaze as his smouldering eyes moved across her upturned features. 'If I could have thought of *anything* but you when we were making love…' He paused, sucking in a deep breath. 'If I could have thought of anything but burying myself in your body we would not be discussing the possibility of a child now.'

The earthy admission sent a thrill through her receptive body.

'As for me seeking a willing...what was your word?' He arched a sardonic brow. 'Ah, yes, incubator. That is not going to happen.' He felt some of the tension slip from her shoulders. 'I am angry with myself, not you.'

'That makes two of us,' Gabby said, feeling a little soothed but still very raw emotionally.

With an arm around her shoulder he led her back to the divan. 'Your first lover should not be someone like me who is not...who is not in it for the long haul,' he finished, with a dry laugh that broke her heart. 'And I could have left you with a child. What if something happens to me before you even know for sure?'

She shook her head in fierce rejection. 'It won't.' *It can't.*

'We have to consider the possibility.'

Gabby shook her head mutely, unsure she could speak for long enough now to explain exactly why she couldn't be pregnant without bursting into tears.

'The only way I know to protect you is for us to get married. Even with no baby, you were an innocent.'

She looked up, aghast, her brain working slowly to process the reality that he had just proposed marriage.

'You asked me to be selfish and say what I wanted. I want this.'

'Moral blackmail really is your forte, isn't it, Rafiq?

Just tell me—if there was no baby, if there never *would* be a baby, would you still want to marry me?'

She was totally confident of his answer. Rafiq's survival instincts had kicked in—not for himself, but for his country. He had been taught from birth that the well-being of an entire land and people were his responsibility, and now all his energies were focused on that end. This was about a baby, an heir.

'Yes.'

Her face fell. *'Yes?'*

He held her eyes and said again firmly, 'Yes.'

'But *why*?'

'The only woman I wish to sleep with is you. I was hoping that this was an experience you would like to repeat.' Finger under her chin, he tilted her face up to his. 'If it helps, my motivation is not political—just sexual.'

'You know I want to sleep with you again,' she said, her eyes filling with tears. 'Damn!' she muttered, brushing them away with the back of her hand. 'I never cry. But we can sleep together without getting married.'

'You were an innocent and that changes matters. You could be carrying my child.'

'You want me to be?'

He didn't deny it.

'It would make you happy?'

He stilled and scanned her face, sensing a change in her attitude but unable to pin it down. 'Of course it would,' he agreed.

Suddenly it seemed simple.

Wasn't that what she wanted to do? Make the man she loved happy? If she wasted that opportunity she would never be able to forgive herself. All it would take was a tiny lie. He would never know and he would be happy—she could live with the guilt. She could live with him asking her to marry him out of a sense of duty because she knew that the only way Rafiq was going to do something for himself would be if he could justify it as being for the greater good!

'Fine. If you still want me to, I will marry you.'

Part of Gabby wished she could truly do what he wanted. But how could she? A child should be the result of love. And their child would have the crushing responsibility that had been Rafiq's burden all his life. Their child would have no father to support him and guide him.

He expelled a long sigh. 'That is a sensible decision.'

She laughed, and he looked at her oddly. 'It doesn't feel like that. I have one condition.' *That you love me*, she wanted to say, but didn't.

He looked wary. 'Condition?'

'That nobody knows.'

'Knows when you become pregnant?'

Gabby felt a stab of guilt but did not lower her gaze.

'That might not happen, Rafiq,' she said quietly. It would not happen, because Gabby would not allow it to happen, but while Rafiq thought it might there was a chance of him actually snatching a little of the happiness he deserved.

The alternative was Rafiq spending the precious time he had left striving to achieve the impossible—to groom his brother to replace him. The fact was some people really *were* indispensable—and Rafiq was one of them.

'I know that, Gabriella.'

He knew it, but she could see in his face he didn't believe it. Was she doing the right thing?

'What is your condition?'

'That nobody knows that we are married.'

That way, afterwards… She pushed past the protective mental block that slid into place every time she thought of losing Rafiq. She had to think ahead. Afterwards she could simply go back home. There would be no need for anyone to know they had been married. She didn't want to gain anything from Rafiq's death; she just wanted to creep away when the time came and lick her wounds.

She refused to acknowledge the wave of crushing despair that washed over her. Time later for her to grieve. Now her priority had to be making Rafiq happy.

Rafiq was shaking his head, his expression discontented. 'But if we live as lovers here my people are going to think you are my mistress,' he protested, visibly unhappy with the prospect.

Her shoulders lifted. 'So?'

'But they would—'

'You've had mistresses before.' It wasn't a subject she much liked to think about.

'I've had lovers.'

'And they stayed here sometimes?'

'Yes,' he conceded irritably, 'in my private quarters. My father never met any of them. They never attended any official engagements.'

'Well, I'm hopeless at official engagements, so where is the difference?'

'A world of difference. You will be my *wife*.'

'Are you saying that your mistress would not be treated with respect?' Gabby knew that his people would not dare be anything else but respectful—at least to her face. But this was a society where women were still split into two distinct camps: wives and mistresses.

'Of course not. But—'

'There are no buts about it, Rafiq,' she said quietly. 'This is a deal-breaker. I want a secret quiet civil ceremony.'

He looked unhappy but resigned as he admitted, 'My wedding would be a full state occasion.'

'And they can't be thrown together in five minutes.'

'True,' he conceded.

'And you need to conserve your strength.'

'For making our baby.'

Gabby agreed, guilt stabbing her, but a clear conscience was a luxury she could not afford. If a lie was what it took to make the time he had left happy, she would lie. To make Rafiq happy she would have done a lot worse.

# CHAPTER FOURTEEN

THE civil ceremony took place the next day in a neighbouring state. They flew straight back and were in the palace just as the sun was setting over the desert.

Gabby discovered that her things had been moved to Rafiq's private apartment during their absence. A beautifully prepared supper was laid out on the terrace.

'This is lovely,' she said, picking up one of the rose petals that had been scattered artfully across the white linen cloth.

To Rafiq her manner was not that of a wife but of a polite child, saying the right thing. As he pulled her chair back for her to take a seat he bent forward, his lips brushing her ear as he voiced the question that had been building inside him all day.

'Are you regretting it?'

At his question she turned her head, her startled eyes wide. 'No!'

The response was immediate enough to soothe his fears slightly. It did not alter the fact that she had barely said a word all day, and nothing at all during the flight back in his private jet. When he had caught her looking pensive she had smiled, but the smile had never touched her eyes.

Rafiq was very conscious that theirs had not been the sort of wedding most girls dreamed of. Even he had found the civil ceremony painfully impersonal. It was hard to tell what Gabby had thought of it. She had made her responses like a sleep walker.

'No, I don't regret it,' she said. 'It does seem kind of surreal, though. We're really married… Which reminds me…' She pulled off the heavy antique gold ring that he had slid on her finger and produced a chain from her pocket. 'We don't want people to see this.'

Rafiq watched, his expression closed and struggling hard with his pride, as she put the ring on the chain and fastened it round her neck.

'No one will know it's there,' she said, dropping it down the softly gathered neckline of the simple sheath dress she wore.

'I will know,' he said, envying the ring its resting place against her breasts. 'And I have no problem with others knowing. I really don't understand why—'

'I'm just happier this way. We're legal—isn't that what matters?'

Rafiq looked half inclined to argue the point, but to Gabby's relief after a moment he shrugged. 'If that is the way you wish it. But whether you use the title or not, you are the Princess.' He laughed at Gabby's expression. 'Had you not realised?'

She shook her head. 'No.'

'Princess Gabriella.'

She shook her head. 'Hush—someone might hear you.'

'I have to tell you, Gabriella, that all this subterfuge is beginning to be wearing. Anyone would think you were ashamed to be my wife.'

The emotion in Gabby's throat thickened. 'I'm not. It's just all happening so quickly and—'

'It's not the way you imagined it would be when you got married?' He cut in.

'I never imagined getting married.'

She hadn't trusted herself to speak during the ceremony. The solemnity of the occasion had awed her, and brought her emotions so close to the surface that she had been scared she would say something she shouldn't—that some of the private dialogue going on in her head would slip out.

Rafiq had looked so incredible, standing next to her when they exchanged vows, and she loved him so totally that she had felt as though her heart was bleeding.

Her feelings had see-sawed dramatically all day, covering the full emotional gamut from fear and sadness to joy and love. Every time she'd looked at Rafiq she had wanted to tell him she loved him. It had been a constant struggle to contain her emotions.

'You haven't eaten anything,' he said as she pushed aside her plate.

'I'm not really hungry.'

'Neither am I—not for food.'

Gabby shivered as the air thickened with a sudden eruption of sexual tension.

He got to his feet and pulled out her chair. Her skin prickled even though he wasn't touching her. She turned and lifted her face to his. The darkness in his eyes drew her in.

'Our wedding night…' she said.

'A special night. But I will make all our nights special, Gabriella. I promise.'

Tears filled her eyes as he took her hand and led her to the bedroom. She stopped on the threshold and caught her breath. She had never been in Rafiq's bedroom before, and like most of the rooms in the palace its proportions were massive.

The furniture was for the most part antique and dark. White drapes fluttered in the breeze that blew in through the open doors. A large bed with an elaborately carved wood headboard dominated the room, but it was not the furniture, the décor, or even the hundreds of lit candles that covered every surface and cast a golden glow that brought a fresh rush of tears to Gabby's eyes. It was the scent.

A trail of ankle-deep rose petals led to the bed, which was itself liberally strewn with the same sweet-smelling petals.

'You always make me think of roses. Your skin smells of roses.' He bent and, inhaling deeply, kissed the side of her neck.

Gabby turned in his arms and linked her hands around his neck. Emotion clogged her throat. 'Thank you,' she said, her heart in her eyes.

Rafiq must have seen it there, because he stiffened and pulled back from her. 'Do not fall in love with me, Gabriella. The knowledge that we don't have long makes things more…*intense*. It's easy to mistake feelings.'

Too late!

His rejection hurt more than she would have

thought possible. But then her self-preservation instincts kicked in, and from somewhere she dredged a mocking smile.

'You're irresistible, Rafiq, but I will do my best.'

The smile stayed in place while his dark gaze swept her face, and then, unable to endure his scrutiny a second longer, she slipped off her shoes, took his hand and stepped onto the rose petal path.

She threw a challenging look at her tall husband. 'This is our wedding night—are we going to spend it talking?'

Rafiq responded to the challenge, scooping her up into his arms and carrying her to the bed.

The words she wanted to say stayed locked in her heart, but at least in their lovemaking Gabby was able to find a physical release for the emotions she was forbidden to express. Rafiq taught her many ways she hadn't known existed to express them, and it wasn't until he slept, just as dawn was breaking, that she allowed the dammed-up tears to fall.

Two weeks passed, and Gabby slipped into some sort of routine. Her presence in the palace was accepted, and her relationship with Rafiq—so long as she didn't use the forbidden L word—was perfect.

Her main aim at the moment was to reconcile the two brothers. Rafiq had banned Hakim and his new wife from the palace, and Gabby felt responsible. She had said so to Hakim when they had spoken on the phone.

'Why should I blame you? Between the pair of you, you pushed me to do the best thing that's ever happened to me. I just wish Rafiq had someone like Carrie to help *him.* But I will be there when he wants me. Knowing Rafiq, it's better to let things settle before we talk.'

Gabby had seen his point. Rafiq was quick to anger but slow to forgive.

She watched covetously now, as he walked out of the bathroom, his hair still wet from the shower.

'Would you like me to come with you?' she asked.

He sat down on the edge of the bed and rubbed the towel that was looped around his neck over his hair. 'Where to?'

Gabby knelt on the bed behind him, sliding her arms around his waist and pressing her body close into his. She rubbed her cheek against his hair-roughened cheek and kissed his neck. 'You know where. You have an appointment to see your doctor this morning—unless it's slipped your mind that you had him flown in by private plane yesterday?'

'It is a pointless exercise. What else can he tell me? I'm dying—I already know that.'

Gabby closed her eyes and moved away from him. She sat back on her heels and pressed her hands to her face. He peeled her hands away, but Gabby turned her head when he tried to kiss her. 'I hate it so much when you talk that way.'

'I will see the doctor and undergo his battery of tests if that is what you wish.'

Gabby gave a watery smile. 'Thank you. If it's any comfort, you don't *look* like an ill man.' Head tilted to one side, she studied his face. It was probably wishful thinking, but it seemed to her that his face was less gaunt than it had been two weeks previously, and his skin had a healthy glow.

He reached out and, cupping the back of her head in one big hand, drew her to him. 'I don't feel like an ill man when I'm with you.'

Gabby wrapped her arms around his neck. She pressed a series of open-mouthed kisses to the strong brown column of his throat. She reached his mouth and stopped, her lips a tantalising whisper away from his.

'Do you think it's possible...?'

'Do I think what is possible?' he husked, tangling his fingers in her hair and breathing in the sweet scent of her.

She took a deep breath and asked the question that had been on her mind for days. 'Do you think maybe you could be in remission?'

Rafiq stiffened and muttered a curse, unfastening her hands from his neck. 'I thought we had agreed we will not do that?' A nerve clenched beside his jaw as he struggled to speak calmly. 'The doctor was clear. There is no chance of remission.'

'But there might be,' she persisted, unable to drop the subject. 'You said yourself this is the first time in months you've slept properly, and you're not tired the way you were.'

Rafiq looked stern as he got to his feet. 'Enough!' he thundered. 'We will speak of this no more.'

'But—'

He cut off her protest with an imperative wave of his hand.

'Don't tell me when I can and can't speak,' Gabby said. 'Why can't you even consider it?'

'There is nothing to consider.'

Gabby subsided onto the bed, her knees drawn to her

chin as he stalked back towards the bathroom. Well, that went well…she thought.

Rafiq's anger burned itself out almost before he had turned on the tap and put his dark head beneath the gushing flow of cold water. He straightened up and shook his head, sending showers of icy droplets across the mirror in front of him.

Wiping the surface with his hand, he leaned forward and looked at his reflection in the smeared surface.

He smiled to himself. The power of suggestion was a marvellous thing. It would be easy to look in the mirror and see what he wanted to see.

Rafiq sighed as he felt a wave of remorse.

He hadn't meant to be so tough on her, and he knew her intentions were good, but he had to protect her from hope.

The idea of watching her face when she had those hopes dashed tore him apart. Better to be brutal now than let her nurse false hopes.

Dragging both hands through his hair to remove the excess moisture, he turned and contemplated the selfish thing he had done. If he really loved her he would have let her go.

And now he couldn't.

His face dark with self-recrimination, he bent to pick up a towel. As he did so his elbow hit a half-open drawer hard, and the contents spilled onto the marble floor.

He glanced at them, but made no move to pick them up—until a small box caught his eye, or the name on the prescription label did. Was Gabriella ill?

Concern creased his brow and quickened his heart-rate as he bent to pick it up. He read the label several times before it actually registered.

Gabby turned at the sound of the bathroom door opening. 'Have you cooled down?'

Her eyes widened. Obviously not. The glitter in his eyes as he approached the bed where she still sat cross-legged was steely. She could tell he was furious by the tension in his magnificent body and the ultra-controlled way he moved. He stopped at the foot of the bed and looked at her, his lips curled into a condemnatory sneer.

He stood there long enough for Gabby's spine to stiffen with apprehension. She was utterly bewildered. But along with the bewilderment came anger—how *dared* he look at her that way?

'Would you like to explain this?'

Gabby's glance slid from his face to the packet he had flung down on the bed. She didn't pick it up. She knew immediately what it was. Her heart sank somewhere below her knees.

'Ah.'

'Is that all you have to say?'

She shrugged, and his nostrils flared. 'It's the contraceptive pill.'

'It is used. I checked.'

'Yes, my doctor prescribed it a month ago.'

'You were never going to be pregnant.'

A week ago—even a few days ago—Gabby would have agreed with him. Now she wasn't so sure. It was a subject she had been trying not to think about. That aside, Rafiq was in essence right.

'No.'

He swallowed, seemingly nonplussed by her lack of denial. 'You let me think there was a possibility.' His deep voice splintered into husky outrage.

'That was the idea, yes,' she agreed.

'You lied by omission.'

'Again true…'

'Are you going to grace me with an explanation, or should I draw my own conclusions?'

His tone brought a belated militant spark to her eyes. 'You appear to mistake me for one of your underlings who has been conditioned to act with unthinking subservient grovelling to win your approval, Your Royal Highness. As for drawing your own conclusions—I'm sure you'll do that anyway.'

'So this is not what it looks like?' Rafiq was amazed at how badly he wanted to be convinced otherwise.

'Yes, it is. If you want to know if I lied, then, yes, I did—and I meant to lie. You have so little time, and you were using it all up in this useless, pointless crusade. You couldn't let go. When you thought there might be a baby you stopped, and spent some time enjoying yourself. That's what I hoped would happen.'

The brazen admission left him speechless.

Now the truth was out Gabby felt relief. She hadn't appreciated until that moment what a strain it had been.

'And while I'm confessing—' she couldn't seem to stop '—I told Hakim that you are ill.'

The casual admission drew an audible gasp from Rafiq.

'I think that's what sent him back to Paris. He knew that he needed support—not from me but from the woman he loves. He'd help if you'd let him, but I don't suppose you will. Because you're so emotionally self-sufficient, so stupid and so *pig-headed*!' she bellowed. 'You push anyone who cares for you away. I think you'd crawl on your hands and knees through the desert rather than admit you need help—and that isn't strong, it's stupid!'

Rafiq was looking at her as though he couldn't quite believe what she was saying.

'You have spoken to Hakim?'

'Oh, yes—it's regular conspiracy. You know, I would have *loved* to have a baby,' she admitted with a wistful sigh. She lifted her eyes to his face and added, '*Your* baby, Rafiq.'

She saw him swallow. He looked like a man who had just felt the world under his feet shift. A voice in the back of Gabby's head was screaming *stop* but she was too far gone now to pull back. Her reckless what-have-I-got-to-lose? mindset was firmly in the driving seat.

'But not for the reasons *you* wanted a baby.' She shook her head sadly. 'No, that would have been utterly wrong. I wanted your baby because I love you. There you go. I've said it.' *Now you've blown it*, said the voice in her head. 'You look amazed,' she said.

Actually, he looked as if she'd just walked up to him and slapped his face.

'Why did you *think* I married you, Rafiq? For the title and the money?'

It could have been worse—he could have said yes. Instead, Rafiq turned on his heel and walked out of the room.

Gabby was so emotionally drained by her outburst

of honesty that she sat there for ten minutes before she even moved.

Well, what did you expect when you screamed you loved him like some lunatic? she asked herself. Did you really think that he'd suddenly confess that he loves you back?

Not think, but hope. She had definitely hoped.

The first step to recovery was admitting you had a problem. Perhaps there were classes for recovering optimists?

'My name is Gabby and I'm an optimist.'

She fell back on the bed and began to laugh hysterically.

## CHAPTER FIFTEEN

RAFIQ sat on one side of the desk, oblivious to the oddness in the doctor's attitude to him.

The doctor, on the other hand, had noticed the oddness in his patient. It made him want to delay breaking the news, even though he had the results of the second set of blood tests in his hand, and he worked up the courage to admit his mistake.

'Sorry, Your Royal Highness, to keep you waiting.' He consulted the figures in front of him and smiled.

Rafiq didn't notice the smile. The only thing he could see was Gabby's face when she had asked, *'Why did you think I married you, Rafiq?'* He couldn't get the look in her eyes out of his head.

Well, Rafiq, why *did* you think she married you?

It was an obvious question to ask—logical, and he prided himself on logic. And now he could see the question had been there in his mind all along, unacknowledged and ignored.

Ignored because he had known the answer.

And if he had admitted to himself that he knew his

honour would not have allowed him to marry her, or to keep her with him.

He was a dying man with nothing to offer the woman who loved him but pain. The only honourable thing would have been to send her away—and Rafiq had been subconsciously looking for a way *not* to do that to do from the moment they'd met.

He could see that now.

He could see a lot of things.

He hadn't wanted an heir—he had wanted Gabriella.

He buried his head in his hands.

The doctor leaned across the table. 'I know it must be a shock, and I am sorry for all the anxiety.'

Rafiq lifted his head. 'Shock…?'

'These days we rely so heavily on computers, and the figures on your original blood samples led us to believe…' His eyes slid guiltily away from those of the tall Prince. Were the Zantaran royal family litigious? 'Once we discovered the problem with the machine's calibration we rechecked all the results. Your own case, Your Highness, was in fact the only one where the result was affected. You had a mild form of the disease, and in some cases this milder form can progress to the more severe type that we thought you had. In others it can— for want of a better word—vanish, or go into total spontaneous remission…a miracle,' he added with a laugh of false jollity. 'But that is an emotive term, and one I would not normally use.'

Rafiq picked up on the word. 'Miracle? What miracle are we speaking of, Doctor?'

'It must be hard for you to take in.'

Especially when he wasn't listening. 'Do you mind repeating yourself? I'm not sure I have this straight…'

'Of course—and I understand your caution. The faulty calibration on the computer analysing your blood samples has led to a false diagnosis. You had a mild form of the disease and it has now cured itself. I double-checked the results and there is no doubt your blood is totally normal. There are no abnormalities. As I say, I am very, *very* sorry.'

Rafiq swallowed. 'So you are saying…?'

'There is no trace of illness in your blood—no trace of illness anywhere,' he revealed happily.

'I'm not going to die?'

'Not in the immediate future. Although as we like to err on the side of caution with your permission we will organise some regular checks.'

'For weeks I have thought I was dying!'

The doctor winced and nodded, his medical aplomb replaced by trepidation as he met the furious and incredulous glare of the very angry Prince.

Rafiq's chest swelled. 'If you are the best…show me the worst! I could have told my father…it might have killed him. My life has been… This mistake has—' He stopped dead. The computer's mistake had given him Gabby.

His desire to strangle the man was replaced by an urge to hug him.

'I'm not dying.' Rafiq, his chest rising and falling like a man who had been running, stared at the doctor. Slowly a smile radiated across his face. 'Thank you,' he said, enfolding the shocked older man's hand in a crushing grip. 'Next time I will ask for a second opinion.'

The older man flushed and nodded. 'I am very happy for you,' he said, weak with relief.

Happy did not begin to describe the feelings roaring inside Rafiq. He felt released. He had his freedom and his future. He had—he hoped—his love.

'Excuse me, Doctor, but I have somewhere I need to be.' *And someone I need to be with for the rest of my life.*

Oblivious to the stares that followed him, the Crown Prince of Zantara ran full-pelt across the courtyard and down the corridors until he reached his private apartments. He paused outside, gathering his thoughts.

He found Gabriella in the courtyard. She was watching the water in the fountain fall, her expression pensive.

'Gabriella?'

She turned at the sound of her name. 'I know what you're going to say.'

'You do?'

She nodded. 'Well, I'm not going away—because whether you'll admit it or not you need me. I'm your wife. You can't make me go away—I have legal rights.'

'I don't want you to go away.'

She regarded him warily. There was something different about him, but she couldn't quite put her finger on it.

'You don't? Well, that's good. Because I *did* take the pill, but it looks like maybe there *might* be a baby... I feel different, and I did forget to take the pill on the—'

'A baby?' he cut in. 'That's nice.'

'Nice!' she choked, staring at him. He was smiling—and not in a nasty snarly way. 'Is that all you can say? You married me to have a baby.'

'No, I married you because I wanted to keep you with

me. The baby was an excuse—because a dying man isn't allowed to be in love, and he isn't allowed to let anyone love him.'

'Love…' Gabby swallowed, hardly daring to believe what she was hearing. She pressed a hand to her throat, where her heart was trying to climb its way out of her chest. 'You said—'

Rafiq was by her side in two strides. His arms closed like steel bands around her as he lifted her off the ground. 'I love you—and I'm allowed to say it because I'm not a dying man. I'm going to live—*we* are going to live, happily ever after.' He rained kisses over her face until she was gasping for breath.

'Stop… Stop…' It made a change for her to be begging him to *stop* kissing her.

He placed her down on her feet and cupped the back of her head in one hand, stroking her hair with the other. 'I love your hair…'

'What has happened? Tell me *slowly*.' He was generating enough energy to light up a small country—the air crackled with it. 'I can't keep up—my head is spinning.'

'You were right, my love, when you observed that I did not look ill. Apparently there is no trace of disease in my body—there was a mistake.'

'You're not ill?' A smile spread like the sun across her face, the only shadow appearing when she added anxiously, 'Permanently?'

'Who knows? I for one have learnt that a man should live in the present, and not delay the things that are important to him.' A wicked smile spread across his face. 'And right now it is important to me to kiss you.'

He did so, with a ruthless efficiency that robbed Gabby of the ability to speak for some time. She just stood in the shelter of his arms, feeling protected and cherished while she tried to take it all in.

Rafiq loved her and they had a future. She cried. Who would not cry when their dreams had come true?

'I'm so happy,' she said between sobs.

Rafiq blotted a tear with his thumb, and smiled at her with such tenderness that her heart skipped a beat.

'It's a miracle.'

'You always believed in miracles. It was I who was the sceptic. I should have believed, because I have seen a miracle first-hand—you, my lovely and most dear Gabriella, are my living, breathing miracle.'

The wedding party was scheduled for three weeks after the day Rafiq had been told he had a life.

It was a lavish affair, with family from both sides and all their friends.

Rafiq had needed all his diplomatic skills to soothe his father when he had revealed the full story—or most of it—to the King, but in the end the monarch of Zantara had been so shaken to learn he might have lost Rafiq that he was inclined to look benevolently on any slight irregularities in both his sons' marriages.

Hakim was there, and it had been a weight off Gabby's mind to see the two brothers reunited. Hakim's new wife was older than him, and nothing like the women he had dated previously. Gabby took to her immediately, and her small son was delightful—a future playmate for their child.

Rafiq and Gabby had decided to keep this news private for the time being, but soon she would have no choice but to reveal her condition.

The wedding party went on long into the night, and it was still in full swing when Rafiq took her hand and led her out of a side door.

'We can't leave—it's our party,' Gabby protested half-heartedly.

'I have a more private party in mind.'

The glow in Rafiq's eyes as he looked at her sent Gabby's pulses racing. 'That sounds like an interesting idea,' she admitted huskily.

Outside the bedroom door, Rafiq paused. 'Close your eyes.'

Gabby shook her head. 'Why?'

'Humour me?' he suggested.

Giggling nervously, she did, and he led her by the hand into their bedroom.

'You can open them now.'

He had recreated the rose petal trail of their wedding night.

Gabby turned and looked up at her tall, handsome husband, her luminous eyes shining with love.

'It should have been perfect and it wasn't. I told you not to love me, do you remember?'

Gabby nodded. She would never forget.

'Now I am saying—no, I am begging you to love me, Gabriella. Because I love you with all my heart and soul.'

It was a request that Gabby was only too happy to satisfy. The only complication was getting the words past the emotional lump in her throat.

'I love you, Rafiq,' she said huskily.

Rafiq gave a satisfied sigh. 'When I think what might have been and what is, I know I am a blessed man. I have you, and I have our child.' He pressed a big hand to her still flat stomach. 'This is how it is meant to be.'

'Though possibly not rose petals every night.'

'On our anniversary?'

'Which one?' she laughed. So far they had celebrated weekly—the day they'd met, the day he'd found out he was going to live, and their wedding day—the first one.

'All of them, my princess. Now come on,' he said, catching her hand. 'I want to wrap you in rose petals and wrap myself in your hair.'

The mental image worked for Gabby—as did the wicked gleam in his eyes as he sat her on the bed. He began to slowly roll down the lacy-topped stockings she wore under the floaty sea-blue dress he had said made her look like a bird of paradise.

'You're doing some serious damage to my nervous system,' she confessed, gasping as he ran his finger along the arch of her foot.

'It is intentional,' he revealed with a wicked grin. With a light push she was tipped over into the rose petals.

Gabby gave a sigh of utter contentment. She knew that this was one of life's great moments. She also knew that life was not all rose petals. She knew that there would be other moments that were not so great, but while she had Rafiq at her side she felt totally confident about facing life's up and downs.

A gurgle of laughter left her throat as Rafiq threw himself down beside her, sending up clouds of rose petals.

'You do realise that only a man who is very secure with his masculinity would risk walking around smelling like a rose bush?'

'Oh, my love,' he purred, sliding over her and ripping off his shirt at the same time. 'I am very secure... Come—let me show you how secure.'

Gabby did—and quickly concluded rather breathlessly that he had every right to be secure. Crown Prince Rafiq Al Kamil was all male!

\* \* \* \* \*

# The Marcolini
# Blackmail Marriage

## MELANIE MILBURNE

**Melanie Milburne** says: One of the greatest joys of being a writer is the process of falling in love with the characters and then watching as they fall in love with each other. I am an absolutely hopeless romantic. I fell in love with my husband on our second date and we even had a secret engagement, so you see it must have been destined for me to be a Harlequin Mills & Boon author! The other great joy of being a romance writer is hearing from readers. You can hear all about the other things I do when I'm not writing and even drop me a line at: www.melaniemilburne.com.au

**Don't miss Melanie Milburne's new book,**
*The Venadicci Marriage Vengeance*,
**coming in May 2009 from Modern™.**

To Pauline Samson for all the work she does for swimming in Tasmania and nationally.
She has sat on various pool decks tirelessly timing both my and other people's swims for the National Aerobic Trophy. Winning it in 2007 was a great achievement for such a small but dedicated club, but really all the credit must go to Pauline, for there is only one thing worse than swimming eight hundred metres of butterfly and that is sitting there timing it!

# CHAPTER ONE

IT WAS the very last thing Claire was expecting. She stared at the lawyer for several seconds, her brain whirling, her heart suddenly beating too fast and too hard. 'What do you mean, he wouldn't agree to it?' she said.

The lawyer gave her a grim look. 'Your husband flatly refused to sign or even to accept the papers for a divorce,' she said. 'He was absolutely adamant. He insists on a meeting with you first.'

Claire gnawed at her lip for a moment. She had hoped to avoid all contact with Antonio Marcolini during his lecture tour of Sydney. It wasn't supposed to happen this way. Five years had passed; a divorce after such a long separation was surely just a matter of a bit of paperwork? Leaving it in the lawyer's hands was meant to make it easier for her to move on.

She *had* to move on.

'Unless you have specific reasons not to meet with him, I suggest you get it over with—and soon,' Angela Reed advised. 'It may well be he wants to end things on a more personal note, rather than formally through the legal system. Ultimately he will not be able to prevent a divorce, of course, but he could make things drag on—which would incur even more legal fees for you.'

Claire felt a familiar twist of panic deep inside at the thought of more bills to pay. She was sailing far too close to the wind as it was; a long drawn-out legal process would just about sink her. But why on earth would Antonio want to see her after all this time? The circumstances under which their relationship had ended were hardly conducive to a friendly cup of coffee and a chat about old times.

She took a deep breath and met the lawyer's speculative gaze. 'I guess one face to face meeting won't hurt,' she said, with a sinking feeling deep in the pit of her stomach.

'Think of it as closure,' Angela said, as she pushed back her chair and rose to her feet, signalling the consultation was at an end.

*Closure*, Claire thought wryly as she made her way out to the street a short time later. That was why she had activated the divorce proceedings in the first place. It was well and truly time to put the past behind her. She owed it to herself to embrace life once more.

The phone was ringing as she unlocked the door of her flat and, dropping her bag and keys on the lumpy sofa, she picked up the receiver. 'Hello?'

'Claire.'

Claire gripped the phone in her suddenly damp hand, trying to suppress the groundswell of emotion that assailed her as soon as she heard the smooth, even tones of Antonio's accented voice. Oh, God, if this was how she was going to be just listening to him, how on earth was she going to cope with seeing him? Tiny beads of perspiration broke out on her upper lip; her heart was hammering and her breathing becoming shallow and uneven.

'Claire.' He repeated her name, the velvet stroke of his deep tone making every pore of her skin lift beneath the layers of her winter-weight clothes, and the blood to kick start in her veins.

She swallowed tightly and, closing her eyes, released his name on a stuttering breath. 'Antonio...I was... er...just about to call you...'

'I take it you have spoken with your lawyer?' he asked.

'Yes, but—'

'Then you will know I will not take no for an answer,' he said, as if she hadn't spoken. 'No meeting, no divorce.'

Claire felt her back come up at his arrogance. 'You think you can order me about like some sort of puppet?' she asked. 'Well, damn you, Antonio. I am not—'

'Face to face, Claire,' he said, in the same indomitable tone. 'I believe there is no better way to do business.'

Claire felt tiny footsteps of ice-cold fear tiptoe up her spine at his words. 'I—I thought you were here for a lecture tour, not to socialise with your soon to be ex-wife,' she said, trying for a cool and unaffected tone but failing miserably.

She glanced to where she had left the newspaper announcing his arrival, lying open, even though every time she walked past, it drove a stake through her heart to see his handsome features smiling as if everything was right with his world.

'It is true I am spending the next three months in

Australia, lecturing and operating for the charity I began in Italy,' he said.

It had not been the first time Claire had read about his charity, called FACE—Facial and Cranial Endowment—which raised millions of dollars for the surgical reconstruction of patients with severe facial injuries. She had followed the progress of some of the cases he had operated on via his website, marvelling at the miracles he performed for his patients. But then miracles only seemed to happen to other people, Claire reminded herself bitterly. Her brief marriage to Antonio had taught her that if nothing else.

'But I must say I find it rather strange you did not expect me to want to see you in person,' he continued.

'I find it inappropriate, given the circumstances,' she returned a little coldly. 'We have nothing to say to each other. I think we said it all the last time we were together.'

And how, Claire thought as she recalled the bitter words she had thrown at him. Angry, bitter words that had done nothing to ease the pain of her loss and the final barbarous sting of his betrayal. He had been so cold, so distant, and clinically detached in that doctor way of his, making her feel as if she had no self-control, no maturity and precious little dignity.

'I beg to differ, Claire,' he countered. 'The last time we were together you did the speaking, and all the accusing and name-calling, if I recall. This time I would like to be the one who does the talking.'

Claire's already white-knuckled fingers tightened around the phone, her heart skipping in her chest. 'Look, we've been separated for five—'

'I know how long we have been separated,' he interrupted yet again. 'Or estranged, as I understand is the
more correct term, since there has been no formal
division of assets between us. That is one of the reasons
I am here now in Australia.'

Claire felt her stomach tilt. 'I thought you were here
to promote your charity…you know…to raise its
profile globally.'

'That is true, but I do not intend to spend the full three
months lecturing,' he said. 'I plan to have a holiday while
I am here, and of course to spend some time with you.'

'Why?' The word came out clipped with the sharp
scissors of suspicion.

'We are still legally married, Claire.'

Claire clenched her teeth. 'So let me guess.' She let
the words drip off her tongue, each one heavily laced
with scorn. 'Your latest mistress didn't want to travel all
this way so you are looking for a three-month fill-in.
Forget it, Antonio. I'm not available.'

'Are you currently seeing anyone?' he asked.

Claire bristled at the question. How he could even
*think* she would be able to move on from the death of
their child as he had so easily done was truly astonishing. 'Why do you want to know?' she asked.

'I would not like to be cutting in on anyone else's territory,' he said. 'Although there are ways to deal with
such obstacles, of course.'

'Yes, well, we all know how that hasn't stopped you
in the past,' she clipped back. 'I seem to recall hearing
about your affair with a married woman a couple of
years back.'

'She was not my mistress, Claire,' he said. 'The press always makes a big deal out of anything Mario and I do. You know that. I warned you about it when we first met.'

To give him credit, Claire had to agree Antonio had done his very best to try and prepare her for the exposure she would receive as one of the Marcolini brothers' love interests. Antonio and Mario, as the sons of high-profile Italian businessman Salvatore Marcolini, could not escape the attention of the media. Every woman they looked at was photographed, every restaurant they dined at was rated, and every move they made was followed with not just one telephoto lens, but hundreds.

Claire had found it both intrusive and terrifying. She was a country girl, born and bred. She was not used to any attention, let alone the world's media. She had grown up in a quiet country town in Outback New South Wales. There had been no glitz and glamour about her and her younger brothers' lives in the drought-stricken bush, nor did Claire's life now, as a hairdresser in a small inner-city suburb, attract the sort of attention Antonio had been used to dealing with since he was a small child.

That was just one of the essential differences that had driven the wedge between them: she was not of his ilk, and his parents had made that more than clear from the first moment he had brought her home to meet them. People with their sort of wealth did not consider a twenty-three-year-old Australian hairdresser on a working holiday marriage material for their brilliantly talented son.

'I am staying at the Hammond Tower Hotel.'

Antonio's voice broke through her thoughts. 'In the penthouse suite.'

'Of course,' Claire muttered cynically.

'You surely did not expect me to purchase a house for the short time I will be here, did you, Claire?' he asked, after another short but tense pause.

'No, of course not,' she answered, wishing she hadn't been so transparent in her bitterness towards him. 'It's just a penthouse is a bit over the top for someone who heads a charity—or so I would have thought.'

'The charity is doing very well without me having to resort to sleeping on a park bench,' he said. 'But of course that is probably where you would like to see me, is it not?'

'I don't wish to see you at all,' Claire responded tightly.

'I am not going to give you a choice,' he said. 'We have things to discuss and I would like to do so in private— your place or mine. It makes no difference to me.'

It made the world of difference to Claire. She didn't want Antonio's presence in her small but tidy flat. It was hard enough living with the memories of his touch, his kisses, and the fiery heat of his lovemaking which, in spite of the passing of the years, had never seemed to lessen. Her body was responding to him even now, just by listening to his voice. How much worse would it be seeing him face to face, breathing in the same air as him, perhaps even touching him?

'I mean it, Claire,' he said with steely emphasis. 'I can be at your place in ten or fifteen minutes, or you can meet me here. You choose.'

Claire pressed her lips together as she considered

224 THE MARCOLINI BLACKMAIL MARRIAGE

her options. Here would be too private, too intimate, but
then meeting him at his hotel would be so public. What
if the press were lurking about? A quick snapshot of
them together could cause the sort of speculation she
had thankfully avoided over the last five years.

In the end she decided her private domain was not
ready to accept the disturbing presence of her estranged
husband. She didn't want to look at her rumpled sofa a
few days hence and think of his long, strong thighs
stretched out there, and nor did she want to drink from
a coffee cup his lips had rested against.

'I'll come to you,' she said, on an expelled breath of
resignation.

'I will wait for you in the Piano Bar,' he said. 'Would
you like me to send a car for you?'

Claire had almost forgotten the wealth Antonio took
for granted. No simple little fuel-efficient hire car for
him—oh, no—he would have the latest Italian sports
car, or a limousine complete with uniformed chauffeur.

The thought of a sleek limousine pulling up to collect
her was almost laughable, given the state of her own
current vehicle. She had to cajole it into starting each
morning, and go through the same routine at the end of
the day. It limped along, as she did, battered and bruised
by what life had dished up, but somehow doggedly determined to complete the journey.

'No,' she said, with a last remnant of pride. 'I will
make my own way there.'

'Fine. I will keep an eye out for you,' he said. 'Shall
we say in an hour?'

Claire put the phone down after mumbling a reply,

her heart contracting in pain at the thought of seeing Antonio again. Her stomach began to flutter inside with razor-winged nerves, her palms already damp in apprehension over what he had already said to her, let alone what else he had in store.

If he didn't want a divorce, what did he want? Their marriage had died, along with the reason it had occurred in the first place.

A giant wave of grief washed over her as she thought about their tiny daughter. She would have just completed her first term in kindergarten by now—would have been five years old and no doubt as cute as a button, with her father's dark brown eyes and a crown of shiny hair, maybe ink-black and slightly wavy, like Antonio's, or chestnut-brown and riotous like hers.

Claire wondered if he ever thought of their baby. Did he lie awake at night even now and imagine he could hear her crying? Did his arms ache to hold her just one more time, as hers did every day? Did he look at the last photograph taken of her in the delivery suite and feel an unbearable pain searing through his chest that those tiny eyes had never opened to look at his face?

Probably not, she thought bitterly as she rummaged in her wardrobe for something to wear. She pulled out a black dress and held it up for inspection. It was three or four seasons old, and far too big for her, but what did it matter? She wasn't out to impress him. That was the job of the supermodels and socialites he partied with all over Europe.

# CHAPTER TWO

THE HAMMOND TOWER HOTEL was close to the city center, with stunning views over the harbour, and the sail-like wings of the iconic Sydney Opera House visible from some angles. But, unlike the other hotels the Hammond competed with, it had an old-world charm about it; the art deco design and furnishings and the immaculately uniformed attendants made Claire feel as if she was stepping back in time, to a far more gracious and glamorous era that few modern hotels could rival, in spite of their massive stainless steel and glass towers.

Claire left her car with the valet parking man, trying not to wince in embarrassment when the engine coughed and choked behind her as he valiantly tried to get it to move.

The doorman on duty smiled in greeting and held the brass and glass doors open for her. 'Good evening, madam,' he said. 'Welcome to the Hammond.'

'Thank you,' Claire said with a polite smile in return, and made her way towards the plush Piano Bar on legs that felt uncoordinated and treacherously unsteady.

Antonio was sitting on one of the leather sofas and

got to his feet when he saw her approach. Claire felt her breath hitch in her throat like a bramble brushing against soft fabric. He was so commandingly tall; how could she have forgotten how petite she'd always felt standing in front of him? He towered over her, his darker than night eyes probing hers without giving anything away.

'Claire.'

That was all he said, just her name, and yet it caused a reaction so intense Claire could barely get her brain to work, let alone her voice. Her gaze consumed him greedily, ravenously, taking in every detail of his features in that pulsing nanosecond of silence. Would he touch her? she wondered in a flash of panic. Should she make the first move so as to keep things on her terms? Or should she lift each cheek in turn for the kiss she had learned was commonplace while living in Italy? Or stand stiffly, as she was doing now, her arms by her sides, the fingers of her right hand tightly clasped around her purse, her heart thumping like a bass drum as she delayed the final moment when she would have to meet his black-as-pitch gaze?

He had barely changed. He still had no signs of grey in his raven-black hair, even though he was now thirty-six years old, and his skin was still tanned, his jaw cleanly shaven. The classic lines of his Italian designer business suit did nothing to hide the superb physical condition he was in. Broad-shouldered and lean-waisted, with long, strong legs and narrow hips—all speaking of a man who took his health and fitness seriously, in spite of the long hours he worked.

'A-Antonio…' She finally managed to speak his name, but it came out barely audible and distinctly wobbly. She could have kicked herself for revealing how much his presence unsettled her. Why couldn't she be cool and sophisticated for once? Why did she have to feel as if her heart was in a vice, with someone slowly but surely turning the handle until she couldn't breathe?

'Would you like to sit down?' He gestured towards the sofa he had just vacated.

So polite, so formal, Claire thought as she sat down, keeping her legs angled away from his as he resumed his seat.

'What would you like to drink?' he asked as the drinks waiter came over.

'Something soft…mineral water,' she said, clutching her purse against her lower body like a life raft. 'I'm driving.'

Antonio ordered her a mineral water, and a brandy and dry for himself, before he sat back to look at her. 'You have lost weight,' he said.

A spark of irritation came and went in her blue-green eyes. 'Is that a criticism or an observation?' she asked.

'I was not criticising you, Claire.'

She folded her arms in a keep-away-from-me pose. 'Look, can we just get this over with?' she asked. 'Say what you want to say and let me get back to my life.'

'What life would that be, I wonder?' he asked, leaning back, one arm draped casually over the back of the sofa as his dark gaze ran over her lazily.

She narrowed her eyes at him, two points of colour firing in her cheeks. 'I have a life, Antonio, it's just I choose not to have you in it.'

Antonio smiled to himself. She had such a cutting

tongue when she thought she could get away with it. But now he was here he had ways and means to bring her to heel, and bring her to heel he would. 'We have things to discuss, Claire,' he said. 'We have been apart a long time, and some decisions have to be made about where we go from here.'

'I can tell you where we go from here,' she said. 'We go straight to court and formally end our marriage.'

He paused for a moment, taking in her flashing blue-green gaze and the way her soft-as-a-feather-pillow mouth was pulled into a tight line. The skin of her face was a pale shade of cream, with a tiny dusting of freckles over the bridge of her *retroussé* nose, giving her a girl-next-door look that was captivating. He had already noted how every male head had turned when she had come into the bar. She was either totally unaware of the effect she had on the male gaze, or she very cleverly ignored it to enhance her feminine power.

'What if I told you I do not want a divorce?' he said after a measured pause.

She put her mineral water down with a sharp little thwack on the nearest coffee table, her eyes going wide as she stared at him. 'What did you say?'

He gave her an indolent half-smile. 'You heard me.'

She sucked in a breath and threw him a flint-like glare. 'That's too bad, Antonio, because I *do* want one.'

Antonio kept on pinning her with his gaze. 'Then why have you not done anything about it before now?'

She shifted her eyes from his. 'I…I couldn't be bothered,' she muttered in a petulant tone. 'You were out of sight and out of my mind, as far as I was concerned.'

'But now I am back you suddenly want to put an end to our marriage?' he snapped his fingers. 'Just like that.'

She looked at him with icy disdain. 'Our marriage ended five years ago, Antonio, and you damn well know it.'

'And why was that?' Antonio asked, not bothering to disguise his simmering anger this time. 'Because you wanted to blame someone for anything and everything and I was the nearest scapegoat?'

She glared at him heatedly. He could see a pulse leaping in her neck, and how her fingers were so tight around her purse. Each and every one of her knuckles looked as if the tiny bones were going to break through the fine layer of her skin.

'You betrayed me,' she said in a low hard tone. 'You betrayed me when I was at my lowest point. I will never forgive you for that.'

Antonio clenched his jaw, the pressure making his teeth ache. 'So you are still running with that fairy story about me being unfaithful to you in the last few months of our relationship, are you?'

Her eyes flashed with pure venom. 'I know what I saw,' she hissed at him in an undertone, so the other drinkers in the bar wouldn't hear. 'You were holding her in your arms, so don't bother denying it.'

'I would not dream of denying it,' he said. 'Daniela was and still is a close family friend. You know that. That is something else I told you when we first met.'

'Yes, but you neglected to tell me you were her lover for the eighteen months prior,' she tossed back. 'A minor detail but a rather important one, I would have thought.'

Antonio put his drink down. 'I did not want to upset you with talk of my ex-lovers,' he said. 'It did not seem appropriate since you were without similar experience.'

'Yes, well, I certainly got all the experience I needed living with you for almost a year,' Claire said, with an embittered set to her mouth.

His eyes warred with hers for a tense moment. 'Why don't you say it, Claire?' he said. 'Why don't you tell everyone in this bar what it is you really blame me for?'

Now she had made him so blisteringly angry Claire wasn't sure she knew how to handle it. She was used to him being cold and distant, clinically detached, with no hint of emotion ever showing through his mask-like expression.

She became aware of the interested glances of the other guests in the bar and felt her face begin to crawl with colour. 'Would you mind keeping your voice down?' she asked in a terse whisper. 'People are staring at us.'

'Let them bloody well stare.'

Claire cringed as she heard someone snicker close by. 'Could we at least go somewhere a little more private?' she said in desperation.

Antonio got to his feet. 'Come with me,' he said, and set a brisk pace towards the lifts situated on the other side of the marbled foyer.

Claire followed at a slower pace, on account of her heels, stepping into the lift he was holding for her, moving to the back of it, as far away from him as the space allowed.

She watched as he swiped his security pass for the penthouse floor, her nerves jumping and leaping beneath her skin as the doors whooshed closed and the lift began to climb each floor.

The silence apart from the mechanical whirr of the lift was palpable; it seemed to grow teeth, snapping at her where she stood in her corner.

Claire could feel her heart thumping irregularly, the blood racing through her veins at breakneck speed. She felt the faint knocking of her knees, and the on-off clench of her insides as the lift finally came to a smooth halt.

Antonio held the doors open for her and she slipped past him, her breath locking in her throat as she caught a faint trace of his lemon-based aftershave, an evocative fragrance that brought a host of memories to the forefront of her brain. Memories of her body pinned beneath his, her skin smelling of him, the taste of him salty and sexy in her mouth, all her muscles relaxed in the afterglow of their shared passion. Each vision made her body glow with heat; she could feel the creep of colour in her cheeks and wondered if he knew what had put it there.

He unlocked the door of his suite with the security card and silently gestured for her to enter, his dark eyes unreadable as they followed her every movement. Claire lowered her gaze and moved past, the gentle swish of her skirt brushing against his trouser legs, making her even more acutely aware of him.

The sound of the door closing behind her made her skin pepper all over with goosebumps, and to disguise her reaction she took a leisurely wander over to the bank of windows, looking down at the view as if that alone was what she was there for.

She sensed him come up behind her, the hairs on the

nape of her neck rising to attention one by one. She suppressed a tiny shiver, and concentrated on watching a brightly lit ferry go under the Harbour Bridge.

'So you want a divorce?' he said, as if she was an employee who had just asked for a raise that was not going to be forthcoming.

Claire turned and faced him combatively. 'You can't deny me one, Antonio. We've been separated for too long for you to contest it.'

'I realise that,' he said, holding her gaze with the dark intensity of his. 'And if that is what you want then I will grant you one. But only after the three months of my stay.'

'I'm not sure I'm following you,' she said, frowning at him guardedly. 'Are you suggesting some sort of temporary reconciliation?'

His eyes continued to watch her steadily. 'I would like us to try again, Claire,' he said. 'This time on your territory, not mine.'

Claire felt the stungun-like blows of her heart inside her chest cavity as his words gradually filtered through her brain. 'You're serious about this…aren't you?' she said. 'My God, Antonio, you are out of your mind if you think I would agree to something like that.'

His expression had more than a hint of intractability about it. 'Three months is not a long period of time, Claire,' he said. 'If things do not work out then what has been lost? This way we can both be assured we are making the right decision.'

She sent him a querulous look. 'As far as I am concerned I made the right decision when I caught that plane back home to Sydney.'

'You made that decision in the heat of the moment, after a particularly harrowing time,' he returned.

Claire gaped at him in rapidly rising rage. 'That's how you refer to her now, is it? "A particularly harrowing time"?'

He drew in a breath as he raked a hand through his hair. 'I knew you would be like this,' he said. 'It is impossible to discuss anything with you without you twisting everything I say to imply I did not care about our daughter. Damn you, Claire, you know that is not true. I wanted her more than anything.'

Claire clenched her jaw, her emotions beginning to spiral out of control. Yes, he *had* wanted their baby; it was just his wife he hadn't wanted as part of the bargain. 'Say her name, for God's sake. Say her name—or have you forgotten it? Is that it, Antonio?' Her voice rose to a shrill level. 'Have you forgotten all about her?'

He set his mouth. 'Do not do this, Claire. It will not bring her back.'

Claire swung away, biting the inside of her mouth to stop herself from becoming hysterical as she had so many times in the past. He was so good at keeping his emotions at bay, which made her loss of control all the more humiliating. How she hated him for it. How could he stand there so coldly and impersonally, assuming she would fall in with his plans, as if by crooking his little finger she would run back to him as if nothing had happened?

'I am serious about this trial reconciliation, Claire,' he said into the thrumming silence.

She turned back, her eyes flashing at him defiantly. 'Well, I hate to inform you, Antonio, but you've got

your work cut out for you—because the very last thing
I will ever agree to is resuming the position of your
wife. Not for three months, not for three weeks, not
even for three days.'

He gave her a long, studied look, his dark eyes centred
on hers. 'You might want to rethink that position after
you have spoken with the authorities about the situation
one of your half-brothers has just landed himself in.'

Claire felt her eyes rounding in alarm. 'W-which
one?' she asked, silently praying it wasn't Isaac. *Oh,
please God don't let it be Isaac.* Callum was no angel,
having had a few run-ins with the law in the past, but
he was on the straight and narrow now. Isaac, however,
was the vulnerable one—young and hot-headed, and
fiercely loyal at times, which had got him into trouble
more often than not.

'Isaac,' Antonio answered.

Claire swallowed, and hoped the despair wasn't
showing on her face. 'What has he…um…allegedly
done?' she asked with a lift of her chin.

He slanted one brow in a wry manner. 'I see you are
no stranger to the legal vernacular when it comes to the
behaviour of your sibling.'

She drew in a breath and forced herself to hold his
gaze. 'I am the first to admit Isaac has some behav-
ioural issues,' she said. 'But I fail to see what they have
to do with you.'

'Actually, his behaviour on this occasion has everything to do with me,' he said, with a purposeful glint in
his dark eyes. 'And you too, when it comes to it.'

*Don't ask*, Claire tried to warn herself, but even so

the words left her lips in a stumbling stream. 'What do you mean?'

'Your brother took it upon himself to steal my hire car from the hospital car park earlier this afternoon and take it for a joy-ride,' he said.

*Oh, dear God*, Claire thought in rising despair. Of all the cars in Sydney, why pick Antonio Marcolini's? She knew Isaac was still in the city; he had come down from the country to go surfing with some friends. He had come to see her only a couple of days ago. He had stayed overnight, and she had given him some money to put towards a new wetsuit.

'Um...was there any damage?' she asked, with a thread of hope holding her voice almost but not quite steady.

'None that three months living with me as my wife will not rectify,' he said, his eyes boring into hers with steely intent.

Claire stared at him, her heart doing a pretty fair imitation of her car's recalcitrant engine on a cold morning. *'You're blackmailing me to come back to you?'* she choked out.

'The word blackmail implies a lack of choice,' he said, with an enigmatic tilt of his lips that was close to a smile. 'In this instance I am giving you a choice, Claire. You either return to our marriage for the duration of my stay in Sydney or I will press charges against your brother. What is it to be?'

# CHAPTER THREE

CLAIRE felt the arctic-cold water of shock trickle drop by chilling drop down her spine as she stood gaping speechlessly at the man she had once loved more than life itself. What he was suggesting was unthinkable. But the alternative was even more horrifying. If Isaac went to prison, or even a detention centre, how could she ever forgive herself, knowing she'd had the means to prevent it? Callum had once described some of the things that went on in remand centres, and none of them had anything to do with justice.

But returning to the marriage that had brought her such heartache and unmitigated despair was surely going to test her limits. How on earth would she do it? What strength of character would she need to draw on to see it through?

Hatred clogged her veins as she sent Antonio a castigating glare. 'You've really surpassed yourself this time, Antonio,' she said. 'I thought your callous, unfeeling treatment of me in the past set the benchmark, but this is way above that. You couldn't have thought of a better revenge than this.'

He responded coolly. 'I am merely offering you an escape route which will be of benefit to all parties concerned.'

Claire rolled her eyes again, only because she knew it would annoy him. 'Pardon me,' she said, 'but I fail to see how *I* could possibly benefit from this outrageous plan of yours.'

Anger flickered in his gaze as it pinned hers. 'Have you ever thought of the sort of damage your brother could have done this afternoon?' he asked.

Claire lifted her chin. 'So your precious prestige hire car got a scratch or two? So what?'

His mouth stretched into a thin, flat line of fury. 'Do you have any idea of how many faces I have had to reconstruct over the years?' he ground out. 'Beautiful, perfect faces, permanently damaged by fools like your brother, whose idea of fun is to do burnouts and wheelies in city streets with no thought or regard to whoever else might be on them. That is what my life's work is all about, Claire. Not that you have ever shown a moment's interest, of course.'

'That is just so typical of you,' she threw back. 'I gave up my whole life for you and your career—not that you ever noticed. I was stuck at home day after miserable day, with only your mother and very occasionally your father dropping in just often enough to remind me none too subtly how I wasn't good enough to be their precious firstborn brilliant surgeon son's wife.'

His jaw tightened like a clamp. 'That is not how my mother tells it,' he bit out. 'She tried her utmost to help you settle in, but you refused to give an inch.'

'Here we go again,' Claire said with a curl of her lip. 'Her version and mine—and you still can't make up your mind which one to believe.'

Antonio thrust his hands into his trouser pockets in case he was tempted to pull her into his arms and kiss her into submission. She was so damned infuriating. No one could make him angrier than she did. He was master of his emotions, he always had been—and needed to be during the long hours of complicated surgical procedures where a cool, calm head was essential. But five minutes with Claire in this mood was enough to set his blood on the boil.

The very fact she had demanded a divorce the moment he stepped foot in the country showed how much of a gold-digger she had become. He could not stomach her getting half of his inheritance. He would do anything to prevent it. She had already taken enough. It still infuriated him to think of her demanding money from his mother the day she had left him.

Their blazingly hot affair had suddenly changed gear when she had informed him she was carrying his child. He had stood by her, marrying her promptly even though he had always had some misgivings over the true state of her feelings. She had claimed to love him, but he had always suspected it was the lifestyle she had fallen in love with, not him at all. From the little she had told him, he knew she came from a relatively poor background. Money had been scarce and luxuries almost unheard of. She had certainly acted a little starstruck on more than one occasion. Her wide-eyed wonder at the way he and his family lived had amused him at first, but after a while he'd realised he had become a passage for her to a new life, a life where each day wasn't a struggle for survival. That was until fate had stepped in with its most devastating of blows.

Thinking of that time always twisted his insides. He had been so busy, so very distracted. The surgical career pathway was strenuously demanding at the best of times, but juggling the needs of a young wife during an unplanned pregnancy and long hours of study and operating had been crippling, to say the least. His mother had told him many times how she had found Claire still in her dressing gown, moping about the villa, unwilling to make the slightest effort to adjust to being a surgeon's wife. Claire had obviously expected him to be at her beck and call, a nine-to-five sort of husband, when he had been anything but.

His own feelings he hated examining too closely, although he had to admit if he had loved her half as much as he had lusted after her maybe things would have been different. Love was a word he had never been quite comfortable using when it came to Claire, or indeed any other woman he had been involved with. He had decided long ago he was not the falling in love type.

The trouble was he still wanted her. He had never stopped wanting her. It was like a thrumming pulse in his body every time he was near her. His blood pounded in his veins as he thought of the ways she had pleasured him in the past. What she had lacked in experience she had made up for in enthusiasm. He had never had a more satisfying lover. Something about Claire and her responses to him, and his to her, made him feel as if he would never be content until he got her out of his system once and for all. And this was the perfect opportunity to do it.

'Claire,' he said locking his gaze with hers, 'is it possible for us to put aside the past for a moment and discuss this like mature adults?'

The look she sent him was contemptuous. 'I fail to see what is mature about forcing me back into your life when you didn't want me in it in the first place,' she said. 'All you really wanted was an heir, and I once I failed to provide one you moved on to the next person who could.'

Antonio silently counted to ten to control his temper. 'So I take it your decision is to send your brother to prison? Is that correct?'

She turned away from him, folding her arms across her chest like a shield. 'You know I would do anything to stop that happening,' she said. 'No doubt that's why you're playing that particular card from the deck.'

'This is not a game, Claire.'

She turned to look at him again, her expression cynical. 'Isn't it?'

He blew out a gust of breath. 'I am thirty-six years old,' he said. 'I want to settle down at some point, but I cannot do that until things are finalised between us one way or the other.'

Claire felt a sensation akin to a sharp pain beneath her ribcage. 'So…' She ran her tongue over the sudden dryness of her lips. 'So you're thinking of getting married to someone else…once we get a divorce?'

His eyes gave little away, his expression even less. 'That is not an unlikely scenario,' he answered. 'I have been thinking about it a lot lately.'

'Are you…' Claire swallowed against the aching restriction in her throat. 'Are you planning on having children?'

Again his expression was shuttered, totally and frustratingly unreadable. 'It is a goal of mine, indeed of most people my age, to have a child or two if it is at all possible.'

'Then I'm not sure why you are wasting your time on our relationship, given it has already failed once,' she said, holding his gaze with an effort. 'Wouldn't you be better placed looking for a replacement wife, instead of trying to refashion the one you've got and don't really want?'

'I do not recall saying I did not want you,' he said, with a look that would have ignited tinder. 'On the contrary, you would not be here right now if that was not my primary focus.'

Claire's eyes widened, her heart skipping a beat. 'So…so what you're saying is…you still want me… as in…*sex*?'

A corner of his mouth lifted in a smile that set her pulse racing out of control. 'You find that surprising, *cara*?' he asked.

'Actually, I find it totally insulting,' she tossed back, desperate to disguise her reaction to him. 'You haven't spoken to me in five years, other than via an occasional terse e-mail in the first few months of our separation, and now you're expecting me to dive headfirst into your bed. What sort of woman do you think I am to agree to something as deplorable as that?'

'You do not have a current lover, so I do not see why this will not work between us—for the time being at least.'

Claire narrowed her eyes in outrage. 'How do you

know I don't have a lover? Have you done some sort of background search on me?'

'You are still legally married to me, Claire,' he said. 'I believe it is very much my business to know if you are involved with anyone at present. Particularly if we are to resume a physical relationship.'

'That is a very big if,' she said, folding her arms. 'Anyway, what about you? How many women have *you* had during our separation?'

'I have had the occasional date, but nothing serious.'

Claire wanted to believe him, but knowing him as she did, or at least had, she couldn't imagine him remaining celibate for five years. He was a full-blooded male, healthy and virile, with a sex drive that had left her shuddering in his arms each and every time. She could feel that virility and potency now. The sensual spell he cast was woven around her like an invisible mist. She couldn't see it but she could feel it dampening her skin, making her aware of his maleness as no one else could. She could feel her breasts stirring against the lace of her bra, the tightness of her nipples reminding her of how his hot, moist mouth had suckled on her, his teeth tugging at her in playful little bites that had made her toes curl. Her belly quivered, the hollow ache of her womanhood pulsing with longing to be filled with his length and thickness again and again, driving her to the cataclysmic release she had silently craved for every one of the days, months and years they had spent apart.

It shamed her to be confronted by her own weakness where he was concerned. What sort of gullible fool would she be to go back for a second helping of betrayal and heartbreak?

He had never wanted their relationship to be anything other than a short-term affair, but her accidental pregnancy had changed everything. It had taken her almost a month to summon up the courage to tell him. Claire still remembered the total look of shock on his face when she had. But then to her surprise he had insisted they get married. It was only later she'd realised it had not been because he loved her, but because he had wanted an heir.

Claire had always known Antonio wasn't anywhere near as serious about her as she was about him. She had heard the adage far too many times to ignore it: Italian men slept with foreigners, but when it came to settling down they married their own countrywomen. But even so she had been caught up in the fairytale of it all: having a handsome man who lavished her with gifts and took her on exciting dates, not to mention one who initiated her into the heady pleasures of the flesh. It was all like a dream come true to a shy country girl from the Outback of Australia.

Claire had always been so careful with men in the past. She hadn't wanted to repeat the mistakes of her mother, pregnant and abandoned at a young age, spending most of her life looking for love in all the wrong places, and going on to have two other children, none of whose fathers had stayed around long enough to have their names registered on the birth certificates.

Claire hadn't slept around like most of her peers. Instead she had saved up the money from the three part-time jobs she'd juggled in order to put herself through hairdressing college. She had graduated as student of the year, and spent the next year or so saving for a holiday abroad, wanting to see the world before she settled into an upmarket salon.

But then she had met Antonio.

He had come in for a haircut, and as Riccardo, her flamboyant boss, had been double-booked due to a mistake one of the apprentices had made, he had asked her to wash and cut Antonio's hair for him.

Claire had smiled up at the tall, gorgeous-looking man, introducing herself shyly. 'I am so sorry about the mistake in the appointment book,' she said. 'Riccardo has spoken to you about me filling in for him?'

Antonio smiled. 'It is not a problem,' he said. 'You are from England, *si*?'

'No.' She felt herself blushing and gushing. 'I'm actually Australian, from Sydney...well, really the country, not the city...a rural district...you know...cows and sheep...that sort of thing.'

'Ah, Australia,' he said, taking the chair she held out for him. 'I have distant relatives there. In fact my younger brother has been there several times. I have been promising myself a trip out there some time. It is the land of opportunities, *si*?'

Claire draped the cape around his impossibly broad shoulders, her nerves fizzing as her fingers accidentally came into contact with the raspy skin along his jaw. 'Um...yes...I guess so. If you're prepared to work hard,' she said, trying to avoid meeting his coal-black eyes in the mirror.

'Do you speak Italian?'

'*Non parlo Italiano*,' she said with an apologetic

grimace. 'But I would like to learn. I've been thinking about taking some classes.'

He met her eyes in the mirror and held them. 'I will give you a lesson for free if you agree to have dinner with me tonight.'

Claire's fingers stilled amongst the silky strands of his sooty black hair. 'Um…I'm not sure if Riccardo agrees with his staff fraternising with clients,' she faltered.

'He will agree when it comes to me,' Antonio said, with the sort of easy confidence that would have presented itself as arrogance in anyone else.

'Would you like to come over to the basin?' she asked, trying for cool and calm but not quite pulling it off.

Antonio rose from the chair, his height yet again dwarfing her. 'Riccardo must think a lot of your skill if he has shunted one of his best clients into your hands,' he said. 'Will I be safe?'

Claire responded to his flirting as any other young woman would have done. 'Only if you behave yourself, Signor Marcolini,' she said with a smile. 'I make a habit of keeping all of my customers satisfied—even the most demanding ones.'

'I am sure you do,' he said, and put back his head so she could wash his hair.

Claire had to drag herself out of the past to concentrate on the here and now. She didn't want to remember how it had felt to run her fingers through his hair, to massage his scalp for far longer than any other client before or since. She didn't want to remember how she had agreed to have dinner with him—not just that night but the following night as well. And she certainly didn't want to remember the way he had kissed her on their third date, his mouth sending her into a frenzy of want that had led to her lying naked in his arms only moments later, his body plunging into hers, her muffled cry of discomfort bringing him up short, shocked, horrified that he had inadvertently hurt her...

*No.* Claire shoved the memories back even further. It had been the first time he had hurt her, but not the last. And there was no way she was going to think about the last.

'I find it hard to believe you have been without a regular bedmate for the last five years,' she said, voicing her doubts out loud.

'Believe what you like,' he said. 'As in the past, I have no control over the unfathomable workings of your mind.'

Claire ground her teeth. 'You know, you are really going to have to dig a little deeper on the charm front to get me back into your bed, Antonio.'

He gave her an imperious smile. 'You think?'

She took a step backwards, her hands clenched into fists by her sides. 'What do your parents and brother think of your dastardly little scheme to lure me back into the fold of the Marcolini family?'

A shadow passed through his dark eyes. It was just a momentary, almost fleeting thing, and Claire thought how she could so easily have missed it. 'My father unfortunately passed away a couple of months ago,' he said, with little trace of emotion in his voice. 'He had a massive heart attack. Too many cigarettes, too much stress, and not enough advice taken from his doctors or his family to slow down, I am afraid.' He paused for a moment, his dark eyes pinning hers in a disquieting manner. 'I thought you would have read about it in the press?'

'I…I must have missed it,' she said, lowering her voice and her gaze respectfully. 'I am so sorry. Your mother must miss him greatly. You must all miss him…'

'My mother is doing the best she can under the circumstances,' he said after another slight pause. 'My brother Mario has taken over my father's business.'

Claire brought her gaze back to his in surprise. 'What? You mean your father didn't leave you anything in his will?'

An indefinable look came into his eyes. 'Mario and I are both partners in the business, of course, but due to my career commitments I have by necessity left most of the corporate side of things to him.'

'I am sure your brother was shocked to hear of your intention to look me up while you are here,' Claire commented with a wry look.

Antonio continued to hold her look with an inscrutable one of his own. 'I have spoken to my brother, who told me rather bluntly he thinks I am a fool for even considering a rematch with you. But then he has always been of the philosophy of one strike and you are out. I am a little more…how shall I say…accommodating?'

Claire could just imagine his playboy younger brother bad-mouthing her to Antonio. His parents had been the same—not that Antonio would ever believe it. That last degrading scene with his mother had been filed away in Claire's do-not-go-there-again-file in her head. She had kept the cheque in her purse for weeks, folded into a tiny square, frayed at the edges, just as her temper was every time she thought of how she had been dismissed, like a servant who hadn't fulfilled the impossible expectations of her employer. But then she had finally cashed it, without a twinge of conscience. As far as she was concerned it had been money well spent.

'How do you know it was my brother who took your car?' Claire asked, looking at Antonio warily. 'You've never met any of my family.' *Thank God*, she thought. What he would make of her loving but totally unsophisticated mother was anyone's guess, but her brothers— as much as she loved them—were way beyond the highbrow circles Antonio moved in.

'When the police caught him he identified himself,' Antonio said. 'He made no effort at all to cover up the fact he was my young brother-in-law.'

Claire felt her stomach drop.

'Wh-where is he?' she asked. 'Where is my brother now?'

'I have arranged for him to spend a few days with a friend of mine,' he said. 'He runs a centre for troubled youths on the South Coast.'

She clenched her fists by her sides. 'I want to see him. I want to see my brother to make sure he's all right.'

'I will organise for you to speak to him via the telephone,' he said, and reached for his mobile.

Claire sank her teeth into her bottom lip as she listened to him speak to his friend before he handed her the phone. She took it with a shaking hand and held it up to her ear, turning away so he wouldn't see the anguish on her face, nor hear what her brother had to say.

'Isaac? It's me, Claire.'

'Yo, sis. What's up?'

Claire mentally pinched the bridge of her nose. 'I think you know what's up,' she said, stepping further out of Antonio's hearing and keeping her voice low. 'Why did you do it, Isaac? Why on earth did you take Antonio Marcolini's car?'

Her brother muttered a filthy swear word. 'I hate the way he treated you. I thought it would help. Why should he drive around in such a cool-dude car when yours is a heap of rust?' he asked. 'Rich bastard. Anyway, I thought you were going to divorce him?'

Claire cringed as the sound of her brother's voice carried across the room. Turning away from Antonio's livid dark brown gaze, she said, 'I'm actually considering…um…getting back with him.'

Her brother let out another swear word. 'Get *out*. Jeez, why didn't you tell me that the other day?'

'Would it have made a difference?' she asked.

There was a small silence.

'Yeah…maybe…I dunno. You seemed pretty cut up about that article and the photo in the paper.'

Claire squeezed her eyes shut. Why hadn't she thrown it in the rubbish, where it belonged? 'Look, I just want you to promise me you'll behave yourself now you've been given this chance.'

'Don't 'ave much choice, locked up here,' he grumbled.

Claire frowned. 'You're locked up?'

'Well…sort of,' Isaac said. 'It's some sort of youth reform centre. It's kind of all right, though. The food's OK, and they've given me a room to myself and a TV. The head honcho wants me to think about teaching

some of the kids to surf. I might take it on; I've got
nothing better to do.'

'Just stay there and do as you're told, Isaac,' she
pleaded with him.

'So you're dead serious about getting back with the
Marcolini bloke, huh?' Isaac asked.

She lowered her voice even further, but even so it
seemed to echo ominously off the walls of the plush
suite—just as her brother's damning words had. 'Yes,'
she said. 'I am as of this moment going to return to
Antonio and live with him as his wife.'

# CHAPTER FOUR

CLAIRE handed back Antonio's phone with a look of grim resignation on her face. 'Would you like me to lie down on the bed now, so you can get straight down to business?' she asked. 'Or would you like me to perform a strip show and really get your money's worth?'

Anger flared like a struck match in his dark eyes. 'There is no need to prostitute yourself, Claire,' he said. 'We will resume a physical relationship only when I am convinced it is what we both want. Right at this moment I can see you would much rather rake your nails down my face than anything else.'

Claire felt relief tussling with her disappointment, making her feel disconcerted over what it was she actually felt for Antonio. She had told herself so many times how much she hated him, and yet standing before him now she found that hatred proving frustratingly elusive. Other feelings had crept up on her—dangerous feelings of want and need. She could feel the traitorous beat of her pulse, the hit and miss of her heartbeats reminding her of the sensual power he still had over her.

'So...' She tried to keep her voice steady and her ex-

pression coolly detached. 'This three-month reconciliation... Am I supposed to move in here with you, or do
I get to keep my own place?'

'You are renting at present? Is that correct?' he asked.

Claire wondered again how he knew so much about
her current circumstances when their contact had been
so limited. In the first weeks after she had left he had
called and left message after message on her mobile, but
she had deleted them without listening. He had e-mailed
her several times, but she had not responded, and in the
end had changed her e-mail address and her mobile
number. She had assured herself if he really wanted to
contact her he would find some way of doing so. But
after some months had gone by, and then a couple of
years, and then another couple, she'd resigned herself
to the fact he had well and truly moved on.

'Claire?'

'Um...yes,' she said. 'I'm renting a place in Glebe,
not far from the salon.'

'Do you own the salon outright?'

She frowned at him. 'What, do you think I am made
of money or something?' she asked. 'Of course I don't
own it outright. I work for a friend, Rebecca Collins.'

Antonio searched her features for a moment. 'So if
you do not own a share in the salon, and you rent where
you live, what exactly did you do with the money my
mother gave you?' he asked.

Her shoulders went back and her blue-green eyes
flashed flick knives of resentment at him. 'So she told
you about that, did she?' she asked.

'She reluctantly informed me of it a couple of weeks

after you left,' he said, keeping his expression deliberately shuttered.

'I looked upon it as a severance payout,' she said. 'After all, you no longer required my services once you'd hooked back up with Daniela Garza.'

Antonio ignored that little jibe to ask, 'Is that why you refused to accept money from me, even though I offered it repeatedly in my e-mails and phone calls?'

She gave him another castigating glare. 'Do you really think I would have accepted money from you after what you did?' she asked.

His lip curled in disdain. 'And yet you demanded it from my mother.'

Shocked, she stared at him with wide eyes. '*What* did you say?'

He let a three beats of silence pass.

'I think you heard what I said, Claire,' he said. 'You blackmailed my mother, forcing her to pay you a large sum of money to stop you going to the press about your marriage to me.'

She was looking at him as if he was speaking another language. But Antonio was well aware of how manipulative she could be, and still had his suspicions about her plans to take him for what she could get. Yet no one looking at her now would think her guilty of such a scheme. Her eyes were wide, feigning shocked innocence, her mouth trembling and her face pale.

'You have not answered my question,' he said.

Her back visibly stiffened, although her tone sounded calm and even. 'What question is that?'

'What did you do with the money?'

She let out her breath in a long hissing stream. 'What do you think I did with it?'

He frowned at her darkly. 'I would have given you money, damn it, Claire. But you always refused it.'

She turned her back on him. 'It was less personal taking it from her,' she said. 'I didn't want anything to do with you.'

'So what did you do with it?'

She turned after a moment, her expression as cold as the night air outside. 'I spent it on myself,' she said, with that same razor-sharp glint in her eyes. 'That's what gold-diggers do, isn't it, Antonio?'

He drew in a breath as he reined back his temper. She was deliberately goading him, as she had done so many times before. Yes, he had proof she had blackmailed his mother, even though she now staunchly denied it, but he understood how she would have seen it as some sort of payback for him not being there for her in the way she had wanted him to be.

He had come to a time in his life now where he wanted to put down roots. His father's sudden death had no doubt got a lot to do with it—not to mention his mother's deterioration since. And, since his brother Mario had no intention of settling down and producing a Marcolini heir, it was up to Antonio to make some important decisions about his own future. He could not move on until he had tied up the loose and frayed ends of the past. God knew he owed it to his beautiful little daughter, who hadn't even had the chance to take her first breath.

Antonio swallowed against the avalanche of emotion

he felt whenever he pictured that tiny, perfect, lifeless face. He had helped so many people during the long, arduous course of his surgical career. He had saved lives, he had changed lives, he had restored health and vitality to people who had stared death or disfigurement in the face—and yet he had not been there when his daughter and Claire had needed him most.

It tortured him to think he might have been able to do something. Claire had gone into labour far too early. He had ignored the signs when she had mentioned her concerns that morning. He had no excuse, not really. The truth was he had been distracted with the case scheduled first on his list that day. A young girl of only seventeen, who had just landed herself a lucrative modelling contract, had been involved in a horrific traffic accident some weeks earlier. Antonio hadn't seen anyone quite so damaged before. He'd had to concentrate on preserving crucial facial nerves during surgery that would decide whether she would ever smile her beautiful smile at the camera again. He had perspired beneath his surgical scrubs; it had run like a river down his back as he'd worked with his dedicated team for twelve, nearly thirteen hours, to put her face back together the best they could—hoping, praying she would still be able to live the life she had mapped out for herself.

And he had done it. Bianca Abraggio was still modelling today—her face her fortune, her gorgeous smile intact, her life on track, while Antonio's was still in limbo.

'I do not recall referring to you at any time as a gold-digger,' he said.

She lifted her chin, her eyes flashing at him like shards

of blue-green glass. 'You didn't need to. Your family made it more than clear that's what they thought I was.'

'Look,' he said, dragging a hand through his hair, 'I admit they were not expecting me to produce a daughter-in-law for them quite so soon. I was in the middle of my final fellowship training and—'

She cut him off. 'They never accepted me. They thought I wasn't good enough for you. I was a foreigner. I couldn't even speak their language. Not to mention I spoke with a broad Australian accent.'

'That is not true,' Antonio said. He had seen time and time again how both of his parents had tried their level best to get on with Claire, but she had been so fiercely independent they had eventually given up trying to include her. 'Anyway, it was not up to them, it was up to me who I spent my time with. It is still up to me.'

'What would *you* know of how it was for me?' she asked. 'I couldn't bear going through it all again. It has taken me this long to move on.'

Antonio could feel his frustration building, and couldn't quite disguise it in his tone. 'Get used to it, Claire, because you and I are going to spend the next three months together—otherwise you will be personally responsible for sending your brother to jail where he belongs.'

She glared at him furiously. 'I thought you had devoted your life to saving the lives of others?' she said. 'If you send my brother to prison you might as well be signing your name on his death certificate. He won't last a day inside. He'll get bullied or beaten up or something. I know he will.'

The look he gave her was merciless. 'Then do not

make me do it, Claire, for I will if I have to. It is in your hands. Do not forget that.'

She threw him a hateful glare as she snatched up her purse from where she had flung it earlier. Fighting to control her anger was like trying to rein in a bolting horse with nothing but piece of string. She had never thought it was possible to hate someone so intensely— especially someone she had loved so much before. Antonio was a ruthless stranger now, a man without mercy, a man who was prepared to go to unbelievable lengths to have her bend to his will.

'When do you wish to start this ridiculous charade?' she asked.

'Have you had dinner?' he asked.

'Um…no, but I'm not hungry.'

'There is a very fine restaurant within a block of here,' he said. 'I suggest we have dinner together, so as to ease back into our relationship.'

'I don't think I could eat a thing.'

'It looks like you have not eaten a thing in days.'

She gave him a cutting look. 'Is there anything else you would like to criticise me about while you're at it?' she asked.

Antonio's eyes glittered determinedly as they held hers. 'One thing I would like to make very clear from the outset,' he said. 'You can say what you like to me when we are alone, but while we are in the presence of other people I expect you to act with the dignity and decorum befitting your role as my wife.'

'Yes, well, that's all it's going to be,' she snipped back. 'An act—and not a particularly attractive one.'

'I will make sure there are certain compensations,' he said. 'A generous allowance, for one thing, which will mean you can cut back your hours at work—or quit altogether while I am here.'

She stood as stiff as a broom handle. 'You can keep your stupid allowance, and I am *not* giving up my job for you,' she said. 'I want to maintain some element of independence.'

'If that is what you want then I have no issue with it,' he said. 'I just thought you might be glad of a break from the long hours you work. You certainly look like you could do with one.'

Claire knew she had dark shadows under her eyes, and she was at least a couple of kilos lighter than she should be, but did he *have* to make her feel as if she had just crawled out from beneath a rock?

'Would you like me to get a paper bag to place over my head before we are seen in public together?' she asked. 'No doubt I fall rather short of the glamorous standard of the legions of other women you have enjoyed over the last five years.'

He held her challenging look for a tense moment. 'I was merely commenting on how stressed and tired you look, *il mio amato*,' he said. 'There is no need to feel as if everything I say to you is a veiled insult.'

Claire had to hastily swallow to keep her emotions in check. Her heart recognised the term of endearment and swelled in response. *My beloved one.* Of course he didn't mean it. How could he? He had never said he loved her. He had not once revealed anything of how he felt about her apart from at the start of their affair, when his desire for her had been so hot and strong it had left her spinning in its wake.

But then he had left her grieving the loss of their baby to find solace in his previous lover's arms. He had always denied it strenuously, and she might have believed his version of events if it hadn't been for Antonio's mother Rosina confirming her son's clandestine relationship.

'Do we have to do this tonight?' she asked now, with a hint of petulance. 'Why can't we meet for dinner tomorrow, or even the day after?'

'Because I have limited time available,' he said. 'I have a large operating list tomorrow, which could well go over time. And besides, I know what you will do if I give you a reprieve. You will more than likely disappear for the next three months so as to avoid further contact with me.'

Claire shifted her gaze so he wouldn't see how close his assessment of her had been. She had been madly thinking of various escape routes, mentally tallying the meagre contents of her bank account to figure a way of covering her tracks until he left the country. But she could hardly leave Rebecca in the lurch—not after she had always been so supportive of her over the years.

'I know how your mind works, Claire,' he said into the silence. 'You would rather walk over hot coals than spend an evening with me, would you not?'

Claire returned her gaze to his, surprised at the bitterness in his tone. What did *he* have to be bitter about? She hadn't destroyed their marriage, he had—and irreparably. 'You surely don't expect me to be doing cartwheels of joy about you forcing your way back into my life, do you?' she asked.

The line of his mouth tightened. 'I can see why you have lost so much weight,' he said. 'It is no doubt due to that chip on your shoulder you are carrying around.'

Claire gripped her purse so tightly her fingers began to ache. 'You don't think I have a right to be upset?' she asked. 'I'm not an emotional cardboard cut-out like you, Antonio. I feel, and I feel deeply. Not a day goes past when I don't think about her—about how old she would be now, what she would look like, the things she would be saying and doing. Do you even spare her a single thought?'

His eyes darkened, and the tension around his mouth increased, making a tiny nerve flicker beneath the skin of his rigid jaw. 'I think of her,' he said, his voice sounding as if it had been scraped across a serrated surface. 'Of course I think about her.'

Claire bit the inside of her mouth until she tasted the metallic sourness of blood. She didn't want to break down in front of him. She didn't want him to see how truly vulnerable she still was around him. If he reached out to comfort her she would betray herself; she was sure of it. Her arms would snake around his neck; her body would press up against his in search of the warmth and strength only he could give. Her flesh would spring to life, every cell in her body recognising the magnetism of his, drawing her into his sensual orbit, luring her into lowering her guard until she had no defences left. The sooner she was out of this suite and in a public place the better, she decided firmly.

She drew in a scratchy breath and forced herself to meet his gaze. 'I guess dinner would be OK,' she said. 'I missed lunch, and breakfast seems like a long time ago.'

He picked up the security card and slid it into his wallet. 'I will not keep you up too late, Claire. I am still getting over my jet lag.'

Claire noticed then how tired he looked. His dark eyes were underscored with bruise-like shadows, and the grooves either side of his mouth looked deeper than usual. He still looked as heart-stoppingly gorgeous as ever—perhaps even more so. Maybe it was because she hadn't seen him for so long. She had forgotten how compelling his chocolate-brown eyes were, how thick and sooty his long lashes, and how his beautifully sculpted mouth with its fuller bottom lip hinted at the passion and potency she had tasted there time and time again.

She had to wrench her gaze away from his mouth, where it had drifted of its own volition.

'So…what's this restaurant like?' she asked as they made their way out of his penthouse. 'What sort of cuisine do they offer?'

He reached past her to press the call button for the lift, and Claire felt her breath come to a stumbling halt in her chest. The near brush of his arm had triggered every nerve in her body, until she could almost sense how it would feel to have him touch her again. Her breasts ached for the press of his hands, the brush of his lips, the sweet hot suck of his mouth and the roll and glide and tortuous tease of his tongue. Was she so pleasure-starved as to be suddenly craving the touch of a man she hated? Her mind was playing tricks on her, surely? He had accused her of blackmail, and yet she couldn't quite stop her heart from skipping a beat every time his gaze meshed with hers.

The lift arrived with an almost soundless swish of doors opening, and Claire stepped in, moving to the back, out of temptation's way.

'Come here, Claire,' Antonio commanded.

Claire held her purse like a shield against her traitorous pelvis, where a pulse had begun beating. 'Why?' she asked. 'There's no one else in the lift.'

'No, but as soon as we hit the ground floor there will be. So it is better to start as we mean to go on,' he said.

She frowned at him as suspicion began to crawl beneath her skin. 'How do you know there will be someone there?' she asked.

He held her narrowed gaze with equanimity. 'I took the liberty of releasing a press statement earlier today.'

Claire felt anger rise up within her like a cold, hard substance, stiffening every vertebra of her spine. 'You were *that* sure I would agree to this farce?' she asked.

His eyes glinted as they held hers. 'I was sure you would not like to see your brother face the authorities. I was also sure you would do it for the money.'

The despair she felt at that moment almost consumed her. It was so hurtful to realise how badly he thought of her, how for all this time he'd believed her to be an avaricious opportunist, when all she had ever wanted from him was his love. How could he have got it so wrong about her? Hadn't he seen how much she had adored him? Claire knew she had been a little goggle-eyed at his lifestyle to begin with, but as their relationship had progressed she'd thought she had demonstrated how little his fame and fortune meant to her. Was his heart so hard and impenetrable he was unable to recognise genuine love when he saw it?

'Come here, Claire,' he commanded again, holding out his hand for her.

Claire released her tightly held breath and pressed herself away from the back of the lift, where she had flattened her spine. She took his hand, struggling to hide the way his fingers curling around hers affected her. His hands—his so very clever, life-saving hands—felt strong and warm against hers. They had been one of the first things she had noticed about him all those years ago in Riccardo's salon. Antonio had strong, capable hands—tanned, lightly sprinkled with hair, broad and yet long-fingered, his nails cut short and scrupulously clean from the hundreds of washes he subjected them to in order to operate.

She looked down at their entwined fingers and suppressed a tiny shiver. Those hands had explored every inch of her body. They had known her intimately; they had taught her everything she knew about sexual response. She could feel the warmth of him seeping through her skin, layer by layer, melting the ice of her resolve to keep herself distanced and unaffected by him.

The lift doors opened and a camera flashed in Claire's face as she stepped out hand in hand with Antonio. She cringed, and shielded her eyes from the over-bright glare, but within seconds another journalist had rushed up and thrust a microphone towards her.

'Mrs Marcolini,' the young woman said, struggling to

keep up with Antonio's determined stride as he pulled
Claire towards the front of the hotel. 'Is it true you are returning to your husband after a five-year estrangement?'

Antonio gently but firmly moved the microphone
away from Claire's face. 'Do you mind giving my wife
some space?' he asked.

The journalist took this as encouragement, and
directed her line of questioning at him instead. 'Mr
Marcolini, you are reputed to be here in Sydney for a
limited time. Does that mean your new relationship with
your wife will be on a set time-frame as well? Or do you
intend to take her back to Italy with you once your
lecture and surgical tour here in Sydney is completed?'

Claire looked up at Antonio, her breath catching in
her throat, but he was as cool and collected as usual, the
urbane smile in place, his inscrutable gaze giving no
clue to what was ticking over in his mind.

'That is between my wife and I,' he answered. 'We have
only just sorted out our differences. Please give us some
space and privacy in which to work on our reconciliation.'

'Mr Marcolini.' The young female journalist was
clearly undaunted by his somewhat terse response. 'You
and your wife suffered the tragedy of a stillbirth five
years ago. Do you have any advice to parents who have
suffered the same?'

Claire felt the sudden tension in Antonio's fingers
where they were wrapped around hers. She looked up
at him again, her heart in her throat and the pain in the
middle of her chest so severe she could scarcely draw
in a much needed breath.

'The loss of a child at any age is a travesty of nature,'

he answered. 'Each person must deal with it in their own way and in their own time. There is no blueprint for grief.'

'And you, Mrs Marcolini?' The journalist aimed her microphone back at Claire. 'What advice would you give to grieving parents, having been through it personally?'

Claire stammered her response, conscious there were women out there just like her, who had been torn apart by the loss of a baby and would no doubt be hanging on every word she said. 'Um…just to keep hoping that one day enough research will be done to make sure stillbirths are a thing of the past. And to remember it's not the mother's fault. Things go wrong, even at the last minute. You mustn't blame yourself…that is the important thing. You mustn't blame yourself…'

Antonio, keeping Claire close, elbowed his way through the knot of people and cameras. 'Just keep walking, *cara*,' he said. 'This will die down in a day or two.'

'I can't see why our situation warrants the attention it's just received. Who gives a toss whether we resume our marriage or not? It's hardly headline material.'

Antonio kept her hand tucked in close to his side as he led the way down the sidewalk to the restaurant he had booked earlier. 'Maybe not here in Australia,' he said. 'However, there are newshounds who relay gossip back to Italy from all over the world. They like to document whatever Mario and I do—especially now we are at the helm of the Marcolini empire.'

'So what is Mario up to these days?' Claire asked, not really out of interest but more out of a desire to steer the conversation away from their unusual situation. 'Still flirting with any woman with a pulse?'

Antonio's smile this time was crooked with affection for his sibling. 'You know my brother Mario. He likes to work hard and to play even harder. I believe there is lately someone he is interested in—an Australian girl, apparently, someone he met last time he was here—but so far she has resisted his charm.'

'Yes, well, maybe he could try a little ruthlessness or blackmail,' she said. 'Both seem to run rather freely in the Marcolini family veins.'

He turned to face her, holding her by the upper arms so she couldn't move away. 'I gave you a choice, Claire,' he said, pinning her gaze with his. 'Your freedom or your brother's. You see it as blackmail, I see it as a chance to sort out what went wrong between us.'

She wrenched herself out of his hold, dusting off her arms as if he had tainted her with his touch. 'I can tell you what went wrong with us, Antonio,' she said. 'All I ever was to you was a temporary diversion—someone to warm your bed occasionally. You had no emotional investment in our relationship until there was the prospect of an heir. The baby was a bonus, and once she was out of the equation, so was I.'

Antonio clenched and unclenched his fingers where hers had so recently been. He could still feel the tingling sensation running up under his skin. 'I fulfilled my responsibilities towards you as best I could, but it was never enough for you. So many men in my place would not have done so. Have you ever thought of that? I stood by you and supported you, but you wanted me to be something I am not nor ever could be.'

She sank her teeth into her lip when it began to tremble. Moisture was starting to shine in the blue-green pools of her eyes, making him feel like an unfeeling brute for raising his voice at her. How on earth did she do it to him? One wounded look from her, just one slight wobble of her chin, and he felt the gut-wrenching blows of guilt assail him all over again.

He let out a weighty sigh and captured her hand again, bringing it up to his mouth, pressing his lips warmly against her cold, thin fingers. 'I am sorry, *cara*,' he said gently. 'I do not want to fight with you. We are supposed to be mending bridges, *si*?'

She looked at him for a stretching moment, her eyes still glistening with unshed tears. 'Some bridges can never be mended, Antonio,' she said, pulling her hand out of his.

Antonio held the restaurant door open for her. *Let's just see about that*, he thought with grim determination, and followed her inside.

# CHAPTER FIVE

A FEW minutes later, once they were seated at a secluded table with drinks, crusty bread rolls and a tiny dish of freshly pressed olive oil placed in front of them, Claire began to feel the tension in her shoulders slowly dissipate. She could see Antonio was making every effort to put her at ease. His manner towards her had subtly changed ever since that tense moment outside the restaurant.

The earlier interaction with the press had upset him much more than she had thought it would. He was well used to handling the intrusive questions of the paparazzi, but this time she had felt the tensile strain in him as he had tried to protect her. It had touched her that he had done so, and made her wonder if his motives for their reconciliation were perhaps more noble than she had first thought.

The waiter took their orders, and once he had left them Antonio caught and held Claire's gaze. 'Did you blame yourself, Claire?' he asked, looking at her with dark intensity.

Claire pressed her lips together, her eyes falling away

from his to stare at the vertical necklaces of bubbles in her soda water. 'I don't suppose there is a mother anywhere in the world who doesn't feel guilty about the death of her child,' she said sadly.

He reached for her hand across the table, his long, strong fingers interlocking with hers. 'I should have arranged some counselling for you,' he said, in a tone deep with regret.

Claire brought her eyes back to his. 'Would you have come to the sessions as well?'

His eyes shifted to look at the contents of his glass, just as hers had done a moment or so earlier. 'I am used to dealing with life and death, Claire,' he said, briefly returning his gaze to hers. 'I lost my first patient, or at least the first one I was personally responsible for under my care, when I was a young registrar. It was unexpected and not my fault, but I blamed myself. I wanted to quit. I did not think I could carry on with my training. But my professor of surgery at the time took me to one side and reassured me that a surgeon is not God. We do what we can to save and preserve lives, but sometimes things go wrong. Things we have no control over.'

'Is that why you chose plastic surgery rather than general surgery?' Claire asked, wondering why she had never thought to ask him that before.

'I was never really interested in plastics as such,' he answered. 'I understand how many people are unhappy with the features they are born with, and I fully support them seeking help if and where it is appropriate, but I never saw myself doing straight rhinoplasty or breast augmentations or liposuction. Reconstructive work has always appealed to me. Seeing someone disfigured by an accident or birth defect reclaiming their life and their place in the world is tremendously satisfying.'

'I've seen some of the work you've done on your website,' Claire said. 'The before and after shots are truly amazing.'

He picked up his glass, his expression somewhere between quizzical and wry. 'I am surprised you bothered looking at all. I thought you wanted me out of sight and out of mind.'

She twisted her mouth. 'I guess intrigue got the better of me. From being an overworked registrar when we met to what you are now—a world leader in reconstructive surgery… Well, that's a pretty big leap, and one I imagine you might not have achieved if I had stayed around.'

A frown tugged at his dark brows. 'That seems a rather negative way of viewing yourself,' he said. 'The early years of surgery are punishing, Claire. You know that. It is like any other demanding profession. You have to put in the hard yards before you reap any of the rewards.'

'I suppose some of the rewards, besides the financial ones, are the hordes of women who trail after you so devotedly,' she put in resentfully.

He made an impatient sound at the back of his throat. 'You really are determined to pick a fight every chance you get, are you not? Well, if it is a fight you want, you can have one—but not here and not now. I refuse to trade insults with you over a table in a public restaurant.'

Claire twisted her hands beneath the table, her stomach tightening into familiar knots. 'I don't see that it is necessary for me to move in with you,' she said, nervously moistening her dry lips. 'Surely we can just see how it goes from day to day? You know…go on the occasional date or something, to see if things work out.'

He looked at her with wry amusement. 'Come now, Claire, surely we have moved well past the dating stage, hmm? You have shared my bed and my body in the past. I am quite sure you will not find it too difficult to do so again, especially since there is financial gain to be had.'

Claire had to look away from his taunting gaze. She felt shattered by his chilling assessment of her. He was treating her like a gold-digger, someone who would sleep with him for whatever she could get out of the arrangement. 'I don't want your money,' she said stiffly. 'I have never wanted it.'

He put his glass down so heavily the red wine splashed against the sides, almost spilling over the rim. 'That is not quite true, though, is it, Claire?'

She twisted her hands even more tightly together, forcing herself to hold his accusatory gaze. 'I wanted your time,' she said. 'But you were always too busy to give it to me.'

'I gave you what I could, Claire,' he said, frowning at her darkly. 'I know it was not enough. You did not always get the best of me; my patients back then and now still have that privilege. Most truly dedicated specialists feel the same way. We have lives in our hands. It is a huge responsibility, for they are all someone's son or daughter, husband or wife, brother or sister.'

'What about your own daughter, Antonio?' she asked, tears filling her eyes. 'The specialist you recommended I see failed to get there on time, and so did you. I felt let down. You both let our baby down.'

Antonio hated going over this. They had done it so many times in the past and it had achieved nothing. All it did was stir up a hornets' nest of guilt in his gut. 'Leave it, Claire,' he said. 'We have to let the past go and move forward. It is the only hope we have to get things right this time around.'

Claire pushed her barely touched food away. 'We wouldn't even be sitting here now if I hadn't asked you for a divorce. You couldn't stand the fact that I'd got in first— just like you couldn't stand the fact that I was the one who left you, not the other way round. And now you have the audacity to use my brother to blackmail me into being with you. I can't believe how ruthless you have become.'

'Your brother has nothing to do with this,' he said, releasing a tight breath. 'I was going to contact you in any case and suggest a trial reconciliation. He just gave me the means to make sure you agreed to it.'

Claire sat in stony silence, wondering whether to believe him or not. He had certainly taken his time about contacting her; she had heard nothing from him for years. But then she began to wonder if it had something to do with the death of his father. Could Antonio have an ulterior motive for chaining her to his side? Suspicion began to make her scalp prickle. No wonder he had looked at her with such fury in his gaze while she had been talking to Isaac, and when she had questioned him about whether his father's estate had been divided between his brother and himself. She was starting to think Antonio would do anything rather than divide up his assets—even if it meant reconciling with his runaway wife.

'You have been on my mind a lot over the years, Claire,' he said into the silence. 'When this offer to come to Australia came up I decided it was a perfect opportunity to see if anything could be salvaged from what was left of our relationship. You had not pressed for a divorce, so I felt there was a chance you might still have feelings for me.'

'Well, you were wrong,' Claire said, tossing her napkin to one side and glaring at him as her anger towards him raced with red-hot speed through her veins. 'I feel nothing for you.'

He held her caustic look without flinching. 'That is not true, *cara*. You feel a lot of things for me. Anger and hate to name just two of them.'

'And that's not enough to send you and your blackmailed bride scheme packing?' she asked, with vitriol sharpening her voice to dagger points.

'Not until I know for sure there is no hope,' he said, with an intransigent set to his features. 'And the only way to find out is to start straight away—from tonight.'

Claire felt her eyes flare in panic. 'You can't mean for me to spend the night with you? Not yet. I'm not ready. It's too soon.'

He gave her an imperious smile, like someone who knew the hand they were about to spread out on the table was going to be a royal flush. 'You want to pull out of our deal?' he asked, reaching for his mobile. 'I can call Frank and tell him the police will be there in half an hour to pick up your brother and press charges on him.'

Claire clenched her hands beneath the table again. 'No, please,' she choked. 'Don't do that… I…I'll stay with you…'

His dark eyes travelled over her face for a pulsing moment. 'I will not force myself on you, Claire,' he said. 'You surely do not expect me to act so boorishly towards you, do you?'

She compressed her lips, waiting a beat or two before she released them. 'I'm not sure what to think…' she confessed. 'We're practically strangers now…'

'Even strangers can become friends,' he said. 'If nothing else, would that not be a good outcome of this three-month arrangement?'

Her eyes were wary as they met his. 'I can't imagine us exchanging Christmas cards and newsy e-mails, Antonio. Besides, we come from completely different worlds. I honestly don't know what I was thinking, getting involved with you in the first place.'

'Then why not tell me about your world?' he said. 'You hardly ever mentioned your family when we were together. You did not even want them to come to our wedding, though I offered to pay for their flights. I have never even seen a photograph of any one of them.'

Claire felt a tide of colour creep into her cheeks. 'They are my family, and I love them,' she said, knowing she sounded far too defensive. 'They're not perfect— far from it—but things have not been easy for any of them. My mother in particular.'

'What is she like?' he asked. 'You told me so little about her in the past.'

She tucked a corkscrew of curls behind her left ear,

wondering where to begin. 'She's had a hard life. She lost her mother when she was in her early teens, and I guess because she felt so rudderless got pregnant at sixteen. Like a lot of other girls left holding the baby, she looked for love in all the wrong places, with each subsequent relationship producing a child but no reliable father. As the eldest and the only girl I kind of slipped into a pseudo-parenting role from an early age. My brother Callum is doing OK now, after a bit of a wild time in his teens, but it's Isaac I worry about. He's a little impulsive at times. He acts before he thinks.'

'He is young, and will eventually grow out of it if he is pointed in the right direction,' Antonio said. 'Frank Guthrie will be a good mentor for him. It sounds like your brother needs a strong male influence.'

Claire lifted her eyes back to his. 'Where did you meet this Frank guy?' she asked. 'I don't recall you mentioning him in the past.'

'I operated on his brother Jack about eighteen months ago,' he said. 'He was involved in a head-on collision just outside of Rome. There was a lot of facial damage. We had to put plates and screws in his forehead and cheeks, and rebuild both of his eye sockets. He was lucky to survive. No one thought he would come through, and certainly not without heavy scarring or disfigurement. I got to know Frank, who had flown over to be with him. He spent a lot of time at the hospital, so we often had a coffee and a chat after my ward rounds.'

'It must be very rewarding, seeing people recover from something like that,' she said. 'Your parents...I mean your mother...must be very proud of you.'

He gave her a wry half-smile. 'My father made it very clear when I first announced I was going to study medicine that he would have preferred me to take up the reins of his business. And my mother complained for years about the long hours I work. But I have always wanted to be a surgeon for as long as I can remember.'

Claire picked up her soda water again. 'How is your mother coping after your father's death?' she asked.

A shadow passed through his gaze as it met hers. 'She is doing as well as can be expected under the circumstances,' he said.

Claire was even more certain now that his father's death had everything to do with Antonio contacting her about this trial reconciliation. There would be certain expectations of him as the firstborn son of a wealthy businessman. An heir would be required. But he could hardly provide one whilst still legally married to his estranged wife.

A divorce between them had the potential to be messy, and no doubt very public. In their haste to marry close to six years ago, when Claire had announced her pregnancy, there had been no time for drawing up a prenuptial agreement. Antonio could not be unaware of how the family laws in Australia worked. She would be entitled to a considerable share of his wealth, including that which he had just inherited upon the death of his father, even though they had been living apart for so long.

She toyed with the edge of the tablecloth, struggling to keep her expression shuttered in case he saw how confused she was. It would be different if she still loved him. She would take him back without hesitation. But her love for him had died the day she had seen him in Daniela Garza's arms.

Or had it?

Claire looked at his face, her heart giving an unco-ordinated skip as her gaze came into contact with his coal-black eyes. She had been aware of a disturbing undercurrent the whole time they had been together this evening. Every time her eyes met his she felt the zap of attraction—unwilling, almost resentful, but no less unmistakable, and it definitely wasn't one-way. Her body recognised him as her pleasure-giver. She had not known such pleasure before or since, and while she imagined in her most tortured moments he had experienced physical ecstasy with many other women, she was more than aware of his ongoing desire for her. She could see it in his eyes, in the way they locked on hers for a second or two longer than necessary. She had felt it in the way his fingers had wrapped around hers in that possessive way of his, their warmth seeping into the coldness of hers. She could only imagine what would happen if he should kiss her at some point. Her lips could almost sense the gentle but firm pressure of his, and her tongue snaked out to try and remove the sensation. She didn't want to remind herself of all she had felt in his arms. She had locked away those memories. They were too painful to recollect.

They were far too dangerous to revisit.

'Have you finished playing with your meal?' Antonio asked.

Claire put down the fork she had been using to move around the seafood risotto she had been vainly trying to push past her lips. 'I guess I'm not as hungry as I thought I was,' she said, her shoulders going down on a sigh.

He took out his wallet and, signalling the waiter, placed his credit card on the table in anticipation of the bill. 'I will give you a night of reprieve, Claire,' he said. 'Go home and get a good night's sleep. If you give me a spare key to your flat I will send someone over tomorrow to shift your things to my suite at the hotel. Do not worry about your lease or the rent for the next three months. I will see to that. All you need concern yourself with is stepping back into your role as my wife.'

He made it sound so simple, Claire thought as she drove back to her flat a short time later. All she had to do was pack a bag or two and slip back into his life as if she had never been away.

Even more worrying—how many nights would pass before he expected her to slip between the sheets of his bed?

# CHAPTER SIX

THE salon was fully booked the following day, and it seemed as if every single client of Claire's had seen the press item documenting her reunion with Antonio Marcolini. All were intent on expressing their congratulations and best wishes. She smiled her way through each and every effusive comment, hoping no one would see through the fragile façade she'd put up.

Claire had refrained from telling Rebecca, her friend and employer, the finer details of her reconciliation with Antonio. How could she tell her closest friend that her estranged husband had more or less blackmailed her back into his life for the next three months?

But Rebecca must have sensed something in Claire's demeanour, and, cocking her head on one side, gave her a penetrating look. 'Claire, are you sure you're doing the right thing?' she asked. 'I mean, according to the papers he's only here for a limited time. What happens when he leaves at the end of August? Is he expecting you to go back to Italy with him?'

Claire bit her lip as she turned to fill the kettle in the small kitchen at the back of the salon. 'We haven't got around to discussing those sorts of details,' she said. 'We're taking it one day at a time, to see how things work out between us.'

Rebecca folded her arms, giving Claire a cynical look. 'So at any point he could just say *Forget it, it's over, I want a divorce.* Aren't any alarms bells ringing in your head?'

Claire puffed out a sigh. 'Look, I know it sounds a bit shaky, but he…*we* both feel it's worth a try. As he said, we were on his territory last time, and emotions were running high when we parted—or at least mine were. This way we can see if there is anything left to rebuild what we had before…before…things went wrong…'

Rebecca gave Claire's nearest arm a squeeze. 'If you need some time off to sort things out, just tell me,' she said. 'I can get Kathleen to come and fill in for you. She's been asking for the occasional day now her son's at preschool. You wouldn't be putting me out—not at all.'

'Thanks, Bex,' Claire said, with an attempt at a convincing smile. 'I'll see how it goes for now.'

Not long after her last client had left the salon door opened, and Claire looked up to see Antonio come in. She felt the ricochet of her reaction ripple its way through her as her eyes met his. Her stomach felt light and fluttery, her heart began to race, and her breathing intervals shortened.

Conscious of Rebecca's speculative look from the behind the reception desk, Claire was uncertain whether to greet him with a kiss or not. For five years she had thought of his kisses—those barely-there nibbles that had made her spine loosen, or the slow, drugging movement of his lips on hers that was a prelude to a drawn-out sensual feast, or the sexy sweep and thrust of his tongue, or the fast-paced pressure of his mouth grinding against hers as desire raced out of control.

No one had kissed her since him, Claire realised with a little jolt. She couldn't even bear the thought of anyone else claiming her lips. It didn't seem right, somehow, and not just because technically she was still married to him.

She looked up into his face, her heart giving a little kick against her breastbone when his gaze dropped to her mouth.

He slowly bent down and brushed his lips against hers, a light touchdown that made her lips instantly hungry for more. She opened her eyes to find his were half closed in a broodingly sexy manner, his focus still trained on her mouth. She moistened her dry lips with the tip of her tongue, her heart going like a piston in her chest as his mouth came back down.

It was a firmer kiss this time, purposeful, and with just the right amount of passion to awaken every nerve of awareness in Claire's body. Lightning bolts of feeling shot through her, tightly curled ribbons of need unfurling deep inside her, making her realise how desperately she still wanted him.

'Ahem…' Rebecca's discreet but diplomatic reminder that they were not alone came just as Claire had started to wind her arms around Antonio's neck.

She stepped out of his hold with a rush of colour. 'Sorry, Bex, I forgot to introduce you,' she said.

'Antonio, this is Rebecca Collins. Bex, this is Antonio Marcolini…my…er…husband.'

Claire watched as Antonio took Rebecca's hand with a smile that would have melted stone. It clearly went a long way to melting any cynical animosity Rebecca had felt previously, for she smiled back widely, congratulating him on coming to claim Claire.

'I'm so happy for you both,' she said, just short of gushing. 'I hope it all works out brilliantly for you. I've told Claire if she needs time off to spend with you, then that's fine. I have back-up. She needs a holiday in any case. She works far too hard as it is.'

Antonio drew Claire closer with one of his arms about her waist. 'I am looking forward to spending some downtime with her once the first rush of my lecture tour is over,' he said. 'I thought we might go on a second honeymoon in a few weeks' time, to somewhere warm and tropical and totally private.'

Claire fixed a smile on her face, her body already on fire at the thought of spending tonight with him in his hotel suite, let alone days and nights at a time in a tropical paradise.

There hadn't been time for a proper honeymoon the first time around. Claire had been suffering with not just morning sickness but all-day sickness, and Antonio had been sitting his final exams. Looking back, she wondered how they had lasted the year even without the tragedy of losing their baby girl. It seemed from the start everything had been pitted against them. Although in time Antonio had seemed to look forward to having their child, Claire had still felt his gradual pulling away from her. His increasing aloofness had made her overly demanding and clingy, which had achieved nothing but to drive him even further away. When she'd failed to produce a live heir he had let her go with barely a protest. That was what hurt the most. He hadn't fought for her. She had secretly hoped he would follow her back to Australia, demanding she come back to him, somehow circumventing the obstacles she had put in his way, but he had not.

Until now.

Antonio led Claire outside a few minutes later, to where she had parked her car. 'This is your car?' he asked, frowning at her.

Claire lifted her chin. 'It gets me from A to B,' she said, adding silently, *Mostly*.

She could tell he was angry, but he seemed to be working hard to control it. 'Claire, if you have been having trouble making ends meet why did you not contact me?' he asked with a brooding frown.

She shifted her eyes from his. 'I didn't want your money,' she said. 'I just wanted to get on with my life.'

No, Antonio thought with a bitter twist of his insides. She hadn't wanted *his* money, but she had thought nothing of taking his mother's. If it took him every day of the three months he was here he would find out what she had done with it.

He gave her car—and that was using the word loosely—another scathing look. She clearly hadn't been spending up big in that department. In fact, there was no indication from what he had seen so far that she lived anything but a low-key life. She owned no real estate, either private or commercial, and her work at the salon was permanent, not casual. She dressed well, but if there was anything new and crafted by a high street designer in her wardrobe he had yet to see it. The black dress she had worn the evening before he had recognised as one he had bought for her in Paris. But then someone as naturally beautiful as Claire did not need the trappings of *haute couture* to showcase her assets. He had seen her in nothing but her creamy skin and he could hardly wait to do so again.

'I forbid you to drive this heap of rust,' he said, taking her keys from her hand before she could stop him.

She glared at him. 'Give me my keys!'

He pocketed them and, capturing her outstretched hand, led her back down the street. 'I will have someone move it later,' he said. 'And I will have a new car delivered to the hotel for you tomorrow.'

She trotted alongside him, tugging at his hold, but his fingers tightened. 'I don't want a new car,' she said. 'I don't want anything from you.'

He shot her a trenchant look as he turned her round to face him. 'If I want to buy my wife a new car, I will. For God's sake, Claire, you are driving around in a death trap. Does it even have airbags?'

She pulled her mouth tight. 'No, but—'

He swore viciously and continued striding towards his own car, parked in a side street. 'I suppose you have done it deliberately?' he said, using his remote to unlock the upmarket vehicle.

'What the hell is that supposed to mean?' she asked.

His eyes lasered hers. 'Do you have any idea of what

the press would make of you driving around in that coffin on wheels? For God's sake, Claire, I am here to teach other surgeons how to repair the sort of damage people get from being drivers and passengers in unworthy road vehicles such as yours.'

'It's not an unworthy vehicle,' she said. 'It passed its registration inspection last year.'

He clicked the remote control device once they got to his car. 'How?' he asked with an indolent curl of his lip. 'Did you bribe the mechanic by offering *him* a service?'

The blue in her eyes burned like the centre of a flame as they warred with his. 'Only someone with your disgusting moral track record would think something like that,' she bit back furiously.

He held the passenger door open for her. 'I am not going to discuss this any further,' he said. 'You are not going to be driving it any more and that is final.'

Claire waited until he was behind the wheel before she spoke through tight lips. 'If you think by buying me a flash new car it will get me back into your bed, then you are not only wasting a heck of a lot of money but your time as well.'

He sent her a challenging look. 'I could get you into the back seat right now, Claire, and have you writhing beneath me within seconds.'

Claire felt her face fire up, and a traitorous pulse began deep and low in her belly. 'You would have to knock me out first,' she said with a derisive scowl.

He laughed and gunned the engine. 'I am looking forward to making you eat every one of those words, *tesoro mio.*' He thrust the car into gear. 'Every single one of them.'

Claire sat with a mutinous set to her mouth, but inside her stomach was quivering at the thought of becoming intimate with him again. When he looked at her in that smouldering way she felt as if she was going to burst into flames. Heat coursed through her. She was annoyed with herself for being so weak. What sort of wanton woman was she, to be allowing herself to fall all over again for his lethally attractive charm? Hadn't she learned her lesson by now? He was using her to keep her hands off his money. He thought far more of his inheritance than he did of her. He didn't care one iota for her. He never had. What other proof did she need? Hadn't she always known it in her heart? As much as she had longed for him to love her, she knew it was not going to happen. Not then, and not now.

Not ever.

After a few minutes of nudging his way through the clogged city streets, Antonio pulled into the parking bay of the hotel. One of the attendants opened Claire's door, while the valet parking attendant took Antonio's place behind the wheel.

Antonio took Claire's hand and led her inside the hotel to the bank of lifts. He didn't speak on the ride up to his penthouse suite, but Claire was aware of the undercurrent of tension building between them. She could feel it in his fingers where they were curled around hers, the warmth and the sensual strength searing into her flesh like a brand.

He swiped his security card and held the door of his

suite open for her, waiting until she had moved past him before he closed it with a click that made her nerves jump.

'Relax, Claire,' he said, reaching up to loosen his tie. 'I am not going to throw you to the floor and ravish you, even though I am tempted.'

Claire chewed at her lip and watched as he shrugged off his jacket, his broad chest and lean, narrow hips making her want to press herself against him and feel every hard plane of his body.

He laid his jacket over the back of one of the sofas. 'Your things were brought over from your flat earlier today,' he informed her. 'One of the housemaids has placed them in the wardrobe in my bedroom.'

Claire looked at him with eyes wide with alarm. '*Your* bedroom?' she asked. 'You mean you expect me to share your bed...like...' she gulped before she could stop herself '...straight away?'

He gave her a bland look. 'Is that going to be a problem for you?'

She let out her breath in a gust of outrage. 'Of *course* it's a problem!'

'It is a big bed, Claire,' he said. 'I am sure I will hardly notice you are there.'

'Thanks,' she said with a resentful glare. 'That makes me feel as if I should just cover up all the mirrors right now, in case they shatter to pieces if I so much as happen to glance into them.'

His dark eyes glinted with amusement as he closed the distance between them. He pushed up her chin to lock gazes with her. 'You are searching for compliments, *si*?' he asked. 'Then I will give you one.' He brought his mouth down to hers, his lips moving against hers in a leisurely fashion, exploring, tasting and teasing.

Claire couldn't hold back her response when his tongue stroked the seam of her mouth for entry; she opened her lips on a sigh, her body sagging against his as he pulled her into his hardness. His tongue explored her thoroughly, reacquainting himself with every contour of her mouth, leaving her breathless with need when he finally lifted his mouth from hers.

'Now,' he said, with that same glint of amusement darkening his eyes, 'do you feel beautiful and desirable again?'

Claire looked into his eyes and felt her resolve slip even further away. Her mouth was still tingling all over from the sensual assault of his, her heart-rate so hectic she could feel it pumping against her breastbone.

She was unable to move out of his embrace, her body locked against the rock-hard wall of his, the unmistakable probe of his erection sending her senses into overdrive.

She lowered her eyes to look at his mouth, her belly giving a little flip of excitement when she saw his tongue move out to sweep over his lips, as if he was preparing to kiss her again.

She drew in a breath as his head came down, a soft whimper escaping from her lips just before his mouth sealed hers. The pressure was light at first, but within moments it subtly increased, his tongue going in search of hers, taking the kiss to a whole new level of sensuality as his groin pulsed against hers with growing need. She could feel the rigid outline of his erection, the length of him so familiar it felt like coming home. She rubbed herself against him, relishing in the feel of him, the way he groaned deep and low in the back of his throat as his hands cupped her bottom to bring her even closer.

His kiss became even more fervent, and her response was just as fiery as their tongues duelled and danced with each other. Her breasts felt achingly alive, tense and tingling with the need to feel his hands and mouth on them.

His hands moved from her bottom to slide up under her top, his palms deliciously warm as they skated over her quivering flesh. He unhooked her bra and she let out a breath of pure pleasure when his hands cupped the weight of her breasts, his thumbs pressing against the tight buds of her nipples.

He lifted his mouth from hers and brought it to her naked breast, that first moist stroke of his tongue evoking a sharp cry of delight from Claire's throat. He suckled on her then, softly at first, his teeth scraping gently, before drawing on her with hot, wet need. The raspy skin of his jaw was like fine sandpaper over her silky skin, but it only made her need for him all the more unbearable. She writhed impatiently against him, her body telling him what she was too proud to admit out loud. Desire flowed like a torrid flame, licking along her veins, igniting her passion to fever-pitch, making her breath come in short sharp gasps as his hands moved down between their pressed bodies and cupped the swollen heat of her feminine mound. Even though two layers of fabric separated his hand from her, Claire nearly exploded with need. He stroked her through her clothes, slowly, tantalisingly, until she was arching her back, desperate for more.

'You want me, *cara*?' he asked as he brought his mouth within a breath of hers.

Claire couldn't speak, and whimpered instead, her teeth nipping at his full bottom lip in tiny, needy bites.

He smiled against her lips. 'I want to hear you say it, *mia moglie poco passionale*—my passionate little wife. Tell me you want me.'

'I want you,' she said without hesitation this time. 'Oh, God, I want you.'

The light of victory shone in his eyes, but instead of bringing his mouth back down to hers he released her and, turning his back, strode casually across the room to the mini bar. 'Would you like a drink?' he asked over one shoulder.

Claire stared at him speechlessly, her arms crossing to cover her naked breasts, her heart feeling as if it had slipped from its rightful position in her chest. He couldn't have orchestrated a more devastating way to demonstrate how weak she was where he was concerned. Kissing her into submission only to walk away as if the erotic interlude had had no effect on him at all.

'No, thank you,' she said, and with fumbling fingers tried to do up the buttons on her blouse. But her vision suddenly blurred, making the simple task impossible.

'Here,' he said, coming back over to where she was standing. 'Let me.'

Claire's heart thumped harder and harder as his steady fingers slowly but surely refastened each tiny button, her mouth trembling slightly when he got to the last ones, between her breasts. She dragged in a breath, the expansion of her chest bringing his fingers into contact with the slight swell of her right breast.

His eyes meshed with hers for a pulsing moment. 'It *will* happen, Claire,' he said, sliding his hand to the nape of her neck in a light but possessive touch that sent another shiver of sensation racing up and down her spine.

She swallowed again, not sure she would be wise to contradict him, given what had almost happened moments earlier.

*It will happen.*

Oh, how those words set her senses on full alert! She could almost feel him plunging inside her, the length and breadth of him filling her, stretching her, making her shatter into a thousand pieces of ecstasy. How many times in the past had she been his willing slave to sensuality? One look, one touch, and she had been on fire for him, her body feeling as if it was going to explode with pleasure as soon as he nudged her trembling thighs apart.

'But then,' he said, moving his hand to trail his fingers down the curve of her cheek, 'sex was never a problem for us, was it?'

Claire compressed her lips, her eyes skittering away from his. She was not going to fall for that again, to openly admit her need of him just so he could gloat over the sensual power he still had over her. He wanted to grind her pride in the dust, but she was going to do everything possible to thwart him. It would take every gram of self-control, but she would do it.

His hands settled on her waist, bringing her close to

his body. 'We were good together, were we not, Claire?' he said. 'Better than good, in fact. Do you remember the way you used to relieve me with your mouth?'

Claire's whole body quivered in response to his erotic reminder of how she had pleasured him in the past. She had been an eager learner and he had taught her well. She had done things with him she had never thought she would do with anyone. The carnal delights he had given and taken still made her blush. His eyes had always scorched her with one look—just as they were doing now.

'Don't do this…' she said, struggling to keep her voice even.

He gave her a guileless look. 'Don't do what?' he asked.

She moistened her lips, hardly realising she was doing it until she saw his eyes drop to her mouth and follow the movement. 'You're trying to destroy my pride. I know you are. It's all a game to you, isn't it? Making me admit I still want you just so you can leave me dangling.'

'I am entitled to recall our most intimate moments together, am I not?' he asked. 'I can hardly erase them from my memory. I just have to look at that soft full mouth of yours and I want to unzip my trousers and push your head down.'

'Stop it,' Claire said, putting her hands over her ears to try to block the incendiary temptation of his words. 'Stop doing this. It won't work.'

He pulled her hands away from her head and brought her up close, pelvis to pelvis, his hot, hard need against her soft, moist ache. 'What are you frightened of, *cara*?' he asked. 'That you might discover you do not hate me as much as you claim? Is that it?'

Claire refused to answer. She clamped her lips together, glaring at him, her heart pounding with a combination of anger and out-of-control desire.

'The fact is you do *not* hate me, Claire,' he said. 'You just hate the fact that you still want me.'

'I do hate you,' she said, wrenching out of his hold. 'You slept with that—'

'Damn you, Claire.' He cut her off. 'How many times do I have to tell you there was nothing going on between us?'

'Your mother told me,' Claire said, putting up her chin at a combative height. 'She told me you had been lovers for a long time and were planning to marry, but that I had ruined everything by falling pregnant. She said you would never have married me if it hadn't been for my accidental pregnancy. She said that Daniela had been unofficially engaged to you for years.'

Antonio felt every muscle in his body tense. He had broken things off with Daniela a couple of months before he had met Claire. Daniela had taken it well, having come to the conclusion herself that their relationship had run its course. She had seemed to understand his need to focus on his career. Yes, they had once or twice laughed off their respective parents' none-too-subtle hints that a marriage between them would be more than agreeable, but he had never been in love with her, and as far as he could tell she had not been in love with him.

The afternoon Claire had seen them together had been as innocent as it had been coincidental. He had been having a quiet non-alcoholic drink with a colleague, both being on call, when Daniela had turned up, having seen him from the street outside. His colleague had left after a half an hour and Daniela had stayed on, expressing her concern over how Antonio was coping with the strain at home. It had been no secret he and Claire were having problems after the stillbirth of their baby. The last couple of months had been particularly dire, with Claire's shifting moods. He had done everything in his power to help her, but it had seemed nothing he said or did was what she wanted. She had oscillated between bouts of hysterical accusation and cold stonewalling, shutting him out for days on end.

Daniela had been supportive, and, knowing him as she had for so many years, had understood his private and internal way of processing the pain of his grief in a way Claire had not been ready or willing or even able to understand.

When Claire had come across them in the foyer, hugging as they had said goodbye, she had immediately misconstrued the situation. Daniela had made a diplomatic exit, but Claire had drawn him into a blazing row out on the street, which had been interrupted by an emergency page from the hospital, where one of his patients had begun bleeding post-operatively. By the time he'd got home the following morning, after more than twelve hours of horrendously difficult surgery, Claire had packed her bags and left.

As to what Claire had just intimated about his mother, there was no way Antonio could verify that now. As far as he knew Claire had demanded a large sum of money from his mother, and once his mother had written the cheque Claire had taken it and left the country. He had arrived at the airport just as her plane had taken off. The anger he had felt at that moment had carried him through the weeks and months ahead, and it had been refuelled every time Claire had refused to answer her phone or respond to his e-mails. Pride had prevented him chasing after her, even though not a day had gone past when he hadn't considered it. He knew it had been stubborn of him, leaving it so long, but he was not the type to beg and plead. He had finally accepted she had moved on with her life, and he had more or less done the same. It had only been when she had started the divorce process that he'd realised what was at stake—and not just his money. They had unfinished business between them, and this time around it was going to be done on his terms and his terms only.

'Perhaps you misunderstood what my mother said,' Antonio offered. 'Her English is not quite as good as it could be.'

Claire's blue-green eyes sent him a caustic glare. 'I know what I heard, Antonio,' she said. 'And besides, your mother speaks perfectly understandable English. Why don't you ask her what she said to me that night? Go on—call her up and ask her. Put the phone on speaker. She can hardly deny it with me standing right here listening to every word.'

Antonio sent splayed fingers through his hair again, releasing a breath that caught on something deep inside his chest on its exit. 'I do not wish to upset my mother right now,' he said. 'She has not been well since the death of my father.'

She gave a disdainful snort. 'You Italians really

know how to stick together, don't you? I know blood is thicker than water and all that, but Marcolini blood is like concrete.'

'It is not about taking sides, Claire,' he said. 'The issues that brought about our estrangement need to be addressed by you and me personally. I do not want to drag in a jury on either side to complicate things any further.'

'What about Daniela?' she asked. 'Have you spoken to *her* lately?'

'No, not lately,' he answered. 'She got married about a year ago, to a friend of one of my cousins who lives in Tuscany. She is expecting a baby; I am not sure how far along she is now—pretty close to delivery, I should think. I have not spoken to her since my father's funeral.'

Claire tried to ignore the deep stab of pain she felt every time she heard of someone else's pregnancy. She seriously wondered sometimes if she would ever be able to feel happy and hopeful for another mother-to-be. How could they be so complacent, so assured of a healthy delivery? Did they really think a good diet and moderate exercise would guarantee them a live baby? She had done all that and more, and look where it had led. She had gone home empty-handed, shattered, shell-shocked. Every tiny bootie and delicately embroidered and knitted outfit had screamed at her from the walls of the beautifully decorated nursery she had seen to herself: where is the baby for all this stuff?

There had been no baby.

Instead there had been a tiny urn of ashes which Claire had carried all the way back to Australia, to give her daughter the interment she felt her baby deserved.

'If my mother somehow misinformed you about my relationship with Daniela, I am deeply sorry,' Antonio's voice broke through her painful thoughts. 'The only excuse I can offer on her behalf is that she was probably concerned our marriage was on the rocks, and thought it would help you to come to some sort of decision over whether or not to continue with it.'

Claire hugged her arms close to her chest, her teeth savaging her bottom lip as she thought about Antonio's explanation for his mother's behaviour. It sounded reasonable on the surface. Their marriage certainly hadn't been a rose-strewn pathway, and they hadn't exactly been able to hide it from his family. Claire cringed at the thought of how often she had sniped at Antonio in their presence towards the end.

Doubts started to creep up and tap her on the shoulder with ghost-like fingertips. What if she had got it totally wrong? What if what she had seen that day had been exactly as Antonio had tried to explain it at the time?

Claire's own insecurities, which had plagued her from the beginning of their hasty marriage, had made her vulnerable to suggestion. She had immediately jumped to the conclusion Daniela and Antonio had enjoyed a mid-afternoon tryst in the hotel that day. She had not for a moment considered any other explanation. But then maybe she hadn't wanted to? Claire thought in retrospect. Maybe Antonio was right about his mother. Rosina Marcolini had been concerned her daughter-in-law was miserably unhappy, and had been so from the start. She had probably assumed Claire was no longer in love with her son, so had given her a way out of the situation. Rosina had obviously told her son it was Claire who had asked her for money, not she who had offered it, but proving it now was going to be difficult— unless she could challenge his mother face to face.

Claire looked up at Antonio. 'When you didn't come home at all that night I assumed you were with Daniela.'

He frowned at her. 'But don't you remember I got an emergency page to go back to Theatre?' he asked. 'When I saw how bad things were with the patient I asked one of the theatre staff to call you to let you know I was going to be late. She tried several times to call, but each time it was engaged or went through to the message service. In the end I told her to give up, as I did not want to be distracted from the difficult case I was working on. The patient was in a bad way and I needed to focus.'

Claire bit her lip again. She had been so angry and upset she had turned her mobile off and left the landline off the hook. It had only been after Antonio's mother had dropped by and had that short but pointed conversation with her that she'd decided to pack her bags and leave.

Antonio came closer and took her hands in his. 'I got home at six in the morning to find you had gone,' he said. 'I lost valuable time thinking you had gone to stay with one of the friends you had made from the Italian class you attended. By the time it was a reasonable hour to call one of them to check you had already boarded the plane. I got to the airport just in time to see it take off. I was angry—angrier than I had ever been in my life. I could not jump on the next plane to follow you as I had patients booked in for weeks ahead. So I decided to let you go. I thought perhaps some time with your family would help you. God knows nothing I did ever seemed to work. But when you consistently refused to take my calls I realised it was over. I thought it was best you got on with your life while I got on with mine.'

Claire lowered her gaze to look at their linked hands. There were no guarantees on their current relationship. He had not made any promise of extending their reconciliation beyond the three-month period. She knew he desired her, but then he was in a foreign country without a mistress at the ready. What better way to fill in the time than with his wayward wife—the one who had got away, so to speak? A man had his pride, after all, and Antonio Marcolini had more than his fair share of it. Claire had done the unthinkable to him. Walking out on him without once begging to be taken back.

This set-up he had orchestrated might very well be a cleverly planned plot to serve his own ends. He knew a divorce would be costly; he no doubt realised he had to keep her sweet as so much was now at stake—his father's millions, for one thing. A temporary affair would stall divorce proceedings for several months. Long enough for him to find some way out of handing her millions of dollars in settlement.

She pulled her hands out of his. 'I think you did the right thing in leaving me to get on with my life,' she said. 'We both needed time to regroup.'

'Perhaps,' he said, looking at her for a long moment. 'But five years is a long time, Claire.'

'Yes, and I needed every minute of it,' she said, with another lift of her chin.

His mouth thinned. 'How many lovers have there been? How many men have come and gone from your bed?'

Her eyes flashed at him. 'I hardly see what business that is of yours.'

He reached for her hands again, tethering her to him with long, strong fingers. 'How soon did you replace me?' he asked, holding her gaze with the searing heat of his.

She tried to get out of his hold but his fingers tightened. 'Why do you want to know?' she asked, glaring up at him.

His jaw tensed, a nerve at the side of his mouth pulsing like a miniature hammer beneath his skin. 'Have you had casual affairs, or something more permanent?' he asked.

'There's been no one permanent,' Claire said, tugging at his hold again. 'Now, let me go. You're hurting me.'

He looked down at his hands around her wrists and loosened his hold without releasing her. His thumbs began a slow stroke of the underside of each wrist, making her spine lose its rigid stance. Claire closed her eyes against the tide of longing that flowed through her. His body was so close she could feel its tempting warmth. The urge to feel his hardness against her again was suddenly irresistible, and she tilted towards him before she could stop herself. It was a betraying movement, but she was beyond caring. For some reason his demonstration of jealousy had stirred her, making her wonder if he felt something for her after all. It had been so long since she had felt anything but this aching sadness and emptiness inside. Would it be so very wrong to succumb to a moment of madness? Making love with Antonio would make her forget everything but the magic of his touch, how he could make her feel, how he could make her body explode time and time again with passion. It was what she wanted; it was what they both wanted.

Antonio held her from him. 'No, Claire,' he said firmly. 'Not like this. Not in anger and recrimination.'

Claire looked up at him in confusion. 'I thought your whole idea was to get me back into your bed as quickly as possible?'

His expression left her little to go on. 'I am not denying my intention of resuming a physical relationship with you, Claire, but if I were to follow through on your invitation just now I am sure you would hate me all the more tomorrow.'

She raised her brows at him. 'Scruples, Antonio?' she asked. 'Well, well, well—who would have thought?'

He stepped away from her, his mouth once again pulled into a taut line. 'If you would like to shower and change, we have a charity function to attend this evening,' he said. 'The dress is formal. You have just under an hour to get ready.'

Claire frowned. 'You expect me to come with you?'

His look was ruthlessly determined. 'I expect you to be by my side, as any other loving wife would want to be. No public displays of temper, Claire, do you understand?'

She pressed her lips together in resentment, not trusting herself to speak.

'I said, do you understand?' he repeated, pinning her with his coal-black gaze.

She lifted her chin. 'I hate you, Antonio,' she said. 'Just keep thinking about that tonight, while I am hanging off your arm and smiling at the cameras like a mindless puppet. I *hate* you.'

He shrugged off her vitriol as smoothly as he did his jacket; he hooked his finger under the collar of it, his eyes still holding hers. 'Just think how much more you are going to hate me when I have you begging in my arms, *tesoro mio*.'

Claire swung away from him, anger propelling her towards the bathroom. She slammed the door behind her, but even under the stinging spray of the shower she could still feel the promise of his words lighting a fire beneath her skin. Every surface the water touched reminded her of how he had touched her in the past: her breasts, her stomach, her lower back and thighs, and that secret place where the tight pearl of her womanhood was swollen with longing for the friction of his body. She hated herself for still wanting him. It made her feel like a lovesick fool who had no better sense than to get her fingers burned twice. That she had been a lovesick fool the first time round was more than obvious to her now. Antonio had probably been laughing at her gaucheness from the start of their affair. She had been a novelty to him—a girl from the bush, an innocent and naïve girl who had been knocked off her feet by his sophisticated charm.

Claire turned off the shower and reached for a towel with grim determination. She would show him just how much she had grown up and wised up over the last five years. He might think he could cajole her back into his bed as easily as he had the first time, but this time around she was not going down without a fight.

# CHAPTER SEVEN

ANTONIO was flicking through some documents on his lap when Claire came out of the bedroom, close to forty-five minutes later. She felt his gaze run over her, taking in her upswept hair, the perfection of her understated make-up, and the flow and cling of her evening dress, in a fuchsia-pink that highlighted the creamy texture of her skin and the blue-green of her eyes.

He put his papers to one side and rose to his feet. 'You look very beautiful, Claire,' he said. 'But you have forgotten something.'

Claire frowned and put a hand up to check both her earrings were in place. 'What?'

He picked up her left hand. 'You are not wearing your wedding and engagement rings.'

Claire felt her stomach go hollow. 'That's because I no longer have them,' she said, not quite able to hold his look.

He brought up her chin with the end of his finger, locking his gaze with hers. 'You sold them?' he asked, with a glint of anger lighting his eyes from behind.

'No,' she said, running her tongue across her lipgloss. 'They were stolen not long after I got back from Italy.

My flat was broken into one day when I was at work. My rings were the only things they got away with. The police said the burglars had probably been disturbed by someone and took what they could and bolted.'

His finger stayed on her chin for several heart-chugging seconds. 'Were the rings covered by an insurance policy?'

'No…I couldn't afford it, and—'

'That is not true, though—is it, Claire?' he said, with that same glitter of simmering anger in his diamond-hard gaze. 'You could well afford it, but you chose to spend the money my mother gave you on other things.'

Pride made Claire's back stiffen. 'So what if I did?' she said. 'What are you going to do about it?'

His hand dropped from her face as if he didn't trust himself to touch her. 'We will be late if we do not leave now,' he said tersely.

Claire followed him out to the lifts. The smooth ride down was conducted in a crackling silence. As soon as the doors swished open he put a hand at her elbow and escorted her to a waiting limousine. She pasted a stiff smile on her face for the benefit of the hotel staff and their driver, but inside she was seething. Acting the role of his reconciled wife was going to be much more difficult than she had first imagined. There was so much bitterness between them, so much ingrained distrust and resentment.

Antonio leaned forward to close the panel separating them from the driver. As he sat back one of his thighs brushed Claire's, and she automatically shifted along the seat.

He gave her a smouldering look that sent a shiver down her spine. 'You did not find my touch so repulsive an hour or so ago, Claire.'

She sent him a haughty glare in the vain hope of disguising her reaction to him. 'I must have been out of my mind. I can think of nothing I want less than to sleep with you again.'

He smiled a lazy smile as he moved closer, until he was touching her thigh to thigh, his hand capturing one of hers. Claire flinched at his touch, and he frowned and looked down at the faint bracelet of fingertip bruises he had unknowingly branded her with earlier.

His smile disappeared and a heavy frown furrowed his brow. He picked up her other hand and turned it over, ever so gently. '*I* did this?' he asked in a husky tone as he met her eyes.

Claire swallowed tightly. His touch was achingly gentle now, his fingers like feathers brushing over the barely-there bruises. His eyes were so dark, intensely so, as if the pupils had completely taken over his irises. Her heart began to thud, in an irregular rhythm that made her chest feel constrained.

'It's n-nothing…' she said with a slight wobble in her voice. 'I probably knocked myself against something…'

He was still frowning as he looked back at her wrists. 'Forgive me,' he said, low and deep. 'I had forgotten how delicately you are made.'

Claire held her breath as he lifted each of her wrists in turn to his mouth, the soft salve of his kisses stirring her far more deeply than the words of his apology could ever do. His lips were a butterfly movement against her sensitive skin, a teasing of the senses that made her realise how terribly unguarded she was around him. Her heart shifted inside her chest like a tiny insect's wings, beating inside the narrow neck of a bottle.

His eyes came back to hers, his fingers loose as they held her hands within his. 'Do they hurt?' he asked in a gravel-like tone.

She shook her head, still not trusting herself to speak. She felt choked-up, emotion piling right to the back of her throat in a great thick wad of feeling she couldn't swallow down, no matter how hard she tried. Her eyes began to burn with the effort of keeping back tears, and she had to blink rapidly a couple of times to stave them off. This was the Antonio she had fallen so deeply in love with all those years ago. How was she supposed to resist him when he sabotaged her resolve not with force but with tenderness?

Antonio released her hands with a sigh. 'We have to sort this out, Claire. I know you think I have engineered this to my advantage, but we both have to be absolutely sure about where this ends up.'

Claire could already guess where it was going to end up. She was halfway there already: back in love with him, back in his arms, dreaming of a happy ever after when there were no guarantees she would ever have a nibble at the happiness cherry again. She could almost taste the hard pip of reality in her mouth. He didn't love her. He had never loved her the way she longed to be loved—the way her mother had never been loved, even after three desperate tries to get it right. Was Claire facing the same agonising destiny? A life of frustrated hopes? Girlhood dreams turned to dust as thick as that lining the roads of the Outback where she had grown up?

The limousine purred to a halt outside a convention center, and within moments the press were there to capture the moment when Antonio Marcolini and his wife, newly reconciled, were to exit the vehicle.

Claire thought she had hidden her discomfiture well as she got out of the car with Antonio by her side, but somehow, in the blur of activity and the surging press of the crowd, she met his gaze for the briefest of moments and realised she had not fooled him—not even for a second.

He offered her his arm and she looped hers through it with a smile that tugged painfully at her face. 'Do we have to do this?' she whispered with a rueful grimace. 'Everyone is looking at us.'

He picked up a tendril of her curly hair and secured it behind her ear. 'We have to, *cara*,' he said, meshing his gaze with hers. 'We need to show ourselves in public as much as possible.'

Claire drew in a scratchy breath and, straightening her shoulders, walked stride by stride with him into the convention center. But for some reason she felt sure he hadn't been referring to the glamorous evening ahead, but more about the night that was to follow…

The table they were led to was at the front of the ballroom, where the other guests were already seated. Each person stood and greeted Antonio formally, before turning to greet her with smiles of speculative interest.

Drinks were served as soon as they sat down, and Claire sipped unenthusiastically at a glass of white wine as convivial conversation was bandied back and forth around her. She smiled in all the right places, even said one or two things that contributed to the general atmosphere of friendliness, but still she felt out on a ledge. She didn't belong here—not amongst his colleagues, not amongst his friends. She had never belonged, and somehow sitting here, with the lively chatter going on around her, it brought it home to her with brutal force. Even listening with one ear to one of the women at the table describing the latest antics of her toddler son felt like a knife going through Claire's chest. Her mind filled with those awful moments after her baby had been delivered, the terrible silence, the hushed whispers, the agonised looks, the shocking realisation that all was not as it was supposed to be.

'Claire?'

Claire suddenly realised Antonio was addressing her, his eyes dark as the suit he was wearing as they meshed with hers. 'Would you like to dance?'

She sent the tip of her tongue out to sweep away yet another layer of lipgloss. 'Dance?'

He smiled—Claire supposed for the benefit of those around them, watching on indulgently. 'Yes,' he said. 'You were very good at it, I seem to remember.'

Claire lowered her gaze to stare at the contents of her glass. 'I haven't danced for ages...'

'It does not matter,' he said, taking her by the hand and gently pulling her to her feet. 'This number is a slow waltz. All you have to do is shuffle your feet in time with mine.'

She had a lot more to do than shuffling her feet, but

after a while Claire relaxed into it, relishing the feel of Antonio's arms around her as he led her in a dance that was a slow as it was sensual. Each step seemed to remind her of how well-matched their bodies were, the union of male and female, the naturalness of it, the ebb and flow of moving in time with each other as if they had been programmed to respond in such a way. His thigh pushed hers backwards, hers moved his forwards, and then they moved together in a twirl that sent the skirt of her long dress out in an arc of vivid pink.

'See?' Antonio said, smiling down at her as he led her into another smooth glide across the floor. 'It is like riding a bike, *si*? You never forget the moves.'

Claire could feel her body responding to his closeness. His pelvis was hard against hers, with not even the space for a silk handkerchief to pass between their bodies. She felt the stirring of his body, the intimate surge of his male flesh that made her ache for his possession all over again. She tried to convince herself it was just a physical thing: he was a virile man, she was a young healthy woman, and the chemistry that had brought them together in the first place had been reawakened. Sex with an ex or an estranged partner was commonplace. The familiarity of the relationship and yet that intriguing element of forbidden fruit made resisting the urge to reconnect in the most elemental way possible sometimes unstoppable. She could feel that temptation now; it was like a pulse deep in her body, a rhythm of longing that would not go away no matter how much she tried to ignore it.

'You are starting to tense up on me,' Antonio said. He

ran his hands down the length of her spine as the number came to an end, and an even slower, more poignant one took its place. 'Relax, *cara*, there are people watching us.'

How could she possibly relax with his hands resting in the sensitive dip of her spine like that? Claire felt as if every nerve was set on super-vigilance, waiting for the stroke and glide of his next touch. Her belly quivered and her skin lifted in a fine layer of goosebumps as she met his dark, intense gaze.

'I'm not used to such big crowds these days,' she said. 'I haven't been out for ages. Compared to you, I live a very quiet life.'

He rested his chin on the top of her head as they moved in time with the music. 'There is nothing wrong with living a quiet life,' he said. 'I sometimes wish mine was a little less fast paced.'

Claire breathed in the scent of him as they circled the floor again. It felt so right to be in his arms, as if she belonged there and nowhere else. The trouble was she wasn't sure how long she was likely to be there. He seemed very intent on sorting out the train wreck of their previous relationship, but his motives for doing so were highly suspect.

It was so hard to tell what Antonio was thinking, let alone feeling. He had always been so good at keeping his cards close to his chest. She, on the other hand, wore her heart on her sleeve and had done so to her own detriment. She had made herself far too vulnerable to him from the outset, and now she felt as if she was doing it all again. He knew he had her in the palm of his hand. He knew she would not do anything that would jeopardise her brother's well-being. That was his trump card, and she was too cowardly to call his bluff, even though she dearly wanted to.

But even without the threat of Isaac facing the authorities, Claire suspected she was in too deep now to extricate herself. She couldn't quite get rid of the nagging fear she had got her wires twisted over his alleged affair with Daniela Garza. If so, she had ruined both of their lives by impulsively leaving him. The very thing she lectured her brother Isaac on time and time again was the very thing she most hated in herself: acting before thinking. How would she ever be able to forgive herself if she had got it wrong?

Antonio skilfully turned her out of the way of another couple on the dance floor, his arms protective around her. 'You look pensive, *cara*,' he said. 'Is something troubling you?'

Claire worried her bottom lip with her teeth, finally releasing it to look up at him. 'If you weren't having an affair with Daniela, why didn't you share the same bed as me after we lost the baby? You never came to me—not once.'

His expression tightened, as if pulled by invisible strings underneath his skin. 'That was because I thought it better to leave you to rest for the first couple of days, without me taking calls from the hospital late at night and disturbing you. It was clear after a while that you did not want me to rejoin you. You seemed to want to blame me for everything. I was damned no matter what I did, or what I said or did not say.'

Claire felt the dark cavern of her grief threatening to open up and swallow her all over again. He was right—

she *had* blamed him for distancing himself. But hadn't she done the very same thing? She had been so lost, so shell-shocked at her loss, it had made it so hard for her to reach out to him for comfort. She had wanted to, many times, but when he'd taken to sleeping in the spare room, or staying overnight at the hospital, she had lain in the sparse loneliness of the bed they had shared and cried until her eyes had been almost permanently red-rimmed and swollen.

She had never seen him shed a single tear for their tiny daughter. She knew people grieved in different ways, but Antonio and his family had all seemed much the same in dealing with the stillbirth. They'd simply got on with their lives as if nothing had happened. Apart from the first day after Claire came out of hospital the baby had never been mentioned—or at least not in Claire's presence. There had been a brief christening in the hospital, but there had been no funeral. Antonio's parents had not thought it appropriate, and in the abyss of her grief she had gone along with their decision because she had not wanted to face the heartbreaking drama of seeing a tiny coffin carried into a church. It had only been later, once she was back in Australia, that she had felt ready to give her daughter a special place to rest.

The music had stopped, and Claire grasped at the chance to visit the ladies' room to restore some sort of order to her emotions. She mumbled something to Antonio about needing to touch up her lipgloss and, conscious of his gaze following her every step of the way, made her way to the exit.

She locked herself inside one of the cubicles in the

ladies' room and took several deep breaths, her throat tight and her eyes aching with the bitter tears of regret.

For all this time she had relished placing the blame for the collapse of their relationship on Antonio. She had so firmly believed he had betrayed her. But in hindsight she could see how immature and foolish she had been right from the start. She had been no more ready for marriage than he had; she had been too young—not just in years, but in terms of worldly experience. He at least had had the maturity to accept responsibility for the pregnancy, and he hadn't even insulted her by insisting on a paternity test, as so many other men might have done. How had she not realised that until now? He might not have loved her, but at least he hadn't deserted her. He had stood by her as much as his demanding career had allowed.

Was it really fair to blame him for not being there for the delivery? He was a surgeon, for God's sake. He had the responsibility of other people's lives in his hands every single day. She hadn't even asked him why he hadn't made it in time. She had jumped to the conclusion that he had deliberately avoided being there because he hadn't wanted the baby in the first place—which was yet another hasty assumption she had made. He might have been initially taken aback by the news of her pregnancy, but as the weeks and months had gone on he had done his best to come with her to all of her prenatal appointments and check-ups. She had even caught him several times viewing the ultrasound DVD they had been given of the baby, wriggling its tiny limbs in her womb. He had bought a baby name book for her, and had sat with his hand gently resting on her belly as they looked through it together.

Claire had never realised how physically ill remorse could make one feel. It was like a burning pain deep inside, gnawing at her, each savage twinge a sickening reminder of how she had thrown away her one chance at happiness. Yes, they had experienced a tragedy, one that neither of them would ever be able to recover from fully, but this was the only opportunity she would get to do something to heal the disappointment and hurt of the past. It was optimistic, and perhaps a little unrealistic, to hope that Antonio would fall in love with her this time around, but she had three months to show him her love was big enough for both of them.

When she came out a few minutes later, Antonio rose from the table to hold out her chair for her, his dark eyes moving over her features like a searchlight, a small frown bringing his brows together. 'Is everything all right, *cara*?' he asked. 'You were away for so long I was about to send someone in to find you.'

Claire shifted her gaze and sat down. 'I'm fine; there was a bit of a queue, that's all.'

The woman seated opposite leaned forward to speak to her. 'I read about the reconciliation with your husband in the paper this morning. I am sure you'll be very happy this time around. I've been married to John for thirty-five years this September. We've had our ups and downs, but that's what marriage is all about—give and take and lots and lots of love.'

Claire stretched her mouth into a smile. 'Thank you.

I am sure there will be plenty of hard work ahead, but, as you say, that is what marriage is all about.'

'My husband is a plastic surgeon as well,' the woman who had introduced herself as Janine Brian continued. 'He's very impressed with some of the new techniques Antonio is demonstrating. You must be very proud of him. He has brought new life and hope to so many people all over the world.'

'Yes…yes, I am,' Claire said, glancing at Antonio, who was now deep in conversation with one of the other guests at the table. She felt her breath lock in her throat as he turned his head to look at her, as if he had sensed her gaze resting on him.

She couldn't stop staring at him; it was like seeing him for the very first time. She marvelled at how handsome he looked in formal dress, how his tuxedo brought out the darkness of his eyes and hair, and how the stark whiteness of his dress shirt highlighted the deep olive tone of his skin. His mouth was tilted at a sexy angle, as if he knew exactly where her thoughts were leading. How could he possibly know how much she wanted to explore every inch of his body as she had done so often in the past? Could he see the hunger in her eyes? Could he sense it in the way her body was tense and on edge, her hands restless and fidgety, her legs crossing and uncrossing under the table? Desire was an unruly force in her body. She felt it running like a hot river of fire beneath her skin, searing her, branding her inside and out with the scorching promise of his possession.

'You two are just so romantic,' Janine said with an indulgent smile. 'Look at them, John.' She elbowed her husband in the ribs. 'Aren't they the most-in-love couple you've ever seen?'

Claire felt a blush steal over her cheeks as Antonio came back to sit beside her. He placed an arm around her shoulders, drawing her close. 'I was a fool to let her get away the first time,' he said. 'It will not be happening again, I can assure you.'

'Well, you know what they say: there's nothing better than making up in the bedroom,' Janine said. 'That's how we got our three kids, wasn't it, darling?'

'Janine…' John Brian frowned.

'What did I say?' Janine frowned back.

'It is OK, John,' Antonio said, giving Claire's shoulder a little squeeze. 'Claire and I cannot expect everyone to be tiptoeing around the subject of children for the rest of our lives.'

Janine Brian's face fell. 'Oh, dear…I completely forgot. John did tell me about… Oh, how awfully insensitive you must think me. I'm so, *so* sorry.'

Claire gave the distressed woman a reassuring smile, even though it stretched at her mouth uncomfortably. 'Please don't be upset or embarrassed,' she said. 'Each day has become a little easier.'

The conversation was thankfully steered in another direction when the waiter appeared with the meals for their table. Claire forced herself to eat as if nothing was wrong for Janine's sake, but later she would barely recall what it was she had eaten.

After the meals were cleared away, Antonio was introduced by the chairman of the charity. Claire watched as he moved up to the lectern, which had been set up with a large screen and data projector. After thanking the chairman and board members, Antonio spoke of the work he carried out in reconstructive surgery under the auspices of FACE. He showed pictures of some of the faces he had worked on, including several from Third World countries, which the charity had sponsored by bringing patients to Rome for surgery to be performed.

Claire looked at one of the young children he had worked on. The little girl, who was seven or eight, had been born with hyperteliorism, a congenital condition which presented as a broad face with wide, separated eyes and a flat nose. Fixing it required major cranial-facial reconstruction, with a team of three surgeons: a neurosurgeon, a facial maxillary surgeon and a plastic surgeon. In this case it had been Antonio. The team had operated for twelve hours to give the little girl a chance at a normal life, without shame or embarrassment over her unusual appearance. The before and after photographs were truly amazing. So too were the happy smiles of the child's parents and the little girl herself.

Once Antonio had finished his presentation he took some questions from the floor before returning to the table to thunderous applause.

The band began to play again and Antonio reached for Claire's hand. 'Let's have one more dance before we go home,' he suggested.

Claire moved into his arms without demur, her own arms going around his neck as his went around her back, holding her in an intimate embrace that perfectly matched the slow rhythm of the ballad being played.

'I thought you handled Janine Brian's little slip very graciously,' Antonio commented after a moment or two.

She looked up at him with a pained expression. 'Thank you,' she said. 'But you're right in saying we can't expect people to avoid the subject of babies all the time. I have friends with little ones, and I have taught myself to enjoy visiting them, even babysitting them without envy.'

He looked down at her for a beat or two. 'That is very brave of you, Claire.'

She gave him another little grimace before she lowered her gaze to stare at his bow tie. 'Not really... There are days when it's very hard...you know...thinking about her...'

Antonio felt the bone-grinding ache of grief work its way through him; it often caught him off guard—more lately than ever. Being with Claire made him realise how much losing a child affected both parents, for years if not for ever. The mother bore the brunt of it, having carried the baby in her womb, not to mention having the disruption of her hormones during and after the delivery. But the father felt loss too, even if it wasn't always as obvious as the mother's. Certainly the father hadn't carried the child, but that didn't mean he didn't feel the devastation of having failed as a first-time father.

Antonio had grown up with an understanding of the traditional role of husband and father as being there to protect his wife and children. He might have gone into marriage a little ahead of schedule, due to the circumstances of Claire's accidental pregnancy, but when their baby had died it had cut at the very heart of him. He had felt so helpless, swamped with grief, but unable to express it for the mammoth weight of guilt that had come down on top of it.

He wondered if Claire knew how much he blamed himself, how he agonised over the 'what if' questions that plagued him in the dark hours of the night. He still had nightmares about arriving at the delivery suite to find her holding their stillborn baby in her arms. A part of him had shut down at that point, and try as he might he had never been able to turn it back on. He felt as if he had fallen into a deep, dark and silent well of despair, locked in a cycle of grief and guilt that to this day he carried like an ill-fitting harness upon his shoulders.

The music changed tempo, and even though she didn't say a word Antonio felt Claire's reluctance to stay on the dance floor with him. He could feel it in her body, the way she stiffened when he drew her close. Whether she was fighting him or fighting herself was something he had not yet decided. But then he had the rest of the night to do so, and do so he would.

He felt a rush of blood in his groin at the thought of sinking into her slick warmth again. The tight cocoon of her body had delighted him like no other. It made his skin come alive with sensation thinking about her hands skating over him the way they'd used to, tentatively, shyly, and then boldly once her confidence with him had grown. The feel of her soft mouth sucking on him that first time had been unbelievable. He had felt as if the top of his head was going to come off, so powerful had been his response. He wanted to feel it all again, every single bit of it—her touch, her taste, the tightness of her that made his body tingle for hours afterwards.

'Time to go home?' he asked as he linked his fingers with hers.

Her cheeks developed a hint of a blush. 'Yes…if you like…' she said, her gaze falling away from his.

Antonio led her back to the table, from where, after a few words of farewell to the other guests, he escorted her out to the waiting limousine. It would take them back to his hotel, where she would have to share his bed in his arms or spend the night alone on the sofa.

It would be interesting to see which she chose.

# CHAPTER EIGHT

IT WAS a mostly silent trip on the way back to the hotel.

Antonio looked at Claire several times on the way, but each time she had her gaze averted, and her fingers were restless as they toyed with the catch of her evening purse.

'Do I unsettle you so much, *cara*?' he asked, as the car purred to a smooth halt outside the hotel.

She turned her gaze on him, a shadow of uncertainty shining in their ocean-blue and green depths. 'A little, I guess,' she confessed as he helped her out of the car.

Antonio led her into the hotel, his hand at her elbow, his stride matching her shorter one. He pressed the call button for the lift, and as he waited for it to come turned to look at her. 'I told you, Claire, we will not resume a physical relationship until we are both ready. I am not going to force myself on you. You can be absolutely sure of that.'

She rolled her lips together as she lifted and then dropped her gaze again. 'I'm not sure what I want... that's the problem...I feel confused right now...'

He tipped up her chin with the end of his index

finger. 'I want you,' he said. 'I think you know that. That is something that has not changed in the last five years.'

'But is this right…what we're doing?' she asked, the tip of her tongue sneaking out to sweep over her lips. 'It seems to me we're back together for all the wrong reasons.'

The lift came to a stop at Antonio's penthouse floor, and he held the doors open with his forearm for Claire to move past.

He swiped his key and led her into the suite, closing the door behind him. 'We have a past, Claire,' he said, securing her gaze with his. 'We have to deal with it one way or the other.'

She bit her bottom lip, her throat moving up and down over a little swallow. 'But is this the right way?' she asked. 'What if we make more problems than we've got now?'

'Like what?' he asked, pulling at his bow tie.

She gnawed at her lip again, releasing it after a second or two to say, 'I don't know…it's just I don't want any misunderstandings to develop between us.'

He tossed his bow tie and his jacket on the nearest sofa. 'The whole point of this exercise is to see if what we started out with is still there, hidden under the sediment of our separation,' he said heavily. 'I do not want to go through the messy process of a divorce only to take the same unresolved issues to another relationship.'

Claire felt her heart clamp with pain. 'So this arrangement you've orchestrated between us is basically an experiment?' she asked, frowning at him.

He held her look for a moment before he blew out a sigh. 'I want to get on with my life, Claire. You need to get on with yours. Neither of us can do that until we work through this.'

She pulled herself upright and faced him squarely. 'So what you're really saying is you need to have a three-month affair with me to see if there is anything worth picking over before you move on to the next woman you want to get involved with. Is that it?'

He gave her a brooding look. 'No, that is not it at all.'

Claire felt as if her hopes and dreams were about to be shattered all over again. Would she ever be anything more than a fill-in for him? Was it too much to ask him to care something for her?

Her rising despair made her voice come out sharper than she had intended. 'Then what the hell is it about, Antonio? I just don't know what you want from me.'

He took her gently but firmly by the shoulders, his dark eyes almost black as they pinned hers. 'I think deep down you know exactly what I want from you, *cara*,' he said and, swooping down, captured her mouth with the searing warmth of his.

Claire had no hope of resisting such a potently passionate kiss. Flames of need licked along her veins, sending her heart-rate soaring as Antonio's tongue probed for entry, the hot searching heat of him making her whimper in response. She could feel her lips swelling under the pressure of his, her body melting into his embrace as he pulled her closer. She felt the erotic ridge of his erection against her—a heady reminder of all the passion they had shared in the past and how earth-shattering it had been.

His mouth continued its sensual assault on her senses

as his hands went from her waist to her lower back, the gentle pressure of his hand against her lumbar region bringing her right up against the hard probe of his arousal. Her belly quivered at that intimate contact, her legs becoming unsteady as a raging tide of desire flooded her being.

His kiss became deeper and more insistent, and Claire responded with the same ardour. She took his full bottom lip in her teeth, gently tugging, then sucking, and then sweeping her tongue over it in a caress that brought a groan from deep inside him.

His hands pressed her even harder against him; even the barrier of his clothes did not lessen the sensation of feeling the potent length of him so close to the heart of her need. Her body was already preparing itself; she could feel the slick moistness gathering between her thighs, her breasts tight and aching for the feel of his mouth and hands.

His kiss became even more urgent as she moulded herself against him, his tongue more insistent as it mated with hers.

She reached between them and shaped him with her fingers, her mouth still locked under the scorching heat of his. He made another guttural sound of pleasure, and she increased the pace of her stroking, up and down, glorying in the licence to touch him, to feel him pulsing with such intense longing for her.

He dragged his mouth from hers, looking down at her with eyes so dark with arousal they looked bottomless. 'Are you sure this is what you want, *cara*?' he asked in a husky tone. 'We do not have to continue with this if you do not feel ready.'

Claire moistened her passion-swollen lips as she held his gaze. 'I'm not sure about anything,' she said. 'I can't seem to put two thoughts together in my head when you are around.'

His wry smile was intoxicatingly sexy. 'Then maybe we should not think, but instead concentrate on feeling,' he said, moving his hand to the zipper at the back of her dress and slowly but surely sliding it down until the satin pooled at her feet.

Claire felt her breath catch as his dark gaze ran over her, taking in her naked breasts, the flat plane of her stomach, the slight flare of her hips and the tiny black lace panties she was wearing.

Her breathing almost stopped altogether when he trailed a fingertip down between her breasts, circling each one before he bent his head and took each tightly budded nipple in his mouth. It was torture and pleasure rolled into one, and the sparks of fiery need shooting up and down her spine at the rasp of his tongue made every rational thought fly out of her head.

He lifted his head and, locking his gaze on hers, sent his fingertip down to the cave of her belly button, and then lower, tracing over the cleft of her body through the lace that shielded her. 'Take them off,' he commanded in a toe-curling tone.

Claire kicked off her heels and peeled off the tiny lace garment, her heart kicking in excitement as he began to undress. Becoming impatient, she helped him with the buttons of his shirt, stopping every now and again to press a hot, moist kiss to his chest, then lower and lower, until she came to the waistband of his trousers.

He shrugged his shirt off and stood with his thighs slightly apart as she undid his belt, pulling it through the loops until it joined her dress on the floor.

She heard him draw in a breath as her fingers pulled down his zipper, and then she felt him jerk in awareness when she peeled back his underwear to touch him skin on skin.

He was like satin-covered steel under her fingertips, and so aroused he was seeping with moisture. She blotted it with her fingertip and then, lifting her eyes to his, brought her finger up to her mouth and sucked on it.

'*Dio*, you are driving me crazy,' he growled, as he heeled himself out of his shoes, his trousers and underwear landing in the same heap as his belt and her dress.

Claire drew in an uneven breath as he walked her backwards towards the bed, his hands on her hips, the heated trajectory of his body setting her alight all over again. She could smell his arousal, the hint of salt and musk that was as intoxicating as the notes of citrus she could pick up from his aftershave.

'Tell me to stop, Claire, otherwise I will not be able to,' he groaned as his mouth brushed against hers.

She linked her arms around his neck, pushing her pelvis against his. 'I don't want you to stop,' she said in a breathless whisper. 'It's been such a long time...'

'You are right about that,' he said as he eased her down on the bed, his eyes devouring her all over again before he joined her. 'It has been far, far too long.'

Claire shivered as his long, strong legs brushed against her smooth ones. The arrant maleness of him had always made her heart race with excitement. The hardness of his body against her dewy softness made her feel light-headed with anticipation. She arched her spine in invitation, aching for him to pin her body with his, to drive her towards the paradise she craved.

'Not so fast, *cara*,' he said, stroking his hands over her belly, thrillingly close to where she pulsed for him. 'You know how it was between us before. It was always much more intense when we took our time.'

Claire sucked in a breath as he bent his head to her breasts, his mouth and tongue inciting her passion to an almost unbearable level. The hot trail of his kisses continued down her sternum to the tiny dish of her belly button, and then over the faint stretchmarks on both of her hips, before moving to the throbbing core of her body. Her breath skidded to a halt in her chest as his fingers gently separated her, the tender, honeyed flesh opening to his stroking touch. He set a slow but tantalising rhythm, each movement bringing her closer and closer to the release she could feel building and building inside her. Then she was there: her back lifting off the bed, her senses soaring out of control, as wave after wave of ecstasy smashed over her, rolling her, tossing and tumbling her, until she felt totally boneless, limp with satiation.

Claire reached for him, her fingers circling his hardness before she slithered down to brush her mouth against him. She felt a shudder go through him when she traced him with the point of her tongue. He was still in control—but only just. His breathing was choppy and uneven, each and every one of his muscles taut with tension as she drew him into her mouth, tasting him, tantalising him with the butterfly caress of her tongue.

'No,' Antonio growled suddenly, and pulled her away. 'I want to come inside you. I have waited so long for this.'

Claire felt her insides tremble with excitement as his body settled over her, one of his thighs nudging hers apart, his weight propped up on his elbows as he drove into her with a deep groan of satisfaction. She felt the skin of his back and shoulders lift in a shiver as her body grabbed at him hungrily, the rocking motion he began setting her alight all over again. Electrifying sensations shot through her with each stroke and smooth glide of his body in hers. She felt the tremors begin deep inside her, the ripples of reaction rolling through her as he increased his pace, each deep thrust taking her higher and higher. She felt as if her body imploded, so forceful was the release he evoked. It rocketed through her like a torpedo, making every nerve hum and sing with sensation.

Antonio's breathing quickened, his thrusts now so deep and so purposeful Claire could feel the exact moment his control finally slipped. With a deep groan he burst inside her, his body shuddering against hers as pleasure coursed through him, her tight body milking him until he collapsed in satisfaction above her.

She kept stroking his back, her fingers dancing over his muscled form, hoping the magical spell of sensuality would not be broken too quickly.

Antonio was right: this was the part they had always got right. It was the other details of their relationship they had tripped over: the involvement of relatives, the demands of his career and the loss of her independence, not to mention the vicissitudes of life, which in their case had been particularly cruel.

Antonio shifted his weight to look down at her. 'It has not changed, has it, *cara*?' he said, brushing a damp curl back from her forehead. 'Although perhaps I am wrong about that; it *has* changed—if anything it has got better.'

Claire trembled under his touch, her body acutely aware of his, still lying encased moistly in hers. 'What if it's not enough, Antonio? Physical attraction will eventually burn itself out. Then what will be left?'

His eyes were dark as pitch as they held hers. 'It has not burned out yet, in spite of our five-year hiatus. As soon as I saw you again I realised it. I wanted you back in my bed no matter what it took to get you there.'

'This can't go anywhere,' she said, dropping her gaze from his in case he saw too much of what she was feeling. She was like a toy he had decided to play with for a limited time. She had to keep reminding herself this was not for ever. He was only here for three months.

'It can go where we want it to,' he said. 'For as long as we want it to.'

Claire felt a prickle of alarm run over her bare flesh as she brought her gaze back to his. 'I'm not sure what you're saying,' she said, flicking her tongue out over her lips. 'This is temporary…isn't it?'

His gaze went to her mouth, halted, and then lifted back to hers. 'Are you on the pill?' he asked.

Something dark and fast scuttled inside Claire's chest, making her feel breathless, as if the faceless creature of fear had buried itself in the chambers of her heart. 'Um…no…' she said, unable to hold his gaze.

He nudged her chin up with the point of his finger, his dark eyes drilling into hers. 'No?'

She rolled her lips together, trying to think where she was in her cycle. 'I'm not on it at the moment...' she said, grimacing slightly.

He kept his gaze steady on hers for several heart-chugging seconds. 'Do you think you are in a safe period?' he asked with an unreadable expression.

'Yes,' she said, even though she was not quite sure. It would be disastrous if she was to fall pregnant by him, setting off another heartbreaking cycle of waiting and hoping, and yet...

Oh, God, the thought of another chance at being a mother was so very tempting. Maybe this time it wouldn't end in tragedy, in spite of the information she had sought on the internet. She had learned that after a previous incident of placental abruption the chances of a second occurring was between ten and seventeen percent. The statistics stated that whereas one out of one hundred and fifty deliveries cited a case of placental sep-aration, the severe form, where foetal death occurred, was only one in five hundred.

It was all a matter of chance...

'Are you sure?' Antonio asked, his gaze now darkened with intensity.

She nodded and eased herself away from him, hugging her knees to her chest to affect some measure of decency. 'But even if we had used a condom there's no guarantee it would have prevented a pregnancy,' she said. 'That's how it happened the last time, if you remember?'

'Yes, but only because you had not been taking the pill long enough for it to be effective,' he said.

Claire felt resentment rise up in her like a viper

wanting to strike at its tormentor. 'So you're blaming me for what happened in the past, is that it? It was my fault for being so naïve in thinking I was covered when I wasn't? We would not have had to go through any of what we went through if I had taken the time to read the leaflet in the box? Is that what you are saying?'

A deep crevasse appeared between his brows. 'I did not say that, Claire. An unplanned pregnancy can happen to anyone.'

She still felt herself bristling in spite of his response. 'Then what exactly *are* you saying?'

It seemed a long time before he answered. 'This is probably not the right time to bring up the subject of babies.'

Claire felt the faint hope she had secretly harboured in her chest deflate at his words. He was after a good time, not a long time. He was at a loose end in a foreign country. No wonder he had looked her up—hooked up with her in a blackmail bargain that would see him as the only winner at the end. He wanted no ties, no lasting consequences of their brief encounter. Just like last time he wanted a short, hot, full-on affair to compensate for the punishing hours he worked.

He also wanted revenge, she reminded herself. He wanted to have things on his terms this time. He would be the one to walk away, not her.

'I can't do this,' she said, springing off the bed to snatch up a bathrobe hanging on the back of the door. She thrust her arms through the sleeves and tied the waistband securely before she faced him again. 'I can't do casual, Antonio. I'm not built that way.'

'This is not casual, Claire,' he said, locking gazes with her. 'We are still married.'

She frowned at him, her heart fluttering in panic. 'What do you want from me?' she asked in a broken whisper.

'I want you, Claire,' he said with an intransigent look as he stepped towards her. 'This is not over. You know that. What happened in that bed just minutes ago proved it beyond any shadow of a doubt.'

Claire tried to back away from him but came up against the wall. 'What happened in that bed was a stupid mistake on my part,' she said, flattening her spine against the cold hard surface behind her. 'I got carried away with the dancing and the wine. I wasn't in my right mind. You should have known that.'

He lifted one brow in a perfect arc of derision. 'It seems to me it is only my fault when you do something you later regret,' he said.

'You're trying to make me fall in love with you, aren't you?' she asked.

He came closer, his eyes meshing with hers. 'Is that your biggest worry, *cara*?' he asked as he trailed his index finger down the curve of her cheek, before tracing over her top lip in a nerve-tingling caress.

Claire's biggest worry was how she was going to prevent a repeat of what had just occurred between them. The sex had been mind-blowing and blissfully satisfying. Even now she could feel her body responding again to his nearness. It didn't help that she was totally naked beneath the bathrobe she was wearing. She could feel the way her breasts were pushing against the soft fabric, her nipples still swollen and sensitive from his mouth. She could feel the moistness of his essence between her thighs. She could even smell the fragrance of their coupling—an intoxicating reminder of how she had fallen apart in his arms and how easily it could happen again. She was hard-wired to respond to him. No one else could affect her the way he did. The intimacy they had shared had only intensified her longing. She could feel it building in her; it was like an on-off pulse deep inside.

She was acutely aware of how he was watching her, with that dark, intelligent gaze of his, noting every nuance of her expression, every movement of her body as it stood so close to his.

He placed his hands either side of her head, on the wall behind her, not just trapping her with the brackets of his arms but with his eyes as well. 'Would falling in love with me be a problem?' he asked.

Claire ran the tip of her tongue over her lips, her chest rising and falling on an uneven breath as she looked into his deep dark gaze. 'It…it would only be a problem if it wasn't reciprocated.'

His eyes went to her mouth. 'If we fall in love then we will not need to go through a divorce,' he said, bringing his gaze back to hers. 'A good solution, *si*?'

She tightened her mouth. 'For you, maybe, but not for me,' she said. 'I'm not going to move back to Italy with you.'

He measured her with a cool, appraising look. 'You might not have a choice if you have conceived my child,' he said. 'I am not prepared to be separated by thousands of kilometres from my own flesh and blood.'

Claire felt her heart lurch, panic fluttering like startled wings inside her chest. 'If I have fallen pregnant there is no guarantee it will end in a live birth,' she said, trying to ignore the blade of pain that sliced through her at admitting it out loud. 'If you want to become a father you would be well advised to pick someone who is capable of doing the job properly.'

His eyes held hers for a tense moment before he dropped his hands from the wall. 'I am aware of the statistics, Claire,' he said. 'But with careful monitoring it may not happen again.'

'I am not prepared to risk it,' Claire said. 'If we are going to continue this farcical arrangement I want you to use protection. I will see my doctor tomorrow about arranging my own.'

Antonio watched as she pushed herself away from the wall, her arms around her middle like a shield, her eyes flashing resentment and pent-up anger against him.

He could still feel the tight clutch of her body around him, the way she had convulsed to receive every drop of his seed. He wanted her so badly it was a bone-deep ache inside him; it had never gone away, no matter how hard he had tried to ignore it. And she wanted him, even though she resented it and did her best to hide it. Her body betrayed her just as his had. And it would betray her again. Of that he was sure.

# CHAPTER NINE

CLAIRE slipped past Antonio to the plush bathroom and closed the door firmly behind her. She considered locking it, but upon inspecting the device recognised it was one of those two-way models which could be unlocked from either side of the door—no doubt installed as a safety feature, in case a guest in the hotel slipped and fell in the bathroom. She realised the only lock she really needed was a lock on her heart, but as far as she knew no such item existed. She was as vulnerable to Antonio as she had ever been—maybe even more so now she had experienced such rapture again in his arms.

She stepped into the shower stall, hoping to wash away the tingling sensations Antonio's touch had activated, but if anything the fine needle spray of the shower only made it worse. Her whole body felt as if every nerve beneath her skin had risen to the surface. Every pore was swollen and excited at the anticipation of the stroke and glide of his hands, the commandeering of his mouth. She touched her breasts. They felt full and heavier than normal, and her nipples were still tightly budded, the brownish discs of her areolae aching all over again for the sweep and suck of his mouth.

Her hands went lower, over the flat plane of her belly and down to the cleft of her body where he had so recently been. She felt tender and swollen, still acutely sensitive, the intricate network of nerves still humming with the sensations Antonio had evoked.

She turned the water off and reached for a fluffy white towel. But even after she was dried off and smothered all over with the delicately fragrant body lotion provided, she felt the tumultuous need for fulfilment racing through her body.

The hotel suite was large, but it only contained one bed—and Claire knew she would be expected to share it with Antonio. Because of their history, she also knew there would be no demarcation line drawn down the middle of the mattress.

Antonio was a sprawler. She knew there would be no hope of avoiding a brush with a hair-roughened limb or two. It would be a form of torture, trying to ignore his presence. If it was anything like in the past he would reach for her, drawing her close to him, like two spoons in a drawer, his erection swelling against her until she opened her thighs to receive him as she had done so many times before.

Her mind began to race with erotic images of how he had taken her that way: the breathing of him against her ear as he plunged into her wetness, the pace of their lovemaking sped up by its primal nature, the explosion of feeling that would make her cry out and make him grunt and groan as each wave of ecstasy washed over them, leaving them spent, tossed up like flotsam on the shore.

Claire exchanged the towel for the bathrobe and, tying the belt securely around her waist, took a steadying breath and opened the door back into the suite.

Antonio was sitting with his ankles crossed, a glass of something amber-coloured in his hand. 'Can I get you a drink, Claire? You look as if you need something to help you relax.'

She gave him a brittle glance. 'The last thing I need is something that will skew my judgement,' she said. 'What I need is a good night's sleep—preferably alone.'

His mouth tilted at a dangerously sexy angle. 'There is only one bed, *tesoro mio*. We can fight over it, if you like, but I already know who will win.'

Claire knew too. That was why she wasn't even going to enter into the debate. She eyed the sofa. It looked long enough to accommodate her, and certainly comfortable enough. She would make do. She would *have* to make do—even if it meant twice-weekly trips to a physiotherapist to realign her neck and back as a result.

Antonio got to his feet in a single fluid movement. 'Do not even think about it, Claire,' he said, placing his drink down with a clink of glass against the marbled surface. 'Our reconciliation will not be taken seriously if the hotel cleaning staff come in each day and see we have not been sleeping in the same bed.'

Claire fisted her hands by her sides and glared at him. 'I don't want to sleep with you.'

He gave her an indolent smile. 'Sleeping is not the problem, though—is it, *cara*?' he asked. 'We could sleep in the same bed for weeks on end if we were anyone other than who we are. Our bodies recognise each other. That is the issue we have to address in sharing a bed: whether we are going to act on that recognition or try to ignore it. My guess is it will continue to prove impossible to ignore.'

*I can ignore it,* Claire decided—although with perhaps not quite the conviction she would have liked, given what had occurred less than an hour ago.

Antonio pulled back the covers on the bed. 'I will leave you to get settled,' he said. 'I am going to have a shower.'

She clutched the edges of the bathrobe tightly against her chest. 'Do you expect me to stay awake for you—to be ready to entertain you when you get back?' she snipped at him.

He smoothed the turned-back edges of the sheet before he faced her. 'I expect no such thing, *cara*,' he said. 'You are tired and quite clearly overwrought. Perhaps you are right. I should not have taken advantage of your generous response to my attentions. I thought we both wanted the same thing, but in hindsight perhaps I misjudged the situation. If so, I am sorry.'

Claire captured her bottom lip, chewing at it in agitation. He made it sound as if he had ravished her without her consent, when nothing had been further from the truth. She had practically ripped the clothes off his body in her haste to have him make love to her. She had been as out of control as he had, her need for him like an unstoppable force—a force she could still feel straining at the leash of common sense inside her, waiting for its moment to break free and wreak havoc all over again.

'It's not your fault...' The words slipped out in a breathless rush. 'I shouldn't have allowed things to go so far. I don't know why I did. I don't think it was the wine or the dancing...it was just...curiosity... I think...'

His brows arched upwards again. 'Curiosity?'

Her tongue darted over the surface of her lips, her gaze momentarily skittering away from his. 'I guess, like you, I wanted to know if it would be the same...you know...as it had been before...before things went wrong...'

He came closer and, using his finger, brought up her chin so her eyes met his once more. 'We cannot change what happened,' he said. 'Our past is always going to be there, whether we continue our association or not. We will both carry it with us wherever we go in the future, and whoever shares our future will have to learn to accept it as part of who we are.'

Her eyes misted over. 'Hold me, Antonio,' she whispered as her arms snaked around his middle. 'Hold me and make me forget.'

Antonio held her close, lowering his chin to the top of her silky head, breathing in the freshly showered flowery fragrance of her as his body stirred against her. He wanted her again, but he was conscious that this time her need for him was motivated by a desire for solace, not sensual fulfilment. He closed his eyes and listened to her breathing, feeling the slight rise and fall of her chest against his, every part of him aching to press her down on the bed and possess her all over again.

He'd had to rein in such impulses before. In the weeks following the loss of their baby he had thought the best way to help her heal would be to mesh his body with hers again—to bring it back to life, to start again, to reignite the passion that had flared so readily from the moment they had met. But she had been so cold, so chillingly angry, as if he had deliberately orchestrated the demise of their daughter. Her reaction had been like an IV line plugged into the bulging vein of his guilt, hydrating it, feeding it, until it had flowed through every pore of his body, poisoning him until he finally gave up.

Antonio stroked the back of her hair, the bounce of her curls against his fingers making the task of holding her at bay all the more difficult. She was crying softly, so softly he would not have known it except for feeling the dampness of her tears against his bare chest. He was used to tears. How many patients had fallen apart in his consulting rooms over the years? Time and time again he had handed them tissues and spoken the words and phrases he'd hoped would make the burden they faced a little easier to bear. And most times it had worked. But it hadn't worked with Claire. Not one word he had spoken had changed anything.

He knew his feelings were undergoing a subtle change, but he wasn't ready to examine them too closely. He had been trained to see things from a clinical perspective. He had seen for himself how often emotions got in the way, complicating the decision-making process. What he needed was a clear head to negotiate his way through the next few months.

Divorce was a dirty word just now. It had always been a dirty word in his family. His parents were of the old school, their religious beliefs insisting on marriage being 'until death do us part'. His father's will might easily have been remade in the years since Claire had left, but Salvatore had done nothing. Antonio had told himself it was a simple oversight—like a lot of people his father hadn't expected to die so soon—but he wondered if there had been more to it than that.

Antonio hadn't been particularly close to either of his parents since late adolescence. His desire to be a surgeon had not been met with the greatest enthusiasm, and he had subsequently felt as if he had let them down in some way, by not living the life they had mapped out for him. He had been assured of their love growing up, and certainly they had done everything possible to support him during his long years of study, but the chasm that divided them seemed to get bigger as each year passed.

His father had only once spoken to him about Claire's desertion. Antonio had still been too raw from it all; he had resented the intrusion into his personal life, and after a heated exchange which had caused months of bitter stonewalling between them eventually his father had apologised and the subject had never been raised again. His mother too had remained tight-lipped. Over the last five years he could not recall a single time when she had mentioned Claire's name in his presence.

Looking back now, he realised he had not handled things well. He had allowed his anger and injured pride over Claire leaving him to blur his judgement. He had been so incensed by her accusation of him having an affair that he hadn't stopped to think why she had felt so deeply insecure, and what he had done or not done to add to those feelings. He had believed her to be looking for a way out of their relationship, and he had done nothing to stop her when she took the first exit.

Antonio put her from him with gentle hands. 'Go to bed, Claire,' he said. 'I will sleep on the sofa tonight.'

She looked up at him, her eyes still glistening and moist. 'I don't want to be alone right now,' she said, so softly he could barely hear it.

His hands tightened on her shoulders. 'Are you sure?'

She nodded, her teeth sinking into her bottom lip. 'Please, Antonio, don't leave me alone tonight. I just couldn't bear it.'

Antonio sighed and slid his hands down the length of her arms, his fingers encircling her wrists. 'You make it so hard to say no, Claire,' he said, looking down at the faint marks he had left on her tender skin. 'Everything about you makes it hard to say no.'

She placed her hands on his chest, looking up at him with luminous eyes. 'I want to forget about the past,' she said. 'You are the only person who can make me forget. Make me forget, Antonio.'

He brought his mouth down to hers in a kiss that was soft and achingly tender. The pressure of his lips on hers was light at first, gently exploring the contours of her mouth. He took his time, stroking her lips until they flowered open on a little sigh. His tongue danced just out of reach of hers, tantalising her, drawing her to him, challenging her to meet him in an explosive connection.

Claire could not resist the assault on her senses; her tongue darted into his mouth, found his and tangled with it boldly, while her lower body caught fire against the hard pressure of his holding her against him. She felt the swollen ridge of his erection through the thin barrier of the boxer shorts he had slipped on earlier. Her hand went down, cupping him through the satin, relishing the deep groan he gave as her fingers outlined his length. She felt his breathing quicken, and slowly but surely lowered the shorts until she was touching him skin on skin, her fingers circling him. Delighted with the way he was pulsing with longing against her, she began to slide her fingers up and down, slowly at first, knowing it would have him begging in seconds—and it did.

He growled against her passion-swollen mouth. 'Please, *cara*, do not torture me.'

She smiled against his lips—a sensual woman's smile, not a shy young girl's. 'You want me to go faster?' she asked huskily.

He nipped at her bottom lip once, twice, three times. 'I think you know what I want, *tesoro mio*. You seem to always know what I want.'

Claire left the bathrobe slip from her shoulders, her eyes watching his flare as he drank in the sight of her naked. His gaze felt like a brand on her flesh; each intimate place it rested felt hot and tingling. Her breasts swung freely as she pushed him back onto the bed, coming over him like a cat on all fours, pausing here and there to lick him, her belly quivering with desire as, each time her mouth came into contact with his flesh, he gave a little jerk of response. His hands bunched against the sheets as she came closer and closer to the hot, hard heat of him. She took her time, each movement drawn out to maximise his pleasure. A little kiss here, a little bite there, a sweep of her tongue on the sharp edge of his hip before she nipped at him with her teeth, each touch of her mouth making his back arch off the bed and a gasping groan came from his lips.

Claire had dreamt of this moment over the years. Alone in her bed, miserably unhappy and unfulfilled, she had dreamed of being with Antonio again, having him throbbing with need for her and only her, just as he was doing now. He was close to losing control. She could sense it in every taut muscle she touched with her hands or lips or tongue. But she still hadn't got to the *pièce de résistance* in her sensual repertoire.

She met his eyes; his were smoky, burning with expectation, totally focussed on her. 'If you want me to beg, then keep doing what you are doing,' he said between ragged breaths. 'But be warned, there will be consequences.'

She gave him a devil-may-care look as she moved down his body with a slithering action. 'I can hardly wait,' she breathed, and bent to the task at hand.

Claire sent her tongue over him first, in a light, cat-like lick that barely touched the satin of his strained flesh. But it was enough to arch his spine. She did it again, stronger this time, from the base to the moist tip, her tongue circling him before she took him in her mouth.

He shuddered at the first smooth suck, his hands going to her head, his fingers digging into her curls, as if to ride out the storm of feeling she was evoking.

Claire tasted his essence, drawing on him all the harder, delighting in the way she was affecting him. She could hear his breathing becoming increasingly rapid, the tension in his muscles like cords of steel as he flirted with the danger of finally letting go.

In the end Claire gave him no choice. She intensified her caresses. Even when he made a vain attempt to pull away she counteracted it, pushing his hand aside as she drew on him all the more vigorously. She heard him snatch in a harsh-sounding breath, his fingers almost painful at they held on to her hair for purchase. He exploded in three short sharp bursts, his body shuddering through it, his chest rising and falling, his face contorted with pleasure as the final waves washed through him.

Claire sat back, a little shocked at how wanton she had been, when only minutes before she had been insisting she was not going to share a bed with him. She had shared much more than a bed now, she realised. The act she had just engaged in was probably the most intimate of all between couples.

She could still remember the first time she had done it. She had been shy and hesitant, wondering if somehow it was wrong, but Antonio had coached her through it with patience, all the time holding back his passion until she had felt comfortable enough to complete the act. It had taken a few tries, but he hadn't seemed to mind. And besides, he had done the same to her—many times. The first time he had placed his mouth on the secret heart of her she had nearly leapt off the bed in reaction, so intense had been the feelings. But over time she had learned to relax into the caress of his lips and tongue, forgetting her shyness and simply enjoying his worship of her body demonstrated time and time again.

Antonio pushed her gently back down on the pillows, his ink-black eyes meshing with hers. 'I owe you,' he said.

Claire felt her belly quiver like unset custard. 'I feel like a hypocrite,' she confessed.

'Why is that?' he asked as he brushed his mouth over her right breast.

She pulled in a sharp breath as her nipple tightened. 'I told you I didn't want to sleep with you, but that is clearly not the case—given what just happened.'

'So, who is sleeping?' he asked, looking at her with a smouldering look.

She began to gnaw at her bottom lip again, her brow furrowing.

'Hey,' he said, stroking her lip with the tip of his index finger. 'Stop doing that. You will make yourself bleed.'

Claire ran her tongue over her lips and encountered his finger. The contact was so erotic she felt a tug deep inside her abdomen.

He was giving her that look—the look that meant she was not going to go to sleep tonight without experiencing the cataclysmic release he had planned for her in return for what she had done to him.

'Lie back,' he commanded deeply.

Claire shivered as she eased back down on the mattress. Her nakedness would barely even have registered in her consciousness if it hadn't been for his searing gaze, drinking all of her in. She saw the way his eyes focussed on her breasts, the way his gaze moved down over her belly to where the triangle of her womanhood was barely concealed by the tiny landing strip of dark, closely cropped curls. It was as close to a Brazilian wax as her pain centres had allowed on her last beauty salon visit, but now she wished she had gone the whole distance. She wanted to please him, to surprise him, to show him she was no longer an innocent girl from the Australian Outback, starstruck by his good looks and status. She was a woman now—a woman who knew what she wanted. And what she wanted was him.

If it was only going to be for three months then she would settle for that. She had dealt with loss before and survived. She had made the mistake of living in the past too long. It was well and truly time to move on, to live in the moment as so many of her peers did. They didn't worry about a few weeks of pleasure with a casual lover. They didn't agonise over whether or not they should sleep with a man they were seriously attracted to. They just did it and enjoyed every minute of it.

Claire's life, on the other hand, had become an anachronism; she had locked herself away in a time warp, not moving on with the times, not dealing with the past, stuck in a blank sort of limbo where her true feelings were papered over most of the time—until Antonio Marcolini had reappeared in her life and turned her world upside down and inside out.

From that first moment when she had heard his voice speak her name on the phone everything had changed. The feelings she had tried to squash had risen to the surface. They were bubbling even now, like volcanic mud, great big blobs of feeling, spluttering, popping with blistering heat, unpredictable, driven by forces outside of her control.

He kissed her mouth lingeringly, deeply and passionately, leaving her in a state of mindless, boneless need. Desire rippled through her as his tongue brushed against hers, calling hers into a sensual duel that left her gasping for more and more of his touch.

He moved his way down to each of her breasts, shaping them, moulding them with the warm broad palms of his hands, before taking each puckered nipple into his mouth. He rolled his tongue over the aching points in a circular motion, before sucking on them, his hot, wet mouth a delicious torture of feeling, sending shooting sparks of reaction to the very core of her being.

'You have such beautiful breasts,' he murmured as he trailed his mouth down to her belly button, circling it with the tip of his tongue. 'Everything about you is beautiful.'

Claire melted under the heat of his words. She had always considered herself an average-looking girl—not ugly, not supermodel material, but somewhere in between. Antonio made her feel as if she was the most gorgeous woman he had ever laid eyes on.

When he separated her tender folds with his fingers she flinched in response. 'Relax, *cara*,' he said softly. 'We have done this many times in the past, *si*?'

She still squirmed a little, her muscles tensing in spite of how gentle he was. 'I'm sorry,' she said on a scratchy breath. 'I'm not sure I can…'

'Do not be sorry, *tesoro mio*,' he said, stroking her inner thighs. 'We can take our time.'

Claire felt her heart swell. He was being so patient with her, just as he had been when they had first met. She had been reticent then, shy and uncertain of how to receive pleasure in such an intimate way, but he had patiently tutored every sensory nerve in her body, bringing every secret part of her to earth-shattering life.

After a moment she began to relax under the gentle caress of his hands. The movements against her smooth skin were slow but sure. It became increasingly obvious to her that he recalled all her pleasure spots. He knew just where to touch, how hard, how soft, how fast and how slow. She felt her body respond with small flutters beneath her skin to begin with, and then, as he stroked against her moist cleft, a wave began to build, higher and higher, gathering momentum, until that final moment when he brushed against the swollen pearl of her arousal again and again, in a soft flickering motion, triggering an orgasm so intense she gasped out in shocked surprise and wonder, her hands clutching at him as she rode out the storm of tumultuous feeling.

When she had calmed, Antonio tucked a springy chestnut curl of her hair behind the shell of her ear, his fingers lingering over the curve of her cheek. She looked so beautiful lying there, her dark lashes like tiny fans over her eyes, her breathing still hectic, her mouth still swollen and blood-red from his kisses.

Would he ever get enough of her to be able to let her go for good? he wondered. Was that why he hadn't pressed for a divorce? Was that why he had let things slide, putting his life on hold in a subconscious hope she would one day return to him? He had used her brother as a tool to get her back in his bed, but now he felt as if he had short-changed himself in some way. She was only with him now because she'd believed she had no choice. Once she realised how much she stood to gain if they were to divorce, would she use it against him in an act of revenge?

He drew her closer into his embrace, his body aching to have her again, but she was drifting off to sleep and he would have to wait. Then he felt her hand reach for him, her soft sigh of satisfaction at finding him hard and pulsing making him snatch in a breath of anticipation. He closed his eyes as she worked her magic on him, every sensitive nerve responding to her touch. He let her carry on for as long as he dared before he pulled her hand away and flipped her on to her back, driving into her warmth so deeply she clutched at him to steady his pace.

'I am sorry,' he said, instantly stilling his movements. 'Have I hurt you?'

'No,' she said, kissing his mouth in little feather-like kisses. 'You just took me by surprise, that's all.'

Antonio smiled against the press of her mouth. 'You took me by surprise too, *cara*,' he said, slowly building his rhythm until she was quivering in his arms.

He closed his eyes and felt himself lift off, the convulsions of her body triggering his own release, making him realise again how much he had missed her and how he would do anything to keep her right where he had her.

In his arms, in his bed, for as long as he could.

# CHAPTER TEN

CLAIRE could feel the pain ripping through her, the stomping march of each contraction tearing apart her abdomen. She clutched at her stomach, her eyes springing open when she realised it was flat, not distended.

Sweat was pouring off her—tiny, fast-running rivulets coursing down between her heaving breasts—and the darkness of the strange bedroom only added to her sense of disorientation and deep-seated panic.

'Claire?' Antonio's deep voice came out of the thick cloak of darkness, and she felt the mattress beside her shift as he reached for the bedside lamp.

The muted glow was of some comfort, but Claire could still feel her heart thumping so heavily she was sure it would burst out of her ribcage. She held her hands against her breasts, just to make sure, her breathing coming in choking gasps.

'I…I had a bad dream…' she said through still trembling lips. 'A nightmare…'

Antonio frowned and, hauling himself into a sitting position, reached for her, gathering her close. 'Do you want to talk about it?' he asked against the fragrant silk of her hair.

She shook her head against his chest.

He began stroking the back of her head, her unruly curls tickling his palm. 'Dreams are not real, *cara*,' he said. 'It is just the brain processing a thousand images or more into some sense of order. Some of it makes sense; a lot of it does not. Dreams are not prophetic; they are just the workings of our deep unconscious at rest.'

She pulled back from him and looked into his eyes, hers wide with anguish. 'It's not the first time it's happened,' she said. 'I feel like she's crying out to me. I *hear* her, Antonio. I sometimes hear her crying for me, but I can't get to her.'

Antonio felt his throat thicken. Five years on and he knew exactly what Claire meant. He could fill his days and even his nights with totally mind-consuming work, and yet in those eerie, unguarded moments, late at night or in the early hours of the morning, he could hear her too. A soft mewing cry that ripped at his guts and left them raw and bleeding.

'I'm sorry…' Claire's soft voice penetrated the silence. 'I'm keeping you awake, and you probably have another big theatre list tomorrow.'

He continued stroking her hair. 'Try and go back to sleep, *cara*,' he said. 'I am used to sleepless nights. It is part of my job.'

After a while Antonio heard the deep and even sound of her breathing, but he didn't move her out of his arms. She had her head nestled against his chest, and his left arm was almost completely numb from the press of her slim body, but he didn't dislodge it or her. He lay staring blankly at the ceiling, his fingers still playing with her hair, his heart feeling as if a heavy weight was pressed down upon it.

It wouldn't take her long to realise he had never had any intention of pressing charges against Isaac. Once Claire knew she no longer had a compelling reason to stay with him as his wife, he would have to think of some other way of keeping her chained to his side. Not because of his father's will, not even because of the money she had taken from his mother, but because he wanted to wake up each morning just like this, with her warm and soft against him.

When Claire woke to find she was alone in Antonio's bed she felt a wave of disappointment wash over her. She wasn't sure what she had been expecting. Breakfast in bed with an avowal of love and red roses on the side was the stuff of dreams; it had no relevance to their current set-up.

She flung the covers back and got up, wincing as her inner muscles protested at the movement. It gave her a fluttery, excited sort of feeling inside to remember how passionately they had made love.

*Had sex*, she corrected herself. This was not about love—at least not from Antonio's point of view. This was about a physical attraction that had suddenly resurfaced.

Claire turned on the shower, a frown pulling at her forehead as she waited for the temperature to adjust.

Yes, but *why* had his attraction for her suddenly resurfaced? He had not sought her out until she had

tried to serve those divorce papers on him. And by returning to live with him she had postponed any prospect
of a divorce being processed smoothly. This reconciliation was not about working through the issues of the
past; this was about a very rich man who did not want
his inheritance cut straight down the middle. He could
very well string her along indefinitely; she had already
demonstrated to him how easily she could be won over.
She cringed at how she had responded so freely to him
the night before. She hadn't lasted twenty-four hours in
his company without caving in to her need of him. How
he must have gloated over her ready capitulation. She
might even now be pregnant. She would have that whole
heartache to go through again—tied to him for the sake
of a child, never knowing if he wanted her for her, or
for what she could give him.

When she had showered and dressed she found the
note he had written next to the tea-making facilities in
the suite, informing her he had an early list at one of the
large teaching hospitals and would see her for a late
dinner at around eight to eight-thirty that evening. There
were no words of affection, no *I love you and can't wait
to see you* phrases—nothing for her to hang her hopes
on. She crumpled the note and tossed it in the bin,
annoyed with herself for wishing and hoping for what
she couldn't have.

Downstairs in the car park a few minutes later, Claire
hoisted her handbag over her shoulder and narrowed her
gaze at the parking attendant. 'What do you mean, this
is *my* car?' she asked.

The parking valet smiled and handed her a silver

embossed keyring. 'It is, Mrs Marcolini,' he said. 'Your husband had it delivered late yesterday. If you would like me to go through all the features with you, I would be happy to explain them—'

Claire plucked the keys from his hand. 'That will not be necessary,' she said with a proud hitch of her chin. 'A car is a car. I am sure I will be able to work out where the throttle and the brakes are.'

'Yes, but—'

She gave the young man a quelling look over her shoulder as she got behind the wheel. She took a moment to orientate herself. The new-car smell was a little off-putting—not to mention the butter-soft leather of the seats. Then there was the dashboard, with all its lights and gadgets, which looked as if it had been modelled on the latest space shuttle from NASA. Maybe she had been a little hasty in sending the helpful assistant on his way, she thought ruefully. After her old and battered jalopy, this car looked as if it needed a rocket scientist to set it in gear, let alone start it.

She took a deep breath and inserted the key that didn't even look like a key into the ignition. The car started with a gentle purr of the engine, its side mirrors opening outwards as if by magic, and the seatbelt light flashing to remind her to belt up.

'All right, already,' Claire muttered, and strapped herself in with a click.

OK, so where was the handbrake? It wasn't in between the driver and passenger seats, so where the hell was it?

The parking valet tapped on the window. Claire

pursed her lips and hunted for the mechanism to lower
the window, locking all the doors and popping the boot
open before she finally located the button with the little
window symbol on it.

'There's a foot brake on the left,' the man said with
a deadpan expression. 'And the release is that button on
the right, marked brake release.'

Claire mentally rolled her eyes. 'Thank you,' she
said, stiff with embarrassment. 'Have a nice day.'

The valet smiled and stepped well back. 'Have a
nice drive.'

'Oh, my God.' Rebecca's eyes ran over the showroom-
perfect gunmetal-grey of the vehicle Claire had parked
outside the salon. 'You're driving a sports car?'

Claire dumped her handbag on the counter and sent
her hand through her disordered curls. 'Yes, well, you
*could* call it driving, I suppose,' she said wryly. 'Not that
I had to do too much. The slightest spot of drizzle has
the windscreen wipers coming on without me having to
leaf through the manual to locate the appropriate switch.
Apparently there's some sort of sensor that detects
moisture. Going through the city tunnel, the headlights
came on automatically—and turned off again once I was
back out in daylight. And just now, parking between that
florist's van and that utility, all I had to do was listen to
the beeps and watch the flashing red lights as the parking
assist device told me when I was getting too close.'

Rebecca let out a whistling stream of air through her
teeth. 'Gosh, I wish *my* estranged husband would buy
me a sports car. All he has given me so far is a lawyer's

bill for the division of assets, most of which *I* own, since I was the only one with a full-time job the whole time we were together.'

Claire hid her scowl as she shrugged herself out of her coat and hung it on a hook in the back room. Rebecca was right. She shouldn't really be complaining about such a generous gift. Most women would be falling over themselves to have been given such a luxurious vehicle. Besides, Antonio had openly expressed his concern over her driving a less than roadworthy car. She didn't fool herself his concerns were for her safety, it was his reputation he was most concerned about—he had said as much at the time. But wouldn't it be wonderful if he had done it out of love for her? Money was no object for him, it never had been, so how could he know what such a gift would mean to her if the right motives had been behind it?

'You have a full list of clients today,' Rebecca said, when Claire came out of the back room into the salon. 'It seems everyone wants to be styled by the woman who has stolen the heart of Antonio Marcolini, celebrity surgeon *extraordinaire*.'

Claire organised her cutting and styling trolley with meticulous care. 'He's just a normal man, Bex,' she said, keeping her gaze averted. 'He brushes his teeth and shaves every morning, just like most other men.'

'So what's it like being back with him?' Rebecca asked. 'I read in the paper you've moved into his hotel suite with him.'

Claire lined up her radial brushes with studious precision. 'That's because my flat is too small. He is used to living in the lap of luxury. A one-bedroom flat in a tawdry inner-city suburb is hardly his scene. Moving in with him seemed the best option—for the time being, at least.'

'Have you done the deed with him yet?'

Claire couldn't control the hot flush of colour in her cheeks. In fact she could feel her whole body heating up at the memory of what she had done to him and what he had done to her.

'Bex, don't ask me questions like that,' she said, frowning heavily. 'There are some things even best mates have to keep private.'

Rebecca perched on the nearest stool and crossed her booted ankles. 'So that's a yes,' she said musingly. 'I thought as much. As soon as he came in here I knew you were a goner. He's hardly the sort of man you could say no to, is he?'

Claire put on her most severe schoolmistress sort of frown. 'This is just a trial reconciliation between us,' she said. 'Nothing has been decided in the long term. Just because he bought me a car it doesn't mean he wants me back for ever. For all I know it could be a consolation prize for when he hotfoots it back to Italy without me.'

Rebecca's forehead creased. 'But I thought you were still in love with him,' she said. 'You are, aren't you? Don't shatter all my romantic delusions, Claire. I'm counting on you to get me back into the dating pool with hope not despair as my personal floating device.'

Claire decided to come clean. 'It's a farce, Bex,' she said on an expelled breath. 'I'm not really back with Antonio. Not in the real sense.'

Rebecca narrowed her gaze. 'But you've all but

admitted you slept with him,' she said. 'If that isn't being back together, what is? And what about that kiss in here yesterday, huh? That looked pretty full-on and genuine to me.'

'He's only here for three months,' Claire said flatly. 'There's no way I would go back to Italy with him unless I was absolutely sure he cared something for me, and quite frankly I can't see that happening. He's not the "I love you" type. I had his baby, for God's sake, and he never once said how he felt about me. Doesn't that tell you something?'

Rebecca grimaced. 'I guess when you put it like that…'

Claire blew out a breath. 'His father is dead. He died just a couple of months ago. I have reason to believe that is why Antonio is here now—not just to do the lecture tour, but to see what gives where I am concerned.'

'So what does give?' Rebecca asked with a pointed look.

Claire looked away and started realigning her brushes again, even though they were all neatly spaced on the trolley. 'I'm not sure,' she said, fiddling with a teasing comb, running her fingers across its pointed teeth, the movement making a slight humming noise. 'A divorce has always been on the cards. For all this time I have been waiting for him to make the first move, but he didn't. I decided to take matters into my own hands once I heard he was coming here, but now I wish I had let sleeping dogs lie.'

'Have you ever asked yourself *why* he never asked you for a divorce?' Rebecca asked after a small pause.

Claire continued to turn the comb over in her

hands. 'What happened back then was…' She stopped
for a moment, thinking about why Antonio had not
sought his freedom as soon as he could. If he *had*
been involved with Daniela Garza, why wouldn't he
have activated a divorce as soon as possible, so he
could be with the woman he wanted to be with?
Everything pointed to Claire having got it horribly
wrong about him. It didn't sit well with her to be in
the guilty seat—that was the position she had always
assigned *him*.

'Or, more to the point, have you ever asked yourself
why you didn't divorce him?' Rebecca added.

Claire let out her breath on a sigh. 'I think you have
probably guessed why.'

Rebecca gave her a look. 'So you *do* still love him?
I sort of guessed you did. It's the way you say his name
and the look you get in your eyes.'

Claire dropped the comb back on the trolley. 'All this
time I've been fooling myself I hate him, but I don't. I
love him. I have always loved him. I was so convinced
he'd been having an affair, but he's always denied it.'

'Yeah, well, men do that, you know.'

Claire chewed at her lip. 'I don't know… Antonio is
a good man, Bex. He does a lot of charitable work all
over the globe. The more I think about it the more I start
to doubt myself. What if I made a terrible mistake?
What if he wasn't having an affair? What if he's been
telling the truth the whole time? What have I done?'

'Claire, lots of marriages survive an affair, or even the
suspicion of one,' Rebecca said. 'If he had one it must
be well and truly over now—otherwise he wouldn't be

with you, trying to sort things out. Give him a chance. You love him. Isn't that all that matters?'

'I'm not sure if he will ever feel anything for me,' Claire said. 'You can't exactly force someone to fall in love with you. If it happens, it happens.'

Rebecca raised her brows and flicked her gaze to the shiny new car outside. 'Listen, honey, any man who buys a woman a car like that must feel something for her. Just go with the flow for a while. Stop agonising over what you haven't got and enjoy what you have got. Some men are just not able to put their feelings into words; it's their actions you have to listen to.'

Claire glanced back at the car outside and sighed. How she wished Rebecca was right—that Antonio was showing her, not telling her how he felt. But then she remembered how much was at stake for him if they were to divorce. Was the car part of the buttering-up process, to keep her sweet when it came to finally putting an end to their relationship?

'Oh, I almost forgot,' Rebecca said. 'Your mother called. She said she'd left a couple of messages on your mobile but you hadn't got back to her. I think she's a bit hurt you didn't call her about getting back with Antonio. Like everyone else, she read about it in the paper.'

Claire grimaced. 'I turned my phone to silent. I forgot to change it back. Oh, God, what am I going to say to her?'

'Tell her the truth,' Rebecca said. 'Tell her you love Antonio and are working at rebuilding your marriage. She's your mum, Claire. All she wants is for you to be happy.'

Claire wanted it too—so much that it hurt. But her

happiness was dependent on securing Antonio's love, and unfortunately that was not in her hands.

Maybe Rebecca was right; she needed to learn to go with the flow, to enjoy what she had for as long as it was there to be had. Antonio might have had less than noble motives for bringing about their reconciliation, but perhaps this window of time was her chance to show him how much she loved him—in spite of how he felt about her...

# CHAPTER ELEVEN

CLAIRE didn't go straight back to the hotel from work. She took a detour to the cemetery, stopping to buy a bunch of tiny pink roses first. She cleaned out the brass vase and refilled it with fresh water, arranging the roses with loving care before placing them on her little daughter's resting place. She felt the familiar tight ache in her chest as she looked at the inscription, hot tears blurring her vision so she could hardly read her baby's name.

'Sleep tight, darling,' she said softly as she finally prepared to leave.

The traffic was heavy on the way back, so by the time she got to the hotel it was much later than she had expected.

'Where the hell have you been?' Antonio barked at her as soon as she came in the door.

Claire let her bag slip to the floor. 'I...I was caught up in traffic.'

'For two hours?' he asked, his gaze hard as it collided with hers.

She ran her tongue over her lips. 'How do you know how long it's been?'

'I called in at the salon but you had already left,' he said. 'I made the trip back here and it only took me fifteen minutes—and that was during peak hour.'

Claire slipped off her coat, trying her best not to be intimidated by his brooding demeanour. 'Thank you for the car,' she said. 'It's lovely. I took it for a bit of a drive.'

'Where to?' The question was accusatory, hostile almost.

'To the cemetery,' she said, holding his dark angry gaze. 'To visit our daughter.'

Claire saw his throat move up and down over a tight swallow, one of his hands scoring a rough pathway through the thickness of his hair as his gaze shifted away from hers.

'Forgive me,' he said in a gruff tone. 'I should not have shouted at you like that.'

'I would have told you where I was going, but I thought you were going to be late,' she said. 'You said so in the note you left for me this morning.'

His eyes came back to hers. 'We got through the list faster than I expected. One of the patients had to be put off until next week due to a clotting problem.'

The silence stretched for a lengthy moment.

Claire broke it by saying, 'I need to have a shower. I feel as if I am covered in hair clippings and dye.' She began to move past him, but he captured her arm on the way past, stopping her in her tracks.

'Claire.'

She looked up at him, the weariness she could see in his face making her heart melt. 'Yes?' she said, barely above a whisper.

'I have something for you,' he said, reaching into his trouser pocket with his other hand.

Claire held her breath as he handed her two velvet ring boxes. She opened the first one to find an exquisite diamond solitaire engagement ring glittering there. The second box contained an equally beautiful diamond-encrusted wedding ring. She knew even before she slipped them onto her finger that they would both be a perfect fit.

She looked up at him again once the rings were in place, but his expression was difficult to read. 'Thank you, Antonio,' she said softly. 'They're truly beautiful. They must have cost you a fortune.'

He gave an off-hand shrug of one of his broad shoulders. 'They are just props,' he said. 'I do not want people to think I am not able or willing to provide you with nice jewellery.'

Claire couldn't help feeling crushed, but tried not to show it on her face. 'I am sure no one would think you a neglectful husband after all the money you have spent on me in the last twenty-four hours.'

His eyes studied her for a pulsing moment. 'Why didn't you tell me you made a large cash donation to the neonatal unit at St Patrick's hospital a few weeks after you returned to Australia?' he asked.

Claire rolled her lips together, wondering how he had found out. She had asked the CEO at the time to keep her name off the records. He had assured her no one would ever know who had made the donation.

'Claire?'

'How did you find out?' she asked.

'There are some secrets that are not so easy to keep,' he said, still with that inscrutable expression on his face.

Claire shifted under his steady gaze, absently twirling the rings on her finger. 'You seem to have made it your business to find out everything you can about me.' She looked up at him again and asked, 'Should I be checking over my shoulder for a man in a trenchcoat?'

The line of his mouth grew tense. 'I would like you to inform me of your movements in future.'

Claire felt her back come up. 'Why?' she asked. 'So you can monitor my every move like a prisoner being kept under guard?'

'I would just like to know where you are and who you are with,' he said. He paused for a moment before adding, 'I was worried about you this evening.'

'Worried?' she asked with a lift of her brows. 'About my welfare or about whether I had escaped your clutches?'

His jaw visibly tightened as he held her gaze with the coal-black hardness of his. 'If you are harbouring the thought of leaving just remember it will only take one phone call to put your brother behind bars.'

Claire's gaze flicked to his mobile phone. 'You won't be able to hold that particular gun to my head for ever you know,' she said. 'It's already wearing a little thin, don't you think?'

He stepped towards her, tilting up her face, his eyes locking once again with hers. 'As long as it works for now,' he said, and slowly and inexorably lowered his mouth to hers.

Claire shivered as he deepened the kiss, her arms snaking around his neck, her senses firing on all cylinders. His tongue teased hers into a sexy tango, building her desire for him with each sensual movement. She pressed herself closer, her body singing with delight as she felt his arousal growing hot and hard against her. His hands skimmed down her sides, grasping her by the hips and pulling her even closer.

His kiss became more drugging, the sweep and caress of his tongue making her sigh with mounting pleasure. His hands moved from her waist to the undersides of her breasts, his thumbs close enough to rub across her nipples in tantalising back and forth movements that brought another whimper of delight from her in spite of the barrier of her clothes.

'I want you naked,' he said against her mouth. 'Now.'

Claire quivered as his hands cupped her breasts. 'I really need a shower…'

'Good idea,' he said, and lifted her effortlessly in her arms, carrying her through to the bathroom. 'I need one too.'

Claire wasn't sure who undressed who, but it seemed only seconds before they were standing under the hot spray of the shower, his mouth doing knee-trembling things to the sensitive skin at the side of her neck. She tilted her head and closed her eyes in bliss as his lips and tongue began an excruciatingly slow journey towards the swell of her breasts.

She was gasping by the time he got there, her senses screaming in reaction as his teeth gently scraped her sensitised flesh. He took her in his mouth, drawing on her, sucking and licking until every nerve was alive and jumping with feeling. The rasp of his stubbly jaw against her tender skin as he moved to her other breast made her spine tingle and her legs threaten to fold beneath her.

The steady stream of steamy water intensified the sensual feelings of their bodies rubbing against each other. Claire had showered with Antonio in the past, but she could not remember it feeling as exhilarating as this. Even as her excitement was building he was taking his time, as if he wanted to draw out every second of pleasure, and her body was delighting in it. Her antici-pation grew and grew, making her breath come in breathless little pants as he came closer and closer to possessing her.

'Now…oh, please now,' she said, pressing herself against his hot, hard heat.

He held her slightly aloft, teasing her with his length at her moist entrance. Just waiting for that first plunge into her tight warmth made her heart race in feverish expectation.

'Tell me how much you want me,' he said, rubbing himself against her.

The erotic motion drove every thought but his imminent possession out of her head. 'Don't make me beg, Antonio,' she gasped as he brushed against her again. 'You know how much I want you. I have never wanted anyone but you.'

His eyes gleamed with male satisfaction as he pressed her back against the shower stall, positioning her for his entry.

Claire closed her eyes as he surged forward, her body accepting him with slick wet heat, her tight muscles clamping around him, drawing him in. He started slowly, but his pace increased until she was breathing as heavily as him, her hands grasping at him to keep her upright as her body began to splinter into a thousand pieces, each one trembling, spinning and quivering in a maelstrom of sensation.

He came within seconds of her, his low, deep grunts of pleasure making her skin pepper all over with goose-bumps as he spilled himself. She felt his body shiver under the pads of her fingertips as she ran them lightly over his back, his taut muscles twitching in the aftermath.

Antonio finally stepped back and brushed the wet hair out of her face. 'I will let you finish up in here,' he said, running a gentle fingertip over a patch of redness on the upper curve of her breast. 'I need to have a shave before I take any more of your skin off.'

Claire looked at her breast, the startling contrast of its creamy softness against the dark tan of his finger making her stomach tilt all over again. She drew in a tight little breath as his fingertip brushed over her nipple, and then another as he circled her areola.

His eyes meshed with hers. 'Did you see your doctor about contraception?' he asked.

Claire felt as if he had just turned the cold water on. She stared at him, her heart-rate not quite steady. 'No…I haven't been able to get an appointment.'

'Where are you in your cycle?'

'I'm not sure…'

His eyes were still locked on hers. 'We have had un-protected sex several times now. Has it occurred to you that you could have already conceived a child?'

She swallowed thickly and, reaching past him, turned off the shower. She stepped out of the cubicle and snatching up one of the big fluffy towels, wrapped herself in it. 'I thought you said the other day it was not the right time to be talking about babies?' she said.

He wrapped a towel around his hips. 'That was then. This is now.'

She eyed him suspiciously. 'So what's changed?' she asked.

'We are older and wiser, Claire. Things could work for us.'

Claire searched his face for some clue to what he was feeling, but his expression was mask-like. 'So...' She paused as she moistened her mouth. 'So what you are saying is...you want to stay married?'

'It was never my intention to divorce you, Claire.'

'Why?' she asked. 'Because it could prove too costly for you now your father has died and left you half of everything he owned?'

Something flickered in his eyes. 'That is why you issued me with the divorce papers, was it not?' he asked. 'You saw a chance to take me to the cleaners in return for all the ways I had supposedly let you down in the past. Do not forget I saw the newspaper article too, Claire. It mentioned the recent death of my father. You did the sums, but fortunately for me your brother took matters into his own hands.'

Claire glared at him, her hands going to tight fists by her sides. 'You bastard. The first I heard about your father's death was when you told me at our first meeting,' she said through clenched teeth. 'You arrogant, unfeeling bastard. Right from the start you set out to seduce me back into your bed, hoping once I was there again I wouldn't want to leave. No wonder you've been buying me expensive rings and a car and talking about babies. You wanted to make me think twice about leaving.'

'There is not going to be a divorce, Claire,' he said, with an intransigent set to his mouth. 'I want you to be absolutely clear about that—especially if there is going to be a child.'

'How can you be so clinical about this?' she asked. 'This is not some business deal. This is my life you're talking about. What if I want to spend it with someone else? Have you thought about that?'

His eyes pinned hers. 'Is there someone else?'

She sent him a resentful scowl. 'Why don't you tell me? You're the one keeping tabs on me.'

'I am not keeping tabs on you,' he said heavily. 'I found out quite by accident you were responsible for that donation. It threw me to think you had not thought to tell me. You allowed me to think you had taken money from my mother to indulge yourself; instead I find that you have been responsible for saving perhaps hundreds of premature babies' lives.'

'I didn't ask your mother for the money. She had written the cheque before she came to see me that night. I am not sure why she continues to insist I demanded it from her.'

Antonio released a sigh. 'There is no point in going over this again. If you say that is how it happened, then I am prepared to leave it at that.'

Her blue-green eyes widened in surprise. 'You believe me?'

'If we are to make a success of our marriage this time around we will both have to learn to trust each other,' he said, dragging a hand through his still-damp hair.

She gave him an ironic look. 'You just accused me of trying to take half your assets. Doesn't that imply a lack of trust on your part?'

He looked at her for a long moment. 'Why, after all this time, did you wait until now to ask me for a divorce?' he asked.

She captured her lip, chewed at it for a second or two before she answered. 'I believed our marriage to be well and truly over, that's why.'

Even now Antonio wondered if he could believe her. He had blackmailed her back into his bed, but she was right in saying he couldn't hold the threat of her brother's imprisonment over her indefinitely. He should not have held it over her in the first place. Her brother had acted out of a sense of loyalty—the kind of behaviour he had seen in his own brother Mario time and time again.

Antonio's head was still reeling with the shock of finding out Claire had not used that money for her own gain. Five years of brooding anger had been swept away with a single sentence from a virtual stranger who had known more about his wife than he did.

It was like seeing Claire for the first time; he was discovering things about her he had not noticed before. Like how she kissed with her whole body, not just her mouth. And how gentle her hands were, the way they sent electrical charges through him with the simplest touch. How sweet her rare smile was, how it touched him in a way nothing else had done. How her beautiful eyes glittered with anger and defiance one moment, then brimmed with emotion at the mere mention of their baby daughter the next. She was like a movie or a novel he had not understood the first time around. She had layers and sub-plots that made him appreciate her uniqueness in a way he had never done before.

He had never been comfortable identifying his emotions concerning Claire. He still wasn't sure why. It wasn't as if he'd had a difficult background, or had suffered at the hands of another woman, therefore making it difficult to let his guard down. He just knew he felt something for Claire he had not felt for any other woman.

He tipped up her chin and brushed his mouth with hers. 'It is not over, *cara*,' he said, and unhooked her towel, tossing it to the floor along with his. 'Not by a long shot.'

# CHAPTER TWELVE

THREE weeks later Claire came out of the salon's bathroom to find Rebecca looking at her speculatively. 'Are you going to continue to fob me off by telling me it was something you ate, or are you going to come clean?' she asked. 'That is the third time in as many days you've been sick.'

Claire blew out a sigh as she dabbed at her clammy brow. 'I think I'm pregnant. I haven't had a test yet, but the signs are all there.'

Rebecca's eyes opened wide with excitement. 'Wow, Claire—that's fabulous! Have you told Antonio?'

Claire began to chew at her lip. 'No...not yet.'

'You don't think he'll be pleased?'

Claire met her friend's questioning gaze. 'I think he'll be very pleased,' she said. 'It means a divorce will be out of the question—for the time being at least.'

Rebecca frowned. 'But, hon, I thought a divorce was out of the question now anyway. The last couple of weeks you've been happier than I've seen you in years. I thought it was finally working out between you and Antonio.'

'It's true things have been much better between us,'

Claire said, thinking of how attentive and considerate Antonio had been lately. 'He's been lovely towards me—taking me out to dinners and shows, and buying me clothes and stuff. He even offered to drive to Narrabri next weekend to meet my mother.'

'But?'

Claire gave Rebecca an anguished look. 'Don't you see, Bex? It's happening all over again.'

'I'm not sure I'm following you…'

'The one thing Antonio wants is an heir,' Claire said. 'When I fell pregnant before that's why he insisted on marrying me—to give the baby his name. It wasn't about loving me or wanting to spend the rest of his life with me. It was about securing an heir for the Marcolini empire.'

'But, Claire, things might have changed now.'

'Oh, yes,' Claire said with a cynical twist of her mouth. 'They very definitely *have* changed. He is now in possession of half his father's wealth as well as his own, which is no small fortune, let me tell you. He knows if he divorces me he will have to give me a huge cut of it. What better way to keep his money than to lure me back into his life and get an heir in the process?'

Rebecca shifted her pursed lips from side to side for a moment. 'I'm thinking you haven't told him you still love him. Am I right?'

'Oh, Bex, I have to bite my tongue every single day,' Claire choked, close to tears. 'But that's the mistake I made before. I can't make myself so vulnerable again. If we are to stay together I want it to be on equal terms. I want to be loved not for what I can give him, but for me—just me.'

'Claire, it's only been…what…a little over three weeks or so since you got back together?' Rebecca said. 'And don't forget his feet had barely stepped on Australian soil when you started waving divorce papers under his nose. He's not likely to unveil his feelings in a hurry after something like that.'

'I guess you're right…' Claire said as she sat on the stool at the reception counter and put her head in her hands. 'It hasn't exactly been a textbook reunion.'

Rebecca stood behind her and gave her shoulders a little squeeze. 'Why don't you take a couple of weeks off? You should get some rest in any case. Then, when you're all relaxed and not feeling so unsure of yourself, you can tell Antonio about the baby.'

Claire got off the stool and faced her friend. 'I think I will take a few days off,' she said. 'I don't want anything to go wrong with this pregnancy. I just couldn't bear it.'

Antonio had not long finished his last case when he received a phone call from his brother Mario, back in Rome. He rubbed his hand across the stubble on his jaw as he listened to the news he had been dreading ever since he'd boarded the plane to Australia.

'How long do the doctors think she will last?' he asked as he stripped off his theatre cap and tossed it in the bin.

'It is hard to say—a week, maybe less,' Mario responded. 'She has been asking for you.'

Antonio felt his insides clench. The irony was particularly painful. The last time he had seen his mother she had looked at him blankly, asking the home care nurse who this tall, dark and handsome stranger was. 'I will arrange a flight straight away,' he informed his brother.

'Is your runaway wife coming with you?' Mario asked.

Antonio felt his teeth grind together at his brother's sardonic tone. 'Claire will take some convincing, but, yes, I plan to bring her with me,' he answered. 'And I would appreciate it if you would not mention the past again. We are getting along just fine.'

'So you have so far managed to stop her divorcing you?' Mario asked.

'So far,' Antonio said, thinking of all the times in the last couple of weeks when he had caught Claire looking at him in that covert way of hers, her gaze immediately falling away from his as if she was harbouring a guilty secret.

For all his talk that day of developing trust between them, he could not get past the thought that she might very well be planning the best payback of all. He couldn't quite shake the feeling, no matter how he tried. Even though she shared his bed willingly, with as much if not more enthusiasm as before, she never once mentioned her feelings towards him as she'd used to do so freely in the past. Even her smiles were fleeting and distant, as if her mind was occupied elsewhere. The only place he could get and hold her full attention was in bed. It was there she responded to him without holding back, her body convulsing around his as he claimed her again and again. He had thought his attraction to her would burn itself out, but it had done the very opposite. He wanted her more than he had ever wanted her. His physical need of her was so great at times it was overwhelming. The irony was that it had been all he had wanted from her in the beginning, and yet now, when he was so sure he could have it, he wanted so much more.

When Antonio got back to the hotel Claire was sitting in the lounge with her legs curled beneath her, a magazine in her lap.

'Hi,' she said, closing the pages as he came in.

'Hi, yourself,' he said, bending down to kiss her briefly.

She looked at him warily once he had straightened. 'Is something wrong?' she asked, unfolding her legs and placing her feet on the carpeted floor, her hands gripping the sofa until her knuckles showed through her creamy skin.

'Claire, I have to return to Italy,' he said without preamble. 'I need to go as soon as possible. I want you to come with me.'

'No,' she said, instantly springing to her feet.

He frowned as she suddenly paled before him, her body swaying slightly. He put out a hand and steadied her. *'Cara*, I did not mean to spring that on you like that, but—'

'I don't want to go.' She cut him off, her face still deathly pale.

'What is wrong?' he asked, still holding her.

'I told you from the start I am not moving back to Italy with you,' she said with a stubborn set to her mouth. 'You can't make me go.'

'I thought we had an agreement,' he said, holding her defiant gaze.

She glared at him, but he could see a nerve flickering at the side of her mouth.

'Don't try and blackmail me, Antonio. It's not going to work. I was speaking to Isaac only yesterday. Your friend has helped him apply for a youth worker's course. He starts in a couple of weeks. He told me you were the one who paid his fees. There is no way you would turn him in now—not unless you don't have an ounce of compassion in your soul.'

Antonio silently ground his teeth as he tried to think of another way to convince her. In the end he decided to try another tactic—to reveal a side of him she had never seen before. 'Claire, my mother is dying,' he said heavily. 'I need to go to her. She is asking for me.'

She shifted under his gaze, her tongue darting out to moisten her lips. 'Go on your own. You don't need me there.'

'I would like you to be there, *tesoro mio*,' he said, scraping a hand through his hair. *I need you to be there.*

'I am quite sure your mother would prefer it if I didn't intrude on such a painfully private moment,' she said, but her voice had lost its hardened edge. Her eyes, too, had softened, bringing out the rich blueness of them.

'The point is my mother will probably not even recognise you.'

She frowned at him. 'What do you mean?'

He released a weary sigh. 'My mother is suffering from Alzheimer's. Up until recently she has been cared for at home by a nurse, but early this morning, Italian time, she suffered a stroke. Her memory of the past, which was already rapidly declining, is now virtually non-existent.'

'But I thought you said she specifically asked for you?' she said.

'She did—which is why it is imperative I go to her,' he said. 'Patients with Alzheimer's can still have short periods of lucidity. I want to see her. It is important to me. I was not there for my father. I did not get to say the things I wanted to say. I did not get to hear the things he wanted to say to me.' He paused for a moment. 'I was not there for you and our baby either. That is something I will regret for the rest of my life. I do not want any more regrets, Claire. Please…do this one thing for me.'

Claire felt her rigid stance begin to crumble. She could see this was a very difficult time for him. He had not long ago lost his father, and now his mother was desperately ill. It was impossible for her to deny him this one request. And hearing him speak of their little baby with such emotion in his voice went a long way to healing the hurt she had carried for so long. Although he had said nothing to her about it, she knew he had gone to visit their daughter's resting place. When she had gone there today, after she had left the salon, she had found a teddy bear dressed in a pink tutu propped up next to a huge bunch of flowers, and a card written in both English and Italian: *With all my love, your devoted Papà.*

It had made Claire realise how private a person Antonio was. He had lived most of his life under the intrusive glare of the paparazzi, and when he grieved he liked to do so alone. If only she had recognised that all those years ago. He was not one to express his feelings to all and sundry. He kept things inside, working through them at his own pace, locking a part of himself away to cope with the difficult issues he had to deal with on a daily basis. How could he handle the welfare of his patients if he was to fall apart emotionally all the time? Patients did not need a surgeon to cry with them. They needed a competent, caring specialist who could think clearly and make good clinical decisions about their condition and how best to deal with it.

It was a shock to realise how little she had known Antonio in the past—how little she had understood of him as a man and as a gifted surgeon. She had fallen in love with a small part of him, never realising the true depths of his character until now.

'Claire, I do not expect to be away for more than a week or ten days at the most,' Antonio assured her. 'I still have commitments here, although they have had to be rescheduled for when I return.'

'All right,' she said on a little sigh. 'I will come with you.'

He pressed a soft kiss to the middle of her forehead. 'Thank you, *il mio amato*,' he said. 'I will try and make things as comfortable for you as possible.'

The flight to Rome was long, but Claire slept on and off in the executive suite Antonio had arranged on the plane. She woke once during the flight to find him lying fully clothed on top of the covers beside her, staring at the ceiling, his handsome features so drawn with exhaustion her heart went out to him.

She stroked a gentle hand across his stubbly jaw. 'Why don't you get undressed and lie down for a while?'

He turned his head and gave her a rueful smile. 'If I get into that bed with you, sleep will be the last thing on my mind.'

Claire felt her cheeks start to glow. 'Maybe that's exactly what you need right now,' she said softly. 'Maybe it's what we both need.'

He rolled on his side and brushed her hair back from her forehead, his eyes dark and intense as they meshed with hers. She closed her eyes as his mouth came down, the brush of his tongue against hers setting her instantly alight. With her mouth still locked on his, she worked the buttons of his shirt, pulling it off him with impatient fingers. She attacked his belt and trousers with the same passionate intent, aching to feel his body against hers without the barrier of clothes.

Antonio removed the slip of a nightgown she was wearing, kissing her breasts, rolling his tongue over each ripe berry of her nipples, his teeth tugging and his tongue soothing simultaneously, his mouth a hot brand of possession that drove her wild with need.

His erection was thick and throbbing against her moist entrance, his breathing ragged as he fought for control. 'I should put on a condom,' he said, reaching across to rummage in his bag. 'You will not be totally covered by the pill yet. It has only been a couple of weeks, *si*?'

Claire stroked his arm with her fingers, her eyes falling away from his. She had let him think she had gone ahead with the appointment with her doctor, and now she wished she hadn't lied by omission. But telling him about her pregnancy now didn't seem quite like the right time. She wanted to feel more assured of his feelings for her. Anyway, it was very early days; anything could go wrong at this stage. She hadn't even had it confirmed in case she jinxed something. She wanted to wait until she was absolutely sure she wasn't imagining it before she told him.

'I am sure it will be fine,' she said. 'I want to feel you.'

He positioned himself over her and she welcomed him with a gasp of delight, moving with him, catching his rhythm, her body gripping him greedily. He reached between their rocking bodies to stroke the moist centre of her desire, his fingers finding their target with consummate ease. She was so ready for him, her back arching off the mattress to keep him where she wanted him. He drew out the pleasure for her, changing his touch to tease her into a cataclysmic release. She was approaching the summit. He could feel her inner muscles start to contract, her whimpering cries coming faster and faster as she finally let go. It was impossible for him to hold back. He surged forward with several deep, hard thrusts, spilling himself, shuddering with the sensation of ultimate pleasure as it flowed through him in waves.

The deep and even sound of Antonio's breathing had a soporific affect on Claire. Her eyes felt as if they were weighted by anvils, and after a few attempts to keep them open she gave up with a soft sigh, and fell into a dreamless sleep curled up in his arms.

When Claire woke the pilot announced they were due to land.

The journey through Customs was tiresome, due to a security scare that had happened with a tourist a few days ago. Everyone seemed to be on tenterhooks, which was quite understandable, and the checkpoints took much longer than normal, even for those holding an Italian passport.

Although the building was air-conditioned Claire felt clammy and, using a tissue, wiped beads of moisture from her forehead. Antonio glanced at her as they were being ushered through, his gaze narrowing in concern.

'Are you all right, *cara*?' he asked. 'The crowds are annoying, I know, but we will soon be home.'

*Home*.

He said it so naturally—as if it really was her home as well. But it would never be home for her—not unless she felt loved and accepted by him. She could live anywhere with him if he loved her the way she loved him. His heart was her home and always would be.

The trip to the Marcolini *palazzo* was lengthened by a traffic snarl, but soon enough the familiar sight came into view. The three-storey mansion stood in stately pride, and the lush green of trees and shrubbery, holding a host of hot summer fragrances, reminded Claire of the blisteringly dry and dusty Outback, where her mother vainly tried year after year to coax flowers and vegetables to grow.

The other startling difference from her background was the number of household staff the Marcolinis employed. Housekeepers—both junior and senior—a gardener and a pool maintenance man, not to mention a chauffeur who seemed to be on call twenty-four hours a day.

'Isn't your mother being looked after in hospital now?' Claire asked, automatically lowering her voice to the hushed, whispered tone all the staff she had encountered so far seemed to have adopted.

'No,' Antonio said. 'She expressly wished to be allowed to stay at home with her family around her.'

Claire looked up at the grand marble staircase to see Antonio's brother descending. Taller by an inch or two, he had the same dark good-looks of his older sibling, his body long and lean and toned by the gym and the pool. He had the same dark brown almost black eyes, but while Antonio's were often filled with compassion for the patients under his care, Mario's were hardened with the worldly cynicism he wore like a second skin.

'So the prodigal wife returns,' he said, as he came to the foot of the stairs where Claire was standing. 'Welcome home, Claire.'

Antonio swore at his brother in Italian, changing back to English to ask, 'How is Mamma?'

'Conscious, but not making much sense,' Mario answered. 'She keeps thinking I am Papà.'

'Yes, well, you look more like him than me,' Antonio said, massaging the back of his neck, where he could feel a knot of tension the size of a golfball. 'Has anyone else been to visit?'

'Daniela came by yesterday, with her husband and baby son,' Mario informed him. 'I am not sure if she will be back,' he added, glancing briefly at Claire.

Claire felt her colour rise and bit down on her lip. Was she for ever to be reminded of her stupid mistake in believing her husband had betrayed her?

'I had better spend some time with Mamma,' Antonio said. 'Has her doctor been today?'

Mario nodded grimly. 'There is nothing you can do,

Antonio. You are not her doctor; you are her son. You need to remember that.'

Antonio swallowed the lump of grief that had risen in his throat. 'Can you get Claire a drink and show her to our room? She is tired from the journey. She almost passed out coming through Customs.'

Claire felt her face flame with guilty colour all over again. She was sure Mario thought she had been putting it on, but she did still feel horribly faint and nauseous. A long-haul flight and crossing time zones, even if in the lap of luxury, was not conducive to feeling one hundred percent even without the suspicion of being pregnant. Even the sudden heat after the cool winter in Sydney took some getting used to. Antonio himself looked ashen and tired beyond description, with dark shadows underscoring his eyes like bruises, but then he was facing the sadness of losing his mother so soon after the death of his father.

'What would you like to drink?' Mario asked as he led the way to the *salotto*.

'Do you have fresh orange juice?' Claire asked.

He gave her his playboy, teasing smile. 'Does Australia have bush flies?'

A reluctant smile tugged at Claire's mouth. She had to admit that Mario, when he let his guard down, could be utterly charming. It was no wonder Antonio would not hear a bad word said against him.

Mario handed her a glass of icy cold orange juice. 'So,' he said, running his gaze over her speculatively, 'you are reunited with my brother.'

Claire lowered her gaze. 'Yes…'

'Let's hope it lasts this time around,' he said. 'He has not been the same since you left.'

Claire took a deep breath and met his hardened gaze full-on. 'I love him, Mario. I know you probably don't believe it, but I do. I've been so stupid. I can't believe how stupid I was back then. I know he wasn't having an affair. I feel so sure of it now. I have never stopped loving him. Not for a moment. I love him so much.'

'Have you told him that?' Mario asked, stalling in the process of lifting his glass to his mouth.

'Have you told me what?' Antonio asked as he stepped into the room behind her.

Claire swung around to reply, but before she could get the words into some sort of order she began to wobble on her feet, her vision blurring alarmingly. She tried to concentrate, to hold on to consciousness, but her extremities were already fizzing with the sudden loss of blood pressure. She felt herself falling, saw the marbled floor coming towards her with frightening speed. The glass she was holding slipped out of her grasp, shattering into a thousand pieces.

She vaguely registered Antonio's voice calling out, 'Catch her!' but if Mario did so in time she was totally unaware of it....

Claire woke in a darkened room. Her aching forehead was being stroked with a cool damp cloth by Antonio. 'What's going on?' she asked through dry lips. 'Where am I?'

'*Cara*, you hit your head when you fainted,' he said, concern thickening his voice. 'I want you to go to hospital to have it X-rayed. The ambulance is on its way. You could have fractured your skull.'

She felt her vision blurring again, and his words seemed to be coming from a long way off. Her head was pounding as if a construction site had taken up residence inside. She felt a wave of sickness rise in her throat, but managed to swallow it down just as the sound of a siren approached on the street outside.

As the ambulance officers loaded her into the back of the vehicle, Claire turned her head to look at Antonio, whose face was grey with anguish. 'I don't need you to come with me,' she said. 'You should be with your mother. How is she?'

'She is fine for now,' Antonio said, gently squeezing her hand before tucking it back under the cotton blanket. 'She has even been asking for you.'

She blinked at him, even though it sent another jack-hammer through her skull. 'She's been asking for *me*?' she asked in a shocked whisper. 'She...she knows I'm here...with you?'

'I told her we were together again,' he said. 'I think she wants to say goodbye and to apologise.'

Claire felt her heart contract even as her consciousness began to waver alarmingly again. 'Tell her...tell her to wait for me...'

'I will,' Antonio said, leaning forward to press a soft kiss to the paper-white skin of her brow just as her eyes fluttered downwards.

*'Come è lei?'*

Claire heard Antonio's voice ask how she was. But the answer from the doctor he was speaking with, even though delivered in the rather stilted manner of a non-Italian speaker, she found hard to follow in her disordered state, apart from the words for 'mild concussion.'

'Commozione minimo…um…er… Ma non è tutto… Lei è incinta…er…'

'How far along?' Antonio asked next—in English this time, clearly in an attempt to put his struggling colleague out of his misery.

Claire felt a prickly sensation go through her, as if all of her corpuscles had been injected with tiny bubbles of air, each one containing a particle of joy.

So it had been confirmed at last.

She was pregnant.

'Two weeks—maybe three,' the doctor answered Antonio in English, his lilting accent giving him away as a Scot, obviously on a foreign medical rotation. 'She is obviously sensitive to the change in her hormones. Some women are more so than others, making the symptoms kick in much earlier than normal. The knock on the head will not help the morning sickness, of course, but with adequate rest she should pick up in a few days. I've had a quick look through her records. She will have to be closely monitored, given what happened last time, but it's entirely possible she will have a safe delivery of a healthy wee one this time. We have come a long way in the last five years in maternal health management.'

Claire felt her heart turn over inside her chest as the joy she was feeling began to spread right through her. If everything went right, she would in a matter of months be holding a baby in her arms—alive and breathing. Up until now she hadn't dared think too far ahead. It had been enough to suspect she was carrying Antonio's baby. To find out there was every reason to hope for a healthy delivery was nothing short of a miracle to her.

'*Grazie*,' Antonio said with a hitch in his voice. 'I mean—thank you.'

'No trouble. I am sorry to hear your mother is not well,' the doctor added. 'Perhaps news of a grandchild will be just the tonic she needs right now?'

'You could be right,' Antonio said. 'Thank you again. You have been very kind and attentive. It is greatly appreciated.'

Claire waited until the sound of the doctor's footsteps had faded into the distance before she opened her eyes. Antonio was looking down at her, his dark brown eyes meltingly soft.

'*Cara*.' His tone was gentle. 'The good news is you do not have a fracture of your skull.'

'And…and the bad news?'

He smiled. 'I do not consider it bad news at all. The doctor attending your admission has found you are pregnant. He took a set of routine blood tests and it came up positive. You're pregnant.'

Claire felt the tears rising until they were streaming down her face. She sniffed, and Antonio quickly reached over and plucked a tissue out of the box by her bed. He began to gently mop at her cheeks. 'And here I was, thinking you had gone on the pill,' he said in mock reproach.

'I was going to,' she said. 'I was about to call to

make an appointment when I realised I was a couple of days late. I decided to wait and see.'

He began to frown. 'You *were* planning on telling me, were you not?'

'Of course!' she said. 'Surely you don't think…?'

He gave a rueful grimace. 'It would be no less than I deserved. I have not exactly been the best husband to you, have I?'

Claire lowered her gaze, plucking at the sheet with her fingers. 'I haven't exactly been the best wife…'

He picked up her hand and brushed his lips against her bent fingers. 'I cannot tell you how thrilled I am about the baby,' he said. 'It is the best news I could have hoped for.'

She gnawed at her lip for a moment. 'It's not just about keeping your inheritance?'

'It has never been about my inheritance,' he said, his eyes warm and soft as they held hers. 'I love you, *il mio amato uno*. I have been so stupid not to have recognised it for all this time. I was too proud to admit the woman I loved had left me. I should have fought for you, Claire. I realise that now. I should have moved heaven and earth to bring you back to me.'

Claire's heart swelled to twice its size as she fell forward into his arms. 'I love you too,' she sobbed against his broad, dependable chest. 'I've been such a fool. I can't believe I left you. It was so immature of me.'

'Hush, *cara*,' he soothed, stroking her back with a gossamer-light touch. 'You were still hurting. Losing Isabella was…' His voice caught but he went on. 'It was like being locked inside an abyss of grief so thick and dark it was all I could do to get through each day without breaking down completely. People were depending on me—my patients, my colleagues—and yet in all of it the most important person I should have supported was you. But I was too shell-shocked to face it at the time. Every time I looked at the pain in your eyes I felt my heart being ripped open. In the end I just could not bear to think what I had done to you. I got you pregnant. I did not support you the way you needed. And when Isabella did not make it I felt…I *still* feel…it was my fault.'

Claire lifted her eyes to his dark moist ones. 'You said her name…' Her voice came out on an incredulous whisper of sound. 'For the first time *ever* you said her name…twice…'

Antonio's throat moved up and down as he fought to control his emotions. 'I have wanted to so many times, *cara*,' he said. 'But every time I tried to I felt as if a giant hand had grasped me by the throat, squeezing until I could not breathe.'

Claire hugged him tightly, allowing him the chance to let out the grief that in her own ignorance and pain had not been allowed purchase.

It was a long time before either of them could speak, but when they finally came apart she looked into his red-rimmed eyes and felt a rush of sheer joy for the first time in five long, lonely years.

'My mother wishes to apologise in person for misleading you,' Antonio said. 'She really felt she was doing the right thing at the time. She thought you no longer loved me. That is why she gave you the money— to help you get back on your feet. She thought it might help you to cut loose by hinting Daniela and I were still involved. I hope you will find it in yourself to forgive her. I know it is a lot to ask. I am finding it hard to forgive her myself.'

Claire smiled as she stroked his raspy jaw. 'Of course I forgive her—and you must too. I do not want any bad feelings to get in the way of our happiness. Not after so long apart.'

He smiled and kissed her softly on her lips. 'I am the luckiest man on earth,' he said. 'I am over the moon about you being back in my life, about the baby, about being together again, about being a family.'

'Speaking of family,' she said. 'Isn't it time you got back to yours at the *palazzo*?'

'My family is right here,' he said, kissing her passionately. 'And I am not going to be separated from it again.'

\* \* \* \* \*

# Dante's Blackmailed Bride

## DAY LECLAIRE

Dear Reader,

I've always loved the idea of love at first sight.
That instant attraction. That electric moment that
occurs when you look at someone and just know...
*he's the one!* And then you touch and it's like all
the energy in the world just poured itself into your
hand and created this sizzling arc of electricity that
only exists between the two of you. In that split
second you realise you discovered your soul mate.

The concept of love at first sight is the initial
premise behind THE DANTE LEGACY, only
I had an idea that took it a step further. I started
wondering... What if this family – let's call them
the Dantes – actually had the ability to recognise
their soul mate with a single touch? What if that
ability had been passed down through the Dante
line for as long as anyone could remember? Would
it be considered a blessing...or a curse?

Those questions led to the creation of the Dante
family and their little family secret...The Inferno.
Having these strong, powerful, alpha males
suddenly discover that they're consumed by The
Inferno and completely out of control as a result
– at the worst possible moment in their lives, of
course – intrigued me. How would they react?
What extremes would they go to in order to
meet their soul mates? I invite you to find out for
yourself.

Welcome to THE DANTE LEGACY and the
all-consuming power of The Inferno, where soul
mates connect with just one electrifying touch.

Enjoy!

*Day Leclaire*

*USA TODAY* bestselling author **Day Leclaire** lives and works in the perfect setting – on an island off the North Carolina coast. Living in an environment where she can connect with primal elements that meld the moodiness of an ever-changing ocean, unfettered wetlands teeming with every creature imaginable, and the ferocity of both hurricanes and nor'easters that batter the fragile island, she's discovered the perfect setting for writing passionate books that offer a unique combination of humour, emotion and unforgettable characters.

Described by her editors as "one of our most popular writers ever!" Day's tremendous worldwide popularity has translated to sales totalling well over five million books. She is a three-time winner of both the Colorado Award of Excellence and the Golden Quill Award. She's won a *Romantic Times BOOKreviews* Career Achievement Award, Love and Laughter awards, a Holt Medallion, a Booksellers Best Award and she has received an impressive ten nominations for the prestigious Romance Writers of America RITA® Award.

Day's romances touch the heart and make you care about her characters as much as she does. In Day's own words, "I adore writing romances and can't think of a better way to spend each day." For more information visit Day on her website at www.dayleclaire.com.

**Don't miss Day Leclaire's new book, the next in THE DANTE LEGACY series, *Dante's Stolen Wife*, coming in July 2009 from Desire™.**

To my own soul mate, Frank, with much love for your constant patience, encouragement and sense of humour. It just keeps getting better!

# PROLOGUE

HE REFUSED to lose.

He refused to allow anything—or anyone—to get in the way of his rebuilding Dantes into the formidable empire it had once been.

Severo Dante fought for the calm control that typified his business dealings as he regarded his brothers. He found it more difficult than usual to maintain an impassive facade, perhaps because the next few business decisions would prove vital to their overall future. Passion was the hallmark of the Dante name, of the Dante image. But the head of the company couldn't afford to allow emotion to overrule intellect. Too much depended on his ability to handle all that went on behind the scenes.

Where others provided the creativity that turned the sparkle and glitter of gemstones into the world's most coveted wedding rings, Sev utilized logic and business acumen to drag Dantes back from the brink of ruin and propel its return to the public acclaim it had once known. At least, that had been the plan until he'd hit this latest roadblock.

Sev turned from the panoramic view of downtown

San Francisco and faced his brothers. "Timeless Heirlooms was in the perfect position for acquisition. Dantes should already have it tucked beneath our corporate umbrella. What the hell happened?" he demanded.

The Dante twins, Marco and Lazzaro, shrugged as one. "New designer," Marco explained.

"It's revitalized their company," Lazz added.

"Who is this designer? What's his name? Where did he come from?" To Sev's frustration, no one answered. "We need to find out. Now. Timeless Heirlooms belonged to Dantes until we were forced to sell it off after Dad died. Now that I've solidified our financial position, I want TH back. And I want it back now."

Marco paced restlessly. "Maybe we should reconsider taking over Timeless. Since we're global again, I'd rather go head-to-head with them and crush them where they stand. We've been cautious long enough. Let's get moving," he persisted. "Expand from our wedding ring market into the areas we once owned—not just heirloom and estate jewelry, but all jewelry needs. Earrings, bracelets, necklaces. Hell, tiaras, if there's a demand for them."

Sev shook his head. "It's too soon. We need a really spectacular collection to launch us, and we don't have that collection, or anything close to one. Nor do we have a suitable marketing campaign, even if one should fall into our lap. By taking over TH we corner that particular market in one simple move. Once solidified there, we'll choose our next target. Something bigger and more impressive." He turned his attention to Lazz. "What's our best approach for finding this new designer?"

"TH is having a spring showing—" Lazz checked his notes with typical thoroughness "—tomorrow night. The Fontaines will be featuring their latest designs, as well as the creative geniuses behind them. One of them has created quite a buzz. Once we have the designer's name, we can order a background check. Find his or her vulnerability."

A cunning gleam appeared in Marco's eyes. "Better yet, we can hire him out from under the Fontaines. He'd make a fine addition to Dantes. Then when we've bought out Timeless Heirlooms, he can go right back to what he's doing now—designing contemporary pieces with the look and feel of heirloom and estate jewelry." A hint of ruthlessness colored his words. "Only he'll do it for TH's new owners—us."

"That's a distinct possibility." Sev considered his options before reaching a decision. "Here's what I want. It might look suspicious if we all attend TH's show. Lazz, you handle the background check and give us something to go on. Marco, you're the people person. You and I will attend the showing. I'll speak to the Fontaines directly."

Marco smiled. "While I use my natural charm and sex appeal to get the latest gossip."

Lazz groaned. "The worst part is…he's right. I've never understood how we can look exactly alike and yet women who won't give me the time of day are all over Marco."

A knock sounded at the door, interrupting a discussion that had been ongoing since the twins had crawled out of their respective cradles. Their youngest brother, Nicolò, walked in. Long considered the family "troubleshooter," he took charge when creative answers were needed to sort out a family dilemma. Nic often claimed that he didn't believe in problems, only solutions.

"Primo sent me," Nic said, referring to their grandfather. "He thought you might have a job for me."

Sev nodded. "I want you working with Lazz. He'll fill you in on the latest developments with Timeless Heirlooms. We may need some innovative suggestions in the near future."

Nic inclined his head, his expression reflecting both his interest and his fierce determination. "I'll get right on it."

Sev folded his arms across his chest. "When Dad died and we discovered that Dantes teetered on the verge of bankruptcy, we were faced with some unpleasant choices—"

"*You* were faced," Lazz interrupted. "You were the one forced to make the tough decisions and sell off all the different subsidiaries of Dantes."

"Selling off the secondary holdings saved the core business and allowed us time to recover and rebuild." Sev eyed each brother in turn. "It's been a long road back, but now we're in a position to reclaim what we once lost. I won't allow anything to stand in the way of doing that. We all agreed that the first business we return to the fold is the heirloom and estate jewelry. That's Timeless Heirlooms. If this new designer is all that stands between us and reacquiring TH, then we either find a way to take them over—" his expression fell into merciless lines "—or take them out."

# CHAPTER ONE

FRANCESCA SOMMERS ran a critical eye over the sumptuous ballroom in Nob Hill's exclusive five-star hotel, Le Premier, and struggled to suppress a severe case of nerves. In a little over twenty-four hours she'd have her very first showing. She couldn't believe her good fortune, both in being offered the opportunity to work with Tina and Kurt Fontaine, as well as having her designs among those featured at Timeless Heirlooms' spring show.

As though sensing Francesca's nervousness, Tina came up beside her and slipped an arm around her waist. "You can stop worrying right now," she said. "You'll see. Your pieces will be the hit of the evening. Not to take anything away from Cliff or Deborah's talent and skill—they're both good designers—it's your collection that will take everyone's breath away. It offers the perfect blend of romantic elegance and timeless appeal that are hallmarks of my company."

Francesca relaxed ever so slightly, smiling in delight at the compliment. "Are you sure you don't mean old-fashioned?" she asked with a laugh.

Tina lifted a dark eyebrow, which gave her exotic features an imperious cast. "Period pieces are a Fontaine specialty. We're at the leading edge of the resurgence in popularity for jewelry like this. You'll see. Tomorrow night's showing will put us over the top."

Francesca shook her head. "Catching Juliet Bloom's eye will put us over the top. I don't suppose she's responded to our invitation?"

"Her agent contacted us. She's still out of the country wrapping her latest film. But her agency's sending a representative. And I've learned that Juliet's next movie is another period piece. If this rep likes what she sees…" Tina lifted a shoulder. "We've all done the best we can. The rest is up to fate, as well as those stunning pieces you've designed."

Kurt entered the room and Tina murmured an excuse before joining her husband. Francesca pretended to give her full attention to the various displays currently under construction, but in reality she studied her employers with an intense yearning.

As the brilliant and creative owner of Timeless Heirlooms, Tina couldn't be more different from her husband of nearly thirty years. Small, dark and vivacious, she hurtled through her days, whereas Kurt took life in stride. He also qualified as one of the most strikingly handsome men Francesca had ever met, towering over Tina, his Nordic appearance the polar opposite of his wife's.

Although he held the title of director of operations for TH, his real job consisted of supporting Tina and keeping the nuts and bolts of the business end of the company running smoothly. With his calm, reassuring demeanor, he excelled at both, even during stressful and frantic periods such as this.

Francesca gripped her hands together. Right now Timeless Heirlooms desperately needed Kurt's soothing touch. Despite the Fontaines' attempts to keep everyone in the dark, rumors had reached Francesca of their financial difficulties. They were counting on her—or rather, her designs—to help them recover their footing in the volatile world of jewelry sales. In response, she'd thrown herself, heart and soul, into her job, giving the Fontaines every ounce of her talent and skill. But would that be enough?

For as long as Francesca could remember, she'd wanted to work for one of Dantes' subsidiaries, mainly because it offered an unparalleled opportunity to advance her career and bring her designs to life. But when the Fontaines bought out TH, a far different reason drew her to apply to them for a job, instead of Dantes. A reason she kept tucked close to her heart.

It gave her the opportunity to get to know her father.

Sev's plans for the evening of the Fontaines' show seemed perfect...right up until he saw *her*.

For some inexplicable reason, she drew his gaze the moment he walked into the ballroom and the impact from that one look struck with all the power and sizzle of a lightning bolt flung from on high. Every business plan, every thought about taking over TH, of tracking down this new designer and acquiring him for Dantes, leaked from Sev's brain and puddled at his feet. In its place one imperative remained.

Get. The. Woman.

She stood in the midst of a group of people, a tall, golden swan surrounded by sparrows. Everything about her spoke of old-time grace and elegance, the very embodiment of Timeless Heirlooms' motto—*jewelry that mates past with present.* He knew many beautiful women, but something about this one captivated him on a visceral level. Unremitting desire entangled him in an unbreakable web and refused to let go no matter how hard he struggled to break the bond.

For a split second Sev forgot why he'd come or what he hoped to accomplish. Instead, he felt compelled to follow that primal tug. He would have, too, if Marco hadn't grabbed his arm.

"Hey, where are you going? The Fontaines are in the other direction." He glanced toward the section of the room that held Sev's attention and grinned in sudden understanding. "*Bella,* yes?"

"Yes." The single word—one riddled with desire—betrayed him and Sev shook his head in an effort to clear it. What the hell was happening to him? He never lost focus like this. Nothing ever came between him and business. Nothing. Not even a drop-dead gorgeous woman whose very presence sang with all the promise and allure of a Greek Siren.

Marco straightened his suit jacket. "Since my assignment is to mingle with the guests while you see what information the Fontaines are willing to cough up, I believe the lady in question is on my list." He clapped his brother on the back. "Looks like you're out of luck, Sev."

The mere thought of his brother getting anywhere close to this particular woman had Sev seeing red. Marco, the charmer. Marco, who could entice any and all women into his bed with a single look. Marco, who had never met a woman he hadn't enjoyed to the fullest, before discarding. Marco, with his golden swan.

A faint roaring filled Sev's ears, a noise that deafened him to everything but one increasingly urgent demand. *Get. The. Woman.* "Not her," he ordered. It amazed him that he could still speak coherently, considering the compulsion that infected him and drove him to react in ways in complete and utter contrast to his normal character. "Stay away from her."

Marco still didn't get it. "You're not playing fair," he protested. "Why don't we let the lady decide who she prefers?"

Sev simply turned and looked at his brother. "Not her," he repeated.

Marco held up his hands, the humor fading from his expression. "Fine, fine. But if she approaches me, I'm not sending her away. Not even for you."

Sev's hands collapsed into fists and it took every ounce of effort to keep from using one of them to rearrange Marco's features—arresting features that attracted women to him with lifelong ease, not to mention unparalleled success. "If she approaches you, send her over to me."

Marco frowned. "Have you met this woman before? Do you have a history with her? You know I don't poach my brothers' women. Not unless your relationship's over." His smile glimmered again. "I don't suppose it's over by any chance?"

"It's not over. In fact, it hasn't started." His gaze fixed on his quarry. "Yet. I'm just staking my claim. Now are we clear, or do I have to spell it out with my fists?"

"No, it's not clear. Stake your claim? Spell it out with fists?" Marco's frown deepened. "Have you lost your mind? When have you ever spoken about a woman like that? What's gotten into you?"

Sev drew in a slow breath, fighting to clear his head, with only limited success. What *had* gotten into him? Marco was right. He never reacted like this over a woman. Nothing and no one came ahead of business. But another glance in the blonde's direction caused the desire to erupt in messy waves of molten heat. It filled him with a whispered demand to go to her. To seduce her. To take her and make her his, no matter who or what stood in his way. It overshadowed all else, rooting into his very soul and sending out powerful tentacles that latched on to every part of him and refused to let go.

"Hey! Wake up, big brother." Marco snapped his fingers in front of Sev's nose, concern bleeding into his voice and expression. "I'll tell you what. Why don't we check out the new designs before we get to work? See what we're up against."

"Good idea," Sev managed to say.

Despite the arm his brother dropped on Sev's shoulder, it took every ounce of self-control at his command to turn his back on the blonde and walk away. With every step, he could feel the quicksand of need sucking at his feet and legs. It didn't matter how much distance he put between them, he could still sense her on every level, and that awareness unsettled him more than he cared to admit.

They found the spring collection staged on sweeps of raw silk and took their time studying the pieces. Models also roamed the ballroom, their beauty enhanced by the glitter of diamonds and colored gems. Marco flirted with the models, while Sev assessed the displays. He kept hoping the blonde might gravitate this way. Since she wore one of the premier sets, he assumed she must be a model, as well, especially with her height and regal bearing. But she kept her distance and he couldn't decide whether to be relieved or annoyed.

Marco ended his conversation with a leggy redhead wearing a solid three million dollars' worth of high quality stones and returned to Sev's side. "I don't get it. Nothing I've seen so far is enough to save Timeless from going under," he said in an undertone. "It's all the same old thing."

"No, not all of it. Not this, for instance."

Sev paused by a display unique in its simplicity. Not that the jewelry needed a fancy backdrop to make it stand out. The pieces spoke for themselves. White gold, diamonds and jet formed a sweeping pattern as elegant and sophisticated as any in recent memory. And yet, an air of romance permeated each item, a promise that by gifting this necklace, or this ring, or this bracelet, the recipient would receive a tangible expression of utter love and devotion.

An image of the blonde wearing the gems flashed through his mind. He could see the delicate strands of the necklace encircling her neck, the graceful length accentuated by the simple drop earrings. It would look perfect on her, particularly when complemented by acres of pale, creamy skin and a simple black silk sheath.

"Aw, hell. This is the first I've seen of this designer's work. It's just the sort of collection I had in mind for Dantes' expansion," Marco said. "We are so screwed."

In more ways than one. If Sev didn't get his mind back on business, he might as well kiss Timeless Heirlooms goodbye. "Find out who designed these and get the information to Lazz and Nic," he instructed his brother. "I'll go talk to the Fontaines. Maybe I'll learn something helpful."

Or maybe he should head for the kitchen, grab a bucket of ice and pour it over his head in the hope of dousing the heat rampaging through his system. Dammit to hell! What had that blonde done to him and how had she done it?

Marco grimaced. "Whatever you learn better be helpful, because I have a feeling they no longer need to sell TH."

Unfortunately, Sev had a nasty feeling his brother was right. Still, his conversation with the Fontaines elicited a few interesting facts. They had, indeed, hired three new designers for the express purpose of revitalizing TH. And they had some big deal in the offing, all very hush-hush. Whatever the deal, the Fontaines were convinced it would catapult them into the big times.

Yet, Sev caught a hint of desperation Tina couldn't quite conceal, which told him all he needed to know. Despite tonight's success, they were still vulnerable. He just needed to uncover the source of that vulnerability and exploit it. He headed for the far end of the room where French doors opened onto a shadowed balcony with a stunning view of San Francisco. The light breeze held a final nip of winter's chill, but he found it a welcome relief after the perfumed warmth of the ballroom. Removing his cell phone from his jacket pocket, he flipped it open and pressed the button for voice activation.

"Lazz," he said.

A few seconds later the call went through. "Sev?" A rapid clicking bled through the line, indicating his brother was typing as he spoke. Ever the multitasker. "I just spoke to Marco."

"And?"

Lazz sighed. "You're both at the same party. So why am I the one keeping you two up-to-date?"

"Do I really need to answer that?"

"Okay, okay. Marco has two names for you so far. There's a Clifton Paris and a Deborah Leighton. He's working on the third one, but everyone's being very mysterious. He thinks it's because they're planning some huge announcement in regard to this final designer."

"Which means he's the one we're after."

"Probably. Marco said there's some special deal TH is about to close, also involving this particular designer."

"The Fontaines said the same thing. Does Marco know what the deal is or which designer?"

"Actually…he does, at least in part. They're about to sign a big-name actress."

Sev fought for patience. "There's a lot of big-name actresses out there. Which one are we looking at?"

"Don't know, yet. But the rumor is, she's top-drawer.

If they do sign someone like Julia Roberts or Nicole Kidman or Juliet Bloom, it'll be huge for them. And it'll effectively prevent both a buyout and, quite possibly, our ability to compete with them on the open market."

Sev grimaced at his brother's all-too-accurate assessment. "I need to find out who they're courting and get the agreement delayed. Put Nicolò on it."

"Right away."

"We also need leverage. Call that P.I. we hired last year—Rufio—and have him start an immediate investigation of the designers Marco's already identified. Then call Marco and tell him I want that third name ASAP. Tell him to alert me the minute he has it."

"Check."

Sev flipped the phone closed and pocketed it. Time to gather himself for round two. He glanced toward the glow of lights, where the subdued chatter of voices wafted from the ballroom. To his relief, his reaction to the blonde had eased somewhat. Five minutes and counting without a single image of her short-circuiting his brain and sending the rest of him into overdrive.

Or so he thought until she appeared in the doorway and stared straight at him. For a split second he believed she came in search of him, that the ever-tightening tendrils between them were acting on a subliminal level and drawing her to him. Then he realized that her eyes hadn't adjusted to the darkness that cloaked him. He nearly groaned. She couldn't see him at all. Did she even sense him? Doubtful. This was his insanity, not hers.

She hesitated while light streamed around her, capturing her in its warm embrace. She'd dressed simply, in a silk sheath of palest lilac. No doubt the color had been selected to complement the jewelry she wore—the set unquestionably the work of TH's mystery designer. A delicate rope of silver, studded with the unmistakable glitter of diamonds and Verdonian amethysts, hugged the base of her neck while a simple confection of the same stones flashed discreetly on the lobes of her ears. Understated. Stylish. Sophisticated.

With a sigh of relief she stepped onto the balcony. The light from the ballroom gave her a final caress, slipping through the thin silk to reveal a womanly shape that nearly brought Sev to his knees. Full breasts strained against the low-cut bodice, while a nipped waist and shapely hips gave the simple dress an impressive definition.

She crossed to the balustrade and stared out at the view, absently rubbing her bare arms against the spring chill. Sev found he couldn't move. The rational part of his brain ordered him to return to the gathering and finish the job at hand. But an overwhelming need eclipsed that small voice of sanity. It was as though some primeval part of himself dominated reason and rationale. He'd become a creature of instinct. And instinct demanded that he inhale her very essence and imprint it on his mind and body and soul.

Her instincts must have been as finely tuned as his own, for she lifted her head as though scenting the air. Then, with unerring accuracy, she spun to face him and her gaze collided with his.

"I've been waiting for you," he said.

Francesca froze, every nerve ending sizzling to life in an instinctive fight-or-flight reaction. She couldn't say what alerted her to the man's presence. One second she believed herself alone and in the next heartbeat she sensed him on a purely intuitive level.

She stared at him and the breath hitched from her lungs. He blended into his shroud of shadows so completely that the ebony richness of his hair and suit melted into his surroundings, making him appear part of the night. Only his eyes were at odds with the endless darkness, glittering like antique gold against a palette of black. As though aware of her apprehension, he stepped into a swath of light coming from the ballroom to enable her to get a better look.

His height impressed her. He stood a full two or three inches over six feet with an imposing expanse of shoulders and long, powerful legs. For the first time since childhood, she felt downright petite. Reflected light cut across his features, throwing the patrician lines of his face into sharp relief. Heaven help her. She couldn't remember the last time she'd seen such a gorgeous man.

But something stunned her even more than his appearance—the emotional turmoil he triggered. She'd never responded to a man like this before. Never experienced such an intense, uncontrollable physical reaction. She stood before him, filled with a feminine helplessness utterly foreign to her nature. Desire shook her, the intensity so absolute that she could only stare in bewilderment when he offered his hand.

"You've been waiting for me?" she finally managed to say. "Why?"

"I noticed you when I first arrived and hoped we'd eventually meet. My name's Severo. Sev, for short."

"Francesca Sommers." She took the hand he offered before snatching it back with a startled exclamation. "Good Lord. What was that?"

He appeared equally stunned. "Static electricity?"

She'd felt static electricity before. Who hadn't? In fact, as a child she and the other foster children had often delighted in scuffing their socks on the carpet before chasing through the house in order to shock each other. That brief zap of electricity bore no similarity to this.

She scrubbed her palm across her hip, but after that initial searing of flesh against flesh, the sensation changed. It scored her palm like a brand, though unlike a brand, it didn't hurt. It sank deep into her bones—part tingle combined with a peculiar ticklish itch. She didn't know what to make of it.

"Maybe we should try that again," Sev said.

She took a swift step backward. "Maybe we shouldn't."

His mouth tilted to one side. "I'm sorry. I have no idea how or why that happened. You sure we can't try this again?" He held out his hand. "I promise, if anything bad occurs, I'll keep my distance."

She hesitated for an instant, then reluctantly slipped her hand into his. "So far, so good."

The previous sensation didn't happen again, true. Instead, another one took its place. It felt as though some part of him seeped from his hand to hers and sank into her pores before being lapped up by her veins. It slid deeper with every beat of her heart, imbuing her with his essence. Worse, each beat filled her with forbidden desire.

She fought the sensation, fought to speak naturally. "So, what brings you to the showing, Sev? Are you a buyer?"

"Not exactly, although the set you're wearing is something I wouldn't mind acquiring. May I have a closer look?"

No more than a couple of feet separated them. The single step he took in her direction shrank that distance to mere inches and magnified her reaction to him. Drawing in a deep breath, she tilted her head to one side so he could get a better look at her design, praying he wouldn't take long so she could escape into the relative safety of the shadows surrounding them. The next instant she found escape the last thing on her mind.

His hand brushed her collarbone as he traced the curve of her necklace with his fingertips, branding her with fire. "Stunning. Absolutely stunning."

On the surface his comment sounded simple enough, yet a heavy, old-world lyricism underscored it, filled with the flavor of foreign climes. She could hear the faint strains of a glorious Italian aria, smell the tart richness of ripening grapes, soaked in the heat and humidity of a Tuscan summer.

Unable to help herself, she swayed toward him and whispered his name. His response came in a frantic explosion of movement. He swept her into his arms, locking her against him. Hips and thighs collided, then melded. Hands sought purchase before hers tunneled into the thick waves of his hair and his spread across her hip and spine, flooding her with a heavy liquid warmth. Lips brushed. Once. Twice. Finally, their mouths mated, the fit sheer perfection.

She practically inhaled him, unable to get enough. Not of his taste. Not of his scent. Not of his touch. His hands drifted upward, igniting a path of fire in their wake. The most peculiar awareness filled her as he touched her. Though his caress aroused her, she didn't get the impression his actions were a form of foreplay. Instead, it almost felt as though he were committing the shape and feel of her to memory, imprinting her on his brain.

She pulled back slightly, fighting for breath. "I don't understand any of this. We've only just met. And yet, I can't keep my hands off of you."

"I can't explain it, either." Desire blazed across his face, giving him a taut, hungry appearance. "But, it's happening, and right now that's all that matters. Fortunately, that also makes it easy to fix."

Yes. Thank goodness they could fix this terrifying reaction and make it go away. "Fine. Let's get it taken care of."

He caught her hand in his. "Let's go."

"Go?" She resisted his pull, not that it got her anywhere. He simply towed her along. "Go where?"

"I'll pay for a room here at Le Premier, and we'll spend the night working this out of our systems. Come morning, we go our separate ways, flame extinguished."

Francesca fought to think straight. "This is crazy." Severo, a man she'd met just five minutes ago, had kissed her with a passion she'd never known existed and then casually suggested they book a room at a hotel for a night of mind-blowing sex. He seemed to have missed one vital point. "I don't do one-night stands."

He never even broke stride. "In the normal course

of things, neither do I. For you, I'm willing to make an exception."

Under different circumstances she'd have found his comment amusing. Without the warmth generated by his embrace, the cool San Francisco air allowed her to regain an ounce of common sense and she pulled free of his grasp. "Wait. Just wait a minute."

She watched him fight for control. "I'm not sure I have a minute to spare." A swift grin lit his face with unexpected masculine beauty. "Will thirty seconds do?"

She thrust her hands into her hair, destroying the elegant little knot she'd taken such pains to fashion a few short hours ago. There was a reason she couldn't go with him. A really good reason, if only she could bring it to mind. "I can't be with you. I need to get back inside. I—I have obligations." That was it. Obligations. Obligations to… She released a silent groan. Why the hell couldn't she remember? "I think I'm obligated to do something important."

Sev shot a perplexed glance toward the ballroom. "As am I." His mouth tugged into another charming smile, one she found irresistible. It altered his entire appearance, transforming him from austere man-in-charge, to someone she'd very much like for a lover. "Since you don't know me, you won't appreciate what I'm about to say, but… I don't give a damn about obligation or duty or what I should be doing or saying or thinking. Right now, finding the nearest bedroom is all that matters."

"I'm not sure—"

He slid his arms around her, pulling her close, and her

hands collided with the powerful expanse of his chest.
Everything about him seduced her. The look in his eyes.
The deep warmth of his voice. The heated imprint of his
body against hers. "Perhaps this will convince you."

He lowered his head once again and captured her
mouth with his. Where before his kiss had been slower
and more careful, this time the joining was fast and
certain and deliciously skillful. He teased her lips apart
and then slid inward, initiating a duel that she wished
could go on forever.

Her hands slid upward to grip the broad width of his
shoulders. She could feel the barely leashed power of
him rippling beneath her palms, could sense how tightly
he held himself in check. And she found that she wanted
to unleash that power and break through those protective safeguards. What would his embrace be like if he
weren't holding back? The mere thought had her
moaning in anticipation.

He must have heard the small sound because he
tensed and a compelling combination of desire and determination poured off him. His kiss deepened as he
shifted from enticement to an unmistakable taking. He
wanted her, and he expressed that want with each escalating kiss. If they'd been anywhere else, she'd have
done something outside her realm of expertise. She'd
have surrendered to his seduction and given herself to
him right then and there.

She'd never experienced anything that felt so right,
not in all her twenty-six years. How could she have
doubted? How could she have questioned being with
this man? She belonged here in his arms and nowhere

else. She wanted what only he could offer. More, she wanted to give him just as much in return. As though sensing the crumbling of her defenses, he lifted his head and stared down at her with dark, compelling eyes.

"Come with me," he insisted, and held out his hand. "Take the chance, Francesca."

How could she refuse him? Without another word of protest, she linked her fingers with his.

# CHAPTER TWO

FRANCESCA REMEMBERED little of their passage from the balcony to the front desk of the hotel. She existed in a dreamlike bubble, every word and action touched with enchantment. From the moment she put her hand in Sev's, the insanity that invaded her earlier came crashing back with even greater intensity. After he collected a key card and made a brief stop at the gift shop for supplies, he led her to a private elevator that whisked them straight to the penthouse suite. It wasn't until she stepped inside that a modicum of common sense prevailed.

"Perhaps we could have a drink and get to know each other," she suggested. "Take this a little slower."

To her surprise, he didn't argue. Maybe he felt the same way she did—overwhelmed and off-kilter. Desperate to regain his footing in this strange new land they'd stumbled upon.

"Let me see what they have in stock." He checked the selection of wines and chuckled, the deep, rich sound tripping along her nerve endings. He hefted one of the bottles. "Well, would you look at this. Here's something you might enjoy. They actually carry one of my family's labels from Italy."

"You're vintners?" she asked in surprise.

"My extended family is." He smiled, the relaxed warmth and humor causing her system to react in the most peculiar way. "I have a huge extended family. You probably couldn't mention a single field of interest where I couldn't find one of my relatives in that business."

"Even the jewelry business?" she joked. Since he'd been at Timeless Heirlooms' showing, he must have some connection to the jewelry industry.

He gave her an odd look. "Especially the jewelry business."

Before she could ask the next logical question—why he'd been present at the showing—he handed her the wine. Their fingers brushed and she caught her breath, the sound a sharp, urgent reaction to his touch. The fragile glass trembled in her grasp and without a word she set it on the closest surface. Slowly, ever so slowly, her gaze shifted to meet his and time froze.

How was this possible? How could she experience such intense feelings for a man she knew nothing about? She'd always kept herself guarded, had made a point to develop previous relationships slowly and with great care. Emotional distance promised safety. This—whatever *this* was—promised excitement, yet threatened danger.

Spending the night with Sev would change her, mark her in some indelible fashion. And yet, even knowing all that, an uncontrollable yearning built within, sweeping relentlessly through her, a yearning she had no more power to resist than the tide could fight the forces that drove each wave toward shore.

She gave up the battle. Stepping into his arms, she surrendered to his embrace. Relief surged through her, catching her by surprise. It took an instant to identify the cause and realize that it felt wrong to be apart from him, that on some level she needed to touch him and have him touch her. That without him she felt adrift and incomplete.

Without a word she helped him remove his suit jacket, the heavy silence broken only by the sigh of silk. His tie followed. She tackled the buttons of his shirt next. It felt so peculiar to stand before him and perform such an intimate, domestic chore. This should be a wife's pleasure. Or a lover's. She was neither. Or did a one-night stand qualify her as his lover?

His shirt parted, the crisp white of fine cotton juxta-posed against the tawny darkness of his skin. Her hands hovered for an instant, creating an additional contrast of cream against rich gold, before she flattened her palms against hard, bare flesh. She splayed her fingers across the rippled warmth and slid them upward, sweeping his shirt from his shoulders. Desire hummed through her veins and reverberated in her soft murmur of delight.

"Nice," she whispered.

"I plan to make it nicer."

A laugh escaped her. "I didn't notice before, but you have an accent."

His mouth curved to one side, an answering laugh turning his eyes to a dazzling gold. "Maybe it's because

Italian was our first language, even though my brothers and I were born and raised in San Francisco."

She wanted to ask more questions, to learn everything possible about him. But more urgent demands took precedence. Unable to help herself, she feathered a line of kisses along the firm sweep of his jaw. It wasn't enough. Not nearly enough. Forking her hands into his crisp, dark hair she drew his head downward and found his mouth with hers.

With a moan of pleasure, she sank inward, tasting the single sip of wine he'd consumed before passion had overruled social niceties. He teased her with a series of gentle kisses, at distinct odds with the ones they had shared earlier. These tempted. Suggested. Offered a dazzling promise of hot, sultry nights and endless pleasure. She pressed closer, her silk-covered breasts warm and heavy against the bare expanse of his chest. She reached for the zip to his trousers just as an insistent burr came from the cell phone he'd tucked into his pocket. Startled, she took a hasty step back.

"Wait." Sev fished out the phone and set it for voice mail before tossing it toward a nearby coffee table. It missed, clattering to the floor. "There. All taken care of."

"Don't you need to get that?" she asked.

"It's just my brother. It can wait until morning."

A slight frown creased his brow. Once upon a time he'd have taken Marco's call regardless of the circumstances. On some level he recognized the urgency of speaking to his brother. But that urgency faded to a dull, nagging sensation, one easily dismissed.

Nothing like this had ever happened to him before.

Not this crazed need. Not taking time away from business for a sexual interlude. Not the haste and desperation of making this woman his. From the minute they kissed, nothing else existed for him but a raw, desperate wanting, one he intended to satisfy.

"Forget about the phone." He cupped her neck and urged her closer, forking his fingers into her hair and tumbling the loosened strands into total disarray. "Forget about everything but right here and right now."

She relaxed against him and in the muted light her hair gleamed softly while her dark eyes held mysteries he longed to probe. He found the zip to her dress and lowered it the length of her spine. She released a sigh as the fabric parted. Inch by inch, the silk slid from her shoulders, revealing acres of smooth, pale skin. It skimmed her breasts before drifting downward to cling to her hips. A simple nudge sent the gown floating to the carpet, leaving her standing within his embrace wearing nothing but garter and stockings, panties and heels. And her jewelry. It glittered against a palate of cream.

He cupped her hips, supporting her as he sank downward, brushing a series of slow, openmouthed kisses from the pearled tips of her breasts to her soft belly. He slipped her heels from her feet and tossed them aside. Then he turned his attention to her stockings. It only took a moment to release the light-as-air nylons and roll them down the endless length of her legs, before disposing of her garter belt.

Damn, but she was sheer perfection, with narrow, coltish ankles, shapely calves and long, toned thighs. He paused where lilac silk acted as her final bastion of defense to press a kiss against the very heart of her. She trembled beneath his touch, sagging within his grasp.

"No more," she gasped. "I mean—"

"I know what you mean," he replied roughly.

And he did. If they didn't find the bedroom soon, they weren't going to make it there at all. He rose and her hands flew to his waistband, ripping at his belt and zipper. He backed her toward the bedroom as she fought to strip him, all the while snatching greedy, biting kisses. In the hallway, he kicked off his shoes and stepped free of his trousers. And then he swung her into his arms.

Sev reached the bed in three short steps and returned her to her feet. He cupped her face, his hands sweeping past the necklace she still wore. The feel of cool gemstones against his heated flesh allowed sanity to return for a brief instant, at least long enough for him to recognize his obligation to protect her jewelry from harm. With a practiced flick of his fingers, he removed necklace, bracelet and earrings and arranged them with due care on the nightstand table.

Satisfied, he returned his attention to Francesca, lowering her to the mattress. She lay in a tumble of creamy white against the darkness of the duvet. Opening the box he'd purchased at the gift store, he removed protection and put it within easy reach. Then he stripped off his boxers and joined Francesca on the bed. Lights from the city drifted through the unshaded windows opposite them, tinting her with an opalescent glow that battled the shadows attempting to conceal her from him.

The peaks of her naked breasts reflected the muted light, while darkness flung a protective arm low across her belly where her final scrap of clothing remained. She lay quietly beneath his scrutiny, her face turned toward his. Light and shadow worked its magic there, as well, the moon slicing a band of brightness across the ripe fullness of her bee-stung mouth, while her eyes—eyes the deep, rich brown of bittersweet chocolate— remained hidden from him.

He traced a path from moonlight to shadow, delving into the mysteries the dark kept hidden. Her eyes fluttered shut and filled him with an intense curiosity to know all she fought to hide. "What are you thinking?" he asked.

"I'm wondering how I came to be here." She shuddered beneath his touch and it took her a minute to finish. "One instant my life is simple and clear-cut and the next it has me so confused I can't think straight."

"Then don't think. Just feel."

He kissed her cupid's mouth. Unable to resist, he captured the plump bottom lip between his teeth and tugged ever so gently. His reward came in the low, helpless moan that escaped her.

"Do that again," she urged.

"All night long, if that's what you want."

He teased her lips once more, light, brushing strokes that promised without satisfying, suggested without de-livering. To his amusement, she chased his wandering mouth in greedy pursuit. He finally let her catch him, delighting in the way she coaxed him into a deeper kiss. She gave both promise and satisfaction, delivering on all he'd suggested. He couldn't get enough of the taste of her, of the incredible parry and slide and nibble of lips and tongue and teeth.

With each exchange, the fever within burned higher and brighter, demanding instant gratification. Sev resisted, refusing to rush. Francesca deserved more. For that matter, so did he. He wanted to explore every inch of her, to delve over each luscious hill and into every valley. To commit her to memory, and then repeat the process in case he'd missed something.

"Why have you stopped?" The question came in a whisper, her confusion communicated through the growing tension in her shoulders and back. "Is something wrong?"

"I haven't stopped," he reassured. "I've just slowed down."

"Oh, I get it. You want to drive me crazy."

He chuckled. "Drive us both crazy."

Her tension changed in tenor, no longer a self-conscious nervousness, but a woman's driving desire, full-bodied and certain. A vibrating need sent a burst of urgency through him. Maybe he'd been kidding himself. Slow was guaranteed to kill him.

Her long graceful hands swept across his torso from shoulder to hip, exploring with open delight. Despite her eagerness, he sensed a tentativeness behind each touch, a newness that spoke of sweet inexperience, right up until her hand closed around him with gentle aggression. Okay, maybe not total inexperience. She found the foil packet he'd set aside for their use and ripped it open, sliding the condom over him with deliberate, torturous strokes. Unable to stand another second, he rolled her under him.

Her body gave as only a woman's body could, ac-

commodating the press and slide of a man's passion.
The moonlight shifted, fully baring her to his gaze.
High, round breasts tempted his caress, the nipples
already ripe and taut with need. He gave them his full
attention, each sweep of tongue and hand causing her
breath to hitch and her heartbeat to race. Drifting lower,
he paused long enough to give due attention to an
abdomen that combined the sheen of satin with the
softness of down.

And then he eased her panties from her hips. He
followed their path with a string of kisses, before
drawing the scrap of silk and lace off and allowing it to
drift to the floor behind him. With that final garment
removed, it left nothing between them but heated air.
Thick, honeyed curls shielded the apex of her thighs and
he cupped her there, drawing a single finger along the
damp cleft, inciting a shudder of desperate yearning.

"It's been a while," she warned. He caught the hint
of apprehension she struggled to control. "I haven't—"

He was quick to reassure. "I'll go slow. You can stop
me if I do anything you don't like."

"I won't stop you." Her eyes darkened. "I can't."

"I'm relieved to hear it." He swept her loosened hair
away from her eyes, the dark blond strands framing the
face of an angel. "Slow and easy now, sweetheart. Open
for me," he urged. "Let me in."

To his relief, she didn't hesitate. Her thighs parted,
lifted, exposing her most private secrets to him. Ever so
gently he teased the opening, tracing his thumb across
the very center of her pleasure. She tensed, drawn bow-
string-taut, and the breath escaped her lungs in a moan

of sheer delight. Again he circled and swirled, until he sensed she teetered on the very edge, before he eased between her legs and sank into her.

She fisted around him, hot and slick and tight. He fought for control and a modicum of finesse, while instinct rode him, slashed through him, inciting him to take her hard and fast. To mate. To storm her defenses and shatter them once and for all. But he couldn't hurt her like that. She deserved better. Slowly, ever so slowly, he pressed inward. If she hadn't told him of her previous lover, he'd have sworn she'd come to him untouched.

"Am I hurting you?" The guttural tone of his voice shocked him. He could hear the raw, feral quality of a man teetering on the edge. "Do you want me to stop?"

"No. I need…" A rosy flush of want rode her cheekbones, and her expression in the moonlight revealed a vulnerability to him and him alone. She twined her arms and legs around him, her fingernails digging into his back. "More, please."

He didn't require any further encouragement. He drove home with a single powerful thrust. Her cry of astonished delight was everything he could have asked for and then some. She moved with him, finding the rhythm with impressive speed, riding the ferocity of the storm with him. He slid his hands beneath her, cupped her bottom and angled her in order to give her the most pleasure.

The storm intensified, howling through him with each stroke. Rational thought fled before a single inescapable imperative. Take the woman. Make her his. Put an indelible stamp on her, one that would bind them together from now through all eternity. She belonged to him now, just as he belonged to her. There was no changing that fact. No going back.

The storm reached its zenith, tearing at him, threatening to rip him apart. Even in the midst of the insanity, even at his most frantic, he remained focused on Francesca. Her needs. Her desires. She anchored him, even as she drove him onward, giving and gifting and surrendering. Her unique feminine perfume, the scent of passion, filled his nostrils. He could feel her approaching climax and sealed her mouth with his. She arched upward as it hit, and he drank in her cry of ecstasy as though it were the sweetest of wines.

It was his turn after that, his release unlike any he'd ever experienced before. She'd done that to him. For him. With him. She'd marked him in some ineradicable fashion. Given him something uniquely hers to give, something he'd never known with any other woman.

"Oh, my," she murmured long afterward, the breath still hitching from her lungs. "That was...unexpected."

"Very." As unexpected as it was unforgettable.

Struggling to catch his own breath, he gathered her up and rolled with her to take the weight from her and transfer it to him. She curled close with feline grace, entangling their limbs into an inescapable knot, part feminine silk, part masculine sinew. Full, round curves cushioned hard angles. With the sweet, gusty sigh of a woman well-satisfied, sleep claimed her.

He lay awake for a long time, holding her close. Their joining should have fulfilled him, satiated whatever fever fired his blood and drove him to make this woman his. It hadn't. Not by a long shot. It should be over now, the flame diminished to a mere flicker. It wasn't. It continued to roar like wildfire driven before a gale. Instead of ending things, their lovemaking had rooted the bond between them, weaving the fabric of their connection into a tight, inseparable warp and weft.

Whether she knew it yet or not, this night had made her his.

Francesca stirred beneath the benevolent rays of the early morning sunshine.

Lord, she felt incredible. Warm. Relaxed. Happy. She didn't know what had caused such an amazing sensation, but considering how fleeting such feelings could be, she didn't want to move in case it went away.

A heavy masculine hand skated down the length of her spine to cup her bottom, giving it a loving pat. "Mmm. Nice."

What the hell? Francesca's eyes flew open and she stared in horror at the gorgeous male relaxing inches from her nose. Sunlight slid across the bed and openly caressed a man whose bone structure managed to combine both a masculine hardness and a mouth-watering allure. Thick, ebony hair framed high, sweeping cheekbones and an aristocratic nose. He smiled drowsily, his wide sensuous lips stirring images of all the places that mouth had been. Memory crashed down on her, overwhelming in its intensity.

What had she done? A better question might have been…what *hadn't* she done? In the brief time they'd spent together, they'd made love in every conceivable fashion. Of course, she'd enjoyed every minute. Sev had proven an outstanding lover. But the romantic illusion cast by the glittering evening had faded beneath the harsh reality of morning light. She'd had a job to do last night at Le Premier, and instead she'd—

Francesca bolted upright in bed in a flat-out panic. *Her job!* Oh, damn. Damn, damn, damn. What had she done? How could she have been so foolish? The Fontaines were going to kill her when she arrived at the office. She scrubbed the heels of her hands across her face.

This was not good. What in the world would she say to them? How could she possibly explain what she'd chosen to do instead of representing Timeless Heirlooms at last night's showing? She needed to get home immediately and call them. But first, she needed to return the jewelry she'd worn last night before Tina went into total meltdown. Assuming she hadn't already.

Francesca thrust a tangle of curls from her face and looked desperately around for a clock, hyperventilating when she read the glowing digits that warned she had precisely half an hour to get to Timeless Heirlooms and explain herself to the Fontaines.

"Where are you going?" Sev asked in a sleep-roughened voice. He snagged her around the waist and tipped her back into his embrace. "I have the perfect way to start our morning." A slow smile built across his face. "Funny thing. It involves staying right here."

She wriggled against him. "No. Please let go. You don't understand."

"Mmm." He reacted to her movements in a way she'd have delighted in only hours before. "That feels good."

"I have to get to work."

His hold tightened, locking them together from abdomen to thigh. Heat exploded, and even knowing she may have destroyed her career thanks to one night of stupidity, desire awoke with a renewed ferocity that left her stunned. How was this possible? She squeezed her eyes shut. Why, oh why, did this temptation have to hit last night of all nights? And why hadn't their time together satisfied the unrelenting hunger that accompanied it?

Well, she knew one thing for certain. If she hesitated even one more second, she wouldn't get out of this bed anytime soon. Taking a deep breath, she planted both hands against his chest—Lord help her, what a chest— and shoved. To her surprise, she succeeded in freeing herself. One minute she lay cocooned in warmth and the next she stood beside the bed, naked, cold and vaguely self-conscious. Sev lifted onto an elbow and studied her through narrowed, watchful eyes. Tension rippled through him, and a hint of something dangerous and predatory lurked in his expression.

"I have to get to work," she explained. "Assuming, after last night, I still have a job. I made a huge mistake leaving with you."

His tension increased ever so slightly, and he continued to remind her of a watchful panther debating whether or not to take down his prey. "Which was your mistake? Leaving with me…or leaving with a couple mil worth of the Fontaines' jewelry? I suspect both the Fontaines, as well as your agency, won't be too pleased. If you'd like, I can place a couple of calls and get you off the hook."

Francesca frowned in confusion. "What agency?"

she asked, before waving that aside. "Oh, never mind. More to the point, where's the jewelry?"

Sev gestured toward the diamond-and-amethyst pieces glittering on the bedside table. "Relax. Everything's safe and sound, and more importantly, undamaged."

"Thank God."

She scooped up the set with exquisite care. Since she didn't have the jewelry cases on her, she could only think of one safe place to put them, and swiftly fastened the pieces to her neck, wrist and ears. It wasn't until she finished that she sensed Sev's gaze on her. His hungry look deepened and made her acutely aware that she stood before him wearing nothing but the designs she'd created. Tension filled the room, heating the air between them.

*Her job!* How could she have forgotten…again? The thought propelled her to action. She caught a glimpse of lilac panties peeking from beneath the pleated edge of the dust ruffle and snatched them up before exiting the bedroom. To her dismay Sev followed right behind, wearing even less than she.

The instant they hit the living room, Sev's cell phone emitted a faint buzz from the direction of the coffee table. This time he picked it up and answered it. "What?" His gaze flickered in her direction. "Say that name again? You're certain?"

She spared him a swift glance, concerned by the sudden grimness lining his face. "What? What's wrong?"

He closed his phone with a snap and came after her. "Who are you?" he demanded.

She stepped into her panties and looked around for her dress. "I already told you. Francesca Sommers." She spotted her dress heaped in a silken pool a few feet shy of the couch. A vague memory of Sev's tossing it toward the cushioned back came to her. Clearly, he'd missed.

Before she could snatch it up, Sev caught her arm and spun her to face him. "You're not a model. You're Timeless Heirlooms' new designer."

His statement sounded more like an accusation. She carefully disengaged her arm from his grasp and bent to pick up her dress. It was ridiculous to feel self-conscious after the night they'd spent together. But something about the way Sev stared at her caused her to hold the gown tight against her breasts. "I never claimed to be a model. You must have jumped to that conclusion." She frowned. "What difference does it make, anyway?"

"Did the Fontaines put you up to this? Is that why you followed me onto the balcony last night?" The questions came at her, fast and sharp.

She stared at him in utter bewilderment, combined with a bubble of irritation. "I have no idea what you're talking about. All I know is that if I don't report in to work within the next twenty minutes, I won't have a job. Now, do you mind? I'd like to—"

He cut her off with a sweep of his hand. "I'm talking about a TH employee falling into bed with one of the owners of Dantes five minutes after meeting. I'm talking about you using the oldest trick in the book to gain inside information for the Fontaines."

She jerked backward as though slapped. "Dantes? You work for Dantes?"

"Sweetheart, I *own* Dantes."

The connection hit and hit hard. Her dress slipped

from between fingers that had gone abruptly boneless. "You're a Dante?"

"Severo Dante. CEO and chairman of the board of Dantes."

"Oh, God." She was *so* fired. "I thought you were a buyer." She managed to add two and two, despite working with only half a brain. "You were at the showing last night to scope out the competition, weren't you?"

He looked around. Finding his trousers between the living room and the bedroom, he snatched them up and yanked them on. The man who stood before her now bore little resemblance to the one who'd made such passionate love to her only hours before. With the exception of the unbuttoned trousers riding low on his hips, he wore nothing but an endless expanse of bare flesh.

Desire still hummed between them, calling to her with even more strength and power than the night before. And she might have answered that call, too, if he hadn't used that one word, that single, appalling word— *Dantes*—that had her itching to run in the opposite direction as fast as her wobbly legs would take her.

She wriggled back into the dress she'd chosen with such care for her first showing. She didn't bother trying to hand-press the wrinkles. Nothing would salvage this mess other than a trip to the dry cleaner's. But at least now she could face him on an even footing, or at least on a somewhat even footing.

She planted her hands on her hips. "Okay, let's have this out. You think I came on to you last night so I could find out your plans in regard to TH?" she demanded. At his nod, she glared at him. "How about the possibility of your coming on to me so you could get the inside scoop on TH's plans? After all, you're trying to buy out the Fontaines, aren't you?"

He studied her for a long silent moment. "It would seem we have a problem."

"Oh, no, we don't." She found her shoes kicked under the wet bar and shoved her feet into the spiked heels. At the same time, she thrust her fingers through her hair in an attempt to restore order to utter disaster. "It's very simple from here on out. We avoid each other at all costs and we don't mention last night to anyone. *Anyone*," she stressed. "If I'd known who you were last night, I'd never have taken off with you."

"Liar."

She closed her eyes, forcing herself to admit the painful truth. "Fine. That's a lie. But I wouldn't have gone with you because you're Severo Dante. It would have been despite that fact." She opened her eyes and fought to keep her gaze level and not betray the profound effect he had on her. "I owe the Fontaines more than I can possibly repay. Betraying them with their chief competitor isn't the sort of repayment I had in mind. So, from now on, we're through. Got it?"

He came for her again, closing the distance so that no more than a whisper of space separated them. It would have been so easy to push aside that cushion of air and take another delicious tumble into insanity. Just the mere thought had her body reacting, softening and loosening in anticipation. He was a Dante, she struggled to remind herself. She hadn't realized that fact before, and therefore couldn't blame herself for what had happened the previous night. But now that she did know, she had a duty to keep her distance.

He brushed aside a lock of her hair. Just that slight a touch and she came totally unraveled. "It would seem we have a problem," he repeated.

No question about that. "I've been consorting with the enemy." Still consorted. Still wanted to consort.

He shook his head. "It's a hell of a lot more complicated than that. Whatever this thing is between us—it isn't over." He traced his hand along the curve of her cheek, leaving behind a streak of fire. "It's only just begun."

# CHAPTER THREE

SEVERO LEFT Le Premier, stopping at his apartment only long enough to change, before continuing to Sausalito to confront his grandfather about the events of the previous night. He had questions, questions only his grandfather could answer.

"Primo?" he called, as he stepped through their front door.

Silence greeted him, which meant Nonna was out and he should continue on toward the gated garden behind his grandparents' hillside home if he wanted to find the object of his search. Sev headed for the kitchen at the rear of the house and stepped from the cool dusky interior into a sunlit explosion of scent and color.

Sure enough, he found Primo hard at work on a bed of native Californian wildflowers. Thick gray hair escaped from beneath the brim of a canvas bucket hat and surrounded a noble, craggy face. At Sev's approach, Primo rocked back onto his heels, grunting in pain from the arthritis that had begun to plague him in recent years.

Fierce golden eyes, identical to Sev's own, fixed on him. "Do me a favor." He spoke in his native tongue, his

Italian seasoned with the unique flavoring of his Tuscan birthplace. "Grab one of those bags of mulch and bring it over here. My ancient bones will be forever grateful."

Sev did as ordered. Stooping, he split the bag with a pair of gardening shears and set to work beside his grandfather. Memories from his childhood hovered, other days that mirrored this one, days filled with the scent of cool, salt-laden air combined with rich loamy earth. Long, industrious moments passed before Sev spoke.

"I'm in the mood for a story, Primo."

His grandfather's thick brows lifted in surprise. "You have a particular one in mind?"

Sev spread a generous layer of mulch around a bed that combined the striking colors of golden poppies, baby blue eyes and beach strawberries. "As a matter of fact, I do." He paused in his endeavors. "Tell me what happened when you met Nonna."

"Ah." An odd smile played across the older man's face. "Are you asking out of simple academic interest, or is there a more personal reason behind your sudden interest?"

"Tell me."

Primo released a gruff laugh at the barked demand. "So. It is personal. You have finally felt the burn, have you, *nipote?*"

Sev wiped his brow before fixing his grandfather with an uncompromising stare. "I want to know what the hell happened to me and how to make it stop."

"What happened is Dantes' Inferno," Primo answered simply. "Some call it a family curse. I have always considered it a family blessing."

The name teased at a far-off memory. No, not a

memory. More of a childhood story, carrying a grain of truth amid the more fantastical elements. "Explain."

Primo released his breath in a deep sigh. "Come. The story sits better with a beer in one hand and a cigar in the other."

Brushing plant detritus from his slacks, he stood and led the way into the kitchen. Cool and rustic, huge flagstones decorated the kitchen floor while rough-hewn redwood beams stretched across the twelve-foot plaster ceiling. A large table, perfect for a substantially sized family, took up one end of the room, while a full compliment of the latest appliances filled the other. After washing up, the two men helped themselves to bottles of homemade honey beer and took a seat at the table. Primo produced a pair of cigars. Once they were clipped and lit, he leaned back in his chair and eyed his grandson.

"I did try and warn you," he began.

"You didn't issue a warning. You told us a fairy tale when we were impressionable children. Why would we put credence in something so implausible?"

"It was real. You just chose not to believe. Not to remember."

The quiet words held an unmistakable conviction, one that threw Sev. "So now I'm supposed to accept that you and Nonna took one look at each other and it was love at first sight? A love inspired by this…this Inferno?"

His grandfather shook his head. "Not even close. I took one look at your grandmother and it was lust at first sight." He studied the burning tip of his cigar and his voice dropped to a husky whisper. "And then I touched her. That is when The Inferno happened. That is when the bond formed—a bond that has lasted our entire lives. Whether you are willing to believe it or not, it is a bond our family has experienced for as long as there have been Dantes."

"Lightning bolts. Love at first sight. Instant attraction." Sev shrugged. "All names for the same spice. How is our story any different from thousands of others? What makes it 'The Inferno' versus the simple chemistry most lovers experience?"

Primo took his time responding. When he did, he came at his answer from a tangent. "Your grandmother belonged to another man. Did you know that?" Bittersweet memories stirred in his distinctive eyes. "She was engaged to him."

Aw, hell. "Not good."

"Now that is an understatement if ever I heard one," Primo said dryly. "You need to understand that all those years ago an engagement was as much a commitment as marriage vows, at least in our little village. So, we fled the country and came here."

"Have you ever regretted it?" Sev asked gently.

Primo's expression turned fierce, emphasizing the contours of his strong Roman nose and squared jawline. "Never. My only regret is the pain I caused this other man." His mouth compressed and he lifted his beer for a long drink. "He was *mio amico*. No, not just my friend. My *best* friend. But once The Inferno strikes..." He shrugged. "There is nothing that can stop it. Nothing that can come between those who have known the burn. Nothing to douse the insanity but to make that woman yours. She is your soul mate. Your other half. To deny it will bring you nothing but grief, as your father discovered to his misfortune."

Sev wanted to refute his grandfather's words, to dismiss them as an aging man's fantasy. But he hesitated, reluctant to say anything now that Primo had mentioned Sev's father. And one other fact held him silent. Everything Primo said precisely matched his reactions last night, which created a serious dilemma for him. He had plans for Francesca, plans other than taking her to bed. To restore Dantes to its former glory, he had no choice but to steal her away from the Fontaines.

"When you first saw Nonna—before you touched—what was it like?"

Primo hesitated as he considered and dug bony fingers into his right hand, massaging the palm. Over the years Sev had witnessed the habitual gesture more times than he could count, long ago assuming it resulted from arthritis or some other physical complaint. Now he knew better. Worse, he'd caught himself imitating it over the past few hours. Even now he could barely suppress the urge.

"I had been away at university and returned for the engagement party. The minute I set eyes on Nonna, it was as though we were connected. As though a ribbon of desire joined us. The closer we came, the stronger it grew. When we touched, the ribbon became stronger than a steel cable, binding us together so we could no longer distinguish my heartbeat from hers. We have beat as one ever since."

The story affected Sev more than he cared to admit, probably because it rang with such simple sincerity.

True or not, Primo clearly believed every word. Not that the origins of his grandparents' romance helped with his current predicament. Okay, so he'd felt that connection, the shock and burn when they'd touched, that ribbon of lust, as he preferred to consider it. But ribbons could be cut.

"How do I get rid of it?" he demanded.

Primo drank down the last of his beer before setting the empty bottle on the table with enough power that the glass rang in protest. "You do not," he stated unequivocally. "Why would you want to?"

"Because she's the wrong woman for me. There are…complications."

Primo released a full-bodied laugh. "More complicated than her belonging to your best friend?" He swept his hand through the air, the gesture leaving behind a smoky contrail. "It is impossible to cut the connection. The Inferno has no respect for time or place or complication. It knows. It chooses. And it has done so for as long as there have been Dantes. You either accept the gift and revel in the blessing it offers, or you walk away and suffer the consequences."

Sev stilled. "What consequences?"

"You ignore The Inferno at your own peril, *nipote*." He leaned forward, each word stone hard. "If you turn your back on it, you will never know true happiness. Look at what happened to your father."

"You think The Inferno killed him?" Sev demanded on a challenging note. "Are you that superstitious?"

Primo's expression softened. "No, it didn't kill Dominic. But because he chose with his head instead of his heart, because he married your mother instead of the woman chosen for him by The Inferno, he never found true happiness. And Dantes suffered as a result." He stabbed his cigar in Sev's direction. "I am warning you, Severo Dante. If you follow in your father's footsteps you, too, will know only the curse, never the blessing."

Tina Fontaine threw herself into a chair near where Francesca sat at her drawing board, while Kurt filled the doorway leading into the small office. One look at their expressions warned Francesca that her previous night's indiscretion had left her career teetering on a knife's edge.

"You owe my dear husband a huge thank-you for stopping me from calling the police last night," came Tina's opening volley.

Francesca stared in horror. "The police?"

Tina leaned forward, not bothering to disguise her fury. "It was your big night. And you disappeared with a bloody fortune in gems around your neck without bothering to tell anyone where you'd gone. What did you expect me to do?"

"I'm sorry. Truly. I have no idea what came over me."

The ring of truth in Francesca's comment gave Tina pause. "Where the hell did you go?"

"I think I can guess," Kurt inserted. "Holed up somewhere clutching a wastebasket, were you?"

Francesca stared at him, utterly miserable. She didn't have any choice. She couldn't lie. She had to admit the truth and take whatever punishment they chose to dole out, even if it meant the end of her career at TH. "Not exactly. I—"

From behind Tina's back, Kurt gave a warning shake of his head. "But you were suffering from a severe case of nerves, I assume?" Before Francesca could reply, he continued, "It's the one excuse Tina can sympathize with, can't you, darling? It happened to her on the night of her first show, too."

Tina gave an irritable shrug. "Yes, fine. It happened to me when we opened our first jewelry store in Mendocino. Too many nerves, too much champagne and too little intestinal fortitude." She shot Francesca an annoyed look. "Is that what happened?"

Francesca hesitated, before nodding despite nearly overwhelming guilt. "I'm so sorry. The crowd got to me and I decided to leave early." She kept her gaze fixed on Tina, but caught Kurt's small look of approval. "I promise it won't happen again."

"I suggest it doesn't. Next time I'll fire you." Tina continued to stare with uncomfortable intensity. "How in the world did you evade security? I need to know so in the future our designers and models can't pull a similar stunt."

Francesca kept her gaze fixed on her drawing table. "There's an exit off the balcony," she whispered. "One of the guests escorted me."

"Go on."

Francesca swallowed. "As for the jewelry…I can't tell you how sorry I am that I worried you. I swear I kept it safe." Or rather Sev had. She'd been too far gone by that time to give a single thought to what damage their lovemaking might do to the delicate pieces.

"That's the only thing that saved your job," Tina said

sternly. "If anything had happened to the jewelry, you'd
be cooling your heels in jail."

Tina's assistant appeared before she could say
anything further and leaned into the room around Kurt.
"Call for you," she informed her boss. "It's Juliet
Bloom's rep."

Tina came off the chair as though catapulted and flew
toward the door. She paused at the last instant. "Fair
warning, Francesca." She threw the admonition over
her shoulder. "The rep wasn't happy when I couldn't
produce you last night. If she's calling to blow off our
deal because you were incapable of doing your job,
you're gone."

Francesca fought to draw breath, seeing her career
vanish before her eyes thanks to one night of utter fool-
ishness. "I understand."

"And there's a call for you on line three, Francesca,"
the assistant added, with a hint of sympathy.

"Excuse me for a minute," she murmured to Kurt.
She picked up the phone, not in the least surprised to
hear Severo Dante's voice respond to her greeting.
"How may I help you?" she asked in as businesslike a
tone as she could manage.

"Huh." He paused as though giving it serious
thought. "I'm not quite sure how to answer that. Most
of the possibilities that come to mind would be interesting variations on last night's theme."

She didn't dare respond to the comment. She'd risked
quite enough already, thanks to Sev. "I'm really busy
right now. Could I get back to you in regard to that?"

"In regard to that, you can get back to me anytime you

want. But I'm calling for a different reason, altogether. I want you to meet me for lunch at Fruits de Mer at one."

She spared Kurt a brief, uncomfortable glance. "That's not remotely possible."

"In hot water, are you?"

"Yes."

"Then let's make it tomorrow."

"I'm sorry, that's quite impossible."

"Make it possible or I'll come by the office and let you explain my presence to the Fontaines. Or better yet, *I'll* explain everything to them. Personally."

Oh, God. If he did that, she'd be fired for sure. Painfully aware of her father listening in, she chose her words with care. "You are such a…gentleman."

He chuckled. "You're not alone, are you?" At her pointed silence, he added, "I'm serious. We need to talk. Will you come tomorrow?"

"It would seem I have no other choice. Now, I really have to go." She ended the conversation by returning the receiver to its cradle. "I'm sorry about that, Kurt."

He regarded her far too acutely. "I assume that was your young man from last night?" He held up a hand before she could reply. "I caught a glimpse of you and your mysterious friend leaving together, which is why I didn't worry about your disappearance as much as Tina. I remember some of the antics she and I got up to when we were first dating. I do, however, recommend in the future that you don't mix business with pleasure."

Embarrassed color warmed Francesca's cheeks. "I hope you know that I don't usually… I'm not—"

He waved that aside, but not before she saw his

cheeks turn a ruddier shade than normal. "I helped you out of a tight spot this time because, quite frankly, we need you and what you can do for Timeless Heirlooms. But, I won't bail you out again."

"I understand." It killed her to be having this conversation with her father. More than anything she hoped to win both his approval, as well as his friendship. Instead, he'd helped her lie to his wife and put their relationship at odds. "As I told Tina, it won't happen again."

"Listen to me, Francesca." He took the chair Tina had vacated. "Your six-month contract with Timeless Heirlooms is almost up. Tina and I are both very excited with what we've seen from you so far. Equally as important, we've enjoyed working with you."

She smiled in genuine pleasure. Receiving such a huge compliment from her father meant the world to her. "Thank you. I've enjoyed working with you, as well."

How could she not? She was living the dream of a lifetime, one she wanted more than anything. Thanks to the detective she'd hired, she'd been able to track down her father the minute she'd graduated from college and approach him without anyone being the wiser. To her delight, she discovered that he shared her passion. Even more incredible, the company he and Tina ran was actively hiring designers, if only on a trial basis.

"Tina and I were on the verge of making your position here permanent. But after last night, we simply can't take the risk. Not yet. You understand our predicament, don't you?"

Her smile died. In the past six months she'd struggled to prove herself as both a top-notch designer, as well as a woman he'd be proud to claim as his daughter. It had all gone so well…until last night. And now she'd ruined everything.

"I do understand," she managed to say. "Kurt, I can't thank you and Tina enough for giving me this opportunity. I swear I'll make it up to you."

"I don't doubt that." He offered her a slow, generous smile, one that never failed to fill Francesca with an intense longing. He stood and held out his hand. "We'll give it another couple months. Maybe once we have Juliet Bloom under contract, we'll feel more comfortable offering you a permanent position with us."

Francesca slipped her hand into his bearlike grasp, fighting back tears. Determination filled her. It didn't matter what it took, she'd find a way to win his approval, as well as a permanent job at Timeless Heirlooms. If that meant avoiding Sev—after the lunch he'd forced on her—then that's what she'd do. Because nothing was more important than having the opportunity to get to know her father, even if she could never tell him the truth about their relationship.

"Thank you for offering me another chance," she said with as much composure as she could manage. "You won't regret it."

"All right," Francesca stated the minute she joined Sev at Fruits de Mer. "You blackmailed me into coming here. Now what do you want?"

Sev studied her silently for a long moment. If he could peg her with a single word it would be *defensive*. From the moment she'd stepped foot in the restaurant and spotted him, she'd had trouble meeting his gaze. He could guess why. He'd seen this woman naked. Had taken her in his arms and made love to her, not once or twice, but three times during their night together, each occasion more passionate than the last. It should have ensured an ease between them. And maybe it would have, except for one vital detail.

Forty-eight hours ago they'd been total strangers.

"You expected things to be different," he said. "Didn't you?"

She looked at him, the unremitting darkness of her eyes making a startling contrast to her pale complexion and honey-blond hair. "Today, you mean?" She gave him her full attention, a painful vulnerability lurking in her gaze. "Let's just say that I'd hoped things would be different."

She'd changed toward him since their night together and he could guess the reason. Now that she'd discovered his identity, she'd decided to end things between them—something he refused to allow. "You hoped our reaction to each other would change now that you know who I am. Because you work for Timeless Heirlooms and I own Dantes. You thought that fact would put a stop to what we're experiencing."

"Yes." A slight frown creased her brow. With a swift glance toward nearby tables, she dropped her voice to a whisper. "I need to explain something. I don't know who that woman was two nights ago. I've never—" She took a deep breath. "I'm not making excuses."

"Of course not." He understood all too well. "But that doesn't alter the facts."

She retreated from him, icing over tension and longing with such speed that he suspected she'd had many years of practice. "As far as I'm concerned, whatever happened between us has run its course."

He tilted his head to one side. "Because you say so? Because it would be so much more convenient on the work front?" He couldn't help laughing. "You're kidding, right? This isn't something you can turn off like a light switch."

"I think it is."

He studied her for a moment to assess her veracity. Satisfied she actually believed the nonsense she trotted out, he placed his hands flat on the table. He slid them across the linen-covered surface, inch by inch. When his hands came to within a foot of hers, she released a soft groan.

"Okay," she said, snatching her hands back. "Point made. Maybe this...this—"

"Attraction? Desire?" He lifted an eyebrow. "Lust?"

She waved the choices aside. "Those are just varying shades of the same thing."

"And you're still experiencing each of those shades, as well as every one in between."

He caught the faint breathy sound of air escaping her lungs. "Whatever this is hasn't run its course at all, has it?" she asked.

"Not even a little." He massaged the tingle in his right palm. "I could feel you, you know."

Her brows shot up. "Feel me? What do you mean?"

"When you walked in the room, I didn't even have to see you," he admitted. "I could feel you."

"I don't understand any of this. How is that possible?"

He didn't answer. Couldn't answer. "Is it the same for you? Has it eased off any since that night?"

She wanted to lie, he could read it in the hint of desperation in those huge, defenseless eyes. "Maybe it has." She moistened her lips. "I'm sure it's not quite as bad as the other night."

"There's an easy way to tell." He extended his hand across the table once again. "Go ahead. Touch me."

Francesca hesitated for a telling moment before splaying her fingers and linking them with Sev's. She gasped at the contact, going rigid with shock. The next instant everything about her softened and relaxed, sinking into what he could only describe as euphoria. Then the next wave hit. A hot tide of need lapped between them, singeing nerve endings and escalating desire.

"I want you again." He told her precisely how much with a single scorching look. "If anything, I want you even more than last time."

"We can't do this. Not again," Francesca protested. "I've already put my job in jeopardy by spending the night with you. If the Fontaines find out it was you at the show…that you were the reason I left, they'd fire me on the spot. I won't risk that. Working at TH is too important to me."

Didn't she get it? "You want me to stop?" He lifted their joined hands. "Tell me how. Because I'd love to know."

She leaned forward, speaking in a low, rapid voice. "What I want is an explanation. Maybe if I understood how and why, I could make it stop."

He hesitated, loath to repeat the story Primo had told

him. But she deserved some sort of answer, even one as far-fetched as The Inferno. It didn't matter that he refused to believe what they were experiencing had anything to do with something so fantastical, or that his grandfather's Inferno fairy tale belonged just there…in fairy tales. She should know.

He forced himself to release her hands, despite an almost uncontrollable urge to sweep her up in his arms and bolt from the restaurant with her. More than anything he wanted to hole up somewhere with acres of bed, twenty-four-hour room service and a suitcase full of condoms.

"Look, I think I can explain this, though the explanation is going to sound a bit crazy." Nor was this the venue he'd have chosen to tell a woman about The Inferno. But at least a crowded restaurant would give the illusion of safety once she'd fully ascertained the extent of his family's insanity. He gave it to her straight. "There's a Dante legend that my grandfather swears is true, about an Inferno that occurs when a man from my family touches the woman meant to be his."

Her eyes narrowed, but at least she didn't run screaming from the restaurant. "Somehow I don't think this is the sort of story we should hash out in public. Do you?"

"Not even a little. My place isn't far from here. We can talk there, if you'd prefer."

"Talk?" A swift laugh bubbled free and she regarded him with wry amusement. "That would make a nice change. I don't suppose you can promise that's all we're going to do?"

He shook his head. "I can't promise a thing where

you're concerned." He leaned back, giving her enough room to breathe. Hell, giving them both enough room to think straight. "But I swear, I'll try. Will you trust me enough to come with me?"

She turned those bottomless dark eyes on him in silent assessment. He'd never met a woman quite so fascinating. She faced the world with elegance and strength and feminine dignity. And though he sensed they were integral parts of her, he also suspected they were a shield she used to protect herself from hurt.

Every so often he caught a glimpse of a waif peeking out, nose pressed to the glass, the want in her so huge and deep it amazed him that one person could contain it all. And yet, he also saw the steely determination that carried her through a life that—if he correctly read all she struggled to conceal—had slammed her with hardship while offering little joy to compensate.

After giving his offer a moment's thought, she nodded. "I promised to meet you this one last time before we parted company, and I will. Besides, I always did like fairy tales even though they never come true." A smile played about her perfect bow mouth, tempting him beyond measure. Then she surprised him by lifting a hand and signaling the waiter. "But who knows. Maybe this one will be different."

# CHAPTER FOUR

TEN SHORT minutes later they arrived at his Pacific Heights Georgian residence. "This is your home?" Francesca asked, clearly stunned.

He could tell the size and grandeur unnerved her. Hell, as a child it had unnerved him, as well. Built in the 1920s, his grandparents purchased it during Dantes' heyday, when Primo controlled the reins of the company.

Sev had recently updated the house from top to bottom, taking a diamond in the rough and giving it the glitter and polish it deserved. While still on the formal side, he'd made a point to add a more welcoming feel to the place. From the two-story entry foyer, a curving staircase—complete with wrought-iron railing—swept toward the second story and an endless array of rooms perfect for entertaining.

"When I'm entertaining guests, I stay here. More often I use my Nob Hill apartment. It's more compact. More to my taste." Unable to resist touching her, he slid his hand down her spine to the small hollow at the base and guided her toward the private den he kept exclusively for his own use. "This is my favorite room in the house."

Francesca visibly relaxed as she looked around. Light filtered in from a bank of windows that provided an unfettered view of the bay and Alcatraz Island. Two of the other walls bulged with books that overran the floor-to-ceiling mahogany cases. The final wall, at right angles to the windows, offered a cozy fireplace fronted by the most comfortable couch Sev had ever owned. He used the electronic controls to light the fire and gestured for her to have a seat.

It amused him that she took the precaution to sit as far from him as the couch cushions allowed. Understandable, but still humorous. "Okay, let me give it to you straight," he began.

She listened intently while he ran through Primo's explanation of The Inferno, refraining from asking any questions until he finished speaking. "You said that, in the past, your family experienced this Inferno," she said after a moment. "What about your brothers? Have they felt anything similar?"

"I'm the first," Sev replied.

Wariness crept into her gaze. "That suggests you buy in to all this."

"No, not really." And he didn't, despite Primo's insistence that legend matched reality. "I think it makes for a charming story, but a story, nonetheless."

"Then how would you explain what's happened to us?"

He'd given that a lot of thought and decided to believe the simplest explanation. "It's nothing more than lust. Given time, it'll fade."

Though she took his comment with apparent equanimity, a pulse kicked to life at the base of her throat, betraying her agitation. "But what if it's more than that? Has it ever infected the women in your family?"

"I don't understand. Which women?"

She made an impatient motion with her hands. "Haven't any of the Dante men had daughters? Have any of the Dante women experienced this Inferno?"

Sev shook his head. "There's only been one daughter in more generations than I can recall. My cousin, Gianna. Here…let me show you."

He circled the couch to a cluster of photos on a console table and picked up a panoramic photograph in a plain silver frame that showed a group shot of all the Dantes. Seated in the middle were Nonna and Primo. Sev, his parents and brothers stood to Primo's right, while his Aunt Elia, and Uncle Alessandro, with their brood of four, stood beside Nonna. He handed the picture to Francesca when she joined him, tapping the image of the only female of his generation, a striking young woman with Sev's coloring.

"If Gia's been cursed by The Inferno, she's never mentioned it."

A hint of laughter lightened Francesca's expression. "Cursed? I thought you said Primo called it a blessing."

He couldn't help himself. He leaned toward her, cupping her cheek. "Does it feel like a blessing to you?"

She shut him out by closing her eyes, concealing her inner thoughts. "No, this isn't a blessing. It's a complication I could live without." She eased back from his touch and opened her eyes again, at the same time slamming impenetrable barriers into place. "And what about the other women? The women who are the object of the Dante men's...blessing?"

"Like you and Nonna and Aunt Elia?"

"Yes. What choice do we have? How do we escape this Inferno?"

He gestured toward the image of his parents. "My father escaped by marrying someone else."

Francesca blinked in surprise. "Your mother wasn't an Inferno bride?"

Sev shook his head. "Shortly after they died I discovered letters that indicated he'd been in love with one of his designers, but married my mother, instead."

"Why didn't he marry the woman he really loved?" she asked hesitantly. "Do you know?"

Sev shrugged. "When I confronted Primo about it, he admitted that my mother had invaluable contacts in the industry. It was more of a business arrangement than a true marriage. Not that it did either of them any good."

"What went wrong?"

Maybe it was the hint of compassion he heard in her voice, but he found himself opening up in way he never had with any other woman. "All of my mother's contacts couldn't make up for my father's lack of business savvy." He studied the photograph. God, they looked so youthful. Just six or seven years older than his own thirty-four, he suddenly realized. They also looked remote and unhappy, though how much of that related to their marriage and how much to business difficulties, he couldn't determine. "They were on the verge of a divorce when they died in a sailing accident."

"And you blame that on The Inferno?" she asked in patent disbelief.

"No. I blame it on bad luck." He couldn't tell her the rest. Couldn't admit that he blamed himself for what happened right before and immediately after his father's death. That piece of guilt he kept locked tightly away. "I'd just graduated from college. The day after their funeral, I stepped into my father's shoes. I spent the first year of my tenure dismantling Dantes and the last decade rebuilding it."

"I'm so sorry." She slipped her hand into his and squeezed. Just that, and yet it made all the difference. The connection between them intensified in some indefinable way. Before it had been sheer sex, or so he believed. Now another emotion crept in, one he resisted analyzing. She hesitated a split second before confessing, "I lost my mother, too. I know how painful that must have been for you."

That might explain some of the sorrow he'd seen lurking in her eyes. "How old were you?" he asked.

"Five." Soft. Abrupt. And a clear message that she had no interest in pursuing the conversation.

Not that he planned to drop it. He'd just approach the subject with more care. "It helped that my brothers and I were older, though at just sixteen, Nicolò had a tough time adapting. Fortunately, Primo and Nonna stepped in, which made a huge difference." He paused. "What about you? Did your father ever remarry?"

"My parents weren't together," she admitted, avoiding his gaze. "I went into foster care."

Oh, God. He tiptoed across eggshells. "Didn't the authorities contact him?"

"They didn't know who he was. I didn't find out myself until after I'd graduated from college and hired someone to locate him for me." She picked up the next picture in the line, putting a clear end to the discussion. A slight smile eased the strain building around the corners of her mouth. "Primo and Nonna on their wedding day, I assume?"

"They eloped right before immigrating to the U.S."

The ancient black-and-white showed a couple arrayed in wedding finery. They looked impossibly young and nervous, their hands joined in a white-knuckle grip. But the photographer managed to catch them in an unguarded moment, as they gathered themselves for a more formal pose. They glanced at each other, as though for reassurance, and the power of their love practically scorched the film.

"Nonna didn't want to escape The Inferno, did she?"

"No."

Francesca returned the photograph to the table with clear finality. "Well, I do." She paced restlessly toward the windows. Once there, she glanced over her shoulder. With the sunlight at her back, her expression fell into shadow. But he could hear the tension rippling through her voice. "I'm not interested in you or Dantes' Inferno or having an affair with you. I just want to be left alone to pursue my career. This is a distraction I don't want or need."

"I wish it were that simple. That I could make it go away for you. But I can't."

He wanted to see her, to look into her eyes and know

her thoughts. To touch her and reestablish the physical connection between them. Without conscious thought, he joined her at the windows. The instant he slid his palm across her warm, silken skin, his world righted itself.

"Why can't I just walk away from you and never look back?" she demanded. He heard the turmoil that under-scored her question, as hunger battled common sense. And he understood what she felt since it mirrored his own reaction to their predicament. "Why can't I simply return to the life I built for myself?"

"You can. We both can. The minute we work this out of our systems."

Sev swept Francesca up into his arms and carried her to the couch. She murmured a token protest, one lost beneath the series of tiny, biting kisses he scattered along her throat. They tumbled onto cushions that molded to their entwined bodies and enfolded them in a private world of suede-covered down. The buttons of her blouse parted beneath his hands, revealing a feminine scrap of lace that struggled to contain her breasts. He couldn't help himself. He reared back, drinking in the sight.

Two nights ago he'd seen her by moonlight and thought it impossible for her to look any more stunning than adorned in shades of silver and alabaster. But now, with her hair and skin gilded in sunlit gold, she stole his breath with her beauty. Inch by inch, he lowered himself onto her. And inch by inch, the heat they generated soared, like a thermometer rising. Given the number of promises he'd made and broken, he half expected her to push him away. Instead, she basked in that heat and wrapped him up in an ardent embrace.

It was as though they'd never left off from the night before last. He reacquainted himself with her mouth, plundering inward. She moaned in welcome and met him with a feminine aggression that sent him straight over the edge. There were too many clothes between them. He yanked at his tie and the first few buttons of his shirt, but somehow he'd lost the ability to work past the knot imprisoning him. Instead, he turned his attention to her and unhooked the front clasp of her bra. He filled his hands with her breasts and her breath escaped in a fevered rush.

"We were supposed to have worked this out of our systems by now," she gasped.

"We will." Maybe in a decade or two. "But until then I need your hands on me. I need to be inside you again."

He shifted a knee between her legs and slid the hem of her skirt upward, uncovering acres of smooth, creamy thigh and a tantalizing glimpse of butter-yellow panties. He itched to explore all that lay beneath that scrap of silk. To see those curls gilded with sunlight, as well. He ran a finger along the scalloped edging, stroking inward toward dewy warmth until he found the sweet heart of her.

Francesca groaned in response, a rich, deep, feminine sound that called to him on every level and drove him ever closer to the edge. He knew that sound, had heard her make it countless times during the night they'd spent together. But there was another sound he wanted to hear…needed to hear. The sound she made when she climaxed in his arms.

She shuddered against his stroking touch and he couldn't stand it another minute. He needed her—now.

In a single swift move, he skimmed her panties down her thighs and tossed them aside. Next, he ripped his belt free and unfastened his trousers, pausing only long enough to remove the protection he'd had the foresight to stick in his pocket before their meeting. Her hands joined his, helping to free him from the restriction of his clothing. And then she cupped him, her touch cool against the burning length of him. Instead of easing the raging fire, it only served to intensify it.

He couldn't remember the last time he'd been so desperate to have a woman that he'd been unable to make it to the comfort of his bedroom. But with Francesca... Nothing mattered except to have her, right here and now. He lifted her and slid deep inside. Her legs closed around him as she welcomed him home.

His groan of pleasure mingled with hers, the heavy pounding of his heart in perfect tempo with hers. The breath exploded from her and then he heard her siren's song, signaling her scramble toward the highest of peaks. He joined her there, calling to her, mating with her, locking them together until he could no longer tell where her body ended and his began.

They moved in perfect harmony, continuing a dance that had begun their first night together. The tempo this time around quickened, turning fast and hard and greedy. He couldn't get enough of her, not how tightly she clenched around him or how she cushioned him against the softness of her woman's body or how she met each thrust with joyous abandon. Long before he was ready for the encounter to end, she spasmed beneath him, and he found he couldn't hold back, couldn't resist going up and over the peak with her before crashing down the other side, holding her tight within his arms.

Long minutes passed without either of them moving—maybe because movement proved a physical impossibility. Finally, the breath heaving from his lungs, he levered himself onto his elbows and gazed down at her. Heaven help him, but she was beautiful, her face delicately flushed with the ripeness of passion, her mouth moist and swollen from his kisses, her eyes heavy-lidded and slumberous.

"I can't walk away from you, Francesca. And I won't."

She closed her eyes with a groan. "I shouldn't have agreed to have lunch with you. I should have known we'd end up like this again."

He eased himself up and off of her. Holding out his hand, he assisted her from the couch and helped return a semblance of order to her clothing. "I didn't give you a choice about lunch. And just so you know, I don't plan to give you a choice in the future, either."

She eyed him in open alarm, but didn't ask the question he suspected hovered on the tip of her tongue. Instead, she asked, "Where's the bathroom?"

He directed her, then excused himself long enough to freshen up, as well. He returned to find her fully tucked and buttoned and preparing to leave. "There's something I want to ask you," he told her. "Actually, it's the reason I invited you to lunch."

A smile flirted with her mouth, a genuine one that filled him with fierce pleasure. "You mean, you didn't invite me so we could indulge in a wrestling match on your couch?"

He regarded her with a hint of laughter. "As delight-ful as that was, no." He crossed to her side. Unable to resist, he slipped a hand into her hair. Cupping the back of her head, he took her mouth in a swift, hungry kiss, a kiss she returned without hesitation. "Come work for me," he offered when they broke apart.

Her eyes were alight with a slumberous passion and he suspected she didn't assimilate his offer imme-diately. He saw the instant words connected with comprehension. The passion eked away, replaced by astonishment. "Work for you?" she repeated.

"I can offer you a far better salary than you receive at Timeless, excellent benefits, your own studio. You'll have the Dante name behind your designs." He pressed, determined she see how much more he could do for her than the Fontaines. "I can assist you to become one of the most sought-after designers in the world. Best of all, we won't have to sneak around hiding our relationship from your employers."

She took a hasty step away from him, pulling free of his hold. "Let me get this straight. You're offering me a job so we can continue our affair?"

"Of course not." Honesty compelled him to admit, "Okay, fine. In part. But mostly because you're a damn good designer. Dantes would be lucky to have you."

Her eyes narrowed. "And what happens when we're no longer Infernoed?"

The word provoked a swift smile. "Infernoed?"

"Right now the hot, southern climes of your anatomy are doing your thinking. Once that brilliant mind of yours kicks in, you'll regret any decisions you make while in the throes of this thing. And I'll have thrown away a job I love for a position at Dantes as the ex-mistress of the owner. How long do you think that'll work?"

He struggled not to take offense. Until two nights ago his southern climes had never before overruled the cooler, dispassionate northern half of his body. Yet, he suspected Francesca assumed it happened on a regular basis. It was part of the price he paid for having a Latin name. Emotion over intellect. Total nonsense, of course.

"I won't compromise the family business for anyone or anything," he stated. "My offer is genuine, Inferno or no Inferno. When our affair ends, you'll still have your job, and it'll be a hell of a lot more secure than your future at Timeless."

He could tell she didn't believe him. "Thank you, but I'm happy with the Fontaines."

"Would you at least allow me to make an official offer?"

She dismissed the idea with a swift shake of her head. "I have my reasons for staying at Timeless Heirlooms, and money isn't really one of them. I'm up for a permanent position there. In fact, I would have it already if I hadn't ruined my reputation by spending the night with you. The only saving grace is that they don't know it's you."

He thought fast. "We can be discreet. They don't have to know."

She cut him off with a swift shake of her head. "Forget it. I won't make that sort of foolish mistake again or do anything to jeopardize my standing with the Fontaines. And just so we're clear? Being with you could get me fired and my job's more important than anything else." She spared a swift glance toward the couch where the cushions still showed the imprint of their entwined bodies. "Even that."

"Francesca—"

She waved him silent. "Forget it, Sev. I agreed to meet with you this one last time. I think you'll agree it was a lovely way to conclude our affair. And that's all this was. A brief affair, now concluded. Now, I really need to go." She picked up her purse and slung it over her shoulder. "If I don't come back from lunch in a reasonable length of time, they'll start asking questions I can't answer."

It would be pointless to argue, he could tell. Better to find out what Nic and Lazz had dug up regarding the gorgeous Ms. Sommers. That way he'd be in a stronger position to formulate a new plan, one with a better chance of success. And it had to be quick, before his North surrendered to his South.

"I'll arrange for a cab," he limited himself to saying. "And I'll give you a call later this week."

She gave him a remote smile. "There's no need…on either count."

He watched the delicious sway of her hips as she exited the room, the view threatening to bring him to his knees. "Damn, woman," he muttered. "There's every need. And I plan to prove it to you."

But he'd better figure out how, and fast. Because if he'd learned nothing else as a result of the past few hours, he'd discovered how wrong he'd been about The Inferno and all matters related to it.

He'd been determined to woo Francesca away from

the Fontaines and have her work for Dantes. To tempt her—not with sex—but with the financial advantages of working for Dantes. Or that had been his intention until he'd come face-to-face with one incontrovertible fact. A fact that sent his carefully laid plans crumbling to dust. There was no way in hell he could keep his hands off her now, or anytime in the near future. As of this minute, the plan changed.

Not only did he want to uproot her from Timeless Heirlooms so the company would be more vulnerable to a Dantes' takeover, but he also wanted to transplant Francesca into his bed and keep her there...at least until The Inferno burned itself out.

# CHAPTER FIVE

FOOLISHLY, Francesca assumed she'd seen the last of Sev.

The delusion lasted right up until she decided to eat lunch at her desk, ordering from her favorite deli, a place that offered fast delivery service and thick sandwiches, stuffed with every imaginable delicacy. Within thirty minutes her sandwich arrived, along with a sprig of vivid-blue forget-me-nots, their delicate scent sweetening the air in her tiny office.

"Thank you," she said to the delivery boy before burying her nose in the fragrant blossoms. "What a nice thing to do."

He eyed her speculatively. "Do I get an extra tip for bein' so nice?"

"Absolutely." She handed it over with a smile. "And thanks again."

"No sweat. The flowers weren't from me, by the way. There's a note that came with it. I stuck it in the bag with your sandwich." With a cheeky grin he darted from the office.

She couldn't help but laugh at his audacity. Then curiosity got the better of her. She opened the bag and found a business card tucked inside. To her dismay, her fingers trembled as she glanced at it. Sure enough, the linen-colored pasteboard had Sev's name and business information typed on the front. On the back, he'd scrawled *Remember.*

Somehow he'd figured out where she usually ordered lunch and she spent the rest of the day sniffing the forget-me-nots as she struggled to do as he asked and remember…to remember that dating Sev promised a fast end to a short career. Worse, it would put an even faster end to her burgeoning relationship with her father. And she wouldn't allow anyone—not even a man as sexy as Severo Dante—to interfere with either of those two goals.

The next morning on her way to work, she swung into her favorite Starbucks, desperate for caffeine after a sleepless night of wishing she were in Sev's bed once more. To her dismay, the line stretched long and wide and she schooled herself to patience. Far ahead, toward the front, she caught a glimpse of a distinctive set of shoulders and striking ebony hair. Unbidden, her heart kicked up a notch and the air escaped her lungs in a soft rush.

It wasn't Severo Dante, she silently scolded, and constantly obsessing over him wasn't going to help matters. She refused to see Sev in every man with an impressive build and dark coloring. She needed to get a grip. Deliberately, she forced her gaze away only to catch herself peeking at him as he finished paying and turned to leave.

This time the breath exploded from her in an audible gasp as she realized it *was* Sev. He came directly toward her with the languid grace so uniquely his, carrying a pair of cappuccinos. He handed her one with a warm smile and a quiet, *"Tesoro mio,"* before continuing out the door.

"Oh, God," the woman behind her said with a groan. "Does that happen to you often?"

"No." Francesca stared at the cappuccino, then at the door through which Sev had vanished, before glancing at the woman behind her. "At least…not until recently."

"I don't suppose you know what *tesoro mio* means?" Before Francesca could respond, the woman shouted out, "Hey, who knows what *tesoro mio* means?"

"Italian. It means my treasure," an older woman toward the front of the line called back.

"Wow," Francesca's companion in line murmured. "Oh, wow."

"I couldn't have said it better myself." Francesca knocked back the drink Sev had given her in the vain hope it would pull her out of the sensual stupor fogging her brain. It didn't. Instead, she spent the next twenty-four hours daydreaming about him.

The next morning, Friday, she wasted her entire time in line searching in vain for Sev's distinctive build. She refused to be disappointed when she didn't spot him, and even came up with a handful of reasonable excuses for lingering in the small bistro while she sipped her drink. But he never showed.

When she arrived at work she was stunned to discover a blown-glass vase sitting on her desk with a new flower to replace the forget-me-nots, this time a sprig of orange blossoms. The white star-shaped blooms caressed the flame-red glass, the contrast between the two colors quite striking. Unable to resist, she picked up the vase, the sweet perfume of the flowers flooding her senses while the delicate glasswork warmed within her hold.

It was an incredible piece with sinuous curves that flowed from base to stem and seemed to beg for her touch. Had Sev stroked it, just as she was now doing? Were her fingers tracing the same path his had taken? It was a distinct possibility, since no one who held this gorgeous creation could resist running their fingers along the flowing lines of the fiery glass.

"Oh. My." Tina came to peer over Francesca's shoulder. "I've never seen anything so beautiful. Where did you get it?"

"It's a gift."

"And orange blossoms. *Très romantique!*"

"Really? I didn't know. I just love the scent."

"Mmm. They mean eternal love." Tina's eyes filled with laughter. "Or innocence. I'll let you decide which is more appropriate."

Definitely not innocence. Francesca hastily returned the vase to her desktop. She took a seat and pulled out her sketchpad, determined to get straight to work. Not that she accomplished much. More times than she could count she found herself staring into space with a reminiscent smile on her face while she stroked the vase and inhaled the sweet scent of orange blossoms.

Saturday came and Francesca assumed that she wouldn't have to worry about Sev showing up at Starbucks, or sending her a gift at work, or finding some other way to tempt her into giving in to his blatant seduction. Or so she thought until she opened the door to her apartment to his latest surprise.

"What are you doing here?" she demanded.

Sev lowered the fist he'd been about to use on her door. "I came to talk to you."

"I thought we decided we weren't going to contact each other again," she said. "Nothing can come of this, you realize that, don't you? No matter how much I might want to see you, it means losing my job and I won't risk that."

He stared down at her with such heat that it was a wonder it didn't turn the air to steam. "I'm well aware of that fact. Not that it changes anything." He glanced over her shoulder and into her apartment. "Aren't you going to invite me in?"

"No, I'm not."

"Please, Francesca."

Just those two words and she felt her resolve fading. "What's the point, Sev?" she whispered.

"This. This is the point."

He cupped her face and took her mouth in a passionate kiss. Francesca closed her eyes as Sev made his point, as well as several others, in ways sweeter and more generous than any that had gone before. She gave herself up to sheer rapture, surrendering to desire over common sense. Without even realizing it, she backed into her apartment and Sev kicked the door closed behind them. Endless minutes passed before she surfaced with a groan.

"I can't believe we're doing this again. It's not safe." She fisted her hands in his shirt. "Listen to me, Sev. I'm telling you straight out. You can't show up at Starbucks or send me flowers or any more gorgeous vases—thank you, by the way—or slip me notes in my lunch."

"Fine. I won't. Instead, why don't I steal you away for the weekend?"

She had to give him credit for sheer brazenness, if nothing else. "Forget it. I've already told you—"

He nodded impatiently. "Yeah, yeah. Heard it all before. That still doesn't change anything. We need time together in order to resolve our differences."

"We can't resolve our differences," she emphasized. "There are simply too many obstacles."

"Obstacles we haven't made any effort to overcome. I'd like to try and correct that oversight. I've made reservations. We'll be discreet. No one will find out we've been together."

"And if I say no?" she asked, lifting an eyebrow. "Will you blackmail me again?"

"Would that make it easier for you to surrender?" His voice dropped, reminding her of a certain moonlit night when he'd whispered the most outrageous suggestions in her ear—suggestions he'd then turned from proposition to action. "Come with me, Francesca. Or I swear I'll show up at Timeless and tell everyone who'll listen that we're lovers."

"I don't believe you. You're just saying that because—"

He leaned in, stopping her with another endless kiss. "Don't challenge me." There was no mistaking the warning in his dark eyes. "When have I ever failed to follow through on my word?"

"Right now," she informed him. "All this week. You said—" She hesitated, struggling to recall precisely what he *had* said when they last met. As far as she could remember, she'd done most of the talking that day. He gave her a knowing look and she blew out her breath in an aggravated sigh. "Well…you might not have come right out and said it, but you did agree to end the affair."

He tipped her face up to his. "Does it look like I agree with our ending things?"

Not even a little. "Without question."

His slow, knowing smile proved her undoing. "Go pack a bag. We can finish arguing about it in the car."

She turned without another word and crossed to her bedroom. Five minutes later she returned with an overnight bag, more certain with every step she took that she'd completely lost her mind. And maybe she had, but after five minutes with Sev, she no longer cared. One more weekend and then she'd put an end to their relationship, she promised herself. Just these two days together and then no more. After all…who would it hurt?

To her delight, Sev drove them into wine country, where he'd booked a room at a charming bed-and-breakfast. They spent the day at several of the local wineries sampling the wares before enjoying an impromptu picnic that consisted of generous slices of the local Sonoma Jack cheese and freshly baked bread. That night they dined out at a small, elegant restaurant that specialized in French cuisine, their day together one of the most enchanting Francesca had ever experienced. The sun had long since set when they returned to their room and silently came together.

She'd been waiting for this from the moment she'd agreed to spend the weekend with Sev, had been anticipating it, desire fomenting with each hour that passed.

And now that the moment had arrived, she tumbled, falling headlong into his arms and into his bed, if not into his heart. Because she couldn't quite convince herself that what they felt could be anything more than physical.

"We can make this work," he told her, during the still hours between deepest night and earliest morning. "If we agree not to discuss anything job-related, this will work."

"But for how long?"

"Look… I know TH is after a big-name actress to pull them out of their financial hole. Eventually, I'll find out who she is. But I don't need you for that. There are far more interesting ways to spend my time with you."

She managed a smile, even though she continued to worry. "Our jobs…they mean everything to us. They're as much a part of us as our flesh and bones. We won't be able to share that part of ourselves."

He conceded the point with a swift nod. "So we discuss other things."

"Like what?"

He rolled onto his side to face her. "Like…growing up in foster care. Coming from such a huge family, I can't begin to imagine it. Why were you never adopted?"

She tugged the sheet over her breasts and tucked it beneath her arms. A ridiculous reaction, she conceded, and more than a little telling. But talking about her childhood left her exposed. Any covering, even a sheet, helped compensate for that.

"I almost was," she said in answer to his question.

He traced a scorching finger from the curve of her cheek down the length of her neck. As always, she flamed beneath his touch. "What happened?"

Francesca shrugged. "They were about to adopt me when Carrie unexpectedly became pregnant with twins. The doctor ordered complete bed rest and her husband insisted I be placed elsewhere, that it was too much for his wife. I heard him tell the social worker that taking care of me put their babies at risk, and that the babies were their most important consideration."

Sev swept her hair back from her face, regarding her with heartbreaking compassion. "What happened then?"

"I went through a succession of homes after that. Four, I think." She dismissed the memory with a careless smile and rolled over on top of him. His warmth became her warmth and helped diminish the coldness that streaked through her veins and sank into her bones. A coldness those particular memories always engendered. "Acting out, I guess, because I'd been foolish enough to imagine that Carrie and her husband might actually want me as much as the children they were about to have."

"I'm sorry." He released his breath in a rough sigh, causing the curls at her temples to swirl and dance. "That's such an inadequate thing to say. But I mean it."

"Like I said, don't feel sorry for me." Pity was the last thing she wanted from him. "I survived."

"And found your father. That must have helped." He studied her curiously. "You haven't told me anything about him. What's he like?"

"There's not much to tell," she claimed, aware of how evasive she sounded. "He...he had a one-night stand with my mother. Since he was married at the time—is still married—I didn't feel comfortable intruding in their lives."

Sev swore. "You just can't catch a break, can you?"

"What about you?" She deliberately changed the subject. "You've said that after your father's death you had to dismantle most of Dantes. I gather that included Timeless Heirlooms."

"Yes."

She could tell he didn't want to talk about it, but pushed, anyway. "Which explains why you're so determined to get it back again. That must have been as difficult for you as foster care was for me." She hesitated before asking, "Why has it become such an obsession? I mean…if your father was the one responsible for Dantes' decline—"

He wrapped his arms around her and reversed their positions, bracing himself on his forearms to lessen the press of weight on top of her. "Why have I become so obsessed with rebuilding it?"

He looked so fierce. So determined. "Yes."

"Because my father tried to tell me something about the business the day before he died." His words grew ragged. "And I was too impatient to listen to another of his crazy schemes. Maybe if I had—" He broke off, a muscle jerking in his cheek.

"What?" Her eyes widened in sudden comprehension. "You think he had an idea for saving Dantes? One that didn't involve dismantling the entire business?"

"I don't think. I know. He called it Dante's Heart. Even my mother thought it would work. I—reluctantly—agreed to meet with them the next day when they returned from their sailing excursion."

"Only they didn't return."

He closed his eyes, grief carving deep lines into his face. "No."

"Didn't he write down his idea? Leave some sort of clue behind?"

"I tore both home and office apart looking for it. There was nothing. Nothing except—"

She recalled what he'd told her when they'd visited his Pacific Heights house. "Letters detailing his affair with a designer."

"Yes." His mouth slid into a smile that, without fail, caused her body to quicken in anticipation. "Seems to run in the family."

"And you think that if you'd only taken the time to listen to your father, you wouldn't have had to sell off all the Dante subsidiaries."

His hands swept over her, settling on the softest of her curves. "If you're asking whether I blame myself, I'll make it easy for you. I do."

She fought to speak through her shiver of desire. "Seems we both have something to prove."

"So it does." He traced a path of kisses from the hollow of her throat downward. "The first thing I want to prove is how much I want you." And in the hours that followed he did precisely that.

Their weekend together changed everything, convincing Francesca that maybe she could have it all. Despite the small warning voice she couldn't quite silence, she allowed herself to be talked back into Sev's bed. Or blackmailed there, he frequently claimed with a teasing grin.

As the days slid into weeks, she became more and

more certain that Sev didn't have an ulterior motive—other than to get her in his bed as often as possible. But since that was her motivation, as well, nothing could make her happier. Of course, he continued to offer her a job at Dantes at regular intervals, making the tempting offers as such casual asides that they felt more like a joke than a true offer. Foolishly, she even managed to convince herself that he'd forgotten about identifying which actress Timeless Heirlooms hoped to sign as their spokeswoman.

Or so she believed until he picked her up one evening and handed her a brightly wrapped package. "This is for you. Fair warning, I want major good-guy points for this one."

"That depends." She picked up the box and shook it. "What did you get?"

"Something you mentioned last week. Go on and open it. It's just a DVD." His expression turned gloomy. "It has chick flick written all over it, but for you, I'm willing to take it like a man."

Ripping off the outer wrapping she realized he'd bought her the latest Juliet Bloom release. She stiffened, wondering if this was his subtle way of telling her he knew about the possibility of TH using Bloom as their spokeswoman. "Thanks," she murmured. She cleared her throat, forcing a more natural tone to her voice. "I can't wait to watch this."

"Then we'll do it tonight," he responded promptly. "We'll order in Chinese and crack open that bottle of Pinot Grigio my family sent over from Italy."

But all through the beginning of the movie she

remained on edge, praying she wouldn't do or say something to give away TH's plans. The entire time, Sev remained his normal self. As far as she could tell, he didn't watch her with any more intensity than usual. There were no double entendres or suspicious comments. Halfway through the film, she managed to relax and even enjoy herself—perhaps in part due to the glass of wine Sev kept topped off.

By the end of the movie, she was in her usual position whenever they watched a DVD, on the couch curled up in Sev's arms. Tears filled her eyes as the film reached its stunning climax, a scene in which the heroine stood before the villain, clothed in nothing but defiance and diamonds.

"It reminds me of our first night together," Sev murmured. "You were wearing your amethyst-and-diamond set, remember? Bloom would look stunning in one of your designs."

Francesca couldn't tear her eyes from the film. "Yes, she will," she murmured.

It took a full half-dozen heartbeats before she realized what she'd said. The instant she had, she ripped free of his embrace and stood. "Oh, God."

Sev climbed slowly to his feet. "Honey, don't. Don't overreact. I swear to you, I already knew."

She shook her head, not believing him. "This was a setup, wasn't it?"

"Not even a little."

Tears of anger blurred her vision. "And I fell for it. I got complacent. Even when I saw which movie you'd chosen, I convinced myself not to read anything into it."

The breath hitched in her throat as she looked around for her purse. "I have to go."

"No, you don't," he argued. "You need to stay so we can talk this through."

She ignored him, scooping her purse off the coffee table and crossing to the entryway to snatch her sweater from the antique armoire he used as a coat closet. "Just answer me one question, Sev." She spun to face him. "Are you going to use the information about Juliet Bloom to try and take down TH?"

At least he didn't lie to her. "Yes."

"Then there's nothing left to be said, is there?"

"There's more to be said than you can possibly imagine. But since you're in no mood to listen to me tonight, it can wait until tomorrow."

"You're wrong, Sev." She yanked open the door to his apartment and stepped through. "There is no tomorrow for us."

# CHAPTER SIX

THE ANSWER to Francesca's question—was Sev going to use the information she'd let slip?—came the next morning when she rushed in to work.

A message sat on her desk requesting she report to Tina's office at her earliest convenience. It didn't have anything to do with her slipup, she attempted to convince herself. Not this fast, nor this soon. He'd only had one night to track down the actress or her rep and cause trouble. He couldn't possibly have accomplished that so quickly.

But a feeling of impending doom clung to her as she sprinted up the steps to the executive level of Timeless Heirlooms. The Fontaines shared adjoining offices at one end of the floor and she could hear Tina's voice raised in anger coming from her side of the suite. Not unusual, given her volatile nature. But not welcome, either, all things considered. Kurt's placating voice rumbled in response to whatever Tina said, indicating the two were in there together.

Francesca knocked on the door, not in the least surprised when no one answered. She doubted they heard her over the shouting. Peeking around the door, she asked, "You wanted to see me?"

Kurt waved her in and toward a brilliant magenta sofa at one end of the room. She took a seat and waited. Outside, storm clouds marched across the city skyline, a perfect reflection of the Fontaines' mood.

"I'm serious, Kurt. Something has to be done about them."

"What do you suggest, honey?" He shoved a hand through hair a shade paler than Francesca's own honey-blond. "I've called Juliet Bloom's rep every day since the showing. She's polite, but refuses to commit."

"Because of those damn Dantes!"

Francesca stiffened at hearing her worst fears confirmed. "What have the Dantes got to do with Juliet Bloom?" As if she didn't know.

Tina swung around, only too happy to explain. "Surprise, surprise, they've approached her, too." She slammed her hands down on her desk. "They sell wedding rings, for God's sake, not jewelry sets. But because it's the Dante name, Bloom is listening."

Francesca's heart sank. Oh, God. He'd done it. Somehow he'd used her slip of the tongue to wrestle the Bloom account away from the Fontaines. "When... when did this happen?"

"We're not sure. Bloom's been cagey ever since the show. Promising, but never quite committing. Then this morning we found out why."

Francesca closed her eyes to hide the guilt she knew must be readily apparent. This was all her fault. She should have been up front with the Fontaines from the start. She never should have allowed Sev to convince her to continue their affair, despite the hint of blackmail behind his insistence. But she'd wanted him, wanted him desperately. And so she'd caved when she should have held firm. If TH went under, she'd be the one responsible and they'd never forgive her. Hell, she'd never forgive herself.

"What are you going to do?" she finally asked.

Tina resumed her pacing. "What can we do? We're running out of time." She didn't need to add that a good portion of Timeless Heirlooms' future hung on the actress agreeing to be their spokeswoman and wear Francesca's creations in her next picture.

Kurt glanced at Francesca. "Severo Dante called," he murmured in an aside. "He told us he was behind the delay and upped his offer for Timeless."

Tina glared in frustration. "I don't care what that SOB offers. I'm not selling." Her anger crumbled to panic and she barreled straight into Kurt's arms. "We're in this together, right? United we stand and all that? Because I couldn't do this without you. This place would fall apart if it weren't for you."

His arms tightened around his wife. "I'm not going anywhere. We'll figure something out."

Tears stung Francesca's eyes at the open display of affection. If only… She shook her head, refusing to allow her thoughts to go there. It wouldn't serve any purpose other than to drive her crazy with futile longing. Kurt could never be her father. And Sev would never be anything more than her temporary lover.

After all, it didn't matter that she couldn't claim Kurt

as her father, she decided then and there, or reveal her connection to him. She refused to do anything that might damage the Fontaines' marriage. And finding out that Kurt had not only indulged in an affair in the early years of their marriage, but also that a child had resulted from that affair would do more than damage it. Knowing Tina, it could very well destroy thirty years of wedded bliss. Francesca could barely handle the guilt of her part in bringing down TH. It would destroy her if she ruined Kurt and Tina's marriage, on top of everything else.

Just being this close to her father filled Francesca with more joy than she thought possible. After all the lonely years in foster care, all the years of working every spare minute of every day to hone her craft, she'd settle for whatever she could get. She refused to bemoan her current circumstances. While her connection to family would remain tenuous at best, as long as she worked at Timeless Heirlooms and it remained afloat, she could pursue a career she loved with all her heart and soul. Even better, she could remain in her father's orbit, even if she never became one of his inner circle.

And if that meant helping them beat Sev at his own game, so be it. "Is there anything I can do?" she asked. "Is there some way of convincing Juliet Bloom to go with TH?"

Kurt looked at her over Tina's head. "Put out some feelers among your associates. See if you can find out who this new designer is."

She froze. "I'm sorry. What new designer?"

Tina pulled free of Kurt's embrace. "That's right. We didn't tell her the best part. Wait until you hear this one." She planted her hands on her hips. "Dantes has convinced Bloom's people that they have some hot new designer on the hook who can give Dame Juliet exactly what she wants."

Oh, no. Oh, please don't let it be who she thought it was. "Who? Who's their new designer?"

"We have no idea. We haven't heard so much as a whisper of a rumor."

"That's where you come in," Kurt added. "We'd appreciate it if you'd keep your ear to the ground. See what some of the other designers are saying. It has to be someone they've acquired very recently, since this Bloom deal's only been around for the last few weeks."

"Maybe we should go downstairs and count heads," Tina muttered. "See if any of our designers are missing. It would be just like him to snitch one of them right from under our noses."

Francesca closed her eyes, her world tilting. Aware that the Fontaines waited for her response, she swallowed, struggling to speak around a throat gone bone-dry. "I'll see what I can find out."

Not that it would take much effort. In fact, it wouldn't take much more than a single visit. How many times had Sev offered her a job, each proposition more lucrative than the last? Suddenly, it all made sense. Sev knew that TH was in hot negotiation with some big name. He'd been frank about that almost from the start. Chances were excellent he also knew which designer had piqued that person's interest…had undoubtedly known from the night they first met. If he stole—*seduced*—her away from TH, he'd gain the ultimate prize. He'd land a highly

lucrative account with Bloom—now that he'd romanced
the actress's name out of her—and he'd take away the
Fontaines' best chance at revitalizing the company
Dantes wanted to purchase. If she didn't miss her guess,
Sev planned to use her to accomplish both those goals.

Overhead the storm clouds broke.

Francesca didn't give the assistant seated at a desk
outside Sev's door a chance to stop her. She simply
swept past the stunning blonde and barged straight into
his office. Four men sat sprawled on couches and chairs
in an informal sitting area at the far end of the enormous
room. She recognized them from the photos that decorated the console in Sev's den, as well as the walls of
his apartment.

Sharp light, scrubbed clean from the recent storm,
streamed from the floor-to-ceiling windows and haloed
the twins, Marco and Lazz, who sat opposite each other
like a pair of striking bookends. She pegged Marco by
his wide grin and appreciative gaze, not to mention the
sexual sizzle he gave off with every exhalation. Lazz
regarded her with a cool, analytical stare, everything
about him suggesting a man who kept his emotions
under tight control. And then there was Nicolò, the
youngest at twenty-nine, but according to Sev, the most
dangerous of the bunch. Had he been the one to suggest
her as a creative solution for taking over Timeless
Heirlooms? Finally, her attention switched to Sev.

He knew why she'd come. She saw the knowledge
settle across a face she'd covered with sweet kisses just
a few hours earlier. He jerked his head toward the door

and his brothers stood en masse. Before Nic left, he handed Sev a file folder with her name prominently displayed across the cover.

Sev lobbed the opening volley. "I have one question before you say anything. Have you signed a formal contract yet with Timeless Heirlooms, or are you still on probation?"

She couldn't believe his nerve. "That's none of your business," she retorted, stung.

"Answer me, Francesca." His quiet tone gentled the implacable demand. "Have you signed with them?"

"I intend to, just as soon as I tell you what I think of you."

He simply nodded, but she caught a hint of relief that came and went in his expression. "Would you care to sit?"

"I prefer to do this standing." Her hands curled into fists. "You used me. You used me to try and take over TH. I'm here to tell you that you've failed. And I'm also here to tell you that I think you're despicable."

"Let's set the record straight on several points." He stood, tossing the folder Nic had given him to one side. "When we first met—hell, when we first made love—I had no idea who you were. Maybe if I'd answered my cell when Marco phoned that night, I would have. But if you recall, I was a little preoccupied and he didn't get through to me until the next morning."

She folded her arms across her chest and shook her head. "I'm not buying it. You could have discovered my identity before you ever arrived at the showing."

"It would have been possible, I suppose. But the fact is, I didn't." He stalked closer. "Next point. The

Fontaines and I were already negotiating the sale of Timeless Heirlooms before you and I ever met. Tina knew I intended to buy them out, either when she eventually sold out to me, or after she was forced to declare bankruptcy. That hasn't changed."

"But you hadn't counted on the success of the showing."

"No."

"Or that they might acquire Juliet Bloom as their spokeswoman. Or that she would use their collection in her next film."

"Correction. *Your* collection. And Juliet Bloom has postponed her decision." He paused a beat. "Indefinitely."

Undisguised fury ripped through Francesca. "Because you told her that you had a collection as good as TH's. That you had the perfect designer for her. Me." He didn't deny it and desolation battled with anger. "You thought you could hire me away from the Fontaines and steal the Bloom account so they'd be forced to sell to you."

"Yes."

The simple confirmation cut deep. "You're not even going to deny it?" *Please deny it!*

"Why should I? It's true. If you'd accepted my job offer that's exactly how it would have gone down." For the first time, she saw a businessman instead of her lover. "That's how it's still going down."

She shook her head. "Not a chance in hell. Do you think I'd ever agree to work for you after this? That I'll ever sleep with you again?"

"One has nothing to do with the other. One is

business, the other personal." He shrugged. "The two are mutually exclusive."

Her chin wobbled precariously. Didn't he get it? "One has *everything* to do with the other. I've lived a lifetime of betrayal in one form or another. I can't..." She ground to a halt, correcting herself. "I *won't* be with a man I can't trust."

"Francesca, I didn't seduce you in order to tempt you away from Timeless."

"You actually expect me to believe that?"

"It's the truth. I made you a legitimate job offer for two reasons. First, you'd be an incredible asset to Dantes. You're the best designer I've ever seen, and that's saying a lot."

"And second?" Not that she needed him to spell it out. She already knew.

"Second, having you leave TH makes them more vulnerable to a Dantes' takeover."

Did he really think she'd find his reasoning appropriate? That *A* plus *B* equaled acceptable in her book? He had a lot to learn. "Maybe if you only wanted me because of my talent, I could somehow justify it. Somehow. But that's not the case. You want to take down Timeless Heirlooms and you want to use me to do it. I can't allow that. I can't allow you to do anything that threatens Tina and Kurt."

"Because Kurt's your father."

The breath escaped her lungs in a heady rush and her vision blurred. One minute she stood staring at Sev in utter betrayal and the next he pressed her into one of the nearby chairs. He disappeared from her line of sight for a moment, then returned with glass in hand.

"It's just water, though I have something stronger if you prefer."

She shook her head without speaking and downed the water in a desperate gulp. "How…?"

"Nicolò hired a private investigator." Sev cupped the curve of her cheek and for a brief, insane moment she relaxed into his touch. The instant she realized what she'd done, she jerked back and his hand fell away. "Before we met at Le Premier I arranged to have each designer investigated. Marco and I attended the showing in order to collect names. By the time Nic called the next morning, the P.I. had matters well underway."

"You're going to blackmail me now, aren't you?"

"Yes."

She closed her eyes. Oh, God. He made it seem so simple. So obvious and acceptable. "You're a total bastard, you know that?"

"When it comes to taking care of my family, you're right." She could literally feel the change come over him as he shifted from lover to adversary. "I'd rather you come to us of your own free will. But I'll do whatever necessary to restore Dantes."

She looked at him, searching his face for some sign of the man she'd taken to her bed. If he still existed— if he ever existed—he was lost to her now. "Don't do this," she pleaded. "You don't need TH. Dantes will still be a success without it."

"Their business is failing." She hated the compassion gleaming in his burnished gold eyes. Hated him all the more for being right. "Bloom might revitalize it for a short time, but Tina is too capricious to keep the business going for longer than a few years. She hired three designers, two of whom are worse than mediocre. The fact that she also hired you is more dumb luck than true discernment. The only reason the company hasn't gone under before this is thanks to Kurt's business acumen."

"So now you're the hero? You're going to rescue Timeless Heirlooms?"

He gathered himself, exuding an uncompromising determination that had long been a hallmark of the Dante legend. "Timeless Heirlooms belonged to us. Because of my father's own capriciousness, I had no choice but to sell it off. Now I'm in a position to right that wrong. Do you expect me to walk away without recovering what I lost?" Regret colored his words. "That isn't going to happen and you know it."

"Because you feel responsible for Dantes' fall from grace."

"Because I *am* responsible. You know why I feel that way."

She remembered the night he'd explained it to her, and how sympathetic she'd felt. Not anymore. Not when he demonstrated such ruthless disregard in order to achieve his goal. "So, you'll do anything to return the company to its former glory. No matter who gets hurt. No matter who gets in your way or who you have to steamroll over." She wasn't asking, but acknowledging fact.

"No one has to get hurt. The Fontaines will be in a far better position if they sell out to us now than if I'm forced to collect the broken pieces after their fall."

"Very generous of you, I'm sure."

For the first time, a spark of anger flared to life in his eyes. "It's time to negotiate, Francesca. Will you come to work at Dantes of your own volition?"

"What happens if I refuse? Will you tell Tina that I'm Kurt's daughter?"

For the first time he didn't give her a straight answer. "I don't want to do it that way."

"But you will if you think there's no other option. You will because you know that the news will devastate Tina, since she and Kurt were married at the time of my conception. Knowing how volatile she is, she'll throw him out. And even if they eventually reconcile—which they will since they truly love each other—the damage will have been done. Their neglect will hand you TH."

"That's Nic's assessment of the situation, yes."

"It's a rotten thing to do, Sev."

Pain sliced across his face. "I've been forced to make far more difficult decisions, decisions that have had disastrous impact on people's lives." His voice dropped, landed in some dark, desolate place that echoed through his words. "I've had no choice. There was no one else to make those decisions. And I don't doubt there'll be other occasions when I'm forced to make still more."

She could see the truth in his eyes, see that he'd made an uncomfortable home for himself between that proverbial rock and a hard place. She could also sympathize with him, up to a point. Because from now on she'd have to make difficult decisions as well, to stand on her own without Sev at her back. Well, she'd been there before. She'd lived most of her life with no one beside her when times grew tough. She could do it again. She needed to be strong, to refortify the barriers she'd created years ago to hide her vulnerability and weakness. And she would. There wasn't any other choice.

"If I agree to work with you, I have one request." She didn't allow herself to consider that her statement as good as conceded defeat.

"Name it."

"The Fontaines are to receive full price for TH. I want it in my contract. I won't lift a finger to help Dantes otherwise."

He gave it a moment's reflection. "In that case I want an exclusive two-year contract with you with an additional two-year non-compete clause. If you walk away without meeting the terms of your contract, I won't allow you to work for anyone else in the industry in any capacity, whatsoever, for two full years."

Suddenly she found herself right there with him, a hard place boring into her back, a boulder slamming her from the front. "That seems a bit harsh."

"I have an investment to protect. I have no intention of buying out TH only to have you walk away from Dantes and help the Fontaines start up a competing business."

It hadn't occurred to her to do any such thing. But now that he mentioned it, it would serve him right if she'd planned to do precisely that. "Very well. I agree."

He held out his hand. "Welcome to Dantes."

Francesca realized her mistake the instant she put her hand in his. The Inferno reared its ugly head, darting from his hand to hers and setting her blood on fire. It didn't seep into her bones, but burned inward, branding her more deeply and completely than she thought possible.

She saw a similar kick of reaction fill Sev's expression with a predatory hunger. "Oh, and there's one more detail I forgot to mention."

She didn't have to ask. She knew precisely what detail he'd omitted. "Forget it."

"I can't forget, any more than you can." Sev's eyes turned to molten gold. "I still want you in my bed."

# CHAPTER SEVEN

SEV DELIBERATELY kept his distance from Francesca over the next few days while she gave notice at TH and settled into her new home at Dantes, not wanting to throw any more fuel on a situation already on the verge of a messy explosion. He'd done enough by insisting she return to his bed, as well as come to work at Dantes.

Though she'd accepted the latter with dignified anger, when it came to his former demand, she'd told him in no uncertain terms which dark corner of his body to put his suggestion and precisely how to achieve such an impossibility. Though he regretted the means he'd used to force her compliance on the work front, at some point she'd face facts.

Timeless Heirlooms teetered on the edge of destruction, and not even Francesca's brilliant designs would save it. Not in the long run. He'd rather acquire TH while he and his brothers could still turn it around, rather than attempt to pick up pieces shattered beyond repair. Quite simply, the Dantes were in a position to fix problems. The Fontaines weren't. Unfortunately, he doubted he'd ever be able to convince Francesca of that simple fact.

He'd respected her preferences and kept his distance, missing her from both his life and his bed. But now Sev couldn't stand it another minute. Whatever existed between them—whether The Inferno or simple desire—the craving to have her close at hand threatened everything he'd worked the past decade to accomplish.

A nagging compulsion consumed him, as though an emergency signal lit up the connection between them. He couldn't recall ever being this distracted. After the sixth time he stood with the subconscious urge to track her down, he finally gave in and acted on the impulse.

He found her in the studio he'd arranged for her use, a huge, bright room with every possible amenity at her disposal, right down to a plush sitting area and tiny kitchenette. Giving her door a brief knock, he entered. And then he allowed his senses to consume her, the thumb of his left hand moving automatically to ply the palm of his right.

She sat at her desk, a drawing pad flipped open and a charcoal pencil in hand. He couldn't say whether the sketch she applied herself to with such assiduous attention had anything to do with her job. But whatever she worked on, he suspected she'd lost all awareness of time and place.

Sunlight streamed in from nearby windows and swirled within her hair, spinning the honey-blond strands to pure gold. It also illuminated the creamy tone of her complexion, making her appear lit from within. Even from this distance, he picked up traces of her unique perfume, the scent light and crisp and uniquely hers.

The pressure that had been building over the past few

days eased with his first glimpse of her, forcing him to concede just how tense he'd become without constant contact with her. Every instinct begged him to go to her and carry her off. To take her as far from Dantes and the Fontaines as possible.

"Is there something I can help you with, Mr. Dante?" she asked without looking up.

He lifted an eyebrow. "Mr. Dante?" He leaned against the door, forcing it shut.

"Don't."

Just that one word, but it contained a full measure of pain and disillusionment. She looked at him then, sparing him nothing. He knew he'd hurt her, but refused to consider how badly. Until now. More than anything he wished he could go to her and find a way to ease her despair. But not only wouldn't she welcome it, he suspected she'd tear a strip off his hide if he came anywhere near her.

"Do you have any idea what it's like being here?" she continued. "The untenable position you've put me in?"

He cocked his head to one side. Okay… More was going on than his forcing her to work for him. Something had exacerbated the situation. "What's wrong?" he demanded.

She threw down her pencil and glared at him. "Why did you give me this office?"

He didn't hesitate. "Because it's the best one available."

"Great. Just great. Would you care to know the first question my coworkers asked me?" She didn't wait for his response. "Not my name. Not general questions about my background. Not where I attended school or who I studied with or where I last worked. They wanted to know who I'd slept with to get this studio."

Sev winced. "Hell."

"Oh, it gets better."

She swept a hand toward the pretty little sitting area tucked beneath the windows. "Guess what's now called the 'casting couch'? Of course, my coworkers treat it like a big joke, but I can see the speculation. They're wondering who I am and why I rate such consideration. As far as they're concerned, I'm brand-new to the industry. An apprentice in their eyes. But somehow I've leapfrogged over them and they don't like it one little bit. In a single thoughtless move, you've made it impossible for me to associate effectively with the other Dante employees."

Damn. "I didn't realize."

"Fine. You didn't realize. But now that you do, you have to fix it."

He could guess where this was going. "What do you suggest?"

"Transfer me to one of the other Dante locations. New York. London. Paris. The way things are right now, I'd even take Timbuktu. Just send me someplace else where they don't know me. Where…" She snatched a shaky breath. "Where I don't have to anticipate seeing you around every corner."

Not see her for months on end? He couldn't do it. The mere suggestion threatened what little sanity he had remaining. "Forget it. Not for at least two years."

"Two years?" He hated the cynical light that darkened her eyes to a black both deep and diamond-hard. "Unless The Inferno burns down to ashes before then, right?"

Sev ignored the question. It hit uncomfortably close to home and he hated the thought that his actions could have so base a motivation. "Other than transfer you, what else can I do? Name it and if it's in my power I'll give it to you."

She laughed, the sound so filled with sorrow that he flinched. "You can give me my old life back. You can let me work for the Fontaines again. Live my life the way *I* choose. I want to work with—" Her voice broke. "With my father. Even if he didn't know about our relationship, at least I could see him every day. At least he didn't hate me."

Sev froze. "Hate you?"

She stared at him in disbelief. "Are you really so blind? Didn't it occur to you what would happen when I refused to sign with Kurt and Tina? What would happen when I turned my back on them after all they've done for me? How they'd react when I jumped to Dantes instead of honoring my promise to sign the contract they were on the verge of offering? I betrayed them, Sev. I betrayed them in the cruelest manner possible and they despise me for what I've done to them."

Dammit to hell. He should have anticipated this. His distraction had cost them both. "I'll talk to them."

"And tell them what?" She thrust back her chair and stood, the movement lacking her usual grace. "Don't you get it? I'll be the proximate cause for the Fontaines losing Timeless Heirlooms. I'm the one they'll blame when you take over. Talking to them isn't going to do a bit of good."

He hadn't considered that aspect of the situation for a very simple, yet vital reason. He'd been so focused on his family's business and restoring all he'd been forced to dismantle, that he hadn't fully explored how his decision would impact Francesca. And he could guess why. He didn't dare look too closely or he'd never be able to make the tough calls. Examining the problem from Francesca's side of the fence would also force him to take a long, hard look at his past choices, something he refused to contemplate.

He'd ruined so many lives when he'd sold off the bits and pieces of Dantes. Until then they'd been a premier business, marketing the most exclusive and magnificent jewelry, worldwide. When his father died, he'd been forced into the top position fresh out of college, with little preparation. And even though Primo had come out of retirement during those first difficult days, his grandfather's heart attack, just three short months after the death of his eldest son and daughter-in-law, had put a swift end to his involvement.

From that point on, Sev shouldered the full burden. He, and he alone, had made the tough choices, choices vital to Dantes' survival. He'd been merciless all those years ago. There'd been no other option. One by one, he'd shut down Dantes' subsidiaries, cutting a swath of destruction throughout the company with ruthless disregard for the lives his decisions destroyed. It had been the only way to save the core business. And now here was one more tough choice to add to the lengthy list he'd accepted as part of his "chain of shame."

"I'm sorry," he said, knowing the sentiment to be both inadequate and unwanted.

She turned her back on him. "Is there anything else I can do for you? I need to return to work."

An idea came to him, an idea so outrageous it might have been one of Nic's crazier schemes. He didn't give himself time to consider all the ramifications. To pull this off, he needed to act, and act fast. "Actually, there is something else. It's the reason I came here, as a matter of fact. There's a charity auction this Saturday night. Dantes has donated a few wedding rings to help raise money for the Susan G. Koman Breast Cancer Foundation. I need an escort."

Instantly she shook her head. "No, thank you."

"It isn't a request."

She spun to confront him. "You must be joking." One look at his expression and her mouth tightened. "Dating you is now part of my job description?"

"I don't recall referring to Saturday night as a date. It's a business function. And yes, on occasion you'll be expected to attend them, just as the Fontaines expected you to when you worked for TH."

He could see the frustration eating at her. "Why is my presence so important?"

"Because it aligns you with your new employer in a public setting."

She paled. "Will the Fontaines be there?"

"I assume so." Compassion filled him. "You're going to have to face them sometime," he added gently.

For a brief, heartrending moment, her chin trembled. Then she firmed it and squared her shoulders. "Fine. We might as well get it over with. Where is it, and what time should I arrive?"

"It's at Le Premier again." He sympathized with her slight flinch, understanding that she probably regarded the hotel as the scene of her downfall. Or at the very least, the point where her life took a sharp, painful ninety-degree turn. "I'll pick you up at your apartment at eight."

"Not a chance—"

"Don't." He cut her off without compunction. "You're not going to win, so don't waste your energy fighting me."

Her chin shot up. "It's your way or…what? You'll fire me?"

He didn't bother answering. She knew the terms of their contract without him reiterating them. He approached, drawn by a force beyond his ability to control. "Do you really want to turn our relationship into a war when there are so many better things we could do with our time and energy?"

Passion exploded across her face. Unfortunately anger drove it rather than desire. "I refuse to fall into your arms after you've forced me into this situation. How could you think I would?"

"Then don't fall." He caught her close and offered a teasing smile. "Trip a little and I'll catch you."

Her anger vied with a naked longing and she splayed her hands across his chest to hold him off. "Please don't do this, Sev. Either let me work for you or let me go. But if you keep forcing the issue we'll end up despising each other."

He tucked a lock of hair behind her ear, the silken feel

of her curls rivaling that of her skin. "I could never despise you." His smile tilted. "But maybe that's all you feel for me."

She closed her eyes. "I—I don't despise you."

He knew how hard her confession came. He leaned into her, basking in her feminine warmth. Somehow, someway, he'd find a way to fix this, while still protecting Dantes and all the people who depended on him.

Somehow…

Francesca dressed with more than her usual care. She tried to tell herself she did it for her own peace of mind, that the extra pains she took helped give her the strength and composure she needed to face the Fontaines, as well as others in the industry who felt she'd sold out. But that would be a lie. Everything she did to prepare for the night ahead was with one person in mind.

Sev.

She checked the mirror a final time. The sleek bronze-toned dress hugged her curves, while her hairstyle—a simple knot at the base of her neck—helped draw attention to the topaz chandelier earrings that she'd designed before joining Timeless Heirlooms. In fact, it had been one of the pieces that had convinced Kurt and Tina to hire her. Checking the mirror a final time, she nodded in satisfaction. Simple and understated, while subtly advertising why her talents were currently in such high demand. Or at least she hoped that would be the overall reaction.

Promptly at eight, Sev knocked at her door. His single sweeping look convinced Francesca she'd chosen the perfect ensemble. Hot molten hunger exploded in his gaze. She fell back a step before the wall of heat radiating off him. Heaven help her, when had her apartment grown so small? And when had Sev grown so large? Even worse, after everything he'd done, why did she still long to throw herself in his arms and surrender everything to him? It didn't make a bit of sense.

*"Tesoro mio,"* he murmured. The lyricism she'd come to associate with him caressed the words. "You stagger me."

Good. She wanted him staggered. She wanted to knock him clean off his feet. It seemed only fair considering he'd done the same to her. Not that she'd allow any hint of that to show. Behind her, the bed called to her, whispering such innovative suggestions, it brought a blush to her cheeks. She gathered up her wrap and purse. Time to leave. She didn't dare stay another second in such close confines with Sev. Not with her bed misbehaving.

She suffered the short drive to Le Premier in silence, reluctant to do or say anything that might put her mental and emotional state in jeopardy. The next few hours would prove incredibly difficult and she wanted a few minutes to prepare herself, to slam every barrier she possessed into place. She succeeded beautifully, right up until he helped her from the car.

Leaning down in a sweet, intimate move, he whispered in her ear, "Back to the scene of the crime."

"Yours or mine?" She managed to ask the question with barely a tremor to betray her agitation.

"Mine," he claimed without hesitation. "I accept full blame for what happened here."

"Considering how little resistance I offered, that's rather generous of you."

He gathered her hand in his and tucked it through the crook of his arm. "Not at all. Because if I had to do it over again, I would."

She stiffened in outrage. "You'd blackmail me into leaving the Fontaines?"

He looked down at her, his eyes burning with tarnished lights. "I'd steal you away and make love to you until morning broke." A teasing smile came and went. "And then I'd blackmail you, if only to keep you close."

Francesca didn't know how to respond to his provocative statement, so she remained silent. If he noticed her discomfort, he didn't let on, chatting casually with associates and taking pains to introduce her as "the most talented designer he'd ever met." To her relief, the first part of the evening passed without a hitch. She and Sev wandered through the ballroom, examining the various offerings available for bid. He paused to show her the three pieces Dantes donated to the cause.

They were all wedding rings, of course. The first she saw featured a "fancy" yellow diamond in a vintage setting that whispered of romantic styles from the late eighteen hundreds. A Verdonia Royal amethyst complemented the diamond. The second ring appeared more sophisticated, the diamond solitaire a clear stone in a swirl of platinum with a round brilliant cut. But Francesca found it too cold for her taste. Moving on to the third ring, she froze, not even realizing she held her breath until she released it on a prolonged sigh. Never had she seen anything so beautiful.

"Is this…is this a fire diamond?" she asked in amazement.

She'd heard of them, of course, but had never been fortunate enough to see one, let alone use them in any of the jewelry she designed. She'd read that the fire of its transformation from coal to diamond lingered at its very heart and gave the gemstone its name. Sure enough, she could see the flames that licked outward from the fiery depths. Mesmerized, she could only stare in awe.

"There's only one mine that produces them and Dantes owns it," he confirmed. "They're even more rare than pink diamonds."

The fire diamond was breathtaking in its simplicity, and yet the band lifted it from stunning to extraordinary. Woven together into a gorgeous setting that combined gold with white gold, it provided a perfect backdrop for the stone.

"Two disparate halves made one," he explained.

"Oh, Sev," she murmured. "I wish I'd designed this. It's magnificent."

He shot her a look of amusement intermingled with pride. "Primo will be delighted to hear you think so, since he created it. It's one of a kind."

"And you're auctioning it off?" She stared at him in dismay. "How can you bear for it to go out of the family?"

"It's for a good cause."

Over the next few hours Francesca forgot her animosity toward Sev. She had so much fun examining all the donated items, she didn't even remember the Fontaines and the strong possibility she'd run into them. When the time came for Primo's ring to go up on the block, she waited anxiously to see who would claim it. To her surprise, Sev put in the winning bid at the very last minute.

"Now I know why you weren't worried." She gave a wry grin. "I should have known."

He inclined his head. "Yes, you should. Primo would have killed me if I'd lost that final bid. Wait here for a minute while I retrieve it."

He left her side to go and claim the ring. No sooner had he disappeared from sight than she caught a glimpse of the Fontaines. Every other thought fled as she stood frozen in place, utterly vulnerable to the approaching storm. Before they reached her, Sev reappeared with a ring box bearing the distinctive Dantes logo.

Spotting the Fontaines, Sev dropped a hand to her shoulder. "Look at me, sweetheart," he murmured.

"I'm all right. Really. I'm fine." So why did she feel like a deer caught in headlights?

"You will be." He gently turned her toward him. Lifting her hand he slid Primo's ring onto her finger. "Trust me."

She glanced down, stunned. "What are you doing?"

"I'm trying to fix things. To protect you."

"I—I don't understand."

"I need you to go along with what's about to happen." He spoke low and urgently. "I owe you this much, sweetheart. Hell, I owe you far more."

Before she could demand a further explanation, the Fontaines descended. Sev greeted them with a broad smile. "You can be the first to congratulate us." He held up her left hand. The fire diamond caught the light and burst into flames. "Francesca just agreed to marry me."

"You must be kidding." Disbelief overrode Tina's anger. "This is a joke, right?"

Kurt studied Francesca with open concern. "This is sudden."

Did she look as dazed as she felt? Probably. She'd never handled surprises well. She'd learned long ago that surprises meant something unpleasant…like moving to a new foster home. "I—"

"She's still in shock," Sev said with an understanding smile. "She didn't see it coming."

"You think I believe this?" Tina demanded. "You think I believe you've actually fallen in love with her?"

Sev tucked Francesca close in a protective hold. "Why do you find it so difficult to believe?" A hard note underscored the question. "Do you consider her so unlovable?"

"Just the opposite," Tina snapped. She started to reach for Francesca before realizing what she'd almost done and snatching her hand back. "It's you I don't trust, Dante. She may be too inexperienced to figure out what you're doing, but I'm not. You've romanced her away from Timeless Heirlooms because she's our best designer. You know perfectly well that without her—" Her voice broke.

It was Kurt's turn to pull his wife into protective arms. "Don't, love. At least now we know what happened."

Tears flooded Francesca's eyes. "I'm sorry," she whispered. "You have no idea how badly I feel."

"Give it time," Tina shot back. "You're going to feel a lot worse before he's done with you. The only reason he's romancing you is to facilitate his takeover of TH. You realize that, don't you?"

Francesca couldn't bring herself to respond to the question. How could she when every word Tina spoke was the truth? Her fingers dug into Sev's arm as she struggled to keep from bursting into tears. She needed to get away. Now. "Excuse me, won't you?"

Spinning free of Sev's embrace, she pushed her way through the crowd of people. She needed air, needed time to regroup. She adored Tina and Kurt, had wanted to spend the bulk of her career working for them. At least, that had been her dream. But Sev changed all that, turning her life upside down.

She gazed down at the engagement ring gracing her finger. And now he'd tried to restore her relationship with the Fontaines. To put himself in the line of fire, instead of her. What he didn't realize was how difficult she found wearing this ring. To her an engagement ring symbolized a soul-deep love. A promise that she'd have someone at her side who cherished her and would be her lifelong partner. This gorgeous, incredible, breathtaking ring was nothing more than a sham. It wasn't real.

And more than ever, it left her feeling like an outsider.

# CHAPTER EIGHT

SEV STOOD THERE, annoyed to discover himself acting the part of the stereotypical hapless male as Francesca disappeared into the crowd in one direction, and an infuriated Tina stormed off in the opposite. Sev stopped Kurt before he could charge after his wife. For Francesca's sake he had to find a way to make this right.

"Francesca didn't have any choice," Sev stated. "You realize that, don't you?"

Kurt swung around with a snarl, shaking free of Sev's hold. "I realize that you forced her to quit a promising job with us and go to work for you."

Sev fought for patience. "It wouldn't have worked, Kurt. It would have put her in an impossible position. Because of our relationship, she'd have been trapped between you and Tina, and the Dantes. She'd have had to watch every word she said, both at work and at home, for fear of betraying one side or the other."

"So you made her choose between us."

"Yes. She doesn't deserve your anger. The only thing she's guilty of is falling in love. Her decision hurt you. Trust me when I say that same decision hurt her every bit as much. She adores you and Tina. You've been her mentors. Her friends. Her family. She owes you everything, and don't think she isn't aware of that fact."

Kurt's expression softened ever so slightly, right up until he looked at Sev. "And you?" he asked harshly. "Is Tina right? Is this your clever way of getting your hands on TH?"

"I don't need Francesca to do that. TH will be mine whether she's working for you, or for me."

"Not if I can help it."

"Kurt…" Sev grimaced. "Talk to Tina. The two of you are important to Francesca."

"Important enough to get you to back off?"

Sev couldn't prevent a smile. If circumstances had been different he might have formed a friendship with Kurt. He'd prefer that over their current contentious relationship. "Good try, Fontaine, but it isn't going to happen. Why don't you and Tina make it easy on yourselves and sell out? I'll give you an excellent price."

"Not interested."

Sev shrugged. "I didn't think so, but it was worth a try." He hesitated. "Will you talk to Tina?"

Kurt released his breath in a rough sigh. "Yeah, I'll talk to her. I don't expect it'll change anything. But I will encourage her not to take her anger out on Francesca."

"I'm the one at fault. Tell her to keep me in the crosshairs where I belong, and we'll all do just fine."

With an abrupt nod, Kurt turned and walked away. Sev had no idea whether his plan stood a chance in hell of success. For Francesca's sake, he had to try. She deserved an opportunity to get to know her father, but because he'd been so focused on Dantes and his plans for the business, he'd stolen that opportunity from her. No. Not just stolen. He'd effectively annihilated any chance of it ever happening. If he could restore that much, maybe—just maybe—he could live with the guilt he felt over the rest.

Sev went after Francesca, not in the least surprised to find she'd retreated to the balcony off the ballroom. It was where they'd first met and he struggled not to read anything into her choice. She stood by the railing, her back to him. He could tell she sensed him the instant he appeared in the doorway, her awareness betrayed by the mantle of stillness that settled over her.

He approached. "I'm sorry to spring that engagement ring on you, sweetheart."

"Have you lost your mind?" She threw the question over her shoulder without turning. "What in the world were you thinking?"

"That I was Nic, I guess."

That did prompt her to swing around. "This was Nicolò's idea?"

"Hell, no." Sev scrubbed his hand across his jaw. "I get all the credit—or should I say blame?—for this one. I just meant it's the sort of crazy scheme he'd have come up with."

"I don't understand. Why would you do such a thing?"

He shrugged. "I had to try and fix the problem somehow."

"Because that's your job. To fix things." It wasn't a question.

"It always has been," he answered simply. "Since the

day my father died, I'm all that stood between Dantes succeeding or going under."

"Well, I'm not some business you have to rebuild. You don't have to fix things for me," she insisted. "I've been taking care of myself for a long time now. I don't need you to step in and assume the job at this late date."

Strongly stated. Maybe a bit too strongly. "Just out of curiosity…" He cocked his head to one side. "Have you ever needed anyone since you turned eighteen?"

He caught the faintest of quivers before she stiffened her chin. "No."

He lowered his voice to a caress. "Or should I ask, have you ever *wanted* anyone?"

"Don't do this," she whispered. "It's not fair. I want permanence, not temporary."

"Not a string of foster homes."

She conceded the accuracy of his observation with a small nod. "Growing up I always felt I had to change who I was so I'd fit in, that being myself wasn't good enough. I refuse to do that any longer. I won't pretend to be something or someone I'm not, not any longer." She tugged at the ring he'd given her. "This doesn't belong on my finger. Not until it's the real thing."

He stopped her before she could remove it, closing his hand over hers. "Leave it there for the time being. I forced you to work for me. Caused dissension for you both at Timeless and at Dantes. The ring will help protect you. It may even right a few wrongs."

She hesitated. "What's the point? It has to come off sometime."

"But not yet." Not until he'd had time to come up

with a resolution to their problems. "Listen to me, honey. There's a very good possibility that our engagement will give you the opportunity to reestablish a relationship with the Fontaines. They're less likely to blame you for leaving them if they believe I forced the issue. They could be part of your life again. You might not see your father as often as you would if you still worked for TH. But at least they won't be angry with you any longer."

"Do you really think so?"

Stark longing filled her expression, ripping him apart. "Give it a chance and see," he suggested roughly.

She teetered on the edge of temptation. "How long do you expect me to keep up this charade?"

"For as long as it takes."

"But it's a lie," Francesca protested.

"Is it?"

A single tug had their bodies colliding in the sweetest of impacts. Sev wrapped his arms around her. The mere touch of her body fomented a reaction unlike anything he'd ever felt with another woman. He'd assumed the acuteness of their passion would ease after a few weeks, that eventually they'd both become sated and the sexual intensity would diminish. It hadn't, and from his perspective, neither of them was close to sated.

A tremor swept through her, one so slight he'd have missed it if they hadn't been fused together from hip to shoulder. He recognized that shiver, felt it each time he pulled her into his arms, and it never failed to excite him. It betrayed a sensual helplessness, one reserved only for him. It whispered her secret to him, teased him with the

knowledge that with one touch, her defenses would fall
before his advance.

"Let me in, sweetheart."

She gripped his shoulders, pushing even as she
yielded. "We're through. Whatever existed between us
is over. It ended the minute you forced me into this devil's
bargain with you. Putting a ring on my finger to *protect*
me doesn't change that. You put business ahead of our
relationship and that's the end of anything personal."

"You know that isn't true."

He swept a hand from the base of her spine to the
nape of her neck. Her shiver became a shudder. The give
to her body ripened into a heated abandonment, one that
silently incited him to deepen their embrace. She wanted
him. She might resist it, but nothing could stop the combustible reaction whenever they touched. Not personal
preference. Not logic or intellect. Not even her hurt and
anger at the hideous position in which he'd put her.

The dragon's breath of The Inferno incinerated both
reason and intellect, and left behind a single urge. To
mate. To step into the fire of that joining and allow the
flames to consume them.

He lowered his head, his mouth hovering above hers
so their breath became one. "I wish this weren't happening when it's clear you don't want it. I wish I could do
what you ask and let you go. But I can't."

"You don't have any choice," she asserted. "Do you
really think that after all you've done I could ever trust
you again?"

"I'm not asking for your trust."

"Just me in your bed."

He didn't bother denying the truth. "Yes, I want you there. Or here. Or anywhere I can have you. Any way you'll allow it."

He closed the final gap between them and sank into her mouth. He heard her sigh of pleasure. Felt it. Drank it inward. Their lips molded, shaping themselves one to the other, before parting. Her breathing grew ragged. Or maybe it was his. *More.* The insistent demand sounded in his head, so clear and sharp he almost thought he'd said it aloud. And maybe he did, because she reared back, breaking the kiss almost as soon as it began.

She turned her head a fraction to avoid any risk of their lips colliding again. "Making love to you is too intimate. It leaves me too vulnerable," she told him with devastating frankness. "I can't open myself to you if I don't trust you."

"We'll find a way to make this work."

He'd said the wrong thing. Instantly, she ripped free of his embrace. "There's only one way that's possible. I can work for you or I can sleep with you. But I refuse to do both. It's your choice, Sev."

She gazed at him and he could see the burgeoning hope in the inky darkness, a hope he had no option but to crush. "I believe we've already had this conversation. You work for Dantes."

He forced himself not to flinch at the acrid disillusionment that shattered the last of her hope. Her chin shot up and she embraced her fury. "You're the consummate businessman to the bitter end, aren't you, Sev? No matter who gets in your way or how many get hurt."

He opened the door a crack so she could see inside.

"There's never been any other choice for me. My family has always depended on me to be the ruthless one."

"I'm not in your way, Sev."

He inclined his head. "Not anymore. You need to understand, sweetheart, that my family still depends on me to make the hard decisions. If I don't make them, if I'm too weak to make them, I could put Dantes at risk again."

"Fine. Now you've made one more hard decision. You've chosen Dantes over our relationship." She stepped back. "Just don't expect me to reward you for that decision."

He dared to touch her a final time. He scraped his knuckles along the curve of her cheek and pretended not to see her flinch. "I'm sure that's your intention now. But you will be back in my bed. There won't be any other choice." He smiled, a painful pull of his mouth. "For either of us."

Francesca twisted the engagement ring she'd worn for the past ten days, still surprised to discover it decorating her finger whenever the fire diamond caught her eye. "So who all will be at your grandparents' house for dinner?" she asked.

Sev shot her a quick glance of reassurance, which dashed any hopes that he hadn't picked up on her nervousness. "Just Nonna, Primo and my brothers this time around. I'll save the rest of the family for another occasion."

"Oh." She started to twist her hands together again, but the fire diamond stopped her, flashing an additional message of reassurance. To her amusement, it worked and she found herself relaxing despite herself. "So. Does your family get together often?"

"Once a month without fail."

"Do they know our engagement isn't real?"

"It is real. For now. As far as my family's concerned, you and I are engaged," he warned. "I'd appreciate it if you wouldn't disabuse them of that notion."

Her brows pulled together. "And how did you explain the suddenness of it? Or the fact that I used to work at TH and now work for you?"

"Easy. I told them we had no choice. It was The Inferno." He shrugged. "I didn't need any other explanation after that."

She caught her bottom lip between her teeth. So much for relaxing. Whenever she'd been sent to a new foster home, that first meeting always proved the most difficult for her. Most of the time she walked into situations where the other foster children, or her foster parents' natural children, had already formed tight family units. Sure, they always welcomed her…at first. But she dreaded those early days of adjustment, hovering on the outside of their too jovial camaraderie as she tried to figure out how to best fit in.

This time around they all believed her madly in love with Sev. How could she possibly convince them of that? "I don't think I can pull this off."

"Don't worry about it," he told her softly. "We won't stay long if you're not enjoying yourself."

"I'll be fine." And she would. She could handle the situation. After all, she wasn't a lost child any longer.

And if she'd learned nothing else during those forma-
tive years, she'd learned how to fake it.

To her delight, she discovered she didn't have to fake
anything. From the moment she and Sev walked in the
door, the Dantes welcomed her with open arms. Primo
and Nonna both gave her exuberant hugs, exclaiming in
pleasure over her choice of engagement ring.

"It's a stunning design," Francesca complimented
Primo with utter sincerity. "I told Sev how envious I am
that it isn't my own creation."

"I am honored," he said, clearly moved. "And I am
even more honored that you have chosen this particular ring to wear for as many years as God blesses
your marriage."

The breath caught in her lungs, the weight of his
words pressing down on her. "Thank you," she
managed to answer, shooting Sev a look of clear desperation.

He responded by lifting her left hand to his mouth in
a move that should have come across as hackneyed, but
instead struck her as unbelievably endearing. Her throat
closed as his gaze linked with hers. And just like that,
in front of all the Dantes, The Inferno struck and she
totally melted.

Nonna dabbed at her eyes and smiled at Primo rem-
iniscently. Then she clapped her hands together,
scolding in Italian. As one, the Dante men shuffled
toward the kitchen, where they switched from English
to Italian. Sev was the last to leave.

He ran his thumb along the curve of her bottom lip.
"You okay?" he asked quietly.

She blew out her breath in a sigh, murmuring in an undertone, "Well…I don't think we have to worry about whether or not they believe our engagement is real."

He bent and captured her mouth, no doubt because he knew she didn't dare protest. Not that protesting occurred to her until long after he'd released her. "No, we don't."

Nonna grinned as she watched their parting. "It is good, what you have. Special."

"I think complicated might be a more accurate description."

Nonna nodded in agreement. "With Dante men, it can be nothing less." She gathered Francesca's hand in hers. "He needs you, that one. Oh, you may look at him and wonder. He is so strong. So hard-nosed. He is quite capable of standing on his own. But he has had to be. He has had no choice but to take the one path open to him. Anything else would have meant disaster for his family."

"Because—" Francesca broke off, realizing it might not be politic to mention that her son's poor business skills almost destroyed the business her husband built.

Nonna nodded. "You are tactful. I appreciate that. But what you are thinking is true. Dominic almost destroyed Dantes." Lines of grief couldn't detract from a face still handsome despite the weight of her years. "If not for Severo, Dantes would be no more."

"It couldn't have been easy for him."

"It was more than difficult. The decisions he has made…" Nonna shook her head. "Any man would find them near to impossible. But at so young an age, so soon after the death of his mother and father…" She clicked her tongue in distress.

"You're saying he had to be ruthless." As he'd proven to her on more than one occasion these past weeks.

"Yes." Nonna closed her eyes and whispered a silent prayer. Then she looked at Francesca, joy replacing her sorrow. "But then he found you. He needs you, *ciccina*. You…soften him. And after all that has been forced on him, all the horrible choices, you give him peace. Best of all, you give him The Inferno."

With a grateful smile, she linked arms with Francesca and urged her toward the kitchen. It troubled Francesca to see the situation from Sev's side of the fence. She didn't want to sympathize with all he'd been through.

Worse, rather than fading, her physical and emotional response toward him grew progressively stronger with each passing day. Considering all that stood between them, it would make life easier if it would just go away. She entered the kitchen and spared him a swift look, confirming that those feelings weren't going anywhere anytime soon.

To her surprise, she spotted Primo at the stove, commandeering the burners like an admiral overseeing his fleet, while the Dante men moved in practiced synchronicity, taking care of all the domestic chores in preparation for the meal.

Her surprise must have shown because Nonna grinned. "This is my night off. It is a Dante tradition," she explained, gesturing toward her grandchildren. "They take care of me on family day."

"I like that." Francesca's eyes narrowed in suspicion. "They do dishes, too, right? You don't get stuck with those?"

"No, no." She gave a broad wink. "I am too clever for that. Here. You take Gianna's seat next to me. She's in *L'Italia*. Visiting *famiglia* with her parents and brothers. You will meet them next time."

Assuming there was a next time, Francesca almost said, before catching back the words at the last second. Fortunately, dinner came together just then and the Dante men descended on the table like locusts. After grace, conversation exploded, for the most part in English, occasionally in Italian, as a bewildering array of dishes passed back and forth.

The choices were endless. Marinated calamari vied with panzanella. Cannellini beans cooked with garlic, olive oil and sage competed with stuffed tomatoes. Then the main dishes marched around the table. Chicken Marsala with red peppers, tortellini, pasta with a variety of sauces.

"Save room for dessert," Sev warned as he piled her food high.

She shook her head at the overloaded plate. "I can serve myself, you know."

He gave her a look a shade too innocent. "I just wanted to make sure you try a bit of everything."

She knew him too well to buy into that one. "I think you want to stuff me full of carbs so my brain goes to sleep."

"Now why would I want to do that?" But his mouth twitched, giving him away.

"So I can't think fast enough to argue with you."

He grinned. "But, *cara,* I love arguing with you."

A liquid warmth swept through her again at the teeny-tiny accent that crept through his words. No doubt the setting contributed to it, and the fact that he constantly switched back and forth between English and Italian.

"Ho-ho. What a liar you are," Nonna corrected in Italian. "It is not the arguing you love. It is the making up afterward."

"Well…" Francesca offered judiciously. "He does excel at both."

Silence descended over the table. *"Parlate italiano?"* Nonna demanded in astonishment. "And why did you not tell us this?"

Francesca grinned. "How would I know what you were all saying about me if I admitted I spoke Italian?"

Delighted laughter rang out as they all bombarded her with questions in rapid-fire succession. Primo rapped his knuckles in an effort to regain control. Instantly, silence descended. "I will ask the questions at my own table, if you do not mind," he informed his grandsons. Eyes identical to Sev's fixed her with uncomfortable shrewdness. "You have Italian relatives? This is why you learned Italian?" he asked.

She shook her head. "As far as I'm aware I'm not of Italian descent." A shadow of regret came and went. "I'm afraid I don't know much about my ancestors, so anything's possible, I suppose."

She caught a hint of compassion in Primo's expression, though he didn't allow it to color his voice. "Then why?" he asked. "Why did you learn Italian?"

"Because it's always been my dream to work at

Dantes," she admitted. "So it made sense to learn the language." A subtle shift in attitude occurred after her confession, one that left her somewhat puzzled.

"Figured it out yet?" Sev asked softly.

Her gaze jerked up to meet his. "Figured what out?"

"You'll get there." He gave her a small wedge of *panforte,* a traditional Tuscan dessert filled with nuts, fruit and a hint of chocolate. With it he served her a cup of strong coffee.

"Do you mean…?" She glanced around the table, re-assured to see that a heated discussion about the best time to expand Dantes raged on, preoccupying the rest of Sev's family. "Do you mean have I worked out the change in your family? The change in their attitude toward me?"

"Almost there," he murmured.

She shrugged. "That's easy enough. It's because they found out I speak Italian. I blend in better."

"Not even close."

Startled, she gave him her full attention. "What? They love me now because I told them I've always wanted to work at Dantes? So what? Lots of people would kill to work for you."

"Nope. Come on, honey. You know. You just refuse to accept the significance of it."

He saw too clearly and it left her far too vulnerable. She returned her fork to her plate, before confessing, "It's because I learned Italian in the hopes I'd someday work for Dantes. That I took that extra step."

A slow smile built across his mouth. "I knew you'd get it."

She scanned the table again, realizing that with that simple, painfully honest statement she'd become one of the family, her acceptance into their inner circle absolute. Most important of all, she'd done it by being herself. Even so, the knowledge filled her with guilt. "But it's a lie."

He helped himself to a second slice of *panforte*. "You didn't learn Italian because you wanted to work for me?"

"Not *you*," she stressed. "Dantes. And not *that*." She shoved her left hand under his nose. "*This*. This is a—"

He leaned over and stopped her with a kiss. "We'll discuss that later," he murmured against her mouth. "In the meantime, don't worry. These things have a way of sorting themselves out."

They lingered over their coffee for another hour before Sev stood and told his family they needed to leave. Hugs were liberally dispensed before they made it out the door. The instant they slid into the car, she returned to the concern uppermost on her mind.

"Can't we tell your family the truth? I really like them, and I'd rather not lie to them."

"We're not lying to them. We are engaged."

"You know what I mean." Impatience edged her voice. "They think we're getting married."

"That might prove a problem at some point," he conceded. "But not today." He pulled up outside her apartment complex. After curbing the wheels to keep them from rolling downhill, he threw the car in Park and shut off the engine. A gentle rain tapped against the windshield and blocked out everything but a watery blur of city lights. "Have you really always wanted to work at Dantes?" he asked.

"Yes."

"Then you've achieved your dream. Is a temporary engagement to me so high a price to pay for that dream?"

"No." She touched her engagement ring in an increasingly familiar gesture. "But what I've done to the Fontaines is far too high a price for any dream."

"You need to trust me. It's all going to work out. It may not be a perfect solution. Compromise will be involved. But it's going to work out."

"Because you say so?"

"Because I intend to make it so."

He cupped her face and drew her close. At the first brush of his mouth against hers, every thought evaporated from her head. The Fontaines, the Dante clan, work pressures…they all slipped away beneath the heat of his taking. He played with her mouth, offering light, teasing kisses. But it only took her tiny moan of pleasure for it to transform into something more. Something deep and sensual and unbearably desperate. Passion exploded, fogging the windows and ripping apart both intent and intention. It needed to stop…before stopping became an impossibility.

"You don't play fair," she protested, struggling to draw breath.

"It doesn't pay to play fair." He eyed her in open amusement. "What it does is give me what I want most."

"And what's that?" she couldn't resist asking.

"You." He lifted an eyebrow. "Invite me in and put us both out of our misery."

Did he think it would be that easy to recover the ground they'd lost? Maybe if their embrace had continued for another few minutes. But it hadn't and she still found enough self-possession—somewhere, if she looked around hard enough—to stand firm in her resolve not to tumble back into his bed.

"No, I'm not inviting you in." She gave him her sweetest smile. "I don't play fair, either. As far as I'm concerned, you can sit here and suffer for your sins."

"But not for much longer," he said. Or was it a warning?

# CHAPTER NINE

FRANCESCA FLIPPED through her sketchpad and experienced a sense of accomplishment unlike anything she'd ever felt before. She'd worked on the creations contained on these pages for most of her life.

It hadn't been her first glimpse of the sparkle and glitter of gemstones that had drawn her to jewelry design. Sure, she loved the beauty of them. And she loved the endless ideas that danced through her imagination, ideas for how to combine the different gemstones into stunning patterns. But that hadn't been what snagged her heart.

From the moment she'd understood the true symbolism of a wedding ring and what it stood for... From the instant she realized what her mother never experienced, and no doubt longed to share with the man she loved, Francesca had been drawn to create the dream. And now she had.

She studied her designs one last time, thrilled that she'd completed what she'd set out to achieve all those years ago. She'd given birth to something beyond her wildest expectations, and ironically she owed it all to

Severo Dante. Somehow, at some point, he'd crept into her heart and given her the final spark of inspiration she'd needed to bring her designs to life.

Tears filled her eyes and she shook her head with a smile. How ridiculous to get all weepy over a bunch of drawings. She hadn't even completed a mock-up of them, yet. Not that it mattered. She knew how the finished product would look. She even knew how they could market the collection. An entire campaign existed between the covers of her sketchpad, a campaign that would relaunch Dantes into a full line of women's jewelry, should that possibility interest them.

Flipping her pad closed, she locked it away just as her studio door banged open. Tina stood there, looking more devastated than Francesca had ever seen her.

"Tina? What's wrong?" Francesca asked, half-rising. "What's happened?"

"Is it true?" Tina slammed the door closed behind her, closeting them together in the room. "All this time I thought you were the innocent in this. That Dante had you completely snowed. I actually thought maybe we could work things out between us. But now I'm not so sure."

A sick suspicion clawed at Francesca's stomach. "What are you talking about?"

"I'm talking about my husband." Tina's mouth twisted. "Or should I say…your father."

Francesca felt every scrap of color drain from her face and she sank back into her chair. "You can't be serious. I'm not—"

Tina cut her off with a swipe of her hand. "Don't. At least have the decency not to lie to me." Her heels pounded out a succession of hard staccato raps as she crossed the room. "I have the evidence."

"How?"

"That's not important." She reached the edge of the desk and Francesca could see the wild pain lurking in the older woman's eyes. "You lied to me. To Kurt."

"Only about my connection to him. Only that, I swear."

A wild laugh ripped loose. "Only that? *Only?*"

How could she explain? "I just wanted to get to know him. From a distance," Francesca emphasized. "I never planned to tell either of you the truth."

Fury ignited. "What were you waiting for? To worm your way into our good graces and then spring it on us? Hope Kurt was smitten enough with the idea of having a daughter that he'd give you a piece of my business?" She slammed her palms on Francesca's desk. "*My* business. Not Kurt's. He may keep the production end of things afloat, but I'm the creative force behind Timeless Heirlooms."

Francesca shook her head. "You don't understand. I'd never do anything to cause trouble for you two." Guilt overwhelmed her. She never should have applied for a job at TH. Never should have put her own selfish needs ahead of respecting the sanctity of her father's marriage. "I just wanted to get to know my father," she confessed miserably. "I never planned to tell either of you who I was. Please, Tina. This isn't Kurt's fault."

"I'm well aware of whose fault this is." She stabbed a finger at Francesca. "Yours. You chose to come into our life. You chose to become involved with Severo Dante. You ruined my marriage."

"Ruined?" Francesca shot to her feet. "No, Tina. Don't walk out on Kurt. Not because of me."

"I can add. Better yet, I can subtract. According to our personnel records, you're twenty-six. That means Kurt and I were married three years when he—" She broke off, clearly softened the description she'd been about to use. "When he had an affair with your mother."

"It was a long time ago, Tina. All anyone has to do is look at him to know he's crazy in love with you." Francesca jettisoned every scrap of pride to plead on Kurt's behalf. "After thirty years of marriage, surely that counts for something?"

"Maybe it would have…if not for you. But every time I see you, every time I hear your name or see your designs, it's a slap in the face. Living proof of my husband's infidelity." Tina spun around and stalked to the door. Once there, she paused. "Oh, and by the way? You can thank your fiancé for clueing me in to your true identity. It would seem he'll do anything to get his hands on TH. Even destroy my marriage."

Sev sat behind his desk, papers strewn across the thick glass surface. Some were preliminary jewelry designs, others financial statements from the various international branches, still others proposals for expansion. All of the reports demanded his immediate attention.

A knock sounded at his door just as he reached for the first report. Before he could respond, Francesca entered the room. She shut the door behind her with a tad too much emphasis, warning of her less than stellar mood.

"How could you?" she demanded.

He stilled, studying her through narrowed eyes. "Clichéd, but intriguing nonetheless. Dare I ask…how could I what?"

"Tina knows. Tina knows I'm Kurt's daughter. There's only one person who could have told her."

"I gather that's where I come in." He leaned back in his chair, reaching for calm. For some reason that only served to push her anger to greater heights.

"Don't," she warned sharply. "Don't play with me."

"I'd love to play with you, though not about this." He gave her a level look. "Honey, I haven't broken my promise to you. The only contact I've had with Tina is to up my offer for Timeless Heirlooms."

Francesca shook her head. "You don't get it. You— or one of your brothers—are the only ones who could have told her. No one else knows."

He smiled at that, which might have been a mistake judging by the flash of fury that glittered in her dark eyes. "Someone must know, otherwise we wouldn't have uncovered the information in the first place."

She slowly shook her head. "I hired a private investigator four years ago to find my father. He couldn't. But he did find an old friend of my mother's and she's the one who told me my father's identity. I never told anyone, not even the P.I. So unless someone tracked this woman down and forced her to talk, I have trouble believing the leak came from her."

That caught him by surprise. Shoving back his chair, he stood and circled his desk. Cupping her elbow, he drew her over to the sitting area on the far side of the room. "Are you certain she didn't tell anyone else?"

"Of course I can't be positive." She perched on the edge of the couch and he sat next to her—too close judging by the tide of awareness that washed through her. She struggled to hide her dismay by directing it toward anger. "But I find it highly unlikely she'd call Tina out of the blue and just hand over that information. It doesn't make any sense."

He analyzed what she'd said, looking for alternate explanations. "What about your foster parents? Is it possible they had that information?"

"Not a chance. They'd have turned Kurt's name over to the state to force him to pay child support." She leveled him with a censorious look. "How did you find out about Kurt? Who in your organization knows the truth?"

"We hired a private investigator to check you out," he admitted.

She couldn't prevent the accusation. "You've had me investigated?"

"We had all of TH's designers investigated as a matter of course." He held up a hand to ward off her indignation. "Listen, I'll contact the investigator and ascertain how he came across the information. All I can tell you is that I didn't betray your secret to Tina. Nor did any of my brothers."

She surged to her feet and paced across his office. "This is going to destroy the Fontaines' marriage."

"Maybe. Maybe not." Though, privately, he'd rate it closer to probable, edging toward definite.

"If it does, you'll be able to pick up TH for a song."

He absorbed the accusation. "Which automatically makes me guilty?"

She spun to face him. "Tina claimed you told her. And it makes sense. Who else profits from revealing the truth to her?"

He shrugged. "As far as I know…no one."

"You're not helping yourself." Frustration riddled her expression. "You realize that, don't you?"

"I realize that nothing I say will change your mind. I also realize that you don't trust me. You can't."

"How could I? Why would I?" She thrust her fingers through her hair, tumbling the curls into delicious disarray. "Since the minute we met you've done nothing to inspire that trust."

That got to him, shaving some of the calm from his temper. "Our nights together didn't inspire trust? Our time together hasn't proven the sort of man I am?"

Tears welled in her eyes again. "Those nights meant everything to me, more than they could have meant to you or you'd never have blackmailed me. You'd never have forced me to betray the Fontaines and work for you."

He climbed to his feet to give weight to his words. "I intend to return Dantes to its position as an international powerhouse, no matter what sort of sacrifices that requires. I made that fact crystal clear to you right from the start. I will recover every last subsidiary I was forced to sell off when I assumed the reins of this company. And that includes TH."

She tugged off his engagement ring and held it out. "Take this. I refuse to wear it a minute longer."

He simply shook his head. "That's not happening. If we break our engagement so soon after we announce it, your life within the jewelry world will become unbearable." He held up his hand to stem her protest. "As my fiancée, you have the Dante name to protect you. No one will dare say a word about you, your talent, or where you choose to work. Nor will anyone dare say anything should Tina decide to be indiscreet."

Her mouth trembled. "You…you think she'll tell people I'm Kurt's daughter? You think she'll publicly blame me for TH's demise?"

"A woman that angry is capable of anything. There's no telling what she'll do."

Francesca made a swift recovery, one that impressed the hell out of him. "I don't care about any of that. Let people talk. Let Tina do her worst. Let the world assume whatever they want."

"Right. And maybe you could handle the public fallout. Damned if you don't seem determined to try. But I have Dantes to consider. Becoming engaged one day and ending it only weeks later is not the image I want to project to the general public, my suppliers, or my associates and competitors."

"Then you never should have come up with this scheme."

"Point taken, but it's a little late for that." He offered a wry smile. "When I came up with the idea, my only consideration was you and trying to salvage your relationship with the Fontaines. That's what I get for thinking like Nic."

For an endless moment she wavered between acceptance and rejection. To his profound relief, she released her breath in a sigh of reluctant agreement. "How long? How long do we have to keep up the pretense?"

"For as long as it takes." He ran his hands up and down her arms, picking up on the slight shiver she couldn't quite suppress. "Give it time, sweetheart. Is it really so bad being engaged to me? You liked my family, didn't you?"

Once again, he'd said the wrong thing. Her eyes darkened in distress. "I don't want to fall in love with them."

He could guess why. "Because it hurts too much when it ends and you're forced to walk away."

She didn't deny it. Instead she changed the subject. "What about the Fontaines? You have to promise me you won't take advantage of this latest wrinkle. You have to promise me you're still going to pay full price for TH, even if their marriage falls apart."

He refused to be anything other than straight with her. "If they offer me a good deal, I'm not going to turn it down."

Maybe he shouldn't have been quite that straight. She pulled back and glared. "We have a contract. You have to pay them full price for their business. And I intend to make sure you stick to that agreement."

"Our contract states I'm to pay fair market value. That's what I intend to pay and not a penny more."

"Even if the fair market value drops because Kurt and Tina divorce?"

"Fair. Market. Value," he repeated succinctly.

She stilled and something drifted across her expression, something that had the businessman in him going on red alert. Then she gave a careless shrug. "If that's the best you're willing to do, I guess I have no choice but to accept it, do I?"

He stared at her through narrowed eyes. "That's precisely what I expect you to do, since that's precisely what the contract calls for."

She turned to leave his office without further argument, which worried him all the more. Hell. No question about it. She was up to something, and he suspected he wouldn't like whatever scheme she was busily hatching.

Later that evening, Francesca stood outside Sev's apartment building, her head bent against the rain, soaked to the skin from an unexpected shower. Why had he demanded she come by tonight of all nights? she wondered in despair. Maybe if she hadn't gotten together with Kurt she wouldn't be finding this so difficult. But when she'd suggested waiting until morning to show Sev her latest designs, he'd insisted that he needed to see them tonight.

She shivered uncontrollably, wanting nothing more than to crawl into her bathtub at home and have a long, hot soak in conjunction with an even longer cry. Swiping the dampness from her cheeks—rain, she attempted to reassure herself, not tears—she rode the elevator to the top floor of Sev's apartment building and applied fist to door.

It opened almost immediately. "What the hell…?" Sev took one look at her and swept her across the threshold and into his apartment, ignoring her disjointed protests about dripping all over his hardwood floors. "I don't give a flying f—" He tempered the expression. "A flying *fig* about the damn floors. I care about you. What the hell's happened? Are you all right?"

"I'm wet." She trembled and held out the packet of designs. "Maybe cold, too. I'm shaking so hard it's sort of tough to tell."

He snatched the designs from her hand and tossed them aside. The packet hit the floor and skidded under an antique coat closet. Then he unceremoniously swept her up into his arms and carried her into the master bathroom. She couldn't rouse herself enough to fight him when he stripped first her, and then himself, and pulled them both into the glassed-in shower stall. He turned the jets on high and she stood docilely beneath the blazing-hot torrent and let the water wash away all emotion.

"What happened?" he asked again, more gently this time.

She didn't even realize she spoke until she heard her voice echoing against the tile. "He didn't want me, Sev. My father. He agreed to meet me tonight and then sent me away. He said he was sorry. Sorry!" She covered her face with her hands as she fought for control. "Sorry he had an affair with my mother. Sorry she became pregnant. Sorry Tina found out the truth. He said he couldn't see me ever again."

"He's a fool."

"Why?" She dropped her hands and stared up at Sev. "What did I do wrong?"

He hugged her fiercely. "You didn't do anything wrong. Not a damn thing. It's them, honey. Something's wrong with them. But you have me and you have the rest of the Dantes. And they flat-out adore you. We'll be your family from now on."

"When they find out we're not really engaged, they won't want me, either," she felt obligated to point out.

"They will. I promise." He continued to hold her close while the water poured down on them. "Easy, sweetheart. Let it all out. You'll feel better if you do."

Let what out? Didn't he understand that she felt dead inside? Her father rejected her. She couldn't say why she cared so much. After all, what did one more rejection matter after so many? At long last, Sev shut off the water and left her dripping, naked and alone, in the middle of the tile floor. An instant later he reappeared with an armload of towels. He slung one around his waist and dropped another on her head, before swathing her from shoulders to knees in a third. Then he proceeded to rub her down with a briskness that caused her skin to glow.

"What are you doing?" she asked, mildly curious.

"You're in shock. I need to get you warm."

She peered at him from beneath the towel. "I'm not shocked. I'm not even surprised. I knew what would happen if Kurt and Tina found out the truth about me."

He knelt at her feet, drying her with an impersonal touch that had her responding in far too personal a way. "You'd be rejected, just as you've been rejected so many times before."

"I'm sort of used to it."

"Yeah, I know. That's what kills me."

"Don't let it bother you. It doesn't bother me. Not anymore."

"I shouldn't ask. But I will." He rocked back on his heels and stared up at her, his face set in grim lines. "Why doesn't it bother you anymore?"

She spoke slowly, as though to a backward child. "Because I can't feel." Sheesh. Didn't he get it? "When you can't feel, it doesn't hurt."

For some reason that made him swear. When he'd run out of invectives, he planted a hand low on her back and ushered her from the bathroom. "I don't know about you, but I could use a drink."

"Several, I think."

"Hmm. And something to eat."

Ten minutes later, she was curled up on the floor in front of a fire, dining on a selection of imported cheese and crackers while sipping the smoothest single-malt whiskey she'd ever tasted. Sev lounged beside her, a towel still knotted at his waist. She woke to her surroundings sufficiently to admire the miles of toned muscle rising above the soft white fleece.

Lord help her, but he was the most gorgeous man she'd ever seen. He hadn't bothered to brush his hair, simply slicked it back from his face so it clung damply to the back of his neck in heavy, dark waves. His features reminded her somewhat of Primo, with the same rugged handsomeness and noble bearing. And, of course, the same stunning eye color. But the rest… Oh, my. The rest was pure Severo Dante.

She buried her nose in the crystal tumbler and took a quick sip. Unable to help herself, she peeked at him from over the rim. Memories from their nights together came storming back. They'd made love right here in front of the fire at least a half-dozen times. Several more times on the couch behind them when they'd been too impatient to traverse the short distance from there to the bedroom. Most nights she shared with him a pathway appeared, one strewn with clothes spreading from front door to bed.

How she enjoyed those moments, when she finally wrestled him free of that last article of clothing. He had the most incredible body, lean and graceful, yet powerful enough to lift her with ease, which he often did, then tip her onto silken sheets and cover her with that endless length of potent masculinity.

She drained the last of the whiskey and set the glass aside. "I need you to do me a favor," she informed him.

"If I can."

"Oh, you can." The only question was…would he? "I want you to make love to me. I want to feel something again."

He studied her for a long, silent moment and she could see him preparing a list of excuses. She was too vulnerable. He didn't want to take advantage of her. There were still so many issues unresolved between them. But something in her gaze, or perhaps it was something buried deep in his heart, must have convinced him otherwise.

Instead of turning her down, he tugged the towel free of her hair and tossed it aside before pulling her onto his lap and thrusting his hands deep into her damp curls. Turning her to fully face him, he closed his mouth over hers in a kiss hot enough to leave scorch marks. She opened for him, welcoming him home. The duel was short and sweet, a battle for supremacy that neither lost, yet both won.

"Do you feel that?" he asked.

The question slid from his mouth to hers and she laughed softly in response. "I'm not sure. I might have noticed a slight tingle."

His eyes narrowed. "Slight tingle? *Slight?*"

She blinked up at him with provocative innocence. "Very slight."

"Let's see what we can do about that."

He flipped her off his lap and onto her back. Firelight lapped over his determined face and caught in his eyes, causing the gold to burn like wildfire. She missed this. Missed seeing his abandoned reaction whenever they touched. Missed the romantic soul that blunted the contours of his male sexuality. Missed opening to him— physically and emotionally—in the darkest hours of the night and sharing all she hid within her heart. And having him share what he kept locked away in his. But most of all she missed *this*. The intimacy. The passion. Possessing and being possessed.

He kissed her again. Deeper. More thoroughly. He worshiped her with mouth and tongue until she went mindless with pleasure. "Tell me you feel that," he demanded.

She groaned. "A tickle. Barely a tickle."

"Right. That's it."

Uh-oh. Annoyed obstinance if ever she heard it. He kissed a path downward, mixing the gentle caresses with love nips that had her toes curling into knots. He ripped the towel open and bared her to a combination of firelight and heated gaze. He shot her one last lingering look before applying himself to his appointed task.

He glided his hands along the sides of her breasts, using just the very tips of his fingers so he barely connected with her skin. She shivered at the sensation, shocked that so light a touch could provoke such a strong reaction. Around he circled, edging ever closer to the pebbled tips. She fought with every ounce of self-possession to keep from crying out, almost shooting off the plush carpet when his teeth closed over her nipple and tugged.

If she'd ever questioned The Inferno before, she didn't now. It erupted, low in her belly, spilling over like molten lava. It liquefied everything in its path as it began an onslaught of hunger so deep and all-consuming, she literally shook with the effort to contain it.

He moved lower, touching her belly with his fingers and mouth. Lower. Brushing the nest of curls that protected her feminine core. Lower. Took the heart of her with his mouth. She went deaf and blind as her climax ripped her apart. She fought to draw air into lungs squeezed breathless, barely aware that Sev had left her side.

She still hadn't recovered when he returned, carefully protected, and settled between her thighs. "Do you feel alive now? Do you feel wanted?"

Sensations toppled one on top of another, so intense she couldn't process them all. "Sev..." His name escaped in a husky cry, half concession, half demand. "Please."

He probed inward, a teasing, swirling movement. "Do you feel this?"

"Yes." She moaned as he slid deep, driving all the way home. "I'm definitely feeling something I never have before."

She wrapped her legs around his waist and held on. She'd never felt more alive. Never felt more wanted or cherished. Never belonged with anyone as she did with Sev in this moment. Her climax approached again, every bit as powerful as before. Only this time he joined her. To her amazement, it didn't rip or shred, but melded, uniting them together in something so different, so special, she couldn't at first find the word to name it. And then it came to her and in doing so, overwhelmed her with the devastating knowledge.

In that brief moment, she no longer stood on the outside looking in. Love opened the door and she flew inside.

# CHAPTER TEN

MORNING FOUND Sev in bed wrapped around Francesca in a complicated tangle of arms and legs. He had a vague recollection of scraping her boneless body off the carpet and tossing her over his shoulder before staggering to the bedroom. Or maybe they'd just crawled here.

She stirred within his embrace and flopped onto her back with a groan. He smiled at the sight. She'd gone to bed with damp hair and now it surrounded her head like a fluffy halo. Something told him she wouldn't appreciate her appearance anywhere near as much as he did.

His smile faded as a new and unfamiliar realization took hold. Last night their relationship had changed, a change that went way beyond what it had been before, on either the work front or as former lovers. Somehow, it had shifted them into an entirely new realm, a realm neither of them anticipated.

"Who glued my eyes shut?" She forced one open. "Hey, we're in bed."

"Excellent observation."

"How'd we get here?"

"Beats the hell out of me."

"Maybe I carried you in before I had my wicked way with you. Again."

He grinned. "That's entirely possible."

"Is it just me…" She hesitated, an innate wariness flickering like a warning light. "Or did something peculiar happen to us last night? Even more peculiar than The Inferno, I mean. Although how that's even possible is beyond me."

He framed her face, tracing the delicate bone structure with his fingertips until the shape and texture became as familiar to him as his own. The need to remain in physical contact with her had become an urge he no longer bothered resisting. The Inferno had won.

"I believe we both realized the truth last night," he admitted.

She regarded him with some reservation. "Which is?"

"This isn't going away." He lifted her left hand and studied the engagement ring she wore. The inner fire seemed to erupt from the center of the diamond, fiercer than he'd ever seen it before. "Maybe we should consider making this permanent."

He absorbed her jerk of surprise, felt her heart rate kick up a notch. "Are you serious?"

"I think it's worth discussing, don't you?"

A small smile played at the corners of her mouth. It grew until her entire face radiated with it. "I wouldn't mind," she admitted softly.

On the nightstand table, his cell emitted a soft buzz and Sev swore beneath his breath. "I should have left the damn thing in the other room."

She jackknifed upward and snatched a swift kiss. "Go ahead and take it while I get cleaned up."

"You sure?"

"Positive."

She bounced off the bed and darted into the bathroom. Her muffled shriek of dismay put a grin on his face. Something told him she'd just discovered a mirror. He snagged the phone and flipped it open. "This better be good," he growled.

"It's Lazz. And it's not good. In fact, it's an effing mess. If you'd bothered to come to work this morning—"

"Get to the point," Sev interrupted.

"Seriously, bro, what the hell are you doing and why aren't you here? There is a fan sitting on my desk cranked to high and you can't believe what just hit it."

"What's wrong?"

"It's Francesca."

Hell. He glanced toward the bathroom. Water ran in the sink and he could hear her humming, the sound light and happy and slightly off-key. "What's the problem?"

"Bloom's rep called. They've decided to go with Timeless."

"Not good, but we knew winning that account would be a long shot. What's it got to do with Francesca?"

At the sound of her name, she appeared in the doorway. She'd tamed her hair, much to his disappointment, and—even more disappointing—slipped on one of his shirts. She shot him a questioning look as she rolled up the sleeves, an incandescent happiness pouring off her in waves. After the meeting with Kurt, he didn't think she'd ever find joy again. But she had, and it humbled him that she found it in his arms.

"Francesca's the one who convinced Bloom to go with TH," Lazz said.

Sev shot off the bed. "Not a chance."

"I'm dead serious. Sev, I spoke to the rep. Personally."

He bowed his head and stared at the floor. "She wouldn't have done that. I want you to double-check, Lazz. Triple-check, if that's what it takes. Find out why Bloom's rep would lie to you." And then he looked up, straight into Francesca's eyes. What hovered there in the shadowed darkness had him breaking off with a word he'd never normally use in her presence. He flipped the phone closed. "Lazz doesn't need to triple-check, does he? Bloom's rep told him the truth."

His shirt hung on her, making her appear small and fragile. Or maybe it was the barriers she slammed back in place. He never realized how utterly they enshrouded her until she emerged from their protective folds. Last night she'd bared herself in a way she never had before, not in all the time they'd been together.

Francesca shook her head. "There's no point in his checking again."

"You contacted Juliet Bloom's representative?" At her nod, he hit her with his accusation. "You advised her to go with Timeless."

"Yes. I guaranteed she wouldn't lose if she did so. That it would only benefit her."

He lifted an eyebrow. "Payback, Francesca?" he asked softly.

She tilted her chin to a combative angle and fixed him

with a cool, remote gaze that shot his blood pressure straight through the roof. "I prefer to call it insurance."

"Explain," he rapped out.

"Timeless Heirlooms owns the designs that Juliet Bloom is so crazy about. The ones I created. She wants to wear them in her next film. Dantes plans to purchase TH, not put them out of business, so Timeless will endure regardless of ownership. Once the company is safely tucked back into the Dantes' fold, you'll receive the continued benefit from having someone of Bloom's caliber as your spokeswoman."

"*If* we tuck TH back into the Dantes' fold," he corrected tightly. "*If.*"

"You've already assured me it's going to happen, regardless of me or the Fontaines, or even Juliet Bloom." She lifted an eyebrow. "A lie, Sev?"

His back teeth clamped together. "It's no lie."

"Then what's the problem?" She stepped from the bathroom, wary enough to keep her distance. Smart woman. "All I've done is ensure that you honor the contract we signed and pay the Fontaines a fair price for TH. Now that Bloom's agreed to be the spokeswoman for them, Kurt and Tina will reunite. They'll have no other choice if they want that contract. Knowing Tina as I do, she won't let a little thing like an illegitimate daughter stand in the way of a deal of this magnitude."

"It will, however, make it more difficult for me to acquire TH."

She graciously conceded the point, which had him backing up a step so he wouldn't give in to temptation and throttle her. "But it will happen. And when that day comes, since I work for you, I'm also available to work with Ms. Bloom should she wish to expand the current collection I designed for her, or have me create a whole new one for her at some point in the future. And if you don't buy out TH, Ms. Bloom will most likely jump ship and become Dantes' spokeswoman, since I now work for you. As far as I can tell, everyone comes out of this a winner."

"Except for you."

That stopped her. About damn time. "What are you talking about?" For the first time a hint of uncertainty crept into her voice.

"I'm talking about the fact that I have the option to either fire you, in which case I'll see to it that you don't work in the industry for the next two years. Or I can transfer you to another office. Either way, Bloom will no longer be your problem."

"Which do you intend to do?"

Francesca asked the question so calmly, if he didn't know better he'd have thought she didn't care. But if he'd learned nothing else about her, he had learned that designing jewelry was as much a part of her as her heart or soul. In fact, it *was* her soul. He couldn't take that away from her, no matter how badly her actions had hurt him.

And they had hurt him. This wasn't about business, anymore. In fact, she'd shown a ruthlessness he could almost admire. A ruthlessness he, himself, had been forced to employ on occasion. No, this had become personal. It felt personal. It felt as though he'd risked opening himself to her, only to have her use what she'd learned to hurt him.

"I believe there's a spot open for you in our New York office. I'll make your transfer effective immediately."

She jerked as though he'd struck her, staring at him for an endless moment with huge, wounded eyes. Without a word, she turned on her heel and moved through the apartment, gathering her possessions. Sev hardened himself as he waited for her to finish and leave.

Even so, it tore him apart watching her. One more rejection. One more door slammed in her face. Once more out in the proverbial cold. They made one hell of a pair. He scoured his face with his hands. All the while, The Inferno consumed him, raging with the urge to go to her. To fix this. To take her back into his arms and make her his again. His jaw tightened. The hell with it. This was just one more roadblock. A huge one, granted. But surely they could—

The front door opened and quietly closed, locking behind her. Sev charged into the living room, but she was gone, leaving nothing behind but a cold gleam emanating from the fireplace. Sitting on the hearth he found the engagement ring he'd given her. He crossed the room and picked it up.

Maybe it was his imagination, but he could have sworn the fire deep within the heart of the diamond had dimmed.

Francesca sat at her drawing board in her New York office, an office not that dissimilar from the one she'd occupied in San Francisco. Exhaustion dogged her thanks to an endless round of sleepless nights. She'd only been in New York for a month, but already it felt like a lifetime. She rubbed her eyes, struggling to get them to focus on designs that could only be described as mediocre, at best. For some reason, her heart wasn't in her work anymore.

But then…how could it be? The past few weeks had been some of the darkest and most difficult of her life, far worse than anything she'd gone through in foster care. Worse even than her father's rejection. She'd made a hideous mistake when she'd contacted Bloom's rep.

Why hadn't it occurred to her that by helping the Fontaines, she was betraying Dantes…and more specifically, the man she loved? She'd been so busy easing her own guilt over leaving TH, that she never gave a thought to how her decision would impact Sev, or that thanks to their feelings for each other, he wouldn't see her actions from a business standpoint, but take her betrayal personally. She'd simply reacted to what she'd perceived as an unfair situation, and taken matters into her own hands.

That still didn't explain why he hadn't acknowledged the designs she'd given him on their last night together. She'd hoped he'd understand what they meant. Hoped he'd realize that while she'd won the Bloom account for TH, she'd left him something far more valuable.

A familiar longing filled her as The Inferno gave her a small, petulant kick. Even after all this time the connection remained—stretched thin and taut, granted. Yet, it held with unbelievable tenacity.

The phone on her desk let out a shrill ring and she picked it up, surprised to have her greeting answered with a cheerful, "*Ciao, sorella.* It's Marco."

Pleasure mingled with disappointment at the sound of his voice—pleasure to hear from a Dante and disappointment that it wasn't the right Dante. "It's good to hear from you," she replied. "Though I'm surprised that any of you are willing to talk to me."

"You'd be surprised by how many of us are on your side." He hesitated. "I'm afraid I can't talk right now. I actually called to ask about some missing designs. Sev would like to know what happened to them. They're not in your old office. I don't suppose you took them with you to New York?"

She frowned. "I don't understand. I gave them to Sev."

"When, Francesca?"

"The night—" She broke off. The night they'd last made love. "The night before I transferred to New York. I brought them to Sev's apartment."

"He claims he doesn't have them."

Memory kicked in. "It had been raining the night I gave him the designs and I was soaked through. I vaguely recall he took them and tossed them onto the floor, out of the way." An image flashed through her mind. "I think they slid under that lovely old armoire he has in the entryway. You know the one I mean? He may not have noticed."

"Got it. Thanks, Francesca." He hesitated. "Are you…are you doing okay?"

No. Not even close to okay. "I'm fine."

"Right." She could hear the irony slipping through the line. "About as fine as Sev, I'd guess."

Francesca closed her eyes. "I have to be fine," she whispered. "We both do. There isn't any other choice."

\* \* \*

"You didn't need to come with me," Sev informed Marco. "I'm perfectly capable of looking under my own coat closet."

"I came to try and make you see sense, as you damn well know."

"I always see sense. I'm the most sensible one of the lot of you."

"Not about this. Not when it comes to Francesca."

Sev shoved his key into the front door lock and twisted so hard it was a wonder the metal didn't snap off in his hand. "What's gotten into you, Marco? What part of 'she betrayed us' don't you get?"

"And how many times did you betray her?" his brother shot back. "I know. I know. You had valid reasons. It was all about protecting Dantes. So answer me this, hotshot. What makes that okay and what she did not okay? She was protecting her family the same as you."

That very question had been tearing Sev apart. How could he explain to his brother that it wasn't about business anymore? How could he explain the irrational belief that *this* betrayal felt personal? That this time he'd allowed his emotions to override his common sense? For the first time in his life, he, the Dante who prided himself on cool emotionless deliberation, who used calm logic and rational thinking to govern all of his business decisions, hadn't been able to utilize any of his skills or abilities.

When it came to Francesca he was neither emotionless, nor logical, let alone cool and calm. The very thought of her caused a burning desire so overwhelming that it didn't leave room for anything else.

Marco followed Sev into the apartment. Stooping, he

reached under the coat closet and snagged a large, thick envelope. "Here it is. Right where she said it'd be." He sent the packet spinning in Sev's direction. "Happy now? Glad you didn't accuse her of selling her designs to the competition?"

Sev jerked as though punched. "She'd never—" he said automatically.

"You're right. She'd never." Marco glared at him. "Do you have any idea how lucky you are? Do you have any idea what the rest of us would give to feel The Inferno for a woman like Francesca? To know that we could actually share a life with a woman like her, instead of longing for what we can never have? Instead of settling for second best? I never thought I'd say this to you, of all people, but you're a fool, Severo Dante."

Without a word, Sev ripped open the envelope and pulled out a sketchpad. He flipped it open and spared it a swift glance. And then he froze. "Marco…"

"What now?" He shifted to stand beside Sev, and whistled softly. "If you needed proof how much she loves you, here it is."

Sev nodded. Page after page revealed some of the most incredible jewelry designs he'd ever seen— designs ideal for the expansion Dantes' planned for some point in the future. It didn't take much thought to understand what she'd done…or why.

He understood all too well why she'd left these designs, designs she'd clearly been working on for years. She'd taken with one hand by giving the Bloom account to TH, and given with the other by presenting Dantes with these designs, dispensing a rough sort of justice. Only, she had more than compensated Dantes for what she'd given to Timeless Heirlooms.

She'd left him an incomparable gift, one that decimated the priorities he'd set in stone the day he'd first taken over from his father. A gift that made him realize there could only be one priority in his life from this point forward, and it wasn't Dantes.

The gift she'd given him wasn't the designs contained in her sketchpad. She'd left behind the gift of her heart.

Another month passed after Francesca's conversation with Marco. A month of pain and sorrow and regret. During those weeks, she'd come to the realization that Sev's feelings for her were truly dead, that The Inferno no longer burned for him the way it still burned for her.

Even when she received instructions to return to San Francisco on company business, she'd been unable to summon so much as a spark of hope. After all, miracles didn't exist. She'd learned that at the tender of age of eight when she'd been discarded by the people she'd hoped would one day be her adoptive parents. She knew better than to expect the door to open and for her to be welcomed in. She'd been disappointed too many times. And Sev had made himself abundantly clear before sending her to New York. She no longer belonged to the Dante inner circle.

She crossed to the mirror and examined her dress. She'd been specifically asked by Sev's assistant to wear red in order to fit in with the theme chosen for this evening's festivities. What theme, no one had bothered to explain. So, Francesca picked the brightest, most glorious shade of red she could find.

The fitted bodice glittered with Swarovski crystal beads, while the chiffon skirt drifted outward from her hips to the floor in layers of handkerchief veils that lifted and swirled on an invisible breeze. After some debate, she chose to leave her hair down and it fell in heavy curls to shoulders bared by the halter neckline of the gown.

Dantes had sent over jewelry to wear for the evening. She'd never seen the pieces before, but they were positively breathtaking. The necklace and earrings were simple confections, as romantic as they were elegant, featuring some of the most stunning fire diamonds she'd ever seen. Based on the design of the engagement ring she'd worn for far too brief a time, she would bet these latest items were Primo's creations, as well.

After checking the mirror a final time, she forced herself to leave the relative safety of the suite before Sev sent out a search party. Not giving herself a chance to reconsider, she took the elevator to the lobby and crossed to the steps leading to the ballroom. She hesitated at the threshold, searching for a friendly face. Instantly a hum of desire lit up like a Roman candle and she turned her head, keying in on Sev.

How could she ever have imagined that The Inferno had finished with them, or that her love would dwindle over time? The urge to go to him, to touch him, to have him possess her mouth…her body…slammed through her. It grew so strong, she could do nothing more than obey the silent imperative. She took a half-dozen steps in Sev's direction before a sudden whisper of voices swelled, then faded, leaving behind a thunderous silence.

Her step faltered and she glanced around, only then realizing that while she wore flaming red, everyone else present was dressed in black and white. Only one other person also wore red, if only a scrap of the color. Sev's pocket handkerchief was a rich shade of ruby that stood out against his black suit and white dress shirt. Feeling painfully conspicuous, she held her head high and finished wending her way toward him.

She greeted him with a cool nod, while inside she burned with the hellish fires of desire. "Mr. Dante."

A small smile played about his mouth. "Ms. Sommers. If you'll come with me?"

He led the way to a small dais and approached the microphone. "I'd like to thank everyone for coming this evening to Dantes' launch of a brand-new collection. With me is the creator of that collection, its heart and soul, Francesca Sommers."

She froze in total shock. More than anything she wanted to grab Sev's hand for support, to demand an explanation. She turned to look at him, and every thought slid from her head, except one. She still loved this man. Utterly. Totally. Completely. From this day until the end of days.

"What's going on?" she pleaded.

"Smile, sweetheart," he murmured. "They're all here for you."

"But...why?"

He stepped toward the microphone again. "Please enjoy your evening, as well as our grand launch of..." He swept his arms wide. "Dante's Heart."

From either side of the ballroom, models appeared, each wearing a different one of the designs Francesca had left behind for Sev to use. Designs she'd envisioned as a teenager. Designs she'd worked on for a full decade and never quite brought to life—until she'd opened her heart to love. To Sev's love. Only then had she found the spark that turned her creative flame into a creative inferno.

She began to tremble in reaction. "You're using my designs to relaunch Dantes into a full line of jewelry?" Why had he done this? What did it mean?

"Jewelry for the contemporary woman." His hands settled on her shoulders and he gazed down at her with eyes more vivid than the sun. "You're Dante's Heart, my love. At least you're *this* Dante's heart."

Applause exploded around them and excited chatter swelled as the assembled guests got their first look at the new line. Tears filled Francesca's eyes. "I love you, Sev. More than you can possibly guess. I'm sorry, so sorry for everything—"

He stopped her words with a shake of his head. "Don't apologize. That's for me to do. I never should have put you in such an impossible position. It won't happen again. From now on you are and always will be first in my life." He inclined his head toward the gathering. "Do you hear them, sweetheart?"

She said the first thing that popped into her head. "They're clapping."

He grinned. "How could they not? They're witnessing something extraordinary." He laced his hand with hers and something deep inside gave way, a rending of barriers that had been erected when she'd been a frightened child of five. And in its place, the connection between them expanded and grew, rooting deep and permanent. "Come with me. We need to talk."

She glanced toward the doors leading onto the balcony. "I think I know the perfect location."

Together they left the dais, intent only on escape. Not that they were allowed such an easy out. Family came first, as Primo enveloped her in a huge bear hug, followed by a warm embrace from Nonna. Marco approached, sweeping her into a dizzying dip and laughing kiss full on the mouth. Then Lazz, who settled for a chaste peck on the cheek. And finally, Nicolò, who kissed the back of her hand with old-world gallantry.

Next, friends and associates impeded their progress, raving about the collection and using words that left Francesca choked with emotion. Words like "spectacular" and "unparalleled" and "generation defining." Mere feet from escape, Francesca came face-to-face with the Fontaines. Instantly, Sev's arm wrapped around her, offering strength and protection. She gave his hand a reassuring squeeze, an unspoken message that even though she appreciated his support, she intended to handle this confrontation on her own terms.

"Tina, Kurt." She offered a smile. Not one of apology. Not one of nervousness or regret. But an open smile of genuine affection. A smile from the heart.

To her astonishment, they responded in kind. "Has Severo told you the news?" Tina asked.

Francesca glanced in bewilderment from Sev back to the Fontaines. "What news?"

Sev shook his head. "I was hoping we'd run into you, so you could tell her, yourself."

Tina grinned. "We reached a compromise. Timeless Heirlooms is now a subsidiary of Dantes. But Sev's agreed that we can continue to run it, with a few changes to assist the bottom line."

"Such as Dantes being in charge of acquiring new designers," Sev inserted. "And a few fiscal repairs that Kurt will oversee."

Tina waved that aside. "With Dantes' name behind us and our contract with Juliet Bloom, TH is guaranteed to skyrocket to the top." Ever the businesswoman, she added, "Anytime you want to contribute one of your designs, my dear, you're more than welcome."

Sev gave Tina a pointed look. "I believe there's something else you wanted to tell Francesca."

Tina squirmed. "Oh, right. That." She released a gusty sigh. "I owe you an apology. Sev didn't tell me about your connection to Kurt. His P.I. did. The man tried to double his profit by reselling the information."

"I've since taken care of the matter," Sev added.

The tone of his voice left little doubt in Francesca's mind that the P.I. was bitterly regretting his most recent business decision. "Thank you for clearing that up."

A nervous light appeared in Kurt's soft-blue eyes. "We were wondering… That is, Tina and I were wondering… Perhaps you'd be available some evening for dinner. I'd like the opportunity to get to know my daughter. If you're willing, that is." He visibly braced himself. "After all we've put you through, I'll understand if you'd rather not."

Francesca could feel her face crumpling and knew she teetered on the edge of totally losing it. Only Sev's presence at her back gave her the necessary strength to respond. "I'd like that. I'd like that very much."

Tina broke from her husband's side and gave Francesca a swift hug. "I never wanted children. It's a messy business, one that never suited me. But having a grown stepdaughter sort of appeals. We can—I don't know—do lunch, or something. Shop and have drinks. Or if you'd prefer a more traditional stepmother, I can have you sweep out the hearth and fix me tea and dress you in soot-covered rags."

Francesca grinned through her tears at the Cinderella reference. "Works for me. The first part, I mean. Not the rest."

"Well, then. Fine." Tina cleared her throat, more awkward than Francesca had ever seen her. "We're all good, right?"

Francesca laughed. "Very good."

The instant the Fontaines departed, Sev cupped her elbow and urged her through the double doors and onto the balcony. The night held an unseasonable warmth, soft and balmy. Together they wandered to the balustrade and leaned against it. From their Nob Hill perch they could stare out at the bright lights that glittered below them like a carpet of diamond shards.

"This is where I first saw you," Francesca murmured.

"This is where I first fell in love with you." He turned to face her. "I'm sorry, Francesca. I should have trusted my instincts from the beginning. Hell, I should have trusted you. For most of my adult life it's been my job to protect my family and our business from all threats."

"And you saw me as a threat." Not much question about that.

"The biggest threat, because you were the one person capable of tempting me to forget honor and duty and responsibility."

"I'd never ask you to do that," she protested. "All I've ever wanted is for you to open your heart and let me in."

"It's wide open, love, and just waiting for you to step across the threshold."

"Is that The Inferno talking?"

"Maybe it is. Or maybe The Inferno knows what lies in our hearts and forces stubborn men to see the truth. Because the truth is you're my heart and soul, and always will be. But I'd also like you to be my wife."

All her life she believed herself on the outside, looking in. Now she realized it wasn't true. It had never been true. Fear kept her from taking that final step, from seeing the open doors. They'd always been there, she'd just been too busy protecting herself from hurt to take that leap of faith and walk inside.

She took the step now, hurtling herself against Sev. His arms closed around her, bringing her home. And then he kissed her, telling her without words just how much he loved her. Long minutes passed before they drew apart.

He reached into his pocket and removed a familiar-looking jeweler's box, emblazoned with the Dantes' logo. He thumbed it open, revealing a set of rings. The first was the engagement ring Primo designed, the other the band that mated with it. Maybe it was his imagination, but the fire diamond no longer appeared dim. Now it seemed to rage with its own inner inferno.

He slipped the engagement ring on her finger. "Will you marry me, Francesca, for real this time?"

She positively glowed. "Yes, yes, yes!"

And then he kissed her again, soothing old hurts and offering a promise for the future. Much, much later Francesca rested her head against Sev's shoulder, her happiness a palpable presence. She gazed toward the ballroom, misty-eyed, and then stiffened within his arms. "Sev, look."

He glanced in the direction she pointed and shrugged. "It's Marco. So what?"

"Look what he's doing with his hands."

Sev stared, his eyes narrowing when he saw it. Marco was busy entertaining a guest with one of his stories, and as he talked he dug the fingers of his left hand into the palm of his right. It could only mean one thing. Sometime, someplace…

"My God," he murmured. "Marco's been struck by The Inferno."

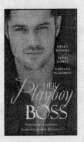

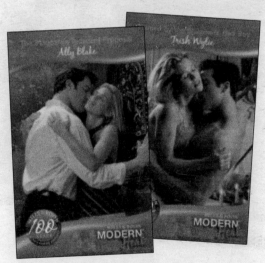